THE WORLD OF
ROBERT JORDAN'S

The Wheel
of Time

By Robert Jordan

THE WHEEL OF TIME
The Eye of the World
The Great Hunt
The Dragon Reborn
The Shadow Rising
The Fires of Heaven
Lord of Chaos
A Crown of Swords
The Path of Daggers
Winter's Heart
Crossroads of Twilight
Knife of Dreams

New Spring

The World of Robert Jordan's The Wheel of Time
by Robert Jordan and Teresa Patterson

The Conan Chronicles 1
The Conan Chronicles 2

THE WORLD OF ROBERT JORDAN'S
The Wheel of Time

ROBERT JORDAN *and* TERESA PATTERSON

www.orbitbooks.co.uk

ORBIT

First published in Great Britain by Orbit 1997
This edition published by Orbit 2000
Reprinted 2000, 2002, 2004, 2005, 2006

The phrases 'The Wheel of Time™' and 'The Dragon Reborn™'
and the snake-wheel symbol are trademarks of Robert Jordan.

Interior illustrations by Todd Cameron Hamilton
Maps and ornaments by Ellisa Mitchell and John M. Ford
Maps by Thomas Canty

A CIP catalogue record for this book
is available from the British Library.

ISBN-13: 978-1-84149-026-7
ISBN-10: 1-84149-026-1

Typeset in Berkeley by M Rules
Printed and bound in Great Britain by Clays Ltd, St Ives plc

Orbit
An imprint of
Little, Brown Book Group
Brettenham House
Lancaster Place
London WC2E 7EN

A member of the Hachette Livre Group of Companies

www.littlebrown.co.uk

To Harriet
with love

Table of Contents

Preface

THIS COMPILATION OF the world's geography, sociology, and history uses information dating from the earliest available records of the Age of Legends through the current era. Reliable sources are limited. Almost all documents from before the War of the Hundred Years survive only as copies, or copies of copies, etc., and thus may well include mistakes made by the scribes. Few complete books or manuscripts of any kind survive from the War of the Hundred Years. The earlier period, from the end of the Trolloc Wars to the end of the War of the Hundred Years, left even less. All information from the time of the Breaking of the World to the end of the Trolloc Wars was pulled from manuscript fragments of varying sizes, sometimes not even consisting of consecutive pages. No books or manuscripts have yet been found dating from before

the Breaking. All the information from the Age of Legends is based on documents from the first few centuries after the Breaking, when the writers might have had access to sources that had survived.

Wherever possible, the information has been at least partially verified by writings contemporary with their contents, but the older a document or manuscript, the harder it is to date pages precisely.

Some difficulties arise not from age or verifiability, but from problems of translation, for the older documents were written primarily or completely in the Old Tongue. Within the Old Tongue, as all scholars know, words have variable meanings, and some meanings have shifted to varying degrees over time.

The authors hope that the reader will forgive the occasional inaccuracy that may arise within these pages and relish instead the immense diversity and energy within the legacy of the Pattern and the World of the Wheel.

The Wheel
and the Power

Chapter 1

The Wheel and the Pattern

 'THE WHEEL OF Time turns, and Ages come and go, leaving memories that become legend. Legend fades to myth, and even myth is long forgotten when the Age that gave it birth comes again.' So begins each saga within the World of the Wheel, a universe in which the major controlling factor is the Wheel of Time and the Great Pattern it spins. A pattern in which light and dark, good and evil, male and female, and life and death struggle for balance within the weave of destiny.

What is the Wheel of Time? Imagine a great cosmic loom in the shape of a seven-spoked wheel, slowly spinning through eternity, weaving the fabric of the universe. The Wheel, put in place by the Creator, is time itself, ever turning and returning. The fabric it weaves is constructed from the threads of lives and events, interlaced

THE DEAD SEA

AILDASHAR

ARAD DOMAN

Toman Head

Almoth
Plain

Fae

TARABON

AMADICI

ARYTH OCEAN

Tremalking

into a design, the Great Pattern, which is the whole of existence and reality, past, present, and future.

Within the influence of this Lace of Ages are not only the earth and stone of the physical world, but other worlds and universes, other dimensions, other possibilities. The Wheel touches what might be, what might have been, and what is. It touches the world of dreams as well as the world of waking.

In this world there is no one beginning or one end, for each spoke of the great Wheel represents one of the seven Ages, receding into the past and returning in the future as the Wheel spins, the fabric of each age changing only its weave and pattern with each passing. With every pass the changes vary to an increasingly greater degree. For each Age there is a separate and unique pattern, the Pattern of the Age, which forms the substance of reality for that age. This design is predetermined by the Wheel and can only partially be changed by those lives which make up the threads within the weave.

No one knows the length of time it takes for a full turning of the Wheel, nor is there a set time for each Age. There is only the certainty that all will come around again, though surely long past the span encompassed by human memory, or even legend. Yet that knowledge provides the basis for the philosophy and history of the known world. No ending, even death, is necessarily final within the turning of the Wheel. Reincarnation is a part of the way of the world. Prophecies are believed and heeded, since they tell as much of what was as of what will be. The only questions are when and in what manner the prophecies will unfold.

In such a world change is simply a predetermined part of the mechanism. Only a few individuals, special souls

known as *ta'veren*, can cause the fabric of the pattern to bend around them, changing the weave. These *ta'veren* are spun out as key threads around which all surrounding life-threads, perhaps in some cases all life-threads, weave to create change. These key threads often produce major variations in the Pattern of an Age. Such major changes are called, in the old tongue, *ta'maral'ailen*, or the 'Web of Destiny.'

Even the *ta'veren* and the Web of Destiny woven around them are bound by the Wheel and the Great Pattern; it is believed that the Wheel spins out *ta'veren* whenever the weave begins to drift away from the Pattern. The changes around them, while often drastic and unsettling for those who must live in the Age, are thought to be part of the Wheel's own correcting mechanism. The more change needed to bring the Great Pattern into balance, the more *ta'veren* spun out into the world.

The Great Wheel is the very heart of all time. But even the Wheel requires energy to maintain itself and its pattern. This energy comes from the True Source, from which the One Power may be drawn. Both the True Source and the One Power are made up of two conflicting yet complementary parts: *saidin*, the male half, and *saidar*, the female half. Working both together and against one another within the True Source, it is *saidin* and *saidar* which provide the driving force that turns the Wheel of Time.

The only known forces outside the Wheel and the Pattern are the Creator, who shaped the Wheel, the One Power that drives it – as well as the plan for the Great Pattern – and the Dark One, who was imprisoned outside the pattern by the Creator at the moment of creation. No one inside and of the Pattern can destroy the Wheel or

change the destiny of the Great Pattern. Even those who are *ta'veren* can only alter, but not completely change, the weave. It is believed that if he escapes his prison, the Dark One, being a creature or force beyond creation, has the ability to remake the Wheel and all of creation in his own dark image. Thus each person, especially each of those born *ta'veren*, must struggle to achieve his or her own best destiny to assure the balance and continuation of the Great Pattern.

Chapter 2

The One Power and
the True Source

THE TRUE SOURCE is made up of two complementary parts: *saidin*, the male half, and
saidar, the female half. Each has separate properties and affinities, working at the same time
with and against the other. Only women can touch *saidar*,
and only men *saidin*. Each is completely unable to sense
the other half of the Source, except as an absence or neg-
ativity. Even the methodologies by which men and
women utilize the One Power that emanates from the
True Source are so completely different that no woman
can teach a man to use the Power, and no man a woman.

In some Ages, such as that called the Age of Legends,
men and women used the complementary and conflicting
halves of the Power together to perform feats that neither
could accomplish separately. In the present Age, part of
the Power, the male half, has been tainted, causing any

man who channels *saidin* to go mad eventually and cause Power-wrought havoc unless he is killed or gentled.

Most people cannot sense or touch the True Source, even though its energy may be manifested all around them. Only a tiny portion of the population, about two or three percent, actually have the ability, once taught, to touch and draw on the One Power, and today many of those cannot utilize its power in any effective manner. The act of drawing and controlling the flow of the One Power from the True Source is known as channeling.

Channeling draws on threads of the One Power and uses them singly or in combination in a weave designed to accomplish the particular task at hand. There are five different threads to the One Power, known as the Five Powers. They are named according to the elements their energies manipulate: Earth, Air (sometimes called Wind), Fire, Water, and Spirit. In many cases only one of the Powers is required to accomplish a task. A weave of Fire alone will light a candle or control a fire. But certain tasks necessitate the weaving of flows in more than one of the Five Powers. For instance, one who wishes to affect the weather must weave a flow combining Air, Water, and Spirit.

Anyone who can channel usually has a greater degree of strength with at least one or two of the Powers, yet they may lack any particular ability at all with some of the others. For example, someone strong in Wind may be all but unable to weave Fire, or may be weak in Earth but equally strong in Spirit and Air. Some few rare individuals have been found to be very strong in as many as three, or in very rare cases four, of the Powers. But since the Age of Legends no one has had great strength in all five. Even then, such individuals were very rare.

Levels of comparative strength also vary greatly from one individual wielder of the Power to another, and from men to women. Using records gathered from the Age of Legends (current data have little usable information concerning the use of *saidin*), it is possible to state certain facts about the strength and distribution of the ability in those men and women who could channel. In general, men were stronger in the use of the Power than women – that is, in the sheer volume of the Power they could handle – though there were certainly individual women who had great strength and individual men who were comparatively weak. By the same token, though some men had great dexterity in the weaving, in general women outstripped men in this regard. Men usually exhibited greater ability with Earth and Fire while women more often excelled in the use of Water and/or Air. Equal numbers of men and women were strong in the use of Spirit. There were, of course, exceptions, but they were rare enough that Earth and Fire came to be regarded as male powers, while Air and Water were considered female powers. Even today women usually exhibit their greatest strength in Air or Water, or both. This probably prompted the popular saying among female channelers: 'There is no rock so strong that water and wind cannot wear it away, no fire so fierce that water cannot quench it or wind snuff it out.' Any equivalent witticism among male channelers has been lost.

Of the tiny percentage of the population who have the potential to channel at all, only a small number have the ability inborn. It usually manifests itself in adolescence or early adulthood, though in general women show the ability at a younger age than men, often much younger. These few talented individuals will eventually channel the

Power with or without guidance, whether or not they wish to do so. In many cases they are not even aware of what they are doing. For such people, touching and drawing on the True Source is completely natural, and potentially deadly.

As far as is known, the One Power is not alive, but is a force of natural energy limited only by the strength of the channeler and the extent of his/her control. One warning must be emphasized: its use is extremely addictive. One unwary of the danger inherent in channeling can easily be seduced into drawing more than he or she can handle, or drawing on it too often. Such mishandling of this Power usually exacts a terrible price on the body and mind.

Drawing *saidar* and channeling it without benefit of guidance or training results in death for four out of five women born with the ability. This death often takes the form of a lingering sickness that saps the individual of her life energy. Those who first touch the Power unintentionally generally feel nothing unusual at the time, but suffer a violent reaction as much as ten days later. This reaction seldom lasts for more than a few hours. Headaches, chills, fever, exhilaration, numbness, dizziness, and lack of coordination are only a few of the most usual symptoms, often occurring simultaneously or in quick succession. These effects return after each incident of touching the Source. Each time, reaction comes closer to the actual act of touching, until the two happen almost simultaneously. At this stage the visible reactions stop, but unless some sort of control has been learned, death becomes a certainty. Some women die within the year, some survive as long as five years, yet without the control that is almost impossible to learn without guidance, all

die. Their final days are usually marked by violent convulsions and screams of agony. Once the last stages are entered, there is no known cure, even with the use of the One Power.

Those women, often called wilders, who do manage to survive and train themselves in the use of the Power usually develop a mental barrier, probably as a survival mechanism, that makes it difficult for them to reach their full potential. Some think that these blocks are partially caused by the social stigma often associated with the use of the Power, and by the unwillingness of the individual to consider or acknowledge the fact that she can channel. Such blocks can sometimes be broken, though not easily, with assistance from those who have proper training. If the barriers are broken, wilders are often among the most powerful of channelers. Many of those who have undergone the training in what is considered the proper sequence look down on the self-taught, using 'wilder' as a derogatory term indicating the unpredictability of a wild talent and the savagery of a wild animal.

Even those with training risk much every time they channel. If a woman draws too much *saidar*, or draws *saidar* too often, she can be burned out or overloaded, losing her ability to channel, or, at worst, killing herself. If she weaves Powers she cannot adequately control, she may cause her own death and damage those around her.

Before the time of the Breaking of the World, men faced much the same risks as women when born with the ability to channel. After the Bore was sealed, that changed. The Dark One, in the last moments of the battle, managed a final counterstroke that tainted the male half

of the One Power. Since the Time of Madness that followed, no man has been able to channel *saidin* without eventually going completely and horribly insane. Even those who do manage to learn some control die from a slow wasting sickness that causes the sufferer to rot alive. In either case, the danger to those around the male channeler is great. Those men who manage to live long enough to go mad usually end up wielding the power of tainted *saidin* in horrible ways, often destroying everyone and everything around them. During the Breaking of the World it was such men who completely destroyed the world and known civilization. It is because of this danger that men are not only not encouraged to learn how to channel; those who do learn, or even try to, are hunted down and rendered harmless or killed.

From the time of the Breaking until very recently, all men born with the ability were by definition wilders, since there was no one to instruct them. Even now, since the founding of the Black Tower, if they survive their initial contact with *saidin*, they are doomed to eventually go mad. It is for this reason – to make certain that the horrors of the Breaking of the World are never loosed again – that the Red Ajah of the Aes Sedai dedicated themselves to finding and gentling all men with the ability to channel.

In the Age of Legends, the process by which a man or woman was rendered incapable of channeling was called 'severing,' as in 'being severed from the True Source.' In the present day, the process is given a different name depending on whether it is done to a man or a woman.

The severing of a man from the True Source is now known as 'gentling.' He can still sense the Power, but is unable to touch *saidin* in any way. He is therefore harmless

to those around him, or 'gentled.' If he is gentled soon enough, the madness and the wasting sickness are also arrested, though not cured, and death by insanity or rot is averted. Unfortunately most who are gentled lose the will to live when their connection to the True Source is severed. They fall into a deep depression and often commit suicide soon after if not forcibly prevented. Those who do not kill themselves usually die within a year or two anyway, for without the will to live the body eventually fails.

For women, the intentional removal of the ability to channel is called 'stilling.' If the ability is lost by accident the process is called being 'burned out,' though the term 'stilling' is sometimes used for this also, a deplorable loss of precision in speech since the Old Tongue fell out of use. In any case, the results of being stilled or burned out are much the same. The stilled woman, like the man who has been gentled, is cut off from the True Source, always tantalized by the sense of *saidar*, yet unable to touch or channel it. The woman who is burned out can neither channel nor sense the Power. Stilling is usually done as punishment for a crime, while burnout occurs through overload or misuse of the power, or is the result of losing to an attack by a greater power while channeling. It is assumed that men are susceptible to burnout as well.

Like the men who have been gentled, women who have been stilled lose the will to survive. In fact, less is known about them than about gentled men, who are held prisoner until they die. Women who have been stilled or burned out usually flee as far as they can from women who retain the ability they have lost. Women who can channel rarely make any effort to find stilled or

burned-out women; the claim is that they should not be taunted in their misery by the presence of women who remain whole, but it should be noted that women who can channel often become queasy, or even physically ill, at the mere thought of the fate suffered by those others, a fate they themselves could also face. It is believed that stilled women live only if they succeed in finding something to fill the void left by the absence of the One Power. Few manage to find a focus that powerful.

All records insist that gentling or stilling cannot be cured, but cases have been rumored of limited healing, using all of the threads of the Power. Historically, however, loss of the ability to channel has been irreversible. Certainly in the Age of Legends, when feats beyond the comprehension of the present day were a matter of course, severing was considered final, beyond all ability to heal.

One of the ways to reduce the chance of accidental stilling or burnout is to use *angreal* and *sa'angreal*, artifacts made during the Age of Legends and perhaps earlier which enhance the channeler's ability to draw and focus the One Power. An *angreal* allows the channeler to safely control a greater amount of the Power than she or he could possibly draw unaided. *Sa'angreal* are similar, but much more powerful. There are considerable variations among *angreal* and *sa'angreal*, but in general a *sa'angreal* can be said to allow one to channel as much more of the One Power over that of the *angreal* as the *angreal* does over channeling unaided. Both *angreal* and *sa'angreal* were keyed during their making for use by either men or women. A woman cannot use one made for a man and vice versa. There are rumors of *angreal* and *sa'angreal* usable by both men and women, but they remain unconfirmed.

Relatively few *angreal* have survived since the Age of Legends, and far fewer, only a handful, of the more powerful *sa'angreal*. The knowledge and skills required for their making was lost during the Breaking of the World.

The most powerful *sa'angreal* ever created were two gigantic statues, one in the form of a man, and the other in the form of a woman. They were made during the War of Power and designed to be used together by a team consisting of a man and a woman, common during that age, as weapons against the Shadow, but they were never actually brought into service before being hidden. It is believed that each separately is more powerful than any other known *sa'angreal*, and that used together they could enable a man and woman to channel enough of the Power to break the world beyond rebuilding. The female *sa'angreal* is the statue of a woman, draped in a flowing robe, holding a crystal globe aloft in one hand. It is currently buried in Tremalking. Its counterpart, in the form of a man, is also dressed in flowing robes with the crystal globe held aloft. The male statue was recently found buried near Cairhien, and is currently being unearthed.

These two statues are also unusual in that they were joined with identical but miniature versions of themselves which are believed to function solely as links between the channelers and the *sa'angreal*. This arrangement was apparently necessary, given the huge size of the *sa'angreal*, to allow the channelers access to the statues without having to transport themselves to the actual site, or worse yet, transporting the immense statues.

Another way to venture beyond the capacity of an unaided channeler is the process of linking several

channelers together. In the current age, drawing and channeling the flow of the One Power is usually a solitary act, but linking, a common technique in the Age of Legends, allows several flows to combine, thus increasing the overall strength and precision of the flow. A group that is linked is called a 'circle,' even when it is only two people. The primary value of the circle is its capacity for singular focus of multiple energies. It is impossible to focus two or more individual flows precisely on the same task, no matter how skilled the channelers, but when linked the person leading the circle can direct and channel the combined flows with the same pinpoint accuracy as if she/he were directing only one flow.

These combined flows handle more Power than any one member could channel alone, with more precision than several separate flows, but the linked flow is not as strong as each of the separate strengths added together. In other words, the link does not combine flows in a purely additive manner. Two women linked can handle more than either could separately, and with much greater control than with multiple flows – because it is a single flow – but they cannot handle as much as the two could separately. This limit holds however large the circle. It is the precision of the circles that makes them so powerful. The exact strike of one chisel can split a stone that would withstand any number of blows from a hammer.

Linking also has gender-based limitations due to the inherent differences of *saidin* and *saidar*. Men have the greater general strength in the Power, but women are essential for linking. Women can initiate a link; men cannot, though they can be part of it and even lead in certain circumstances.

Linking can be learned by any woman who can channel, and one who does not know how to form a link can be brought into one by someone who does know how. Leading a circle, however, depends on both strength and skill, which are not the same thing. The greater the combination of strength and skill, the larger the circle that a woman, or man, can lead.

The one who forms a link is not necessarily the one to lead it. Control can be passed voluntarily, and in the cases of some mixed-gender circles must be passed in order to weave flows.

A circle of up to thirteen female channelers can be linked together without the presence of a man. If a man is added to the link of thirteen women, they can then increase the link to include thirteen more women, or a total of twenty-six women and one man. Two men can take the circle to include thirty-four women. The next total is forty-five, with three men linked with forty-two women, then fifty-four (four men and fifty women), then sixty-three (five men and fifty-eight women), and finally seventy-two (six men and sixty-six women). This last, a circle of seventy-two, is the maximum possible link in terms of numbers.

Other gender mixes are possible in a link as well. The number of men in a circle is limited only by the fact that with the exceptions of the linking of one man and one woman or of two men and one woman (and, of course, two men and two women), there must always be at least one more woman in the circle than the number of men. Thus, three men would need four women to be in a circle together, four men would need five women, and so on. There can also be smaller circles than thirteen, whether of women alone or of men and women.

The cumulative strength of a circle depends on its size, the strengths of the individuals linked, whether or not *angreal* or *sa'angreal* are used, and the balance between male and female members in the circle. Although men are stronger than women, the strongest linked circles were those which contained nearly equal numbers of men and women. A smaller circle with a closer balance can be stronger than a larger, unbalanced circle.

The most powerful circle potentially, depending on the strengths and gifts of those linked, would be one containing thirty-five men and thirty-seven women, achieving the maximum possible size of seventy-two members as well as the greatest possible balance of male and female.

In most cases, either a man or a woman can control the link – this is called leading, focusing, or guiding – but in the case of a circle of seventy-two, a circle of only one man and one woman, or in most circles of up to thirteen which contain more than one man, a man must lead. Excepting the examples given above, and other circles of thirteen or less, a woman must lead where the minimum number of men are present.

Certain fragmentary manuscripts, largely forgotten, contain tantalizing hints about the nature and use of circles in the Age of Legends, but unfortunately only hints. According to what the circle was intended to achieve, members were recruited depending on their strengths in the Five Powers while the leader was chosen more for skill. It also seems that certain balances of male with female were considered best for certain tasks, and also certain sizes of circles. A circle of seventy-two may have been the largest and most powerful combination, but it was not always the best for the desired results. Some tasks

were best accomplished by a circle of one man and one woman, despite its limited strength, while others were more efficiently done with greater numbers. The details remain lost in the ruins of the Age of Legends, although it is possible that there may be sources hidden away in the library of the White Tower.

The Age of
Legends

Chapter 3

The Age of Legends

 THERE WAS A time, before the Breaking, when men and women wielded the One Power side by side with no fear of any taint on *saidin*. In this time there were no wars – even the word for war was lost, known only to scholars – and all manner of wonders were commonplace. This age is now known as the Age of Legends.

It has been well over three thousand years since the end of the Age of Legends, and its origins have been lost in the shroud of time. The little that is known has been gleaned from a few fragmented records which must be puzzled together to form a partial understanding of the Age.

One thing is certain: it was a very long and prosperous period in the history of the world. Huge cities, such as Paaran Disen, M'Jinn, Comelle, Mar Ruois, and Adanza,

arose to glitter as towering technological jewels among the lush greenery and verdant fields of crops which surrounded them. The great research college of Collam Daan, located in V'saine, with its magnificent floating sphere, drew seekers of knowledge from all across the land to study and discover new wonders of science and the One Power. Sho-wings filled the air and jo-cars sped along the ground, leaving little trace of their passage as they carried people and cargo from city to city. Crime was almost unknown, rehabilitation quick and certain. It was a time of idyllic peace, with all the possibilities and wonders of the universe awaiting discovery.

The people of this age had long outgrown any interest in material wealth as a goal unto itself. Status and honor were all-important, and could only be gained through service to the community. All hoped to be allowed to serve according to their gifts and to be found worthy of that service. Several sources mention the fact that even names reflected a person's status and honor. Everyone was born with two names and could earn the third one only through accomplishment, apparently possible in many fields.

The people afforded the most status, though they still had to earn their third name through great individual works, were those whose gifts made them capable of the greatest service: those who could effectively channel the One Power. These men and women were called Aes Sedai, which meant 'servant of all' in the Old Tongue. They were dedicated to using the full extent of their gift for the betterment of their world. Their symbol was a circle, half white and half black with the colors separated by a sinuous line, representing the equal and opposing balance of the *saidin* and *saidar* that made up the halves of the True Source.

Since the ability to channel was a genetic recessive, only two to three percent of the population could channel. Most of them were fairly weak, but the few who had great strength could perform feats that now seem miraculous. The talent was split equally among men and women, with men being stronger in general than women in the use of the Power, though individual strength did not matter greatly, as most Aes Sedai worked in teams.

Oddly, it appears from the fragmented records concerning Aes Sedai that many of them followed vocations which had little or nothing to do with the One Power or being Aes Sedai. When it was necessary to form a circle to perform some task, these Aes Sedai could be summoned from their other careers by the Hall of the Tower to assist with their particular strengths and skills.

Certain professions were primarily dominated by Aes Sedai. All Healers were channelers, called Restorers, able to do far more healing with the One Power than medicine alone allowed. No herb remedy or surgery could match the Restorer for speed or efficiency. No disease or injury, save death, was beyond the capacity of the Power to heal. Death from causes other than old age occurred only when the victim was beyond the reach of an Aes Sedai Restorer.

Mining, as such, was done with Aes Sedai who were strong in Earth. They could find and remove pure ores without any damage to the structure or ecology of the land. They could even use the Power to create alloys far beyond the strength of any constructed otherwise, though

such alloys were rare and highly valued even then. These alloys could be worked using conventional methods.

Farmland produced optimum yield through use of the One Power. In a method called 'seed singing,' Ogier (a separate race of beings gifted with the ability to aid and enhance growing things), Nym, and Da'shain Aiel worked as a team, focusing the One Power to insure perfect growth for every field they 'sang.' Sung crops were immune to blight and impervious to insects. As a result, most crops reached their best possible growth and highest nutritional content. Aes Sedai also manipulated the weather to best advantage. Droughts, floods, and other natural disasters were apparently unknown.

Most technological research and development was done by Aes Sedai. Entire branches of science owed their existence to the use of the One Power.

One particularly interesting fragment records Aes Sedai participating in an avenue of research that led to the development of living constructs made with and/or able to utilize the One Power. Chora trees were one such construct. Their large green trefoil leaves emitted an aura of peace and well-being to any who passed beneath them. Over the centuries, the chora tree has become better known through legend than through experience, for very few of these constructs survived the Breaking or its aftermath. Also known by the Aiel name *Avendesora*, the tree is now extremely rare and highly prized. Only one chora tree, called *Avendoraldera*, has been known to exist outside the Aiel Waste since the time of the Breaking. *Avendoraldera* no longer exists, having been destroyed by King Laman of Cairhien. The tree's destruction heralded the Aiel War and eventually led to Laman's death.

The Nym, another construct, were sentient beings with the ability to utilize the One Power for the benefit of plants and growing things. As a nameless scribe in Paaran Disen wrote, 'Where a Nym touched, all manner of green and growing things thrived.'

Other fields of Aes Sedai endeavor included design and construction of *angreal*, *sa'angreal* and *ter'angreal*. *Angreal* and *sa'angreal*, as mentioned previously, enhanced the ability to channel. *Ter'angreal*, however, were tools made to perform a specific function. Some had to be activated and energized with the One Power, and could only be used by Aes Sedai. Others could be used by anyone.

Some of these artifacts have survived to this day, but the original purpose of many of them remains unknown. Research in this area has been limited by the dangerous nature of many *ter'angreal*. Some channelers have been killed or burned out when attempting to work with these artifacts.

Several of the more unusual surviving *ter'angreal* are doorways or arches. It is not known where, when, or how the person entering is transported, but while the visitor is within their influence everything has the texture of reality.

The tri-arched *ter'angreal* within the heart of the White Tower requires women who can channel to activate it, and aids in testing a novice hoping to be advanced to the rank of Accepted. The arches, each made of silver material and standing just tall enough to walk under, make the initiate face her worst fears, first for what was, second for what is, and third for what will be. A similar *ter'angreal* stands in the Aiel city of Rhuidean and is believed to show the Wise Women who use it their possible futures. No one has been able to determine whether the current usage of either is at all similar to its original purpose.

Perhaps the strangest of all known *ter'angreal* are two tall redstone doorways, similar to yet different from each other in form and function, which do not require the user to be a channeler. Each stands independent of any supporting structure and is twisted strangely so that the eye keeps slipping away from the contour of its shape. One of these, decorated with three sinuous lines that run from top to bottom on each upright, resides in the Stone of Tear. Anyone passing through it enters a strange world where he or she is allowed to ask three questions and receive truthful answers. By an ancient compact with the inhabitants of the other side, no lamps, torches, items made of iron, or musical instruments are allowed within.

The other doorway, found in Rhuidean, is also crafted of redstone with twisting corners, but is decorated with rows of inverted triangles running the length of each upright. As with its counterpart, no device for making light, no iron, and no musical instruments may be brought within. Unlike its counterpart in Tear, what is granted within are three requests, but only at a price. The few who have ventured into it have discovered that the price can be very high.

Almost nothing is known of the worlds beyond the two doorways, except that the answers received are always true, though not always easily understood, and the requests are always granted, though not always as intended by the petitioner. Several ancient legends seem to refer to the inhabitants of the other side of these *ter'angreal*, and to indicate that dealing with them is both delicate and dangerous.

One property both arches and doorways seem to have in common is that they may only be used once by the

same individual, which makes them unlike most other *ter'angreal*, which can be reused as needed.

According to all sources, the Aes Sedai in the Age of Legends had a very loose sort of organization. To what extent that organization was part of the world government is not known; clearly the Aes Sedai were highly influential, with considerable power, at least at times, but equally clearly they were not the entire government and did not necessarily dominate it. They had their own internal governing structure through the Hall of the Servants, which was the core of the guild that controlled and regulated all those who could channel. This guild had branches in every city, town, and village that housed Aes Sedai. In large cities the guild hall was usually an impressive building. In small towns or villages the guild often met in someone's home, temporarily dedicated for that purpose. The main Hall of the Servants, located in the capital city of Paaran Disen, was described in one holographic fragment as having 'massive columned entrances, large ornate doorways, and polished floors of glowing white elstone.'

The Hall of the Servants regulated the Aes Sedai, setting and enforcing the rules that pertained to channelers. Since Aes Sedai of this time often worked in teams, detailed rules of conduct and procedure were essential to the guild. All law and punishment for Aes Sedai were handled within the guild. Little record survives to detail the actual bureaucracy, save that the individual Aes Sedai who was elected to head it was usually styled as 'First Among Servants,' and sat on the High Seat. There are records that, toward the end of the Age, Lews Therin Telamon, who was then First Among Servants, wore the ring of the Tamyrlin and summoned the Nine Rods of

Dominion. The description of the ring and exact nature of the nine rods have been lost, but it seems clear that the Aes Sedai, through the Hall of the Servants, wielded great power and were accorded a very high level of prestige and respect. Some historians, although not all, believe that the Oath Rod of the Aes Sedai may in fact be one of the original Nine Rods of Dominion mentioned in the ancient texts. The Oath Rod is currently held by the Aes Sedai of the White Tower and is used by each Accepted as she gives the oaths that are part of the ceremony of becoming an Aes Sedai. A *ter'angreal*, the Oath Rod is capable of binding a promise 'bone deep' into the one who holds it, so that any oath given cannot be broken unless the swearer is stilled.

The 'servants of all' were themselves apparently served by the Da'shain Aiel. These people were sworn to a covenant that bound them to serve the Aes Sedai and uphold the 'Way of the Leaf,' a pacifistic code of honor. The exact details and history of this covenant are lost, but we can surmise that each Aiel was pledged in service to a particular Aes Sedai, although it was not unusual for an Aes Sedai to be served by more than one Aiel. Their loyalty to the covenant and their service earned the Da'shain a level of respect second only to that accorded to the Aes Sedai.

The Da'shain Aiel had a very specific mode of dress that set them apart from regular citizens. They wore their hair short except for a tail in the back. They usually dressed in plain coat, breeches, and soft laced boots, usually in shades of brown or gray. Sources are not clear concerning whether or not Da'shain Aiel could channel, though they do agree that the Aiel could often enhance channeling, as when adding their voices to the seed singing of the Ogier.

With so few people able to channel, the Power had to be used selectively. Aes Sedai were not expected to maintain or energize machines, for instance, but rather concentrated their efforts on designing and creating the technology for them. Technicians and other skilled non-channelers could then handle the construction and repair; after that, anyone could operate them. The process that enabled the great Sharom, or floating sphere of Collam Daan, to hover high above the university was discovered and refined through the use of the One Power, but the sphere was built by normal people and suspended through use of the world's own magnetic and gravitational fields.

One often-mentioned benefit of Power-based technology was a very clean, aesthetically pleasing environment. Pollution from refining, transport, and industry was unknown, since waste by-products could be dispersed on a submolecular level. This waste-free technology, combined with the culture's need for a harmonious environment wherever possible, led to a lifestyle that focused on beauty and comfort as much as on utilitarian efficiency.

This marriage of aesthetics and functionality was especially evident in the major cities of the age, which were Paaran Disen, M'Jinn, Comelle, Adanza, Mar Ruois, V'saine, Jalanda, Emar Dal, Paral, Halidar, Kemali, Tsomo Nasalle, Devaille, and Tzora, in order of population size and importance. Each of these major metropolitan areas was a work of art unto itself.

V'saine, among the major cities, was best known as the home of the Collam Daan. The great university's silver and blue domes were bested only by the Sharom, a huge white sphere a thousand feet in diameter that floated

serenely above it. Together, the Collam Daan and the Sharom were the world's foremost center for research and development.

The Sharom was one of the classic examples of functional beauty. It might seem impractical to suspend a building high in the air, especially a scientific research facility that required its visitors to use an airborne transport or the One Power, but the designers of Collam Daan did it simply because they could, and because the Sharom was a skyborne pearl that celebrated the triumph of their art.

The coastal city of Comelle, third-largest in the world, overlooked the sea with breathtaking splendor from its mountainside. Its immense glass, crystal, and metal structures clung to the steep rock like a shining flower bursting from the stone. Adanza was reported to 'thrive with a vitality in its beauty matched only by the vitality of its people.' Even Tzora, the smallest of the major cities, was known for its multihued glass towers, in a wide variety of geometric shapes, which glittered like jewels in the sun.

Paaran Disen, central seat of government and crown jewel of them all, not only contained wonders of architectural genius among its spires and towers, but also the Hall of the Servants with its columns and shimmering elstone.

In each city, whether large or small, select use of the One Power allowed such latitude in architectural design and construction that almost every artistic whim could be indulged. Variations on geometric and organic shapes were favored, with gardens, trees, and fountains freely interwoven into the urban fabric. Silvery towers that stretched so high they seemed to touch the sky were often

interspersed with domes and arches that glowed rainbow bright with inset colored glass. Ribbonlike monorails and walkways hung suspended in the air between the structures, as if in an attempt to lace them together.

In every city, tall trefoil-leafed chora trees lined the smooth pavements of the streets and walkways, giving both shade and their unique aura of contentment. It was a saying of the Age that a city without chora trees would seem bleak as a wilderness. Gardens that may have contained red- and white-blossomed calma flowers and night-blooming dara lilies surrounded many of the structures.

Perhaps because of the pleasant nature of the environment, most people preferred to walk from one place to another except when distances were too great or burdens too large. Or when, as in the case with the Sharom, the entrances were high above the ground and required special transport. For these occasions, the people used a wide variety of vehicles.

Most short-range mass transport was handled by large multi-passenger vehicles that used a type of antigravity technology. Jo-cars, jumpers, and hoverflies had a much smaller passenger and cargo capacity. Jo-cars had a very efficient four-wheel design, or, in the floater version, a type of gravitational hovercraft technology. Both jumpers and hoverflies could float suspended above the ground at various distances. The smoothly paved roads made all types of travel, both vehicular and pedestrian, more efficient.

Long-range transport relied primarily on the sho-wing, an airborne vehicle available in several types and sizes. The sho-wing was capable of both short- and long-range flight, sometimes at high rates of speed. All overseas

travel was done via sho-wing. The sho-wing designs were derived from a basic delta-wing pattern, which was varied to suit the specific needs of each individual purpose. Some of them were very large, capable of carrying hundreds of passengers, and some were quite small, for personal use.

For the Aes Sedai, and sometimes those who served them, mechanical transport was unnecessary. Many people who could channel effectively could also Travel, a process which used the One Power to open a doorway that allowed stepping from one location to another at any distance without crossing the intervening space. Anyone could pass through the opening if it was made large enough, but only an Aes Sedai could actually create and hold the doorway. It was a very convenient way to move between locations, but impractical for use by the general public. It has only recently been rediscovered. Like most things having to do with the Power, it is different for men and women. A man must use the Power to bore a hole through the Pattern from his location to the place he wants to be. A woman, however, creates a similarity in the Pattern from her location to where she wants to be. When both places have achieved enough of a similarity at one spot, the places become one and she can simply step through the resulting opening. For either men or women, attempting the method of the other gender often has tragic results. Skimming, a process similar to Traveling, was occasionally used by those less adept. This method involved the use of platforms or steps in the void outside the Pattern to carry the traveler from one point to another.

There are records of people of the Age even transporting to other worlds, both among the stars and in other

dimensions. The Portal Stones are said to be gateways to alternative realities within the Pattern. Portal Stones, activated by the One Power, allowed the users and any who accompanied them to travel to other dimensions and worlds within the universe of the Wheel. Ruins of Portal Stones have been discovered in various parts of the world. Gray stone cylinders approximately three spans tall and a full pace thick, these stones are covered with hundreds of deeply incised diagrams and markings. The knowledge of their use has been lost, but it is believed that Aes Sedai in the Age of Legends used them freely. Indications are that they may predate the Age of Legends. It is doubtful that Portal Stones were used regularly by any other than Aes Sedai, because skill and strength in the Power were needed to activate them.

If the bits of information concerning daily life that have been preserved over the centuries can be believed, even ordinary people had access to a wide variety of technological wonders that seemed to rival the Power itself. It was possible to 'live' stories in your own home by some means no longer known, and entertainment also was brought directly into the home through a three-dimensional imaging process. Live or prerecorded programs took on lifelike form right before the viewer. Communications also made use of this process. It was possible, with a code, to contact anyone who had access to a call unit, and to then see that person, or their logo if they wished to preserve privacy, as a small three-dimensional projection. This process created the illusion of being able to talk face-to-face no matter the actual distance involved.

Heat exchangers maintained interior environments at a constant temperature regardless of the weather.

Glowbulbs provided light without need of recharging or replacement. Energy to propel vehicles and operate devices was dispersed through a broadcast process that made it available to anyone with the proper receiving equipment. Preservation of artifacts or extreme perishables was possible with stasis-boxes. Time did not pass for objects within a stasis-box once the box was activated.

While many fabrics primarily contained natural fibers, some fabrics like streith and fancloth were entirely artificial. Streith was a shimmering material, usually white, that changed color and opacity to match the mood of the wearer. Fancloth created a camouflage effect, able to duplicate its surroundings so faithfully as to make the wearer seem invisible. Both were used in high-fashion garments. These fabrics exist today, but are quite rare, and fancloth, at least, is used for far more practical applications. Fancloaks, made of fancloth, are one of the finest examples of modern practicality deriving from ancient fashion. Designed to cover the wearer from head to foot, these cloaks create an almost perfect camouflage. Because of the difficulty in obtaining fancloth today, it is exclusively reserved for use by the Warders of the Aes Sedai. It is believed to be manufactured in the White Tower by use of a *ter'angreal*.

One badly fragmented text believed to date from this time contains some interesting data regarding health and healing. Because of the use of the Power in health care, most people did not have to fear dying from disease or injury. The average life expectancy was between one hundred and fifty and two hundred years. For Aes Sedai it was considerably longer, since use of the One Power somehow enhanced the youth and durability of

the channeler's body, greatly extending his or her life. There are records of some Aes Sedai being considered barely middle-aged at three hundred years, and some channelers may have lived seven hundred years or more. Since long life spans and excellent health care resulted in large viable populations, it is fortunate that birth-control methods were extremely reliable and without side effects.

This society was supported by a stable worldwide economy; it is doubtful that the people of the Age would have been able to reach such a high level of advancement without it. The global capitalistic economy gave the greatest rewards for the greatest service, and while Aes Sedai handled many important roles, they represented such a small percentage of the community that the majority of jobs was left open to nonchannelers. Financial gain was not difficult to achieve, but meant little in a world where most material things were plentiful. Individuals gained financial reward based on their work and its value to society. Even a person in the least-valued position gained enough money to assure a comfortable standard of living. There was no poverty. Everyone who wished had a place to serve.

Despite the overall harmonious balance within society, crime, including violent crimes and crimes of passion, was not unknown. Society did not believe in any type of restraint unless absolutely necessary. When the perpetrators of violent acts were caught, they were not sent to prison. Rather, they were constrained, in some manner not fully understood, against repeat offenses. This binding made it impossible for the criminal ever to repeat his crime. As a result, criminal acts of any kind were very rare.

The Age's system of government was both strong and responsive. Unfortunately very few details of this government or how it interacted with the population at large and the Aes Sedai are available. The sparse fragmented documents that have been preserved mention a worldwide parliament, or 'council,' of democratically elected officials. They also mention that within the government the ability to channel earned respect, but did not guarantee prominence. From this we can deduce that Aes Sedai were often elected to the council, and were influential, but were not necessarily in charge.

It is easy to understand why major conflicts among people or classes did not exist in the Age of Legends. Most of the motives for conflict had been eliminated: Worldwide economic stability had been established, removing any possibility of poverty or extreme financial inequality. Food harvesting and distribution was enhanced by the high level of technology and the use of the One Power, eliminating starvation and even deprivation. Status was more important than financial gain, eliminating most types of base greed, if not envy. In addition, the most powerful group of people, the Aes Sedai, were seldom tempted to use their abilities for personal gain alone, because they knew that service to others would reap greater rewards and higher status than any political or financial manipulation ever could.

Without economic or survival motivations, conflicts rarely escalated beyond argument, usually solved through mediation. As a result, the concept of war did not exist. At least not until the very end of the Age.

TESTING FOR THE ABILITY IN THE AGE OF LEGENDS

It was considered a great honor to be chosen to train and serve as an Aes Sedai. But only the two or three percent of the population that had that ability to learn to channel could join the elite ranks of the 'servants of all.' To find these gifted people, Aes Sedai regularly tested young people, looking for the spark that meant they might become Aes Sedai.

The testing was not mandatory, though few passed up the opportunity, and it required no special preparation or study. As with everything that dealt with the Power and its separate halves, the male and female abilities functioned differently and manifested themselves at different ages.

In general, women displayed the ability to channel, or to learn, at a far younger age than their male counterparts. For a woman, this ability appeared at any age from puberty, or approximately twelve or thirteen, to twenty-one. If she was tested at twenty-one and the spark was still not there, it never would be. A man usually did not manifest trainability until at least the age of sixteen, but he retained the potential to show the inborn ability to channel until his mid-twenties. In both cases, the ability to learn – as opposed to the inborn spark – would lie dormant until discovered at whatever age. Though relatively few people tested after their early or mid-twenties, some did test successfully at much later ages. These were inevitably people who either had not tested at all when younger or who had given up after a failure or two.

Because the ability to learn could appear at any time during an almost ten-year period, candidates were encouraged to test more than once, though few did. For those

who had the inborn ability to channel, the choice to avoid retesting would not change anything. They would channel eventually without the test. However, those who had the ability to learn, but did not have the inborn talent, might never be aware of that fact if they stopped testing before trainability manifested itself. For such a person to succeed as a channeler, the spark of ability had to be drawn out and carefully honed by Aes Sedai instructors.

The testing process required a trained Aes Sedai in the role of tester. Owing to the nature of *saidin* and *saidar*, the Aes Sedai who tested women had to be female, and the one who tested men, male. No woman could verify a man's ability, and no man a woman's, save through their works.

A man who had the ability to learn gave off a resonance whenever *saidin* was channeled within close proximity. This resonance could be felt only by another man, and only while he was embracing the Power himself. A nonchanneler, or a channeler who was not touching *saidin* at that moment, felt nothing. The candidate himself usually also felt nothing. The testing Aes Sedai usually channeled a very tiny flame while waiting to feel the resulting resonance from the candidate. If he felt the 'echo,' he knew the other man had the spark that meant he might be able to be trained. This usually took about ten to fifteen minutes, if the candidate was focused on the flame, or up to thirty minutes if he was not. Even if the candidate was very resistant, the resonance would still occur, though it might take as much as an hour.

For men, this step was only the beginning. It established only the possibility of touching the True Source. There was no way to tell how much potential ability an individual actually had. Only through training and experience could a man's strength and limitations become

known, for with proper guidance the man's ability continued to grow until he reached those limits.

For women the testing process was not quite as difficult. A female Aes Sedai could feel the inborn ability to channel and relative strength of another woman who could channel within five or ten feet. It was not necessary for either to embrace the Power to feel this 'kindred spirit.'

To find those who could not yet channel but who had the ability to learn, it was necessary to establish a resonance. Like her male counterpart, the female Aes Sedai drew on the One Power to channel a small flame, but it was then up to the *candidate* to try to feel the flow of the Power the Aes Sedai was channeling. If she had any ability to learn, *she* would feel the resonance of the Aes Sedai's flow. At that point the tester was also able to feel the candidate and immediately know her potential strength. Sometimes the woman being tested would actually be led unconsciously to channeling the flow, though only for the briefest time; this was an indication of great potential for quick learning.

In both cases the tester had to be very careful to use only a minute amount of the Power to avoid damage or burnout for the candidate.

The men and women who passed the testing were sent away to a special school to be trained as Aes Sedai. The schooling included as well the regular curriculum of subjects and was free to those who qualified.

Chapter 4

The Fall into Shadow

The Dark One was bound outside of time
by the Creator at the moment of creation.

 It was not until an ill-fated research project produced the Bore that the truth about the Dark One was suspected. During the Age of Legends, no one knew of the Dark One or felt his touch.

The accomplishments of this lost Age seem infinite by modern standards, but at the time, many Aes Sedai chafed under the severe limitations imposed by the natural restrictions of *saidin* and *saidar*. Some dreamed of a source of power that would bypass these limitations.

One team of researchers at the Collam Daan, including in their number Mierin Eronaile and Beidomon, both Aes Sedai, believed they had actually found that source. (There seem to have been other members of the team, but their names have not survived. The record also does not tell us Mierin's position on the team,

though at least one source does mention Beidomon as 'assisting her.')

They had discovered a thin place in the Pattern that appeared to cover an undivided source of the One Power separate from the True Source. This energy did not appear to follow the conventional restrictions of the Power, in that it gave indications of being usable by men and women equally. Such a source, available without limitations, would allow men and women to unite in ways previously impossible. Aes Sedai would be able to perform feats well beyond existing capabilities. It was apparently inaccessible by the means used for the One Power, but they had only to bore a small hole in the Pattern to tap it. Using the One Power, in what was, they hoped, the last time *saidin* and *saidar* would be separated, Mierin and the team bored through to the source of the unusual Power emanations.

The resulting backlash destroyed the floating Sharom, shattering it like the egg it so resembled, and creating ripples in the fabric of reality as shock waves from the breach shook the Pattern. It was not an indivisible source of the One Power the team had discovered, but the place outside of the Pattern where the Dark One had been imprisoned since the moment of creation. The emanations Mierin and the others had sensed with such hope were his dark energies, trapped just beyond the thin place in the pattern that covered his prison. The hole they created has been ever after known as the Bore.

One of the most important finds of recent years, perhaps one of the most important since the Breaking, is no less than a fragmentary history of the world from the drilling of the Bore into the Dark One's prison to the end of the Breaking of the World. The original apparently

dated from early in the first century AB, though no record can be found anywhere of such a history's publication, and it has almost certainly survived purely in single copies. Discovered in a dusty storage room in Chachin, the pages lay in a chest full of old bills and receipts, students' copybooks and private diaries, most so foxed by age and with ink so faded as to be unreadable. The fragment was readable, barely, but the usual problems were present, of course, quite aside from the difficulties of translation and centuries of copyists' errors; such a history would no doubt be a vast, multi-volume work, yet of the 212 surviving pages, the largest section of consecutive pages numbers six, and nowhere else are there more than two. Such dates as are given are totally incomprehensible, as no calendar dating from the Age of Legends has ever been found.

Many pages refer to cataclysmic events (cities destroyed by balefire during the War of the Shadow; whole regions swallowed by earthquakes or covered by the sea almost overnight), but the pages that would tell exactly where these things happened, what their special significance was, and the resolution or end result are usually missing. Why is this collection so important? Fragmentary as it is, it contains more information about the War of the Shadow than any other known source, perhaps as much as all others combined in some ways. But even more, the six consecutive pages and others that must be placed close to them contain the only known account of events surrounding what surely must be the most important single event in the history of the world, in any Age: the sealing of the Bore by Lews Therin Telamon and the Hundred Companions.

At one time, the denizens of the world had only to

deal with the evil within themselves. If motivations for war and hate were removed, then so were the resultant activities. The Bore changed all of that. Like a small finger hole in a prison wall, the Bore was not large enough to allow the Dark One's escape, but it was large enough to allow him to touch the world. His touch subtly altered everything that came within its influence. All the baser motivations and emotional problems of mankind were enhanced and manipulated, enlarging envy, greed, and anger despite lack of any true motivating factors. All those dissatisfied with their lot in life felt that dissatisfaction intensify. Thievery, assault, murder, and even wars began to appear with increasing frequency.

Measures designed to deal with the occasional problems of a peaceful social structure were entirely inadequate in the face of these new problems. The fabric of society began to unravel under the onslaught of the Dark One's influence. A large part of the horror came from the simple fact that for many years, no one knew why this was all happening; chaos seemed to be welling up from nowhere, without cause.

Some people did begin to suspect, and eventually to know, the cause, but unfortunately most of these were people who saw possible gain for themselves in the Dark One's freedom. Before the rest of the world had more than suspected what they faced, the growing numbers of those favoring the Dark One were beginning to organize, and perhaps to communicate with the Dark One; certainly they did so later.

Those who were dissatisfied with their lives or who sought greater power now had a choice. Anyone who thought they had ever been mistreated or passed over, as well as many who just sought change, were drawn to

embrace the Dark. The Dark One offered favor and status above what these people could otherwise achieve. Those who served his cause were given promises of immortality, provided the Dark One was freed. The Dark Lord promised to remake the world in his image once he was unbound from his prison. All who stood by him would then be rewarded for their assistance. Even Aes Sedai, drawn by promises of power, immortality, and, in some cases, revenge, joined the ranks of those sympathetic to the Dark One, adding great strength to his cause. These Aes Sedai came to be known as 'Dreadlords.'

The ranks of those sympathetic to the Dark sowed plots and counterplots into the upheavals already plaguing society. It was during this time that such brutal sports as *sha'je* dueling came briefly into vogue. *Sha'je* duels, held at Qal, involved the use of left- and right-hand daggers, called respectively *osan'gar* and *aran'gar*, tipped with slow poison. There was rarely a clear winner, since both participants usually succumbed to either blade or poison. Yet there were worse. In some parts of the world, in the years immediately preceding the final collapse into war, murder, rape, and even torture became regular parts of many spectator sports.

The Friends of the Dark, as they called themselves, actively recruited additional followers. In some cases they are believed to have deliberately forced individuals in key positions of power to join them, using torture, Compulsion, or a form of linking that would turn any who could channel to the Dark, even against their will.

This period of increasingly dark chaos lasted approximately one hundred years to one hundred and ten years after the drilling of the Bore, and was referred to as 'the Collapse' by several very early sources. It certainly qualified

for the name, as civilization did very nearly collapse, and the order and peace of the world of the Age of Legends certainly did.

Eventually those loyal to the Dark One felt themselves strong enough to act. In a swift strike they made an attempt to free the Dark One completely and take control. This event was the actual beginning of the War of the Shadow, which pitted the followers and minions of the Dark against those who fought to resist, and which soon involved the whole world. During the resulting ten-year struggle, all the forgotten facets of war were rediscovered, in many cases twisted by the Dark.

Fearsome constructs, creatures out of nightmare, and weapons of evil were unleashed on an ill-prepared population. Under the onslaught of the Dark forces, the defenders were forced to turn their technology to the making of weapons of war. Jo-cars were armored and fitted with weapons, hoverflies were altered into deadly flying machines capable of striking from the sky. Shocklances and other tools of long-distance destruction were built along with suitable body armor. Fancloth, formerly used for fashion, became the material for camouflage battle capes and proved invaluable on the battlefield.

Some sports, such as swordplay, formerly considered a tame form of exercise, were reinvented as deadly martial arts. Children were trained from the age of ten to become soldiers. Men and women learned battle tactics and defense strategies where before they had studied art and music. As the entire world had once lived peace, it now became geared for war.

The One Power, previously only used for good, became a deadly weapon. This may be the reason the war was also

known as the War of Power. Air, Water, Earth, Fire, and Spirit produced devastating results. But these flows were mild weapons compared with the vast destructive power unleashed when channelers on both sides discovered balefire. The liquid white-hot fire was invincible, burning anything it touched into nonexistence.

This weapon was used liberally for a year by both sides – until they discovered its hidden cost. The searing energy of balefire did more than kill or destroy – it actually burned threads from the Pattern. Anything destroyed this way actually ceased to exist before the moment of destruction, leaving only a memory of deeds no longer done and souls forever erased from the Pattern. Not only that; whatever had been done because of those vanished actions also no longer had been done. The greater the power of the balefire, the further back in time its victim ceased to exist. During the year of unrestricted use, entire cities were burned from the Pattern, and the world and its universe were threatened by the broken and loose threads. Reality itself was in danger of unraveling.

Faced with the possible dissolution of existence, both sides, without formal agreement or truce, simply stopped using balefire. There was no point in winning a world if the world was utterly destroyed in the process. Even those who supported the Dark Lord wanted something left to rule.

Even without such a destructive weapon, the Dark One still had vast resources to call upon. His armies of ferocious inhuman constructs, often armed with deadly weapons made at the cost of human souls, and combined with those powerful Aes Sedai who had turned to his cause, routinely routed the forces that attempted to stand against them. Though trapped outside the Pattern, the

Dark One inspired unquestioning loyalty and fear among those who felt his touch.

At the onset of the war, the people had turned to the Aes Sedai to defend and guide them. The man who sat in the High Seat of the Hall of the Servants at that time was Lews Therin Telamon, Lord of the Morning, who came to be known as the Dragon. The most powerful man of his time, he was chosen to lead the Ogier (who proved themselves to be as fierce in war as they had been gifted with songs in peace), the human warmen armed with new technology, and the Aes Sedai in the fight to prevent the Dark One from breaking free of his prison. Their idyllic peace and innocence had already been taken. Now, under the Dragon, they struggled to save what was left from ultimate destruction.

Only the Da'shain Aiel, who served the Aes Sedai and the Lord Dragon who led them, remained completely apart from the fighting. Their covenant, the Way of the Leaf, prevented them from taking up arms even in the face of death. The Aes Sedai they served zealously protected them and their covenant, while accepting their service in all non-military matters. In many ways the Aiel represented to them the best of all that had been lost when the Bore was opened. Perhaps it was this mutual service and protection under Lews Therin that led to the Da'shain being called the People of the Dragon.

The War of the Shadow was a seesaw affair. In the first three years, large parts of the world fell under the Dark One's dominion, however indirectly, through human representatives. Over the next four years, under Lews Therin's leadership, much of the territory was retaken, though not without reverses. At that point a stalemate was reached which lasted nearly a year. Then the Shadow

began to advance again, slowly at first but with increasing speed. According to the unknown writer of the fragmentary historical record, 'It was as if with every step forward by the Shadow, disorder and chaos grew, and feeding on that, the Shadow gained strength, so that its next stride was longer, and the next after would be longer still.'

The conflict eventually grew to engulf the entire world. Huge parts of the world were devastated as the war surged back and forth, though little information survives concerning individual battles. It is mentioned that the Dragon soundly defeated Elan Morin Tedronai, the 'Betrayer of Hope,' at the gates of Paaran Disen, but all else concerning that battle has been lost, save that Elan Morin survived his defeat. For the most part Lews Therin seems to have found himself fighting for a losing cause. Some of his most trusted generals, including the favored Tel Janin Aellinsar and Barid Bel Medar, betrayed him to join the Dark, using their considerable talents and strengths against him.

One of the most powerful male *sa'angreal* ever made, *Callandor* is believed to have been constructed during the War of Power. A crystal sword with a curved blade, it is the only *sa'angreal* known to be made in the form of a weapon. Possibly second only to the giant male and female statues, it was believed able to channel enough of the Power to level a city. Perhaps aware of the danger inherent in such a weapon, its makers placed the sword within the Stone of Tear and specially shielded it sometime during the Breaking, probably in an attempt to protect it from maddened male Aes Sedai.

By the final years of the war, the Shadow seemed on a path to inevitable victory. The Shadow was willing to starve or murder much of the population of the conquered

territories to enforce its rule, and the forces of the Light could no longer sustain the protracted war. They were moving toward defeat with increasing speed. If they were to win, they would have to develop a single decisive offensive that could end the war quickly.

One of the more daring plans, proposed by Lews Therin, centered around a direct attack on the Bore itself, to reseal the Bore and cut the Dark One's access to the world. Without the Dark One's touch, the world would have a chance to return to normal. Seven indestructible *cuendillar* disks, made with the One Power and marked with the seal of the Aes Sedai, were prepared to function as 'focus points' (there seems no better translation from the Old Tongue). The strike was to be carried out at Shayol Ghul, the one place on earth where that 'thinness in the Pattern' makes the Bore detectable. A raiding force consisting of soldiers for security and a circle of seven female Aes Sedai and six male would travel there and implant seals held by the focus points.

The plan was risky for a number of reasons. All knew that the Dark One had a certain direct effect on the area close around Shayol Ghul – his touch had already transformed it from an idyllic island in a cool sea to a desolate waste – and it was quite likely that any attempt to channel there would be instantly detected and the raiding party destroyed. Worse, several experts claimed that if the seals were not placed with exact precision, the resultant strain, instead of sealing the Bore, would rip it open, freeing the Dark One entirely.

Most references to the seals concern the seven palm-sized discs marked on top with the ancient symbol of the Aes Sedai, half dead black and half purest white with the two halves separated by a sinuous line. In fact, each of

these discs only serves as a focus for the actual seals on the Dark One's prison, which are weaves of the Power. The discs themselves are *ter'angreal* made of *cuendillar*, or 'heartstone,' designed to absorb any force used against it, including the One Power, and become stronger from the assault rather than break. In recent years these seals have begun to fail. Those that have been found are no longer indestructible. The implications for the state of the Dark One's prison, considering the link between the physical discs and the actual seals, are frightening to contemplate.

Another plan centered around two huge *sa'angreal*, one attuned to *saidin* and one to *saidar*, both so powerful that using them safely required special *ter'angreal*, like miniature versions of the great *sa'angreal*, constructed especially for the purpose. This project had its detractors, too, for the *sa'angreal* were thought to be so powerful that either one might enable a single person to channel enough of the One Power to destroy the world, while both together certainly would do so. Some doubted that so much of the One Power could possibly be handled safely. Against that was the certainty that used together they would provide enough of the Power to defeat the Shadow's forces completely and erect a barrier around Shayol Ghul until a safe way of dealing with the Bore could be determined. Many of the supporters of this plan distrusted the other, and they had no intention of trying to seal the Bore immediately; they feared the same error in precise placement.

Support in the Hall of the Servants for the second plan, and opposition to the first, centered around a woman named Latra Posae Decume. Apparently a speaker of considerable force and persuasion, she gathered many adherents around her, but what assured her victory was

an agreement she reached with every female Aes Sedai of significant strength on the side of the Light. (In the manuscript, this agreement is called 'the Fateful Concord,' but it is doubtful that this was the name by which it was generally known.) Lews Therin's plan was too rash, too dangerous, and no woman would take part in it. Since precise placement of the seals was widely thought to require a circle including seven women and six men, all well above average strength in the Power, the Concord apparently killed the plan. Work on the two huge *sa'angreal*, which would have the form of statues, rushed forward.

Just as the *sa'angreal* were completed, disaster struck. The *ter'angreal* required to use them were being made at a place far removed from the *sa'angreal*, because of the danger of 'uncontrolled resonances during the final stages,' and that region was overrun by Shadow forces under Sammael. Fortunately the *ter'angreal* themselves were hidden and the place where they were made destroyed just before the invasion (it had been a secret all along), so neither Sammael nor anyone else for the Shadow knew that any of the tools of Power were within their grasp. The side of the Light still had the *sa'angreal*, but no safe way to use them; without the *ter'angreal* it was certain that even the strongest Aes Sedai would be burned out by the huge flow of the One Power, probably within minutes.

Lews Therin argued again for his plan, acknowledging the risks but saying that it was now the only chance; yet Latra Posae maintained her opposition. Belief in the danger of misplaced seals had spread, and more female Aes Sedai had pledged to the Fateful Concord, even many who were nowhere near strong enough to qualify for the

circle. Latra Posae managed to have agents sent to attempt to smuggle the access *ter'angreal* out of Shadow-controlled territory.

Almost immediately on the heels of Sammael's advance, and well before Latra Posae's agents had time to reach their objective, armies commanded by Demandred and Be'lal struck heavily, threatening (although perhaps unknowingly) the great *sa'angreal*. At this point in the war, halting the Shadow's advance was the best that could be hoped for; the forces of Light had regained no con-quered territory in over two years. Lews Therin's forces barely managed to contain these two drives, but Demandred and Be'lal kept the pressure on. Sammael began a new offensive, also barely held, and there is men-tion of heavy military activity elsewhere. It was clear that the final defeat was at hand; should any of the three major offensives commanded by Forsaken break through, the end would be only a matter of time, perhaps as little as months. Massive riots swept a number of cities still held for the Light as people panicked in expectation of the Shadow's victory. The Hall of the Servants itself was razed by those once loyal to Lews Therin, and 'the peace fac-tion' reappeared. This faction was apparently a group demanding negotiations with the Forsaken.

The available evidence does not state whether there were several peace factions during the course of the war or only one, with fortunes that waxed and waned. This was not the first time that a faction had pressed for peace with the Forsaken, for the manuscript makes it clear that this group, acting on its own, sent parties to the Forsaken on several occasions to seek a negotiated settlement. In each case, however, members of the returned delegation were later discovered aiding the Shadow's cause.

Apparently they did not heed a saying supposed to have originated during their time: 'There is never peace with the Shadow.'

Latra Posae's opposition to the Dragon's plan continued despite these events, and the female Aes Sedai – perhaps in the manner of animals that, seeing a boulder rushing downhill, freeze in the path of destruction – held to their pledge, making the circle impossible. Lews Therin plainly knew it would be impossible to hold the huge *sa'angreal* long enough for the access *ter'angreal* to be smuggled out, even if the smuggling were successful. In his view, there was no longer any choice, and he resolved to carry out his initial plan without the women.

Unknown to anyone at this point, all of the agents responsible for recovering the *ter'angreal* had been caught and killed, and the artifacts were scattered widely across areas held for the Shadow. News of this tragedy was not received until well after events had far outrun anyone's plans.

A group of powerful young male Aes Sedai, vocal to the point of disrupting meetings at the Hall of the Servants, had supported Lews Therin during the struggle with Latra Posae. This group was popularly called the Hundred Companions, though they actually numbered 113 at this point. With the Hundred Companions and a force of some ten thousand warmen, Lews Therin launched the planned attack on the Bore.

While the exact events of that day can never be known, some of the details have survived. The Dragon and his companions arrived at Shayol Ghul to discover an unexpected bonus: a gathering of the thirteen most powerful leaders of the Forsaken Aes Sedai was taking place at the Pit of Doom deep within the mountain at the same

moment, perhaps summoned by the Dark One for a conference. The Companions struck quickly and mercilessly, sealing the Bore safely, without ripping open the Dark One's prison as many opponents had feared. Forty-five of the Companions were killed in the battle, and apparently the warmen took a much higher percentage of casualties. The strike trapped all the attending Forsaken within the sealing, thus removing with one stroke the Shadow's touch and his leadership in this world. With the seals safely placed, the *cuendillar* disks were carefully hidden.

After the hundred or so years of the Collapse and ten bloody years of conflict, the War of the Shadow was at an end. Though most of the world was still held for the Shadow, many believed that without their leaders the Shadow's followers would falter, all Shadow-held lands would be easily reclaimed, and the Shadow would be extinguished completely. After all, the Dark One could no longer reach the world. Lews Therin, the Dragon, and the forces of Light had emerged victorious, or so it seemed.

No one had counted on the Dark One's counterstroke.

Chapter 5

The Dark One and the Male Forsaken

SHAI'TAN

WHEN THE BORE was drilled into a place outside the Pattern, a dark presence used the opening to touch the world. This presence, which named itself Shai'tan, had been imprisoned outside of time and creation by the Creator of the universe. Since its touch was first felt, it has been called by many names: Father of Lies, Sightblinder, Lord of the Grave, Shepherd of the Night, Heartsbane, Soulsbane, Heartfang, Old Grim, Grassburner, Leafblighter, and, most commonly, the Dark One. Even today, few use its true name, fearing that to do so will call the Dark One's attention to them. Naming the Dark One is considered an evil curse.

Though neither male nor female by known standards, Shai'tan is usually referred to as male. He has no true physical form, being something outside and beyond this

universe, yet he has the ability to affect the physical world. Human motivations are often ascribed to him despite the fact that he is not human and therefore defies our complete understanding. Yet there is one human word which seems to embody Shai'tan – 'evil.'

His followers agree that it is his intention to break free of his prison and come fully into the world, and he has announced his intention to remake all of creation according to his own design when he escapes after Tarmon Gai'don, the Last Battle. There is little doubt that he has the power to do this, since he is a being with godlike abilities, perhaps on a level with the Creator's. Many scholars believe him to be the complete antithesis of the Creator. He does not, however, have the ability to break free of his prison without assistance from our world. The fact that the War of the Shadow began with an attempt by his followers to complete what the Bore began is proof of this limitation. Those followers were and are essential to any possible escape, but since the drilling of the Bore, there have always been those willing to follow the Dark.

When Shai'tan first touched the world, his touch carried a promise of power and dominion beyond the dreams of man. He promised to remake the world and allow those who prepared the way to rule it in his name. Those who served him faithfully would be granted immortality.

DREADLORDS

Some Aes Sedai were extremely susceptible to these promises of domination and glory. It did not matter that the world they would rule would be a world of shadow.

All that mattered was that they would rule, and with immortality their rule could last forever. These Aes Sedai forsook the Light and their oaths of service to follow the wishes of the Great Lord of the Dark. They never called him by name, believing use of his true name to be blasphemy, instead using 'Great Lord of the Dark.' All of these Dreadlords, as they were known, traveled to the Pit of Doom in Shayol Ghul to dedicate their souls to the Dark Lord. The best of them were given power and ability beyond that of others, making them almost demigods. Among themselves they were known as 'Those Chosen to Rule the World Forever,' or simply 'the Chosen.' To all others, they were known as the Forsaken.

THE FORSAKEN

One thing is clear from a number of sources: The Forsaken schemed against one another with almost as much fervor as they schemed for the Shadow's conquest. The greatest goal for all of the Chosen was to be named 'Nae'blis,' the one who would stand above all others, only a half step below the Great Lord himself after the Last Battle. They vied for that position of greatest favor from the day they were sworn to the Dark, hoping to prove their worthiness to the Great Lord. Though other Aes Sedai went over to the Shadow, none who equaled or approached in strength those now called Forsaken was still alive by the last year of the War of Power; yet not one of them is reported to have died by enemy action. These people wanted power, and the desire became an obsession – and it is almost certain that the Dark One encouraged this deadly competition. No doubt the Dark

One wanted only the strongest to serve him, and he prodded his servants to winnow themselves.

The survivors of this winnowing process, the thirteen most powerful of the Chosen, who were caught in the sealing of the Bore, are known in all cases but one by the Old Tongue names men had given them out of contempt. They are Aginor, Asmodean, Balthamel, Be'lal, Demandred, Graendal, Ishamael, Lanfear, Mesaana, Moghedien, Rahvin, Sammael, and Semirhage. The Chosen proudly embraced their new names as symbols of their rebirth in the Shadow, relinquishing the ones with which they had been born. From the War of Power to this day their names have been invoked to frighten children, though the bleakest of the tales told of the Chosen are but pale shadows of the atrocities they actually committed.

Many details of their lives and origins have been lost to time and history while their bodies remained trapped in the seal, but a remarkable amount of information has survived the three or possibly four thousand years since they were imprisoned by Lews Therin. Yet it is also remarkable that so little is known of their doings after their recent reemergence into the world. Whether the Forsaken destroyed any accurate information about themselves that might reveal weaknesses is unknown, but it must be considered a possibility. In any case, the amount of information available on the Forsaken differs considerably from individual to individual.

ISHAMAEL

Foremost of the thirteen who formed the high council of the Shadow's forces was Ishamael, or 'Betrayer of Hope' in

the Old Tongue. Also known as Ba'alzamon, Heart of the Dark, and Soul of the Shadow, he was assuredly the Dark One's top captain-general despite the fact that he never held a direct field command. Believed to be the most powerful of the Chosen in the use of the One Power, he was equaled by none but Lews Therin Telamon himself.

As Elan Morin Tedronai, he was one of the foremost philosophers of his time, possibly the foremost. His books (among them *Analysis of Perceived Meaning*, *Reality and the Absence of Meaning*, and the *Disassembly of Reason*), while too esoteric for wide popularity, were extremely influential in many areas beyond philosophy, especially in the arts. No copies survive, and perhaps the world is better off for it, considering the circumstances. Some particles that have survived of his writings from after he went over to the Shadow – probably letters – indicate that it was his belief that the war between the Shadow and the soul of Lews Therin had gone on since the creation, an endless war between the Great Lord of the Dark and the Creator using human surrogates. According to him, Lews Therin had succumbed to the Dark during other turnings of the Wheel and become the Great Lord's champion. During the war, he fought as hard to turn Lews Therin to the side of the Shadow as he did to defeat him.

Elan Morin certainly was among the first to pledge himself to the Shadow, possibly the first. His public announcement of this, coming from a world-respected figure at a time when famine, plagues, and massive riots were racking an unprepared world, in the middle of a conference called to discuss dealing with the crisis, sparked even greater riots. It was Elan Morin who at the same time first announced to the world what it was that they faced. He called for the complete destruction of the

old order – indeed, the complete destruction of every-thing.

When the Dragon led the final strike against the Dark at Shayol Ghul, Ishamael may have been in some way only partially trapped by the seal on the Bore, leaving him aware and able to touch the world while the others slept within the seal – this according to a recently dis-covered torn manuscript attributed to Aran son of Malan son of Senar (born circa 50 AB). The manuscript, which was apparently incomplete at Aran's death, is based largely on letters and diaries which Aran attributes to Aes Sedai who lived during the Breaking itself. These writings (unfortunately represented today only by small quota-tions within the manuscript) claim that there were sightings of, even encounters with, Ishamael after the Bore was sealed, in fact perhaps as much as forty years after. In no case were the sightings by the women who wrote the diaries, but Aran apparently trusted them implicitly.

Such claims might be thought ridiculous except that Aran is known to have been a writer of strict honesty, one who never cited a source that he could not verify (though both his sources and their verification are long lost to us). He speculated (citing other lost sources) that it may have taken some years for Ishamael to be drawn fully into the trap with the other Forsaken. If this was so, it seemed possible that Ishamael might well be thrown out of the prison holding the others and drawn back again on some regular cycle. During his lifetime Aran made observations based on cycles of various multiples of forty years without discovering any indications that one of the Forsaken was loose in the world at those intervals.

The last pages of the manuscript suggest that Aran had become doubtful of his own thesis, but we have evidence that he may have been right. Interviews with imprisoned Darkfriends revealed that a number of them received instructions from Ishamael long before the other Forsaken were freed (an event generally agreed to have occurred in 997 or 998 NE, and to have been caused by the gradual weakening of the seals). Some claim to have received instructions from him as early as 983 NE, when plainly the seals were still strong enough to hold the others.

It seems entirely likely that Ishamael could have been free in still earlier times, and that the cycle was merely longer than Aran could observe. Certainly two periods of the greatest upheaval humanity has known since the Breaking, the Trolloc Wars and the War of the Hundred Years, would be likely times for one of the Forsaken to be free and working his malevolence. During the Trolloc Wars the name Ba'alzamon, later claimed by Ishamael, was used by a paramount leader, and later by other Dreadlords. No such connection exists during the War of the Hundred Years, but it is hardly impossible given the other evidence. Perhaps some future researcher will determine whether Ishamael was in fact responsible for these two disasters to humankind.

Further evidence of this possibility comes from recent accounts by those who claim to have seen Ishamael before his death. He is said there to have forgotten his true name, and to be more than half-mad and less than half-human, a condition which could be at least partially accounted for by Aran's theory. He was usually dressed all in black with flame in place of eyes and mouth. Whether this was a trick of the Power or the result of his

entrapment is unknown. He was killed by Rand al'Thor in the Stone of Tear in 999 NE, but with the Lord of the Grave, death is not always final.

AGINOR

The second most powerful man, known by the Forsaken name Aginor, came close to rivaling Lews Therin and Ishamael in strength. Before he turned to the Dark, he was Ishar Morrad Chuain, one of the foremost biological scientists of the Age of Legends. If available sources can be believed, he understood 'the most basic structures of living things' better than anyone else in the Age. It is certain that he chafed under the widely held belief that there was nothing left to discover, only an occasional loose end to tuck in. His work apparently concerned new variations of plant life, both as crops and as ornamentals, but he was disciplined more than once for unauthorized work on animals.

Ishar Morrad was one of the first of the Forsaken to go over to the Shadow, probably some time in the first three decades of the Collapse. After becoming Forsaken, he dedicated his energies to the creation of 'Shadowspawn,' living constructs designed to serve the Shadow. His handiwork first appeared in the form of Trollocs, creatures made from combinations of human and animal substance. It is certain that the creation of Trollocs began well before the War of Power, because they appeared in large numbers in its very first days. Prolific breeders, the Trollocs formed the bulk of the Shadow's armies by the end of the war. Soon these were followed by other creations, some of which still exist, such as the Draghkar,

and some known only through historical records, such as the Gholam and the Jumara.

As far as is known, Aginor held no field commands and never served as a governor. He did have complete authority, however, to obtain material for his experiments. It has been estimated that in excess of ten thousand men, women, and children were taken away every day from the very beginning of the War of Power to its end, and this number may have been more than doubled during the last five years of the war.

It is recorded that Aginor went over to the Shadow because only as one of the Shadowsworn would he be allowed to do the sort of research he wanted.

During the closing of the Bore he was caught and bound just beneath the surface of the seal. As a result of his proximity to the world, he was one of the first to awaken and escape back into the world, only to find himself trapped in a body impossibly aged and withered from the grinding of the Wheel over the long years of his captivity. Because of the immortality granted by the Dark Lord, he was alive, but perhaps because of the effects of his imprisonment, his body had suffered the ravages of time. He was also one of the first to die, falling to Rand al'Thor near the Eye of the World in 998 NE.

BALTHAMEL

Balthamel, born Eval Ramman, was a historian specializing in the study of vanished cultures. Though quite strong in the Power, he was unable to distinguish himself enough to earn the coveted third name. Some sources suggest that the quality of his work was not the only

reason he lacked status. He was said to have a wildfire temper that he often could not control. More than once he supposedly came very close to being bound with the Power against doing violence.

He was a good-looking man who enjoyed the company of women and was very popular with them, but despite his position at an institute of higher learning in M'Jinn, he spent a great deal of time in establishments that today would be called taverns of the lowest sort. He enjoyed consorting with the rougher elements of society, even criminals, to a surprising degree. It has been suggested that the main, and possibly only, reason he was not dismissed from his post was his strength in the One Power.

Eval was drawn to the Shadow by the promise of immortality. To live forever and never age; as simple as that. He made his journey to Shayol Ghul to pledge his soul somewhere in the middle years of the Collapse.

Although as Balthamel he stood high in the councils of the Shadow during the war, his exact role is impossible to ascertain. He may have headed an intelligence network which competed with that run by Moghedien. Without doubt he never held a field command, though it is possible that he did serve as a governor. Whatever his position, it is known that he participated in a number of large-scale atrocities, including setting up camps to breed humans as fodder for Trollocs.

After the sealing of the Bore, he was trapped even closer to the surface of the seal than Aginor, and was freed at the same time. Like Aginor, he also suffered from the passage of time, but to a much greater extent. His soul and spirit were still vital, but his once handsome body had rotted to the point that he could not bear to

have it seen. Unable to use his own tongue to speak, Balthamel was forced to cover every bit of his flesh and required Aginor to speak for him. The first of the thirteen to die, he was killed by the last of the Nym, the Green Man, at the Eye of the World.

SAMMAEL

Most of the other Forsaken were trapped deeply enough to remain untouched and undamaged by time, though it made them a little slower to escape than Aginor and Balthamel. They lacked even scars, except for the one worn by the Chosen called Sammael.

Sammael's scar was a livid groove that slanted across his otherwise attractive face, as if a red-hot poker had been dragged from hairline to jaw. In his Age, such things were easily Restored. But he refused to allow his scar to be removed, wearing it as a reminder of the humiliating defeat in which he gained it. It was a badge of hatred and vengeance. An active, solid man with golden hair, blue eyes, and an abrupt manner, Sammael was ruggedly handsome. His compact physique made him seem larger than he actually was. When compared to other men, he was only of average height. This rankled him, for he felt he was judged more often by height than skill, and was usually found lacking.

As Tel Janin Aellinsar, he was a world-renowned sportsman before the war, competing in a number of events, among them archery and a sort of bloodless competition with swords, at which he was the world champion. He was reportedly friends with Lews Therin Telamon, though the closeness of the friendship cannot

be ascertained. With the onset of the War of Power his other talents were revealed, and he soon became one of Lews Therin's best generals. Without a doubt he fell in love with war, and very likely with the honors and privileges that went with being one of the best-known and highest-ranking generals. His greatest ability lay in defense, and those fighting the Shadow were often on the defensive.

In the fourth year of the war he suddenly went over to the Shadow. This was partly because he came to believe that the Dark One would inevitably win – despite his skill as both warrior and tactician, he usually favored committing his forces only when certain of victory – and partly because of hatred for Lews Therin. He believed that he was a better general than Lews Therin and deserved the overall command that had been given to the other man. It was Lews Therin Telamon who gave him his scar, a scar he was determined to wear until Lews Therin lay defeated before him.

Sammael much preferred conquest by military means to the maneuvers of political intrigue or diplomacy, and preferred field commands to service as a governor. Whenever possible he always returned to military action. Certainly the people of his territories were always glad to see him go. In addition to the usual atrocities, his governorships were marked by what might be called absentminded cruelty. His territories quickly degenerated to a point where they were barely able to support the Shadow's war efforts. Filth and hunger were far from uncommon in Shadow-ruled areas – in fact, the lack of them was uncommon, and the use of the Power to cure or maintain the health of civilians was unknown – but Sammael's territories experienced incalculable deaths

through disease and famine, apparently because he could not be bothered with even the bare minimum of attention to sanitation and food distribution. He is recorded as being fond of grandiose schemes, and people and resources assigned to the running of the territory under the previous governor were inevitably ordered into these schemes as soon as Sammael took charge.

In sharp contrast to the civilian population, soldiers under Sammael's command – human and Shadowspawn – were well treated and cared for, though impersonally. It was said that he took care of them as he had taken care of his equipment in his sporting days, so that it would not fail him.

As badly as the civilians fared under Sammael's rule, prisoners of war suffered far worse. Those who did not go to feed Trollocs (and that was the most common fate of soldiers taken prisoner by the Shadow) often found themselves confined with insufficient food and water to sustain life or with none at all. It is known that on one occasion, on being informed that the food provided to the prisoners was only half what was needed to keep them alive, he ordered the immediate execution of half the prisoners.

Sammael was last known to be ruling in Illian, under the name Lord Brend, but his present whereabouts cannot be determined.

RAHVIN

Sammael hated political intrigue, but Rahvin much preferred such diplomacy and manipulation to open conflict.

A tall dark man of large build, Rahvin was quite handsome despite the white hair streaking his temples.

Nothing is known of Ared Mosinel before the Collapse, when he appeared among the highest council of the Dark One's forces, and in truth not a great deal after. There is little doubt that he thirsted for power above all else, and turned to the Dark Lord to satisfy that thirst. It is believed that he used Compulsion discreetly, bending minds and wills to assure his constant control of any situation.

Under the Shadow he held both military commands and political office, and while he was a fair general, it was in the political and diplomatic areas that his abilities blossomed, though with a decided bent toward manipulation. He is credited with causing several regions to surrender to the Dark One's forces without actual invasion. The regions he governed for the Shadow were efficiently if harshly administered, though often with a lack of attention to detail.

Rahvin's two major weaknesses were his love of sycophancy and his fondness for women. Many people gained positions in his administration by flattering him, although he was quick to remove them if they proved too unsuited to the position. And although a handsome man, he could not stand rejection. His lovers were seldom allowed any choice in the matter. Much of the laxity of his administration can be attributed to time spent with his lovers.

Once free of the Bore, he adopted the name Gaebril and seduced Queen Morgase of Andor, using Compulsion to turn her into a besotted pet, and ruling Andor from behind the throne until he was killed with balefire by Rand al'Thor.

BE'LAL

While Rahvin preferred manipulation, the Forsaken known as Be'lal, the Envious, was a master of it, to the point that he was often known as the Netweaver. As Duram Laddel Cham, he was the Age of Legends' equivalent of an advocate, representing people in courts of law. That he was good at what he did is proven by the honorific third name, but not by any other source. He is the Forsaken about whom the least is known.

Some sources suggest that he, like Sammael, had been one of the leaders in the fight against the Shadow before he turned to the Dark, and that he envied and later hated Lews Therin. A tall, athletic man with close-cropped silver hair, he combined and surpassed the strengths of both Rahvin and Sammael, being both a patient and cunning planner and a capable fighter willing to do battle directly with the foe.

He went over to the Shadow during the Collapse, but whether at the beginning or end is not recorded. During the war he held several field commands, apparently proving himself a more than adequate if not outstanding general, and he governed at least one conquered region. His campaigns and his gubernatorial administration were marked by extreme violence and cruelty, but as much might be said of any of the Forsaken. Some fragments indicate that he was among those who razed the Hall of the Servants, destroying it just days before the strike that sealed him, and the other Forsaken, in the Bore.

After his escape from the seal, he carefully made his way into the nobility of Tear, and as High Lord Samon ruled Tear until he was killed by Moiraine Sedai with balefire in the Stone of Tear.

DEMANDRED

Demandred was another of the Forsaken who, like Sammael, turned against Lews Therin in the War of the Shadow for reasons of envy. He hated the Dragon even more than Sammael did, though with much less direct cause.

Before his conversion to the Dark he had been Barid Bel Medar, second only to Lews Therin Telamon as the most honored and influential man of his age. He was tall and reasonably good-looking, though not so tall as Lews Therin, and his hawk nose left him almost, but not quite, handsome.

'Almost' seemed to be the story of his life. Born one day after Lews Therin, he had almost as much strength and almost as much skill. He spent years almost equaling Lews Therin's accomplishments and fame. If not for Lews Therin Telamon, he would have undoubtedly been the most acclaimed man of his Age. He held many high public offices and wrote books on a wide array of subjects that were both critical and popular successes. It was his misfortune that Lews Therin held even higher offices with even greater successes in those offices, and wrote books that achieved greater critical and popular acclaim.

At the beginning of the War of Power, Barid Bel quickly became one of the leading, and highest-ranking, generals in the fight against the Shadow. In a world that had no memory of war and no military, generals had to be created, and the ability to lead in war was found in many places it might not have been suspected. Barid Bel had strategic vision and a tactical flair. At last he had found an area where he could, if not surpass, at least match Lews Therin. There is reason to believe that Barid

Bel thought himself intellectually far superior to Lews Therin, believing him to be an overcautious fool militarily, while he himself was a gambler, willing to play the odds. As a result he was furious when Lews Therin was appointed over him to command the forces opposing the Shadow.

Second once again, his hatred and jealousy of Lews Therin Telamon increased with every honor Lews awarded him. He apparently also made a cold calculation that, with Lews Therin in command, the Shadow was the more likely victor. In the third year of the war, he turned to the Dark Lord to avenge his overwhelming hatred of the Dragon, and was called Demandred.

Demandred was as good a general for the Shadow as he had been against it, winning many battles. Several times he served as the governor over conquered territory, but these periods were short. Each time he quickly returned to the field, not because of any love of war, but because he wanted to be personally responsible for Lews Therin's defeat and destruction. There are some indications that he did not get along well with all the other Forsaken, and was especially cool toward Sammael, perhaps because of their competing military abilities and each one's wish to be the one to destroy the Dragon.

It has been said that he believed that all who dishonored him should be punished, and his view of both his honor and suitable punishment was extreme. During the war he was reported to have captured two entire cities and fed every prisoner, man, woman, and child to the Trollocs just because he believed they had slighted him when he still bore the name Barid Bel Medar.

Awakening from the seal to find that Lews Therin was long dead changed nothing for Demandred. He simply

transferred his hatred intact to Rand al'Thor. Demandred is currently alive and at large.

ASMODEAN

Probably the man among the Forsaken with the most unusual reason for turning to the Shadow is Asmodean. A dark-eyed, dark-haired, handsome man, Joar Addam Nessosin was an acclaimed composer before the War of the Shadow. Born in the small port city of Shorelle (location unknown), he was a child prodigy, in both composition and performance on a wide range of instruments. (Of these only the harp and several sorts of flute would be familiar in the modern era. He also played the shama, the balfone, the corea, and the obaen, but of these instruments nothing remains except their names.)

Joar Addam never fulfilled his early promise, at least never to the extent expected. Works he composed while as young as fifteen were performed in many of the great cities of the world, but he never rose to the exalted heights that many had foretold, and was never ranked among the great composers of the Age. It is reliably reported that his reason for dedicating his soul to the Shadow was the promise of immortality. With eternity at his disposal, surely he would reach that greatness and, perhaps even more important, the recognition of it that had eluded him.

It is believed that he never held any field commands, though he did take part in a number of battles on some level, and he served as a governor of conquered areas. By and large, his administrations were not particularly horrific compared with others of the Forsaken, though it

should be remembered that all the Forsaken did such things as allow Mesaana's mobs of children free rein, cooperate with Aginor's 'harvesters' to gather people, and make men, women, and children available rations for Trolloc garrisons. The one atrocity which was specifically his has been overlooked by some historians because it involved fewer people. It should not be. Artists of all sorts of whom he disapproved were blinded and/or otherwise maimed. Any artist – writer, musician, any at all – could become an object of Asmodean's displeasure, but it was most particularly aimed at musicians and composers who had been considered his rivals before the war. The horror of this can only be compounded by the fact that there was no torture involved, as such; the unfortunate was simply made incapable of producing his or her art again and then released.

After escaping the Bore, he allied uneasily with Lanfear, posing as the bard Jasin Natael, until she trapped him into becoming a teacher for Rand al'Thor. He died in Caemlyn, killer unknown.

Chapter 6

The Female Forsaken and the Darkfriends

LANFEAR

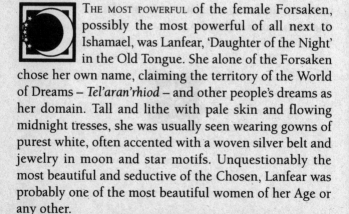 THE MOST POWERFUL of the female Forsaken, possibly the most powerful of all next to Ishamael, was Lanfear, 'Daughter of the Night' in the Old Tongue. She alone of the Forsaken chose her own name, claiming the territory of the World of Dreams – *Tel'aran'rhiod* – and other people's dreams as her domain. Tall and lithe with pale skin and flowing midnight tresses, she was usually seen wearing gowns of purest white, often accented with a woven silver belt and jewelry in moon and star motifs. Unquestionably the most beautiful and seductive of the Chosen, Lanfear was probably one of the most beautiful women of her Age or any other.

Born Mierin Eronaile, she was not world-famous or well known, though she was respected by her colleagues.

She worked at the Collam Daan, the prime center for research into the One Power, located in V'saine. She was, in fact, a member of the team which discovered the Dark One's prison and drilled the Bore while trying to find the new source of power that seemingly could be drawn on by men and women without the divisions of *saidin* and *saidar*.

There is little doubt that she was as surprised as the rest of the world to discover what actually lay beyond the hole she helped create, and she was indeed fortunate to be one of the few to survive the backlash that destroyed the Sharom and most of the Collam Daan.

From various bits of evidence it seems that Mierin was not among the first to go over to the Shadow, but when she did pledge her soul to the Dark One, it was for the most basic of reasons: love and hate.

It is certain that Lews Therin and Mierin were involved with one another for a short time, and that Lews Therin broke off the relationship some years before the drilling of the Bore, partly because she loved her association with the great Lews Therin more than she loved the man, and partly because she saw him as a path to power for herself. Mierin was never willing to accept that break and continued a determined pursuit of him. When Lews Therin, after rejecting Mierin, married Ilyena Moerelle Dalisar, about fifty years before the beginning of the War of the Shadow, Mierin reached her flash point. She attempted to disrupt the wedding ceremony and over the following year made several blatant public approaches to Lews Therin, blaming Ilyena for her 'loss' of him. Shortly after this she embraced the Shadow. She never gave up on claiming Lews Therin eventually; he was the object of a number of plots by the Forsaken, mainly to capture or

turn him in some way, and she was in the forefront of almost all of these.

While never a field commander, Lanfear was very useful to the Dark One both before and during the War of the Shadow. Using dreams, she guided a number of operations that turned people against established authority, creating massive riots. She is credited with winning several battles for the Shadow by the same means. She is credited with driving a number of people mad and driving others to suicide, as well as performing outright assassinations in *Tel'aran'rhiod*.

Aside from these useful pursuits, Lanfear served as a governor of conquered territory at least once. She was involved in many atrocities, perhaps more than most of the Forsaken, but the people she governed had more than the usual horrors of the Shadow to face; they feared sleep itself. Suicide rates were extremely high in her territory, even considering the fact that suicide was endemic in all the conquered territories.

Quite aside from her strength in the Power and her skills, her knowledge of Lews Therin, whom she had studied as a dedicated hunter might study the life and habits of her prey, was an asset to the Shadow.

When Lews Therin sealed the Bore, Lanfear was buried very deeply in the sealing, held in a dreamless sleep beyond the reach of time. As a result the long years did not affect her beauty, or the intensity of her desire for power and for Lews Therin. Upon awakening to the world, she adopted the pseudonym Selene and sought out Rand al'Thor, believing him to be somehow connected with, if not the direct reincarnation of, Lews Therin. As a result she focused most of her energies on trying to win his heart and turn him toward her and the

Shadow. She apparently was killed by Moiraine Sedai when both fell through a *ter'angreal* doorway in Cairhien.

GRAENDAL

The most flashy and decadent of all the Forsaken was the woman Graendal. Though not as beautiful as Lanfear, she was quite stunning in her own way. Blond and somewhat fleshy when compared with her dark-haired rival, she sheathed her voluptuous body in clinging gowns that left little to the imagination, styling her red-gold hair in elaborate bejeweled ringlets, and surrounding herself with gorgeous half-naked servants who doted on her every whim.

Though as one of the Chosen dedicated to sensual pleasure, she had been far different before the Bore. Kamarile Maradim Nindar was a noted ascetic, not only living a spare and simple life, but preaching that others should as well. Kamarile Maradim was famed and loved around the world, if apparently more often by people who had heard of her than by those who actually knew her. Dedicated to curing those with mental illness that the One Power and Healing could not touch, she was possibly the best at subtle manipulations of the human mind who ever lived. Those who knew her well often did not like her. While her public calls for a sparse life were always moderate, in private she was inevitably abrasive and cutting toward anyone who did not live up to her standards of simplicity, which meant toward everyone.

Within ten years after the Bore was drilled, Kamarile Maradim underwent a complete metamorphosis, becoming

the opposite of all she had been. Extreme hedonism replaced her asceticism. Her simple clothes were replaced with the latest and most daring styles, chosen to enhance her appearance. Sensual and sexual pleasures took primacy over everything else.

There is no evidence that this change was caused by the Dark One. Instead, it seems to have stemmed from a realization that the world could never live up to her standards. It may have been her way of showing the world her contempt for what she saw as their way of life, by taking that way to its furthest extremes, though she was reported to enjoy her pleasures greatly.

Given the troubles sweeping the world at that time, the odd behavior of this world-famous woman excited little attention, but that fact is unfortunate. There is considerable evidence that Kamarile Maradim may have been one of the first to discover what the world faced, though not until some years after her change of behavior, when the second of those who came to be called the Forsaken decided to serve the Dark One. She visited Shayol Ghul to make her oaths within the first twenty-five years of the Collapse.

Even after her behavioral metamorphosis, she still retained her worldwide fame, and made use of it, as her new affiliation was not known until she declared herself. In many ways her announcement to the world marked the beginning of the war, for before that day was done, Devaille had been seized by human adherents of the Shadow supported by the first army of Trollocs to be revealed.

Both before and after her announcement she proved to be adept at intrigue, and made use of her skills and knowledge of the mind to further the Dark One's cause.

Before the war, not only much of the general unrest but a number of highly destructive riots can be laid at her feet, and possibly the strangely harmful behavior of several people in high office as well as a number of key people's suicides.

While not a military commander in the field during the war, Graendal apparently was responsible for a number of significant gains and for a variety of successful subversion efforts. One source says: 'Graendal conquered territories as surely as any of the Shadow's generals, but her battlegrounds were her enemies' minds.'

After awakening from the long sleep within the seal, Graendal took over a palace in Arad Doman, staffed it with servants stolen from among the rich and powerful families of the land, and, posing as the ailing Lady Basene, began her pursuit of power.

At this writing she is still alive and believed at large.

SEMIRHAGE

While Graendal had been a healer of the mind beyond compare, the woman to be known as Semirhage, then Nemene Damendar Boann, had been an equally renowned healer of the body. An unusually tall, dark-eyed woman possessed of remarkable calm and grace, Nemene Damendar was known for her ability to heal any injury, even to bring people back from the brink of death when all else had failed. She was often summoned around the world to deal with the most difficult cases, in particular to do with the brain.

In addition to being a Restorer, she was also a sadist. Her pleasure was often exacted along with the healing.

A little extra physical and mental pain was a small price to pay when compared with survival. Most patients were so grateful to be alive they made no comment about the suffering they endured at her hand. Those people she felt society could do without, however, were not so lucky. If they did not die from the torture, she killed them after. She thoroughly enjoyed giving them what she believed to be their just deserts – until the Hall of the Servants discovered her perversion.

It was sometime after the drilling of the Bore that Nemene Damendar's secret became known, though her predilections certainly long predated the Dark One's influence on the world. Confronted by a delegation from the Hall, she was given a choice: to be bound against violence, never to know her pleasures again, or to be severed from the One Power and cast out in disgrace from the Aes Sedai. To her, there was no choice. She became one of the first to make the journey to Shayol Ghul, one of the first to dedicate her soul to the Great Lord of the Dark.

It is certain that she added greatly to the turmoil during the last half of the Collapse. At one end of the scale was the effect of the public revelation that someone as prominent as she had gone over to the Shadow. At the other was her treatment of kidnapped members of the Hall of the Tower. Furious at the Hall for daring to value her victims over herself, Semirhage used her alliance with the Dark Lord to make them pay. She used her knowledge of the human body and her skill at manipulating pleasure and pain as an extremely effective means of torture. Her revenge was exacted every time another councilor from the Hall publicly professed adherence to the Shadow after her attentions. Few recanted that adherence, and then only after long treatment at the hands of Restorers. Even

those who were finally Restored were, for the rest of their lives, more fearful of falling back into her hands than of anything else in the world.

During the war she held several field commands, proving herself a general of only average abilities. She governed several conquered territories, and her administrations were marked by a level of violence and cruelty that stands out even among the Forsaken. She forced the inhabitants of several captured cities to cooperate in torturing one another to death. Yet while these thousands of brutal deaths were very high on the scale of numbers, they were fairly low in sheer cruelty compared with some of her other actions. It was with small groups or individuals that she took the infliction of pain to what might be called an art. She spent many hours 'studying' the ways in which pain could break human will and dignity, and what people could be forced to do to avoid more pain. She claimed there were no limits, except with those who managed to escape her by dying. Semirhage used the techniques perfected on members of the Hall of the Servants, while she was being sought during the Collapse, on captured soldiers and civilians who were then sent on missions against their former comrades. These missions were invariably carried out unless discovered first. Prominent prisoners were always handed over to her to be bent to the Shadow. It was Semirhage who discovered that a circle of thirteen, using thirteen Myrddraal as a sort of filter, could turn anyone who could channel to the Shadow, though she invariably preferred to handle Aes Sedai herself. She hated everyone who called themselves Aes Sedai, and took the greatest pleasure in personally breaking them, by slow increments so they could be fully aware of what was happening to the last.

Semirhage also headed a network aimed at rooting out traitors and spies not only in the captured lands, but among supporters of the Dark One as well. Her reputation was such that special precautions had to be taken to keep prisoners from committing suicide on learning that they were to be handed over to her, whether they served the Shadow or the Light.

Preferring to clothe her perfectly proportioned form in black, possibly as much because Lanfear wore white as to intimidate her 'patients,' Semirhage could appear quite forbidding, or motherly and gentle. When the seal released her, she awakened to a world filled with people even more susceptible to her skills than those of her Age. She is alive and at large.

MESAANA

Unlike Semirhage, or Graendal, the Chosen called Mesaana turned to the Dark Lord because she was not the best in her profession. A woman of average height and appearance, Saine Tarasind was hardheaded, practical, and intelligent, though often taken for being dreamy because of her introspection. It has been said that she was always interested in real power, not the appearance of it. Appearances were never important to her. She wanted desperately to be a successful researcher. She spent her youth working toward that goal, aiming for the cutting edge of exploration. But her dreams were shattered when she was denied a place at Collam Daan. The board labeled her 'unsuited for research,' but agreed to allow her to instruct students.

She found herself lecturing about discoveries made by

others, disseminating old knowledge when she longed to seek the new. She was nothing but a lowly teacher – until she went over to the Shadow, and as Mesaana found a way to teach them all.

During the war she held several field commands for the Shadow, showing herself to be an adequate general at best but as a governor of conquered territories she blossomed. Her administration was orderly and efficient, as such things were reckoned among the Forsaken, which meant that atrocities were as well regulated as taxes and garbage collection. To the usual atrocities, Mesaana added her own refinement. Calling on her considerable skills as a teacher, she set up educational systems that were copied by others of the Forsaken; it is also possible that she administered education in territories other than her own.

These schools corrupted or damaged much of a generation of children in the conquered territories. They were required from the earliest age to spy and report not only on each other, but on their parents and neighbors; this was the least of her harm. Under her direction mobs of children and adolescents were encouraged to destroy anything which they felt might detract from the Dark One's glory, especially museums, libraries, and research facilities. The old order, the old world, was to be rooted up and obliterated. These mobs hunted down teachers from the old schools and institutions of higher learning, scientists from the research centers, librarians and museum curators, and officials of the former government. Many members of these mobs betrayed their own parents and relatives, and in the second half of the war even carried out executions, often impromptu but at times using 'courts' comprised entirely of children. The lasting effect

on the memory of humankind can be seen in one fact. During the Breaking, bands of brigands looted, killed, and destroyed almost as if in a race to see whether they could smash the world before the male Aes Sedai could; the common name for these brigands was 'Mesaana's Children.'

At the time of the sealing of the Bore, Mesaana was considered just in her middle years, a little over three hundred. Upon her escape from that seal she secretly placed herself within the White Tower, where it is assumed she remains.

MOGHEDIEN

Moghedien, the Spider, also avoided gambling or risk taking of any kind, but not because of an innate carefulness. A sturdily handsome dark-haired woman, she was named the Spider because she preferred to lurk unseen in the shadows until her prey was safely caught in her web, rather than facing any kind of open confrontation.

Before going over to the Shadow, Lillen Moiral was an 'advisor for investments,' a profession that no source explains. Whatever the work entailed, it is recorded that she was cautioned a number of times, and even disciplined, for violating its ethics and the laws surrounding it.

She went over to the Shadow long before the War of Power began, but managed to keep her alliance a secret until the war had been raging for several years. During that time she acted as a spy and agent provocateur, having secured a medium-level position in Lews Therin's

command-and-staff structure. Several major disasters in the early years of the war can be directly attributed to her machinations.

Moghedien has been described as a natural-born skulker and as an out-and-out coward who scoffed at those who took open risks, but at the same time envied their achievements and hated them because she was sure they despised her for hanging back. It is known that a number of the other Forsaken did, in fact, look down on her, yet those who discounted her too far usually lived to regret it. Many people did not live to regret it. While she was never known to confront an enemy openly unless she had the upper hand or was forced to, it was said she could remember a slight until the Wheel of Time stopped turning.

How she was revealed to be a supporter of the Shadow is not known, but it is recorded that she barely escaped capture, and that several thousand people, few in any way connected to the attempt to detain her, were killed as a diversion during that escape, a matter of sabotaging a public transport system.

It is known that she headed a very effective intelligence and sabotage network, one which may in fact have been under her control well before this. Some sources say that as many deaths may be laid at Moghedien's feet as at those of any general of the Shadow, but few of her victims were soldiers.

Her greatest asset was her ability within the World of Dreams, *Tel'aran'rhiod*. Within its dimensions her skills surpassed even Lanfear's, despite the latter's claim of sovereignty. She never dared confront or challenge Lanfear in the world of flesh, for there she could not hope to match Lanfear's superior strength.

After escaping the Bore, she was seen masquerading as a servant in Tanchico and Amador. Captured by Nynaeve, she was held prisoner under the pseudonym of Marigan, then freed by the being known as Aran'gar. She is believed to be at large.

OSAN'GAR AND ARAN'GAR

Two new names added to the list of Forsaken are not new members of the thirteen. Rather, two who were killed have been given new life and new bodies by the Great Lord of the Dark. Their identities before rebirth are unknown, save that both were male. They were pulled from death sleep and placed within bodies stolen from the Borderlands – a man, renamed Osan'gar, and a woman, Aran'gar. Both proved that the Lord of the Grave was an apt name for the Dark One; he could defeat even death, so long as it was not death by balefire.

The pair was named after the left- and right-hand daggers in an ancient and deadly form of dueling popular just before the War of Power. Osan'gar was a middle-aged, rather ordinary-looking man. Aran'gar, however, was a beauty. With an oval face set off by sparkling green eyes and glossy black hair, she had a lush, sleek body suitable for a *daien* dancer.

These were the first of the Forsaken to be named by the Dark Lord himself. They were to be tools for his use, much like the poisoned daggers that were their namesakes.

FRIENDS OF THE DARK

Men and women who could not channel were also susceptible to promises of power and immortality. With the Dark touch fueling baser emotions like greed and envy, there were many who would give their oaths. In the beginning, these people styled themselves Friends of the Dark. In modern times they are known simply as Darkfriends. Like the Forsaken, they originated with the Dark One's touch through the Bore. Unlike the Forsaken, they have not known immortality, yet they have survived as a society for over three thousand years, serving and waiting for Tarmon Gai'don: the Last Battle.

There are many levels of commitment among the Friends of the Dark. Some extremists are deeply dedicated to obtaining freedom for the Dark One and thus immortality and dominion for themselves, while those on the lowest level simply want to belong to something greater than themselves, something dark and naughty. Many of the latter do not really believe that they might actually be held to their oaths. Some may not even believe in the existence of the Dark One.

While the current Age contains relatively few Friends of the Dark who are truly dedicated, compared with those who are dabblers, altogether they make up a small but significant percentage of the population. Every major city contains cells of Darkfriends. A city of one hundred thousand probably contains between five hundred to a thousand Darkfriends. Every town or village visited by merchant caravans probably hosts a cell. Other than their sympathy for the Dark, Darkfriends may have very little in common. They include the very highly placed and powerful, as well as those who are servants or even beggars.

Rank within the Darkfriends has little to do with rank in the world; the most powerful noble would be expected to obey a beggar if that beggar gave the proper signs. Even the Children of the Light, supposedly dedicated to the eradication of all Darkfriends, and the modern Aes Sedai are not invulnerable to infiltration by those allied with the Dark One. For protection from discovery, most Darkfriends only know one or two others; and even then often not by true name. Those in vulnerable positions attend gatherings carefully cloaked and veiled so that no one may know too much.

During the War of Power, far more Friends were seriously dedicated to the Great Lord than in modern times, largely due to the high visibility of the Forsaken's leadership, and the numbers of high-ranking figures publicly turning to the Shadow. There was not as great a need for secrecy, the boundaries were clearly drawn, and only spies had to remain completely hidden. Friends of the Dark served as fighters, spies, and servants for the Dark Lord and his commanders.

Though it was known that Friends of the Dark could repudiate their oaths, as 'no one can walk in the Shadow so long that they cannot walk in the Light,' very few sought redemption. Fear of revenge from their Shadow masters upon the breaking of oaths to the Dark One was a major deterrent. Punishments for failure or sloppy work were bad enough; even brave souls did not like to think upon the penalties for oathbreaking. The Trollocs and other constructs had to be fed, and a forsworn Friend of the Dark would do to fill Shadowspawn bellies just as well as any other human.

Renunciation of the Dark did not mean automatic forgiveness for the crimes done while in service to the

Shadow. Friends of the Dark could find redemption, but they would probably also find punishment, often death, for their crimes. For most Darkfriends the thought of gaining redemption only to go to the grave usually left them deciding to stay sworn to the Dark. Life under the Shadow was still life.

Chapter 7

Shadowspawn

 THE WAR OF the Shadow began as a conflict of men against men. But Lews Therin and his supporters soon discovered that the Dark One was more than willing to use inhuman soldiers to fight his battles. Early in the war those opposing the Shadow found themselves suddenly facing not just men, but hordes of dark horrific creatures out of nightmare, and their numbers increased as the war continued. These Shadowspawn were often vaguely human, but with differences born of the dark that made them far less than men, if more deadly.

Many of these creatures were created by the Forsaken Aginor, and others, from existing genetic material. They were designed to breed true whenever possible, since

natural procreation was a more certain and less costly way to produce large populations than were laboratory vats.

TROLLOCS

The Dark One's greatest need was for soldiers. Before the war, his scientists set about combining living human and animal genetic material to create the ultimate warrior, something that was powerful and fierce in battle, fast, hard to kill, and intelligent enough to fight well and take orders. They used naturally aggressive animals such as boars, bears, wolves, goats, wildcats, rams, and eagles in combination with human stock to produce this soldier. The resulting man-beasts, each with face and characteristics of the particular animal from which he was crafted, were called Trollocs.

The Trolloc was and is certainly large and powerful. Standing eight to ten feet in height, with the body of an overlarge, extremely muscular man, they were stronger than either the human or animal part of their heritage and almost as fast as a horse. Vicious by nature, they manifested plenty of ferocity, killing for no other reason than the pure pleasure of it. And their size and strength made them extremely difficult to kill.

However, as an ultimate fighting machine the creature was initially a failure. Trollocs simply did not have the crucial discipline, or the ability to take orders, that characterizes an efficient soldier. Instead, they had the instincts and drives of animals combined with the worst human characteristics and a very limited (by human standards) level of intelligence. They could perform only

comparatively simple tasks, and they had extremely deceitful and unstable personalities. As soldiers they were usually unable or unwilling to follow orders unless driven by fear. Even then, if the Trollocs were more afraid of the foe than of the commanders that drove them, they often turned and ran, sometimes trampling or killing those commanders in the process.

The men and women who first faced these creatures were terrified. Their towering coarse-haired bulky forms loomed over any human, while intelligent human eyes glared evilly out from faces that often bore horns or tusks, and bestial muzzles full of gnashing teeth, or snapping sharp beaks. Some even had the hind legs of the animal they resembled, with hooves or claws in place of feet, though almost all had humanlike hands with thick, heavy nails – the better to carry their deadly weapons. And if they lacked a soldier's true discipline, sheer numbers made up for a great deal.

Their lust for killing made it very difficult for their commanders to take live prisoners, or to use Trollocs in situations that required them to distinguish between friend and foe. It was easier to let the beast-men run free, killing – and often eating – whomever they found, than to use them where any restraint or discrimination was required. Trollocs were omnivorous, but preferred meat: animal, human, or even Trolloc – it did not matter.

Shadowsworn researchers struggled to find a way to make use of the Trollocs' few assets. There had to be a way to motivate and control these killing machines for the benefit of the Great Lord. Ironically, it was the Trollocs themselves that provided the solution, by way of their throwback offspring: the Myrddraal.

*

MYRDDRAAL

Trollocs do not always breed true; instead they sometimes produce throwbacks to either the animal or the human side of their genetics. The throwbacks to the animal half die, but the throwbacks to the human side usually survive, though corrupted by the evil of their original makers, and are called Myrddraal.

Also known as Shadowmen, Halfmen, Lurks, Fetches, Fades, and Neverborn, the Myrddraal resemble men much more closely than do their Trolloc parents in size, appearance, and level of intelligence. Though their names are always in the Trolloc tongue, they are nonetheless vastly different from either human or Trolloc, for the darkness twists them. With tall, muscular, coldly handsome bodies, each of the Myrddraal is as like the others as if poured from the same mold. They move with sinuous grace beyond the capability of any human, and strike with the speed of a serpent. Their skin, instead of being pink, brown, black, or even golden, is the dead fishbelly white of a slug found under a rock, while the blood that runs beneath it is corrosive, and black as the Lord they serve. Black hair, lacking all hint of human gloss or texture, covers only their heads, leaving their pale faces bare.

The most chilling difference between humans and Myrddraal is in their faces, so like a human face but for the complete lack of eyes. Not even a slight indentation mars the cruel smooth planes of Myrddraal faces to mark where eyes should be, yet these creatures can see like eagles in brightest sunlight or darkest shadow. Thus were they also called 'the Eyeless.'

Sight without eyes is not their only inhuman ability – they can also vanish wherever there are shadows, and

travel far distances by stepping into any area of shadow, only to suddenly appear elsewhere, in a shadow far away. Even Aginor, who made the Trollocs and thus, indirectly, the Myrddraal, was not able to discover how they could use shadow to transport themselves.

Possibly the manner of their creation causes them to exist only partly in this world, for mirrors reflect nothing but a misty form where a Myrddraal stands, and their cloaks always hang motionless from their shoulders, no matter how fierce the gale around them, as if the wind of this world dares not touch them. Their only known weakness is a fear of running water. Whenever possible they avoid crossing or traveling on any kind of stream, river, or channel. Only the greatest need can force them to overcome this reluctance. Their fear will not save one who is a direct target for the Shadowman, but often stops any more casual pursuit.

Perhaps their most potent weapon is their eyeless gaze. The stare from one of those cold, merciless faces causes paralyzing fear. Even the most courageous warrior has been known to cower beneath a Shadowman's glare.

It was the Myrddraals' ability to cause fear that helped solve the Trolloc problem. Even Trollocs were (and are) terrified of Myrddraal, and the Halfmen were quite capable of taking and following orders. So it was that the Trollocs were salvaged as soldiers, with the Myrddraal as their commanders. The Halfmen drove them into battle and controlled them there with fear.

In time it was discovered that a Myrddraal could link with a number of Trollocs, completely overriding their bestial nature and taking control of their minds and wills, to create a deadly, well-disciplined fighting force almost as effective as was originally intended. Unfortunately, the

Myrddraal was then the weak link. If it was killed, the Trollocs sharing the link died with it.

Together Trollocs and Myrddraal made a fearsome foe. Organized in fighting units, called fists, of between one and two hundred Trollocs, usually under the command of a Myrddraal, they swept down on many unsuspecting regions, wreaking destruction on anything that stood before them. To a population new to war, the Trolloc armies seemed the personification of the Dark One himself.

While it is certain they wielded more deadly weapons in the Age of Legends, in the present day Trollocs make their own weapons and armor, crude and unfinished compared to the products of human armorers, but quite deadly. They wear no helmets because of the difficulty in crafting adequate protection for the wide variety of mis-shapen bestial faces. Some Trollocs demonstrate individual preferences through tattoos, carved bone adornments, and the way they wear their hair.

Outside of the military unit of the fist, Trollocs are divided into tribelike bands. The known tribes include the Ahf'frait, Al'ghol, Bhansheen, Dhjin'nen, Ghar'ghael, Ghob'hlin, Gho'hlem, Ghraem'lan, Ko'bal, Kno'mon, Dha'vol, and the Dhai'mon. They are the only constructs from the War of the Shadow known to have developed a social structure and tribal system.

As in the Age of Legends, only male Trollocs fight or hunt. Females are cloistered, serving as little more than breeding machines. Fortunately female Trollocs enjoy being pregnant. Trollocs can interbreed with humans, but apparently prefer humans as food. In any case, even if the human mother survives to give birth, the resulting off-spring are usually stillborn, and the few born live do not survive long.

Although Myrddraal are the offspring of Trollocs, they bear little similarity to them, other than having Trolloc names. So far as is known, all Myrddraal are male, probably sterile due to their hybrid nature, and completely lacking in individualistic expression, such as ornamentation or variations in armor or clothing. Where Trollocs have a vile and violent sense of humor, Myrddraal have none. The Shadowmen prefer a comparatively solitary existence and are seldom seen in large groups, avoiding all purely social interaction. They usually hold themselves somewhat apart from the Trollocs they command. Unlike Trollocs, they are capable of working alone with great stealth and cunning to achieve an ordered objective. They are also harder to kill than Trollocs. Even when mortally wounded they do not die completely until the setting of the sun.

It has been said that all Myrddraal are virtually alike, but at least one variation from the norm has been sighted. It is a Myrddraal unlike all others. Its very name, Shaidar Haran, meaning 'Hand of the Dark,' is in the Old Tongue, rather than in the Trolloc language like the names of all other Halfmen. Where most Myrddraal are the height of a tall man, Shaidar Haran stands taller by several feet, towering head and shoulders above man and Halfman alike. Its demeanor is one of arrogance, rather than servitude, even to the point of commanding Forsaken, and it has evinced a definite dark sense of humor, something previously unknown among Myrddraal.

The weapons, armor, and fighting style of Myrddraal are much more sophisticated than those of their parents. Instead of crude chain mail and leather, they wear black articulated plate designed in multiple overlapping strips over black gambeson and breeches, which gives maximum

protection and freedom of movement while enhancing their serpentlike demeanor. A black cloak with deep cowl is worn over the armor and often covers the sword – their primary weapon – as well.

Myrddraal swords are very specialized weapons. Unlike crude Trolloc blades, hammered out from any type of usable metal, these blades are only made at one place in all the world, a gray-roofed forge on the slopes of Shayol Ghul at Thakan'dar, mere yards away from the entrance to the Pit of Doom itself. No mortal smith crafts such foul blades. Only shadow-forgers, animated man-shaped beings apparently hacked from the mountain stone, can work the deadly steel. Though not truly alive, they perform their only task with great skill. Each black shadow-blade is carefully fashioned, quenched in the ink-dark, tainted streams of Shayol Ghul, and seasoned with a human soul.

The smallest wound from any of these corrupted blades brings death to the victim; the wounds fester and will not heal without the aid of the One Power. With such a weapon, little skill is needed, yet the Halfmen are agile fighters and would be formidable foes armed with even plain steel. The black blades make (and made) them almost invincible to the common soldier. But their weapons do wear out, after a time, and must be replaced, and the demand for Myrddraal swords is (and was) not always matched by the availability of materials or live prisoners.

DRAGHKAR

The Myrddraal were an accidental offshoot of Trollocs, but other constructs, equally dangerous, were deliberate

corruptions of human stock. The most fearsome of these is the Draghkar, dangerous not because of any skill in battle – the creature does not fight well, having very thin frail hands and arms unsuited for weapons – but because it has the ability to summon its prey into its lethal embrace. The Draghkar's main weapon is its song, a soft, irresistible crooning that compels its victims to approach. Its touch is not instantly fatal, but survivors are usually far worse than dead.

At rest the Draghkar is easily taken for an overly tall, pale-skinned man wrapped in a large black cloak. Dark shoulder-length hair that is often pulled back in an elegant queue adds to this illusion. In actuality the cloak is a pair of large, batlike wings, capable of supporting the creature's weight in flight. The slender body beneath the wings appears human, except for the too pale, almost white skin and the sharp talons that tip human-looking hands. The face, however, has little of humanity in it. Gaunt cheeks emphasize large dark eyes – much too large for any born man – and a wound of a mouth with brilliant blood-red puckered lips that cover sharp pointed teeth.

Despite the sharp teeth, it is not the Draghkar's bite that is so dangerous, but its kiss. Once it has drawn the intended prey into its embrace, the Draghkar fastens its misshapen lips to its victim in a 'kiss' that slowly drains away the soul. Only when the soul and personality are completely gone does the creature devour life as well. Those it kills have no marks upon their bodies, yet are as cold the moment they fall as if they had been several days dead. Victims unlucky enough to be kissed, but saved before the moment of death, are left as empty, soulless shells – mere parodies of life. Many consider it better not

be rescued at all from a Draghkar rather than to be rescued too late. Even those who only suffered a momentary brush of those lips are forever changed, part of their soul drained away.

During the War of the Shadow, as today, Draghkar were used primarily as outdoor assassins, often in conjunction with a distracting raid by Myrddraal and Trollocs. They use their wings to come upon their prey unseen, preferably at night and when the target is isolated, then drop to the ground and use their song to summon the victim to his or her death. They are less effective as indoor or daylight assassins, as they have difficulty gaining access to sealed areas or dealing with groups of people or sunlight.

DARKHOUNDS

Not all Shadowspawn were designed to appear vaguely human. The Darkhounds were constructed from canine stock corrupted by the Shadow. Resembling hounds only in their basic shape, they are darker than night and as large as ponies. Their voice in full cry sounds much like that of a wolf, but with an eerie wailing tone echoing of blood and death that could never have come from a born creature's throat.

Created as guard-beasts around the time of the War of Power, they were used in later years to hunt down the enemies of the Dark One. They weigh two hundred and fifty to three hundred pounds each, and usually run in packs of ten or twelve. Only single packs are used, as they are more likely to turn on each other than on the intended prey.

It has been speculated that they were slightly shifted out of reality in their creation. This would explain the fact that they make no mark, despite their large size, on even the softest ground, but leave prints in even the hardest stone. Often the smell of burned sulphur accompanies them.

The Darkhounds may have given rise to the legends of Grim or Old Grim – the Dark One – and his 'Wild Hunt.' According to the legend, on clear moonlit nights Old Grim would ride out with his 'black dogs' hunting for souls, the smell of burning sulphur and brimstone marking their trail. With eyes that shone like silver and gnashing teeth gleaming like burnished metal, the black dogs would run their quarry to ground. Rain could keep the Wild Hunt out of the night, but once they were on the trail of a soul, they had to be confronted and defeated or the victim's death was inevitable. Some believed that merely seeing the Wild Hunt pass meant imminent death, either for the viewer or for someone dear to them. It was thought particularly dangerous to meet them at a crossroads, just after sunset or just before sunrise.

It is true that Darkhounds do not give up the chase easily. They do not like rain or thunderstorms, and will not usually venture into them, but if they are already on a trail, the rain often fails to stop them. They have more speed than galloping horses and can maintain it longer than any horse. It is sometimes possible, however, to end the pursuit by placing running water between the prey and the hounds, since they will not cross flowing water. The only other choice is to kill them or be killed, and they have never died easily. Since the Breaking, and the loss of the Age of Legends' technology, only the surest

hand with bow or sword has had any chance, yet this may no longer be enough.

If Darkhounds die hard, they kill with ease. The smallest bite from their terrible jaws is death, just as certainly as if the victim had taken a dagger in the heart. Their blood and saliva are poison. One drop on the skin can kill, usually very slowly and with great pain.

In recent times a new breed of Darkhound has been reported abroad in the world, one that apparently can be slain only with the One Power. Stories tell of the beasts being cut to pieces with power-wrought weapons, only to have their hacked parts melt and reform into whole, living hounds and renew the attack. Should these tales be true, they are ominous.

GRAY MEN

Not all Shadowspawn were constructs. There were some creatures, like those called Gray Men, who were in truth ordinary living men and women. They did not merely pledge their souls to the Shadow, as Darkfriends did, but actually gave them away. To all intents and purposes, although they continued to move and think, they are already dead. These 'Soulless' are extremely effective assassins, for their lack in some way makes them so ordinary-looking that even the most searching gaze can slide right over them. They are literally beneath any notice. This allows them to infiltrate even busy public areas with ease. In many cases the intended victim does not even see them after the strike, and there have been occasions where passersby who watched the victim fall failed to see the killer.

Gray Men are primarily men, though there are occasionally women in their number, and even in the War of the Shadow they had no real use beyond assassination, so far as is known today. It is unknown what promises these people have been given by the Dark Lord to induce them to give up their souls, though the number discovered suggest that the motivation must have been extremely powerful.

ANIMALS AND BIRDS

The Dark One also made use of natural animals and birds that had an affinity for decay, carrion and death. As today, ravens and crows often were spies and killers for the Dark, carrying what they had seen to Myrddraal, who could pull the information from their minds to take to their Lord. In the cities rats and similar vermin performed the same function. As soon as the fact was realized, many areas put a large bounty on these creatures. Then as now it was true that not every rat or raven served the Shadow, but there was no way to be certain which was which. Best to try to destroy them all.

The Breaking of the World

THOUGH LEWS THERIN'S campaign to seal the Bore was technically successful, it also heralded a greater disaster than any of the events of the War of the Shadow, for in the very moment of sealing the Dark One away from the world, a backblast tainted *saidin* even as the Companions drew upon it. Whether this was a deliberate action by the Dark One or a by-product of his efforts to stop the Bore from being sealed may never be known. In either case, this backblast lead to the greatest cataclysm in recorded time, the Breaking of the World.

Lews Therin and the sixty-eight survivors of the Hundred went insane on the instant, perhaps not even knowing that their attempt to seal the Bore had been successful. Within days, these powerful male Aes Sedai, armed with the One Power and completely out of control,

began unleashing their might against anyone or anything that crossed their path or even caught their notice, leaving trails of death and wanton destruction. Thus began the Time of Madness.

Never before had the One Power been used in such a manner. The taint had trapped the minds of all the surviving Companions in twisted dreams of madness, while *saidin* gave them the power to make those dreams instant reality. There is no way to know of individual acts of destruction by most of the Companions, save that they were of a scale previously unknown. Lews Therin's deeds, however, were recorded, and have survived the Breaking to live on in legend, for he is known not only to have wreaked great devastation upon the land, but to have killed every living person who carried any of his blood, as well as everyone he loved. It is for this reason that he has been known ever after as the 'Kinslayer.' It is probable that the other Companions acted in a similar fashion in the throes of their madness, but it was Lews Therin who stood alone, the best of them, as their leader, and it is Lews Therin alone whose name has been recorded in infamy. Even now those who endanger or threaten the people around them or who are close to them are said to be 'taken by the Dragon' or 'possessed of the Dragon.'

Unfortunately, the Companions were not the only ones affected by the backlash. Other male Aes Sedai were touching the True Source continuously for other matters, but although they noticed the taint right away, no one knew what it was; though it covered all *saidin* like a coat of rancid oil, it did not prevent or directly alter the use of the One Power. Unlike the Companions, most male Aes Sedai were not affected immediately. Some time passed before other men began going insane, and still more

before anyone realized the cause. While some sources date the Breaking from the major destruction caused by Lews Therin and the survivors of the Hundred Companions, others put the real beginning as much as ten years later, when so many male Aes Sedai had succumbed to the taint, adding their nightmares to the destruction, that there was no longer any hope of stopping it. If there ever had been.

Civilization maintained some cohesion for a good many years after the strike at Shayol Ghul, of course, though the decline into barbarism was inevitable. But in many ways the Shadowsworn were a more immediate threat than the maddened male Aes Sedai. Deprived of their highest levels of leadership and with the loss of the Dark One's influence, the remaining Shadowsworn fell into struggles for power. Of course the war continued, complete with armies of Trollocs and Myrddraal, but increasingly those armies turned against one another as often as against the forces of the Light. These divided forces were much more easily dealt with than the earlier Shadow armies, but they still were strong enough to prey on a civilization increasingly ravaged by the growing population of mad Aes Sedai. With Lews Therin gone, Latra Posae, the former leader of the Fateful Concord, rose to preeminence, earning the name Shadar Nor, best translated as 'Cutter of the Shadow' or perhaps 'Slicer of the Shadow,' for her valiant fight against the Shadowsworn. She died sometime during the Breaking, but the exact date and circumstances are unknown.

In the end, it was the Breaking that put a finish to the war. The growing devastation forced both the Shadowsworn and those dedicated to the Light to concentrate on the task of survival. More and more male Aes Sedai were

succumbing to the madness, turning the world inside out before they died, and as their numbers rose, chaos grew, and civilization dwindled. During the worst of it, these men, who could wield the One Power to a degree now unknown, caused even the weather to rebel, and the world saw storms of unimaginable fury. Volcanoes erupted fountains of ash into the air as great earthquakes shook the land. Trapped in their delusions, the Aes Sedai leveled mountain ranges, raised new mountains, lifted plateaus where seas had flowed, and made the ocean rush in where dry land had been. Cities crumbled, their surviving inhabitants scattering to hunt for safety in a world of reflected madness.

Eventually every male Aes Sedai went horribly insane, and that insanity changed the face of the earth. Many parts of the world were completely depopulated. The nations scattered to the eight corners of the world. Until the last man who could channel finally died, chaos ruled.

Various fragmentary sources put the actual duration of the Breaking – that is, the major geological and climatic upheavals – at anywhere from 239 to 344 years. Since these sources date from the days between the end of the Breaking and the founding of the Compact of the Ten Nations, it is possible that some of these writers had access to still earlier source material, but none can be taken as definitive.

It is difficult to imagine the horror of those years, especially for those men who could channel, who knew that they faced a sentence of death and were destined to add to the carnage. Each time they touched the True Source, they did so through the rancid taint, and brought the madness that much closer. Once the taint took over, the

victim began to slowly rot. His body decayed around him, his mind failed, and the destructive nightmare eventually devoured him – and many others with him. Sometimes the erosion of mind and body was quite rapid, at other times agonizingly slow. There are indications that many victims knew what was happening, but were powerless to stop it. Many took their own lives before the madness struck, in an attempt to avoid their fate.

Still others tried to avoid the taint on *saidin*. But there were only three ways to do so. The first was simply not to touch the True Source. While seeming to be the simplest answer, it was also nearly impossible. Once trained in the use of the Power, a man trying to avoid touching it was like a man trying to cease breathing. The second solution was to be completely severed from the True Source. Few men were willing to take such a drastic solution, especially since victims of severing, doomed to sense The Power while being forever unable to touch it, usually died soon afterwards.

The third solution was to hide somewhere beyond the reach of the One Power, where one was not aware of the True Source. The only places where the Power did not work and the True Source could not be sensed were Ogier *stedding*. Where the Ogier made their homes, Aes Sedai were completely cut off from the True Source, but without the irreversibility of severing or taunting presence of the Source. Within *stedding*, it was as if an Aes Sedai had never had the ability to channel. Thus the madness could not reach any man while he was within.

Male Aes Sedai began to sequester themselves in *stedding* within a few years of the discovery of the taint and its effects. At first they came while they tried to reason out how to circumvent or remove the taint and later simply to

try to avoid going mad. The number increased once wholesale destruction began, as men attempted to avoid causing it, but even protected from all awareness of the True Source, the sense of loss in those who had felt its Power grew as time passed until it drove them back into danger. Some men slipped away in the hope that the taint had lessened, or so they claimed. Others admitted that they could no longer bear the inability not only to channel, but even to sense the Source. By the end of the Breaking, all the male Aes Sedai who had sought sanctuary in *stedding* had left, and all fell to the taint. Some scholars believe that these men may have prolonged the Breaking and intensified it. Others believe that, by removing themselves from the initial devastation, they may have lessened the disaster by spreading the damage out over a greater time.

Many *stedding* fell to the Breaking, for while *stedding* prevented the use or sense of the One Power, they were vulnerable to upheavals of the earth around them. When the *stedding* shifted, even the Ogier were driven into flight. During the years of the actual Breaking, there were no clear places of safety, and therefore no settled populations. Everyone became a refugee, intent only on surviving for one more day. No matter how safe a resting place looked, there was no guarantee that solid rock might not melt beneath those it sheltered at the whim of a maddened Aes Sedai.

The great cities lay in ruin or had been obliterated from the earth. The seas had moved or boiled away. The population was a fraction of its former size. Mankind's greatest works had vanished. Humanity returned to a primitive existence. Many died because they could not endure the hardships. It was hardest on the Ogier, for

they were bound to the *stedding* in ways still not understood, and they no longer knew where the *stedding* were. As they searched through their Long Exile, the bond became something stronger, and the Longing grew in them. Many died of the Longing before they found the first *stedding* again, and many more before enough were found to shelter the survivors of what had once been a race nearly as numerous as humankind.

In the chaos, the surviving Aes Sedai scattered the seven *cuendillar* seals that held the Bore, lest one of the maddened Aes Sedai, or even one of the Shadowsworn, find them unprotected. Only a few souls knew where they were secreted. Later, during the Trolloc Wars, those who held this knowledge were lost, and with them the location of the seals.

SECTION 3

The World
Since the
Breaking

AFTER THE LAST male Aes Sedai finally died, and the geologic fabric and climate of the earth settled into some kind of normalcy, the survivors found themselves in a vastly changed world without nations or governments. The social structure had vanished over the several hundred years of catastrophic chaos. Geographical features were completely rearranged, with some areas gone or tainted by the Shadow, such as those which came to be known as the Blight and the Blasted Lands.

Civilization had fallen to the most primitive nomadic levels. Only a few groups managed to keep any hold on their culture or traditions. The Aes Sedai, now all female, had been broken and scattered, their numbers greatly reduced by attempts to combat or contain their maddened male counterparts. Over the next several hundred

years, all would struggle to build small communities, then tribes, and eventually new nations and new styles of government from the ashes and rubble of their broken world.

CALENDARS

Since the Breaking of the World, three dating systems have attained enough popular appeal to become standard calendars. The first to come into use after the Breaking was known as the Toman Calendar, so named for its creator Toma dur Ahmid. It used the delineation AB, for After the Breaking, and began with year 1 AB. Because of the tumult of the period, this calendar was not actually adopted until some two hundred years after the death of the last male Aes Sedai (which officially ended the Breaking). Even then, owing to the total chaos during the Breaking and its immediate aftermath, its starting point had to be arbitrarily assigned. The Toman Calendar was in use until the end of the Trolloc Wars.

At the end of the Trolloc Wars so many records had been lost that there was argument about the exact year under the old system. A new calendar, proposed by Tiam of Gazar, was established to date from the end of the Trolloc Wars to celebrate the freedom from the Trolloc threat. It recorded each year as a Free Year, delineated as FY 1, etc. The Gazaran Calendar gained wide acceptance within twenty years of the war's end and remained in popular use until after the War of the Hundred Years. There is still considerable debate among historians over exactly which year of the Toman Calendar should be considered Free Year 1 of the Gazaran Calendar.

After the death and destruction of the War of the Hundred Years, a third calendar, the Farede Calendar, was devised by Urin din Jubai Soaring Gull, a Sea Folk scholar. The Farede Calendar began its dating system from the arbitrarily decided end of the War of the Hundred Years, beginning with year 1 NE (New Era). Urin din Jubai's calendar was promulgated by and named after Panarch Farede of Tarabon, the first Panarch of Tarabon, as part of his attempt to make Tanchico the intellectual center of the known world. By 50 NE the Farede Calendar was in general use, where it remains today. Once again, the loss of records engendered no little argument – among those who argue such things – as to where the year 1 NE should fit according to the Gazaran Calendar.

Artur Hawkwing attempted to establish a new calendar based on the founding of his empire (FF, From the Founding), but it never gained popular use, and only historians now refer to it.

Chapter 9

Formation of the White Tower

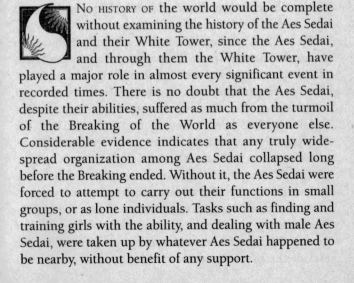 No HISTORY OF the world would be complete without examining the history of the Aes Sedai and their White Tower, since the Aes Sedai, and through them the White Tower, have played a major role in almost every significant event in recorded times. There is no doubt that the Aes Sedai, despite their abilities, suffered as much from the turmoil of the Breaking of the World as everyone else. Considerable evidence indicates that any truly widespread organization among Aes Sedai collapsed long before the Breaking ended. Without it, the Aes Sedai were forced to attempt to carry out their functions in small groups, or as lone individuals. Tasks such as finding and training girls with the ability, and dealing with male Aes Sedai, were taken up by whatever Aes Sedai happened to be nearby, without benefit of any support.

Given the exceedingly long lifespan of Aes Sedai during the Age of Legends, it would seem possible that at least some Aes Sedai who were alive at the beginning of the Breaking, even some who lived when the Bore was drilled, were still living when the Breaking ended. Over the centuries there has been considerable speculation, some rather wild, about this. However, the increasingly violent nature of the times, from the drilling of the Bore to the beginning of the War of the Shadow, the war itself, and finally the centuries of the Breaking, suggest that no Aes Sedai alive at the end of the Breaking had survived that entire span, or even a significant portion of it. The one possible exception may be the Aes Sedai who were involved in the building of Rhuidean, in the Aiel Waste. Tantalizing rumors claim that Aiel Wise Ones and clan chiefs may know something of this, but unless they can be induced to be more forthcoming – and so far, they are rigidly closemouthed – little is likely to be learned beyond the fact that Aes Sedai were involved.

By the first century AB, letters reliably attributed to Aes Sedai already speak of 'forgotten Talents' and 'lost abilities,' and bemoan the 'vast knowledge of the Power that is gone and may be centuries in the rediscovery.' If any Aes Sedai had survived the entire span, or even Aes Sedai who had been raised in the early years of the Breaking, there would have been few or no lost abilities and no need to 'rediscover' them.

The White Tower has always maintained a frosty silence on this subject, at least with outsiders, yet it is clear that as the larger organization of Aes Sedai shattered during the Breaking, a number of the smaller groups that formed became in effect permanent. By the end of the Breaking, each of these groups considered

itself independent of the others. (And let the White Tower make of that what they will!) It should be noted that this is another argument against any Aes Sedai having survived from before the Breaking. Surely they would have managed to overcome any such division.

Almost nothing is known about the organization of Aes Sedai during the Age of Legends, but it is generally accepted that *ajah* played an important part, though apparently they were nothing like the present-day Ajah. In the surviving twenty-three consecutive pages of a dictionary from circa 50 AB, *ajah*, in the Old Tongue, is defined as 'an informal and temporary group of people gathered together for a common purpose or goal, or by a common set of beliefs.' In thirty-one pages all in the same hand, located in the Royal Library in Cairhien, which appear to be random survivors of a larger manuscript reliably dated from the same period, the organization of Aes Sedai in the Age of Legends, or perhaps their manner of functioning, is described as 'a vast sea of *ajah* (note: word deliberately left untranslated), all constantly shrinking, growing, dividing, combining, melting away only to be reborn in some new guise and begin the process once more.' In the first centuries after the Breaking, the nature of *ajah* or *Ajah* changed. We cannot be sure exactly when the change occurred, but another dictionary (circa 200 AB; 219 surviving random pages) defines *Ajah* as 'a sisterhood of Aes Sedai,' and no lower-case form is listed.

When in 47 AB the Aes Sedai decided to build a new city as a center of their power, one cannot reasonably doubt that the decision was reached by negotiation between independent groups. Significant is the following, from a contemporary letter recently discovered

among uncataloged documents in the Royal Library in Cairhien.

'Sitting each for her *ajah*, if they still can be called so as they are, were Elisane Tishar, Mitsora Caal, Karella Fanway, Azille Narof, Saraline Amerano, Dumera Alman, Salindi Casolan, Catlynde Artein, Biranca Hasad, Mailaine Harvole, Nemaira Eldros, Lideine Rajan, and several others.'

Twelve women, not to mention 'several others,' doubtless representing groups too small to be significant, each sitting for her *ajah*! Not yet Ajah, but the 'if they still can be called so as they are' seems particularly meaningful, indicating great changes in the view of *ajah*. Comparing the two definitions and what we know of Ajah today, it seems that the most likely change was from 'temporary' to 'permanent.' Other fragmentary documents found with the letter, which speak of various women threatening to walk out of the meetings, also strongly suggest that what occurred here was a meeting of independent groups. Later events strongly suggest that while the decision to build Tar Valon was an outcome of the conference, the true goal may well have been to unify these separate entities.

Construction on what was to become the central city of Aes Sedai power, Tar Valon, placed on the island of the same name, did not begin until 98 AB. At that time, Ogier, who had taken up stonemasonry after the Breaking, had become the finest of all at the craft. The Aes Sedai may have recognized the brilliance of the largely organic forms the Ogier created, probably because of the Ogier's natural affinity for growing things, for they gave the Ogier masons free rein on many of the buildings. Even in modern times many of these structures still stand as a tribute to their art. It took 104 years of uninterrupted

construction to build Tar Valon, until 202 AB. It is believed to be the first major city built after the Breaking. At the least, it was the first among those surviving today.

From the beginning the city was laid out with intent to grow: even the oldest quarters were more spacious than could possibly have been needed for any population at the time; streets and parks were planned for the entire island of Tar Valon; and the whole island was walled. Northharbor and Southharbor were built at this time, though not by Ogier, and were separated from the city, as it then stood, by considerable expanses of open ground.

By 98 AB the name 'the White Tower' had been in use for some time for the planned central structure, perhaps as long as thirty years, though the Tower itself would not be finished for another hundred years. In that year (98 AB), Elisane Tishar is shown as the Amyrlin Seat, the first to bear that title, one she apparently had held for several years at this point. A Hall of the Tower had been chosen, but a council of seven was recorded as 'closely advising the Amyrlin Seat.' These women were Mitsora Caal, Karella Fanway, Azille Narof, Saraline Amerano, Dumera Alman, Salindi Casolan, and Kiam Lopiang.

Although at this time the term 'Ajah' was still not in use, the fact that there are seven of these advisors is surely significant in view of the later creation of the seven Ajahs. And, of course, that six of the seven women are named in the letter from the Cairhienin Royal Library.

By the end of the second century AB, the seven Ajahs definitely were in existence, each focused on a particular purpose. That is clear from any number of sources. Whatever form the Hall of the Tower had initially, it now consisted of twenty-one Sitters in the Hall, three from

each Ajah. The fact that each Ajah currently chooses its Sitters as it pleases, and that the internal structure and rules of the Ajah vary considerably (if it is not clear exactly in what form), both emphasize their original independent nature.

Once the decision was made to build Tar Valon and consolidate Aes Sedai power, those same Aes Sedai initiated and carried out, between roughly 50 AB and 100 AB, an extremely vigorous campaign against women 'pretending to be Aes Sedai.' It seems that there were a considerable number of such women at this time. Was it that so soon after the Breaking, at a time when more people manifested the ability to channel than do now, great numbers of wilders existed who believed they could claim the title? Or were many of these 'false Aes Sedai' actually Aes Sedai who resisted going along with the amalgamation of independent groups into one whole? Certainly there is evidence that many of these women were 'forced to kneel to the Amyrlin Seat and the White Tower,' at least some were stilled, and a large number joined the Tower and were thereafter accepted as Aes Sedai. Historically Aes Sedai have been very rough with women who pretend to be Aes Sedai, and there is no record anywhere outside this time of any such woman being accepted into the Tower.

One document (part of a letter, reliably dated in 77 AB by internal evidence; the property of a man who wishes to remain anonymous for obvious reasons) may well indicate the answer. It states that 'Lideine and several of her followers were stilled, whereupon the rest submitted themselves, and with that example Mailaine ceased her resistance and led her followers to kneel. The rest must be brought to heel.' Among those listed at the meeting that

reached the decision to build Tar Valon were Lideine Rajan and Mailaine Harvole. While the text is not conclusive, it is certainly suggestive that these two names should be linked in this manner less than twenty years after that meeting. Requests for comment from the White Tower have met with silence.

The White Tower itself is one of the most impressive buildings of the world; certainly nothing known to the writer in the present day compares in any way. Designed by Aes Sedai, and therefore lacking the organic touch found in many of the finest Ogier structures, it was created by Ogier aided by Aes Sedai wielding the One Power. The main tower of the building is constructed entirely of white stone and towers five hundred feet above the ground. It is three hundred feet across at the base, making it the largest structure erected since the Age of Legends. Slightly wider at the base than at the top, the Tower was designed to house the Ajahs in the top half; each within its own pie-shaped section, while leaving the wider bottom half to general purposes. A smaller palace-like structure attached to the back of the main tower was intended for novices and Accepted, while a large building behind the Tower and palace was to function as a library. The front of the Tower faced a great public square, which emphasized the deep broad steps and massive doors of the main entrance. A stone wall, broken occasionally by columns and rails, enclosed the perimeter of the grounds. The square was bordered by various public buildings, many of which were not only Ogier-built, but Ogier-designed, to seem animated by a life and vitality that belied the stone of their construction. Today, the White Tower and the square appear much as they must have then.

There seems little doubt that the Aes Sedai intended their numbers to grow, since the Tower and its related buildings were far larger than needed at the time, with living and working quarters for many more Aes Sedai than there have been – even now – at any one time since the Breaking. The library was certainly intended to house the largest collection of knowledge in the known world, and it may deserve the title as the greatest of libraries just for the value of its secrets.

It is unfortunate that the official histories of the White Tower are unavailable to anyone save Aes Sedai. (This writer will make no comment on why dissemination of their contents to non-Aes Sedai is prohibited by White Tower law.) Despite the destruction during the fourth Trolloc attempt to take Tar Valon during the Trolloc Wars (circa 1290 AB), the minor damage done to the Tower library in the Great Fire of FY 642, and the somewhat greater damage attributed to arson (or possibly an attempt to keep certain records from Artur Hawkwing) in FY 993, the official histories still must contain the closest thing that exists anywhere to an unbroken record from the present day back to the Breaking of the World and possibly even further.

Reliable knowledge of many historical periods is made even more difficult by the Aes Sedai habit, ever since the building of the White Tower, of attempting to gather everything that pertains to their history into the Tower. The Tower's position has always been that this is 'preserving the history of the White Tower and Aes Sedai.' The remark can be taken two ways: either as making sure that nothing of that history is lost or destroyed, or as making sure that the official version of the history prevails over evidence to the contrary. On many historical

subjects the only reply from the Tower is a cool Aes Sedai gaze, and perhaps an answer that upon analysis could mean several things, sometimes mutually exclusive. Still, documents do exist outside Aes Sedai hands, and some pictures can be constructed, however sparsely sketched, of early events. Often pictures which do not please the Aes Sedai.

With the building of Tar Valon and the White Tower, and the formation of the Hall of the Tower, the Aes Sedai were well on their way to creating a new centralized organization to replace that which had been lost. They were also in a unique position to wield influence and power in a world of young and struggling nations.

Chapter 10

Rise and Fall of the Ten Nations

AFTER THE BREAKING it took almost two hundred years, but eventually nations did emerge. Unfortunately many of those sympathetic to the Dark One, as well as many of his creatures from the War of the Shadow, survived to prey upon the people of these nations. The Shadowspawn had retreated to the Blight, but the threat of their presence and that of the Friends of the Dark was very strong. It soon became obvious that no nation could stand alone against such threats. Some kind of unification was necessary, but it could not require that any of those involved give up their sovereignty.

In 209 AB (After the Breaking; the Toman Calendar had been universally adopted about ten years earlier), the Compact of the Ten Nations was formed. This compact, also called the Second Compact, was largely the work of

Queen Mabriam of Aramaelle, reported to be Aes Sedai (as were a number of queens, apparently, between the Breaking and the end of the Trolloc Wars), so it is likely that the White Tower played a large role.

While much information on the Ten Nations has been lost, we know the name of each nation and the ruler who signed the Compact: Aelgar, ruled by King Remedan the Goldentongued; Almoren, ruled by King Coerid Nosar; Aramaelle, ruled by Queen Mabriam en Shereed; Aridhol, ruled by Queen Doreille Torghin; Coremanda, ruled by King Ladoman; Eharon, ruled by King Temanin; Essenia, ruled by First Lord Cristol; Jaramide, ruled by High Queen Egoridin; Manetheren, ruled by Queen Sorelle ay Marena; and Safer, ruled by King Eawynd.

Each of the Ten Nations boasted several cities built by Ogier, and while none of the original Ten remain today, remnants of their cities formed the foundations for several modern cities. The following lists each of the nations, its capital, its other Ogier-built cities, and, where applicable, the name of the modern city that took its place:

Aelgar   Capital city: Ancohima. Other Ogier-built: Condaris, Mainelle (site of Tanchico), Shar Honelle.

Almoren   Capital city: Al'cair'rahienallen (became Cairhien), also Jennshain.

Aramaelle   Capital city: Mafal Dadaranell. Others: Anolle'sanna, Cuebiyarsande, Rhahime Naille.

Aridhol   Capital city: Aridhol (Shadar Logoth). Others: Abor'maseleine, Cyrendemar'naille.

Coremanda   Capital city: Shaemal. Others: Braem (near site of New Braem), Hai Caemlyn (core formed the inner city of Caemlyn), Nailine Samfara.

Eharon   Capital city: Londaren Cor. Others: Barashta (Became Ebou Dar),. Dorelle Caromon (became Illian).

Essenia   Capital city: Aren Mador (site of Far Madding). Others: Dalsande, Tear.

Jaramide   Capital city: Deranbar (became Maradon). Others: Barsine, Allorallen (site of Bandar Eban), Canaire'somelle, Nashebar.

Manetheren   Capital   city: Manetheren.   Others: Corartheren; Jara'copan, Shanaine (site of Jehannah).

Safer   Capital city: Iman (site of Katar). Others: Miereallen (site of Falme), Shainrahien.

The Compact lasted for roughly eight hundred years, protecting all its members against the creatures of the Shadow. During this time culture and social graces began to flourish, for memories of the Age of Legends had not been completely lost. There was still hope that the glories of that past Age could be rebuilt.

Most of these hopes failed when, about 1000 AB, Trollocs suddenly roared south out of the Blight in large numbers to begin a series of wars that would shatter the Compact. These wars, known as the Trolloc Wars, spanned approximately 350 years and spread destruction across most of the continent.

No reason for the Trolloc invasion is known. In most

cases these armies were commanded by Dreadlords –
Shadowsworn who could channel – who were most often
women, many of them believed to be renegade Aes Sedai
(almost certainly Black Ajah, by definition), though there
were no small numbers of male Dreadlords. Without
doubt some of the men were Darkfriends, but it is possible that some turned to the Shadow rather than face
gentling or death.

The Trolloc foot soldiers were usually armed with
spears and hook-tipped axes. Trollocs almost never used
projectile weapons, although, then as now, there were
some few Trolloc archers whose bows fired arrows
roughly the diameter of a large man's thumb. Myrddraal
officers drove the Trollocs toward battle until their thirst
for killing took over. Other types of Shadowspawn functioned as support or assassination troops.

The Trolloc armies of Trollocs and Dreadlords were
often joined by armies of human Darkfriends who, while
not as fierce or strong as Trollocs, were much more adept
and cunning.

The Compact was successful in that each nation rallied
to support the war effort and the other nations, but it
was weakened by each nation's insistence on maintaining

Map 1 (overleaf) Notes.
At this time the Blight did not extend out of the Mountains of
Dhoom. The then-Borderlands (not so called at the time)
Jaramide and Aramaelle had northern borders actually
reaching into the Mountains of Dhoom.

At this time the diamond-shaped area centered around
Tar Valon was land ruled directly from the White Tower. This
area grew in size after the Trolloc Wars, and shrank to the
island itself during Hawkwing's reign.

its own separate armed forces. The White Tower supplied Aes Sedai to assist the armies of the Compact against the Dreadlords, but even those Aes Sedai were under the command of the Tower alone.

At this time the military formed 'banners,' which consisted of roughly fifteen hundred horse, primarily archers, or three thousand infantry. These 'banners' combined into armies under the command of a general, often a noble, and were usually accompanied by a small complement of Aes Sedai.

The Trolloc armies simply overwhelmed their objective with such numbers that it could not help but fall, in almost every encounter severely outnumbering the defenders. Very early in the wars it became obvious that no human army could stand for long head to head against the huge masses sent against it. A different tactic had to be developed, one that would strike the Trollocs' weaker points, their animalistic natures and inability to reason in a tight situation.

Basically, after long harassing actions by cavalry, human infantry took up a defensive position in front of the wave, holding it long enough for mounted archers to move in from the sides and whittle the enemy down safely from a distance. Those Trollocs not destroyed in the pincer broke and ran. Both cavalry and infantry had to be fast, and the infantry had to have the courage to stand against an onslaught by monsters. If the force was too large for the infantry to hold, the human army would pull back to let it pass, then hit it from the sides and rear.

Such tactics worked often enough, though not without heavy casualties among the infantry. When they succeeded, the result was a slaughter of Trollocs; when they did not, it was the humans who were butchered.

There were numerous variations in military organization during the Trolloc Wars, but basically a varying number of banners were grouped together as a 'legion,' which usually combined foot and horse, though it could be of either alone. Banners could be 'heavy' or 'light,' depending on their arms and armor. It was possible for an entire legion to be heavy or light, but more usually they were mixed. A banner of artillery (smaller in numbers than a banner of horse, though apparently no fixed number) comprised catapults and huge crossbows that fired spears, and was often part of the legion as well.

Throughout the Trolloc Wars and into the first part of the War of the Hundred Years, by which time the military arts had reached what many regard as their pinnacle, legions were grouped together in 'grand legions.' An army was usually divided into four grand legions, one of which was normally designated as the reserve.

Other groups attached to armies during this time included each banner's musicians (drummers always, though the style of drums varied, along with pipers, flutists, and/or trumpeters), who after battle served as stretcher bearers carrying wounded to Aes Sedai for Healing, or in the absence of Aes Sedai offering what aid they could themselves, often with the help of whatever hedge-doctors and Wisdoms could be found.

The army always included a supply banner and a logistics corps, often numbering as many men as a grand legion in itself, as well as a miners' banner. The latter was responsible, by the War of the Hundred Years, for everything from building bridges to tunneling under an enemy's fortifications. This banner's men were often assigned individually to various legions for specific

duties. The same was true of the signal banner, whose signal flags, semaphore towers, messenger pigeons, and heliographs transmitted messages.

The banner-and-legion structure disappeared during the latter part of the War of the Hundred Years.

Trolloc incursions managed to reach at various times as far south as present-day Illian and Tear, where several famous sieges of the Stone took place. Tear never fell, but many other cities were not so fortunate.

Each nation of the Compact was at the mercy of its allies for support against the threat. Some handled the responsibility with honor. Such were the fiercely brave warriors of Manetheren, fighting under the Red Eagle banner so fervently for over two centuries that they came to be known as the thorn in the Dark One's foot, the bramble to his hand, and Manetheren herself as the sword that could not be broken. But when at last the Shadow sent concentrated forces to destroy their source, the Mountain Home of Manetheren, no others came to their aid.

King Aemon and his men, after a forced march from victory at the Battle of Bekkar, known as the Field of Blood, held off overwhelming numbers of Trollocs and Shadowspawn for over ten days while awaiting promised reinforcements that never came. The King's battle cry, '*Carai an Ellisande!* For the honor of the Rose of the Sun!' was said to echo over the land until the Rose of the Sun herself, Queen Eldrene, could hear it from the city. Eventually the sword that would not break was shattered by the Dark forces, aided by the faithlessness of allies. Stories record that Queen Eldrene's heart broke the moment Aemon died. An Aes Sedai, she reached out to the True Source, surely aided by a *sa'angreal*, to hunt

down the victors, and supposedly sent balefire to consume the Dreadlords, Myrddraal, and Darkfriends where
they stood. But the effort required more Power than
anyone could wield unaided, and she and the city of
Manetheren died in flames. Those who betrayed the
Mountain Home by leaving her to face the foe alone
escaped unpunished.

Other nations fell from within. Such was the nation of
Aridhol, once closely allied with Manetheren. Its capital
city, also called Aridhol, fell to something dark that was
not of the Shadow. King Balwen Mayel, known as Balwen
Ironhand, in great despair over the course of the wars,
gladly welcomed a man called Mordeth to his court;
Mordeth won Balwen's ear and mind; Aridhol would use
the tactics of the Shadow against the Shadow. It is said
that Aridhol festered under the poison Mordeth spread,
turning in on itself to become hardened and cruel. Its
people spoke of the Light while abandoning the Light.
Eventually, their suspicion and hate created something
unspeakably evil that began to feed on that which created it. Now nothing remains of the people and nation of
Aridhol. The ruined city that was once known as Aridhol
still stands, but it bears a new name: Shadar Logoth, the
Place Where the Shadow Waits. The evil that was born
there still lives, locked in the bedrock beneath the city,
hungering for wayward souls. That evil has been named
Mashadar. Late in the Trolloc Wars, an army of Trollocs,
Myrddraal, Dreadlords, and Darkfriends camped within
the ruins. They never came out. Since that day no
Trolloc or Shadowspawn will willingly set foot in Shadar
Logoth.

Whether vanquished in battle, consumed from within,
or simply weakened by the strain of war, no nation

remained unravaged by the Trolloc Wars. The small periods of peace never allowed the nations to rebuild much of what had been lost, and eventually the wars destroyed most of the civilization that had been so hard restored after the Breaking.

After almost three hundred years of fighting, the Trollocs were soundly defeated at the Battle of Maighande. The victory turned the Trollocs and began the long push that finally drove them back into the Blight, ending the Trolloc Wars.

Many nations were destroyed outright in the Trolloc Wars, and the population shifts were massive. Overall population levels fell drastically, both due to the wars and a decreasing birth rate. Aelgar, Eharon, Essenia, Jaramide, and Safer survived after a fashion, but much weakened and impoverished. Within fifty years of the Trolloc Wars new nations appeared, hammered together from the wreckage of ruined lands.

The century immediately following the wars was one of great turmoil. The five nations that outlived the wars fell to their own internal weaknesses as the new nations struggled to establish firm borders. Only Tar Valon and the White Tower of the Aes Sedai remained whole. Indeed, the White Tower actually gained lands and influence.

Chapter 11

The Second Dragon and the Rise of Artur Hawkwing

 BY FREE YEAR 100, entirely new nations had risen from the rubble of the Trolloc Wars. They were: Aldeshar, Abayan, Balasun, Basharande, Caembarin, Dal Calain, Darmovan, Dhowlan, Elan Dapor, Elsalam, Esandara, Farashelle, Fergansea, Hamarea, Ileande, Indrahar, Kharendor, Khodomar, Masenashar, Moreina, Nerevan, Oburun, Oman Dahar, Roemalle, Rhamdashar, Shandalle, Shiota, Talmour, and Tova.

Since the wars, the Blight had spread out from the Mountains of Dhoom, though it was still far smaller than at present. Rhamdashar's northern border was actually in the mountains, but not so deep as its predecessor's. Elsalam's northern border was in the mountains in the east and the west, with a slight bulge southward in the center. Basharande's northern border

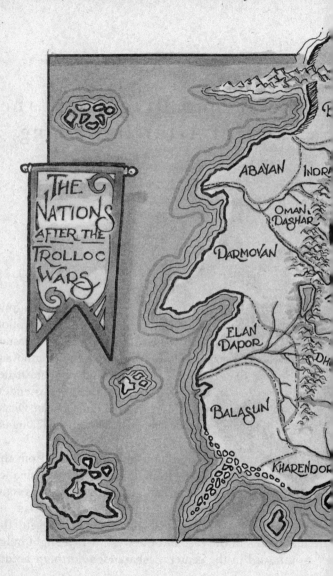

touched the mountains in several places, but it contained a number of southward bulges of varying size. At this point, all of the borders that did not reach the mountains were still within sight of them.

Without the Trolloc threat, these new nations prospered. For almost eight hundred years there were no records of any major problems beyond the usual political squabbles and border conflicts. All that changed when, in the early 900s of the Free Years, two men were born: one a prince of Shandalle who was *ta'veren*, the other born in obscurity with the ability to channel and dreams of greatness.

Artur Paendrag Tanreall was born in FY 912 to Myrdin Paendrag Maregore and Mailinde Paendrag Lyndhal, the King and Queen of Shandalle. In FY 937, at the age of twenty-five, he married his first wife, the Lady Amaline Tagora. At the age of twenty-seven, after an epidemic of the Black Fever which took an estimated one in ten of the population, including his mother and father, he ascended the throne.

It is impossible to tell the history of Artur Hawkwing without beginning with Guaire Amalasan. Early in FY 939, while the snows still fell, Amalasan named himself the Dragon Reborn in Darmovan. He raised a banner which showed the ancient symbol of the Aes Sedai on a field of blue and called those who followed him the Children of the Dragon.

From internal evidence, he was an educated man, with a considerable knowledge of the Prophecies of the Dragon, but strangely for someone who jarred the world to its foundations, almost nothing is known about him. In FY 939 he was young, somewhere in his twenties, with dark, deep-set eyes and a mesmerizing gaze. He had a compelling presence, and it is said that he never addressed a

body of people but they were in his hands. And that is all that is known of a man who shook the pillars of heaven.

Within half a year Darmovan was his. The Black Fever epidemic just then reaching Darmovan certainly contributed to Amalasan's rise, but without doubt he was not just a charismatic leader, but one of the great captains of the time. He took both Balasun and Elan Dapor in less than a year after first proclaiming himself ruler of Darmovan.

During the next three years his conquests continued at an increasing rate as tens of thousands from many nations flocked to his banner. By FY 943 he had added Kharendor, Dhowlan, Farashelle, Shiota, Nerevan, Esandara, Fergansea, and Moreina to his holdings. The Stone of Tear was under siege, resisting only because as many as thirty Aes Sedai had taken refuge there when the rest of Moreina fell. The presence of those Aes Sedai in Tear, which has a history of distrusting channelers dating back to its founding after the Breaking, is of some interest in itself.

Talmour and Khodomar were in danger of falling into Amalasan's hands, and fierce fighting had begun in Masenashar, Dal Calain, and Aldeshar itself. In many cities not under his control, rioting mobs declared that he was the Dragon Reborn.

No nation liked another interfering with its internal problems, and no nation was eager to spend its soldiers helping another deal with a false Dragon, especially if he happened to be far away – but the speed of his conquests convinced rulers that he was a danger. By the summer of FY 941 every nation had sent armies against Amalasan.

Shandalle was a small land, and although it had successfully fought off every invasion by its neighbors, it was not in the same rank with the most powerful nations, Basharande, Elsalam, Rhamdashar, Hamarea, Caembarin,

and Aldeshar. Still, Shandalle, led by young King Artur Paendrag, not yet called Hawkwing, was one of the first to send an army, in the spring of FY 940.

The more powerful rulers and generals soon noted (some sources say 'grudgingly' or 'with irritation') that Artur Paendrag consistently matched Amalasan when they faced one another directly. In fact, Artur Paendrag did not lose a single battle to Amalasan, gaining at worst a stalemate. By FY 942 he was called Hawkwing. His personal sigil was the Golden Hawk, and the banner of Shandalle featured three golden hawks in flight, but all sources agree that the name came from the speed with which he moved his troops. Still, Shandalle was a minor power, and at no time was he in command of the overall war.

The decisive engagements of the war, already being called the War of the Second Dragon, came in the spring of FY 943, between two armies that were unaware of one another until they were so close they had no choice but to fight. Artur Hawkwing was moving south out of Tova, across the Maraside Mountains (along the present southern border of Cairhien), to join the fighting in Khodomar. Various sources differ only slightly in the details. Hawkwing had approximately twenty-three thousand foot and twelve thousand horse, of whom some were probably Tar Valon soldiers, and an indeterminate number of Aes Sedai. Amalasan, with some forty-one thousand foot and twenty-six thousand horse, apparently intended to cross the Marasides and strike into Tova; he was known for leaping past what others considered the obvious battlefield to open battle in his enemy's rear.

Hawkwing came out of the Marasides by the Jolvaine Pass, not far from the small town of Endersole, to find his forward scouts making contact with Amalasan's,

approaching the pass from the south. Whether as the Battle of Endersole or the Battle of Jolvaine Pass, the next two days would be studied avidly by military men over the following thousand years.

The region was, then as now, heavily forested, hilly and rugged, severely limiting the usefulness of cavalry, and Amalasan dismounted a great portion of his, using them as foot. The day went very much Amalasan's way. Both armies suffered heavy casualties, but Amalasan could better afford them. Twice only the quick redeployment of Hawkwing's forces kept him from being outflanked. The Aes Sedai, whatever their number, were barely able to match Amalasan's use of the One Power in the battle, and by nightfall it was a miracle that Hawkwing still held his army together. (Wrote an anonymous contemporary: 'It was only by the Grace of the Light – or else by that Shadow-given gift of making men follow him even to sure and certain death.')

For any other general, the course to follow would have been obvious – retreat through the pass in the darkness with the remnants of his army. Hawkwing, though, was not any other general. He began a retreat north toward the pass; as soon as he was certain that Amalasan's scouts had seen this, Hawkwing's rear guard began fierce skirmishing as if to protect the fleeing army, thus screening the forces from Amalasan's scouts. Hawkwing divided his troops, in contravention of established military thought, and sent them east and west.

Amalasan no doubt believed the reports of his scouts implicitly, and only the most rabidly unfriendly contemporary commentators count it against him as a military leader. Quick retreat through the pass was the best move for an outnumbered and defeated army, and only a madman

would contemplate a flanking attack over that terrible terrain at night. A madman, or a general whose troops would follow him even into the Pit of Doom.

When the first gray light of dawn broke, Amalasan's army was preparing to move on the pass, all attention directed north. It was then that Hawkwing struck. His divided infantry fell on Amalasan's encampment from the east and the west, while his cavalry, having completed a night ride of some fifty miles, struck from the south.

Caught by surprise, Amalasan's forces came very near collapse in the first half-hour. Amalasan could have rallied them and turned the battle his way – he had done as much before – but Hawkwing and his horsemen drove straight for Amalasan's banner, with them the Aes Sedai, and Amalasan was taken. (Given his ability to channel, stories of a man-to-man duel between him and Hawkwing must be discarded; Hawkwing himself always denied it.) Once the news began to spread, Amalasan's army did collapse.

Military doctrine of the time dictated the pursuit of a defeated army, not only to keep it from returning but to destroy it as completely as possible. As so often before and after, Hawkwing ignored 'what must be done'; as quickly as he could pull his forces together, he sped north through the Jolvaine Pass and pressed hard for Tar Valon.

The first recorded conflict between Hawkwing and Aes Sedai came at the border of Tar Valon. By White Tower law, no one could enter its lands with more than twenty armed retainers and a like number unarmed. Hawkwing took his entire army to within a few miles of the bridges leading across the Osendrelle Erinin to Tar Valon itself. Whether he did this in the face of opposition from the Aes Sedai accompanying him, or whether the Tar Valon component of the army had suffered so greatly that those

Aes Sedai actually requested Hawkwing's escort to Tar Valon itself, will never be certain. It is known that the Aes Sedai who came with him, the women who had survived the battle and shielded Guaire Amalasan, went straight from a public heroes' welcome to terms of penance that the Tower kept secret for a number of years.

Within a day of his arrival a curt message was delivered to Hawkwing from the Amyrlin, Bonwhin Meraighdin: he was given five days to rest his army, after which he was to lead them beyond Tar Valon's borders without delay.

News of Amalasan's capture had spread with astonishing rapidity, but while it had caused the collapse of an army already on the point of shattering, its effect elsewhere was very different. Within three days of the Battle of Jolvaine Pass, Sawyn Maculhene set out from Khodomar with an army estimated at fifty thousand men, and Elinde Motheneos marched from northern Esandara with a larger force, both bent on freeing Amalasan. Maculhene was a cavalry leader of both daring and skill, while Motheneos, said in some accounts to be a renegade Aes Sedai (such rumors cluster around most major historical events, though seldom with any evidence), was an expert in siege warfare. One source claims that she brought disassembled siege engines and towers on wagons, but details of their pursuit of Hawkwing are almost nonexistent, although its end is recorded in the library of the White Tower, among other places.

Amalasan was taken into Tar Valon immediately upon his arrival to the White Tower, where he was tried over a space of several days and sentenced to stilling. Meanwhile Hawkwing camped with an army where no army not sworn to the White Tower had ever before been allowed. Despite Aes Sedai attempts to hide the truth, it is clear

that the attack by Maculhene and Motheneos came as a complete surprise, capturing at least two of the Alindrelle Erinin bridges and reaching the White Tower itself before being blunted.

Some non-Aes Sedai sources say that Hawkwing was allowed, or perhaps asked, to bring his army into Tar Valon to help turn back the assault. Among all White Tower sources available to non-Aes Sedai historians (there are, of course, the rumored caches within the White Tower library to which access is restricted even among Aes Sedai) not one mentions the presence of Artur Hawkwing, nor of an army not sworn to Tar Valon camped within sight of the Shining Walls. This fact is in itself most curious.

In any case, the attack was defeated. Both Sawyn Maculhene and Elinde Motheneos died, Maculhene in the fighting, Motheneos either in battle or executed after capture. Their armies were harried mercilessly. All in all, at least forty thousand of Amalasan's supporters died.

By the early summer of FY 943, Artur Hawkwing was back in Shandalle, in what is now considered the first year of the rule of Artur the High King. From that year his future was set. Perhaps it was set the day he crossed the borders on his way to Tar Valon. Or on the first day of Jolvaine Pass.

What part Bonwhin played in the events that followed can only be speculated upon. (What is available to non-Aes Sedai concerning her later deposition and stilling reveals little beyond vague charges of malfeasance. Records of an Amyrlin's trial before the Hall of the Tower are not for non-Aes Sedai eyes, it seems.) The evidence is conclusive, though, that Bonwhin never forgave Hawkwing for entering Tar Valon's territory with an army. An enmity even deeper might be explained by the possibility that Hawkwing did indeed come to the White Tower's rescue

against Maculhene and Motheneos. Bonwhin was an imperious woman even for an Amyrlin, and it is unlikely she would either have forgotten the need for rescue or forgiven the one who provided it.

In the summer of FY 943, Queen Nesaline of Caembarin, King Tefan of Khodomar, and First Counselor Almindhra of Tova simultaneously sent armies into Shandalle. That they should in concert choose that moment for such a move is surprising without the instigation of Tar Valon. Some sources claim that they were fearful of Hawkwing's reputation as a general, and of the intentions of a man who had not only defied White Tower law within the lands of Tar Valon's rule, but had refused an audience with the Amyrlin. Some sources say that it was Bonwhin who refused to grant him audience; Amyrlins have certainly been known to refuse monarchs, while the reverse is practically unheard of.

The world was still very unsettled. Trolloc activity had begun a brief yet violent upswing in the north. Once Amalasan was gentled, his following began to fall apart, but in many of the lands he had troubled, including Khodomar, men and women who had risen with him were trying to hold on to power. And among the common people, Hawkwing was being hailed as the savior who had captured the false Dragon; in a number of lands, people said with varying degrees of openness that they wished he ruled their nations. Whatever their motivation, that last was one of the facts the rulers of Caembarin, Tova, and Khodomar failed to take into account fully. Another was that Artur Hawkwing had showed himself to be one of the great captains of the Age. He was about to show that he was one of the great captains of all time. As a result the period FY 943–963 is called either the Wars of Consolidation or, more simply, the Consolidation.

Although Hawkwing had begun disbanding his army as soon as he returned home, he fought back against the three allies with what he still had and reassembled with surprising speed the men who had been sent home. By the time snows forced an end to fighting, in FY 943, he held nearly half of Tova and considerable parts of Caembarin and Khodomar. He had not been defeated once, though often outnumbered. And thousands of people in all three lands had flocked to his banner, with more coming by the day. Guaire Amalasan had set the example; countless thousands had abandoned the lands of their birth to follow a man, and it could hardly seem unthinkable now.

Even at that point it could have ended. Negotiations led by Tar Valon were the usual end to wars of this era, though of course the victor in the fighting always came out better than the losers. There is no record available anywhere of any attempt at negotiation by the White Tower. Available Tower records themselves are completely silent on the subject. When the thaws came in FY 944, Aldeshar sent men to aid Caembarin, Ileande sent men to Tova, and Talmour to Khodomar.

The next nineteen years were not continuous warfare for Hawkwing, but the periods of respite were so short, never more than a year and seldom so much, that they might as well have been. Nations came against him and were defeated. By FY 963, except for the territory ruled by Tar Valon, Artur Hawkwing was undisputed master of every mile from the Spine of the World to the Aryth Ocean. With the exception of Moreina, where the High Governor of the Stone of Tear declared for Hawkwing and a rebellion by dissident nobles gave him most of the rest of the country, all of that land had been taken by conquest. In all that time he had not lost one battle.

Chapter 12

The Reign of the High King

 ASIDE FROM EVENTS surrounding Tar Valon (recorded later), the next twenty-three years were largely peaceful, notwithstanding nine recorded revolts during that time. Though several of those were quite widespread, apparently none gained any degree of popular support. They grew exclusively among the disgruntled nobility of the conquered lands, and most collapsed as soon as Hawkwing sent forces to deal with them, at least one before those forces even arrived.

The last eight years of Hawkwing's life took on a very different cast, however. Early in FY 986, a massive Trolloc invasion struck into the northern provinces at three points. The seventy-four-year-old Hawkwing moved as quickly as ever the younger one had, and as decisively. In a series of seven major battles culminating at Talidar in

the summer of FY 987, he crushed the invasion so decisively that Trolloc activity along the Blight was diminished for the next fifty years.

Perhaps this brief war with the Trollocs made the martial juices rise again in Hawkwing, or perhaps the death of his second wife, Tamika, from unrecorded causes the autumn after Talidar reminded him of his own mortality. There is evidence that he began massive planning in the winter of FY 989. In FY 992, a force of incredible dimensions (sources vary widely, but a typical one claims two thousand ships of all sizes carrying over three hundred thousand soldiers and settlers) sailed into the Aryth Ocean from the western ports, under the command of Hawkwing's son, Luthair Paendrag Mondwin. Its destination was Seanchan. Surely the world had never seen such a fleet, yet the following year Hawkwing sent out another, reportedly of equal size, from the southern ports. Much less is known of this fleet than of that led by Luthair Paendrag, only that its destination was the lands known as Shara, among other names, and that it was under the command of a daughter of Hawkwing. The fate of the Seanchan expedition is all too well known, now, but of the Shara expedition there is only silence, beyond a few stories of the sort told in village taverns, claiming that Hawkwing conquered 'lands beyond the Aiel Waste.' Sea Folk ships' logs of that time do show that the landings were observed on the coast of Shara in FY 993. Other logs report seeing large numbers of ships burning in late FY 994, primarily in the same bays where the initial landings were recorded.

Perhaps Hawkwing received dire reports from these expeditions – reports are alluded to, but nothing remains of them – or perhaps launching the expeditions was like

the last flowering of a tree before it fails. In early summer of FY 994, Artur Hawkwing was stricken by a sudden illness and went into a precipitous decline. For much of the next month he was fever-ridden and delirious, often shouting for his sword, Justice. According to several sources, he frequently spoke as if Amaline or Tamika or both were in the room. His last words were addressed to them. 'I cannot come, yet. The work is not done. The battle is still to be fought.' At the age of eighty-two, Artur Paendrag Tanreall, Artur Hawkwing, the High King, was dead. Within months the first battles had been fought of what would come to be called the War of the Hundred Years.

That he was loved and respected by the common people cannot be doubted. One source reports that when forces he sent to deal with a widespread revolt in what had been Safer arrived, they discovered that the people of the region had already risen against the revolutionaries and imprisoned the leaders to hand over to the High King's justice. Since several sources record that he never inflicted any penalties on a region where a revolt occurred, only on those people who actually participated (anti-Hawkwing writers are silent on the subject, and they would certainly have leaped on the slightest claim of oppression), it must be taken that this counterrevolt came from the people's own wish to support him. While he raised no monument to himself (even the great monument he built at Talidar did not show his name or image, only the names of those who died in the battle), it seems that every town and village built some sort of monument or memorial to the High King. Unfortunately, all of these monuments were destroyed during the War of the Hundred Years, along with almost everything else that

alluded to the High King or his rule. After he raised the monument at Talidar, a public subscription began for a monument to him, a great statue to be constructed in the new capital that he was planning. Even some sources otherwise critical of Hawkwing agree that this movement began spontaneously among the common people. Hawkwing himself tried to discourage it, even forbade it at first, apparently giving in only when he realized that this was one revolt he could not suppress.

It is clear that Hawkwing was both a good ruler and well loved. Sources that claim otherwise inevitably reveal prejudice; without exception, those writers who can be identified were closely linked with the nobility of the conquered lands. Understandably, many among the conquered nobility did not love him. He made use of them where their abilities warranted (a considerable number served as governors or functionaries in the empire), but this in itself was a sore point with many of them. Men and women who without Hawkwing would have been kings and queens instead found themselves governing provinces in his name or overseeing the construction of flood-control projects or the like. In many ways their titles became irrelevant; those with higher ranks could find themselves serving under those of lower rank, or even under commoners, for Hawkwing appointed strictly according to merit. Additionally, he divided all of the nations into provinces which ofttimes overlapped old national boundaries. While lower-level functionaries in any province always came from the region, no one was appointed governor over a province that held any part of the nation they had been born in, and he made certain that soldiers garrisoned in a province always came from still another region of the empire. These things made it

impossible for any governor to build a personal base of power. And if Hawkwing promoted on merit, he demoted on the same basis. He had small tolerance for incompetence and none for malfeasance or misuse of office; whatever their ancestry, officials guilty of the first were removed immediately, while those guilty of the second often found themselves dragged away bodily, sentenced to periods of hard labor – a common fate for felons at the time, as opposed to imprisonment – and their estates and titles declared forfeit. As bad or worse from the point of view of the nobility, he also abrogated the special privileges that they claimed in various lands. Everyone stood equal in the face of the High King's law.

The legal system under Hawkwing is largely lost to the record, but it is known that he established schools which trained judges and advocates in the law, and that everyone, high and low, had the right to an advocate in appearing before a panel of judges, which sat in threes, and a jury selected from the census roles. Which meant of course, that nobles could find themselves being tried not by their peers, but before judges and jury who were all commoners. Judges and advocates apparently never served in one place for more than six years, and were held to a strict code of ethics. There was also a system for appealing the verdict of a court, with the final appeal being to Hawkwing himself. And that is all that is known of what most historians agree was the most elaborate and finely regulated judicial system the world has ever seen, one in which it was quite possible for a farmer to gain judgment against a former king if the facts were on his side.

That 'a maiden could ride alone and decked with jewels from one end of Hawkwing's kingdom to the other

without fear of harm' has been repeated so often that it has become a cliché, yet it appears to have been very nearly the truth. Hawkwing created a Civil Guard – by the evidence well trained, well disciplined, and held to a strict code of conduct – which not only policed cities and larger towns, but also patrolled the roads. Small parties of what were apparently called 'circuit rovers' (the term is not capitalized in the two sources available) rode a regular pattern of patrol between even the smallest villages.

Of Hawkwing's personal life, again very little can be discovered. His marriage to Amaline Paendrag Tagora was apparently a love-match. Proof of this can be seen from the so-called Amaline Poems, which largely survived the attempted destruction of everything connected with Hawkwing during the first three decades of the War of the Hundred Years. The work of a fair-to-poor poet, they are also plainly the work of a man stricken to the heart by the woman he wrote to. They appear to cover the entire span of their marriage.

It is certain that in FY 942 Amaline gave birth to twins, Amira and Modair, but while she and Hawkwing are known to have had another son and another daughter, nothing survives of them, not even their names. In FY 959 Modair was killed in battle, and though Hawkwing surely mourned ('Loss,' the only one of the Amaline Poems not a love poem, clearly speaks of this time), it was the deaths by poison in FY 961 of Amaline and their three remaining children which came close to undoing him.

Several sources use terms such as 'the Black Years' and 'the Years of Silent Rage' for the period from FY 961 to 965, the final years of the Consolidation and also the near disastrous invasion of the Aiel Waste in FY 964.

Hawkwing is said to have sealed himself away from all human emotion, 'and of these, love and pity he buried most deep.' Even writers plainly favoring Hawkwing agree that his search for the murderers was harsh and unrelenting; and they speak of more than one hundred executions. His initial treatment of Aldeshar, the last nation to fall to him, was certainly cruel: no prisoners taken in a number of battles, the displacement of nearly the whole population to other parts of the empire, the confiscation of all estates with the whole nobility and the entire merchant class reduced to absolute penury and scattered to every corner of the empire. Had such treatment continued, had it been extended to the rest of the empire, there can be no doubt that Hawkwing would have faced a thousand revolts during the rest of his reign instead of the handful reliably documented.

Salvation for the empire, and very likely for Hawkwing personally, came in the person of a woman named Tamika. Extremely little is known of her beyond her first name. All sources agree that she was nearly thirty years younger than Hawkwing. A number claim that she could channel, even that she was a renegade Aes Sedai, though this does not square with reports of her youth. What is certain is that she brought Hawkwing out of the Black Years. At her behest he relented in his treatment of Aldeshar, allowing the people to return, restoring confiscated estates and titles. Because of her, the harshness that had begun to spread from Aldeshar into the rest of the conquered lands vanished like ice at the spring thaw.

Hawkwing met Tamika late in FY 964 on his return from the Aiel Waste and married her one year later. Several sources speak of the Tamika Poems, saying that they showed a man every bit as much in love as in the

Amaline Poems, but of course none of them survive. Tamika can certainly be credited for Hawkwing's return to his earlier policies toward the conquered lands, possibly for several refinements in administration and taxation added after FY 965, and thus in large part for Hawkwing's reputation as a great ruler. Their first son, Luthair Paendrag Mondwin, was born in FY 967. They had either three more children or four, but we know almost nothing of them. At least two of those children were daughters, for one commanded the 'Shara expedition,' and a partial letter in the Royal Library in Cairhien says that 'the great Hawkwing died less than an hour before the news arrived of the tragic deaths of his daughter Laiwynde and her son, the last of Hawkwing's blood this side of the oceans.' Tamika herself died in FY 987; there is no record of the cause.

Tamika's relations with the White Tower were decidedly cool and distant, though certainly not hostile. Openly, at least. But in FY 968 or 969 either Bonwhin refused to receive her or Tamika refused a summons to Bonwhin. The last is unlikely since at this period even Hawkwing himself would have gone. And yet would Bonwhin have refused audience to the Queen and wife to the undisputed ruler of every scrap of land not held by Tar Valon? Unless perhaps rumors that Tamika was a renegade Aes Sedai were true. Rumors of renegade Aes Sedai seem to be a minor staple of history, however, though none has ever been confirmed, and it should be noted that with the sole exception of Tamika every source speaks of swift and dire punishments handed out by the White Tower. Consider the familiar tale of the kidnapping of Queen Sulmara of Masenashar (circa 450 AB). The details differ in the various tellings, but the

end is the same in all versions: Once captured, Sulmara spent the remainder of her life laboring in the White Tower's stables.

While the Firsts of Mayene claim descent from Hawkwing, through a grandson named Tyrn, there is no evidence that any of Hawkwing's blood survived him, and all surviving contemporary records state clearly that none did. On the other hand, given the state of affairs after Hawkwing's death, any living descendant of Hawkwing would have been hidden away as a matter of safety.

No account of Hawkwing should omit his dealings with the White Tower. The loosening and tightening of tensions there can be charted with some rough precision, though hindered by the Tower library's lack of records for the period. Among those available to non-Aes Sedai, at least.

In the beginning Hawkwing showed no animus toward Aes Sedai. He apparently approached Tar Valon seeking help in negotiations with his multiple enemies in FY 944, with no result. Although Tar Valon took no open part in any of the wars against Hawkwing, every ruler who sent forces against him gained Aes Sedai advisors, often as many as four or five, before the ruler made any move against Hawkwing. Whether or not Tar Valon was involved in provocation, the rulers must have seen no choice but to oppose him. Yet Hawkwing must have believed that Tar Valon was, if not inciting, at least aiding his enemies.

By all sources Hawkwing made no open moves against Tar Valon during the Consolidation. Amaline certainly had something to do with this; while it is certain that she was not Aes Sedai and there is no evidence that she could channel, there is some suggestion that as a very young

woman she went to the White Tower seeking training, and many sources report her friendliness with Aes Sedai and her generally pro-Tar Valon stance. To all outward appearances, Hawkwing eventually made a peace with the White Tower, if not one with a signed treaty, of course, for Tar Valon was not likely to admit that it had been opposing him. In FY 954, he accepted an Aes Sedai advisor, Chowin Tsao of the Green Ajah. Rulers fighting him also still had advisors from Tar Valon, of course, but the White Tower had always maintained a public stance of neutrality, and it appears that he accepted this posture at least in public.

Apparently a temporary break occurred during the Black Years. Chowin Tsao is his advisor in a fragmentary letter reliably dated in FY 962, but another letter (probably FY 967, by internal evidence) states that 'after five years the High King has reconciled with Tar Valon and agreed to accept once more a counselor from among the sisters.'

Whatever the reason for the split, the reconciliation was wholehearted while it lasted. By FY 974 Hawkwing was making wide use of Aes Sedai throughout his empire. They held a number of positions of authority and responsibility, even serving as provincial governors. And then, in the autumn of FY 974, Hawkwing curtly dismissed not only his Aes Sedai advisor (name unknown), but all Aes Sedai holding posts within his realm. In the early spring of FY 975 he put a price on the head of any Aes Sedai who refused to renounce Tar Valon – though there is no credible evidence that he demanded they transfer allegiance to him. By the summer of that year, his generals had not only overrun all of Tar Valon's territory, but were laying siege to the city itself.

That siege would last the rest of Hawkwing's life, and even a few months longer. It is generally believed that even with Aes Sedai use of the One Power, Tar Valon would have fallen had it not been for widespread, if unorganized, sympathy, resulting in a fairly steady stream of supplies smuggled into the city via the river. While Hawkwing himself was immensely popular, many people had no antipathy against Aes Sedai and felt that to move against Tar Valon was wrong and even dangerous. In addition, many nobles covertly supported Tar Valon, whether or not they dared do so openly.

Why did he turn against Tar Valon so violently? Many agree that in FY 974 Hawkwing became convinced that Tar Valon was using him to increase its own power; Aes Sedai now governed more than one third of the provinces of the empire, and there seems little doubt that these women took their orders from Bonwhin more than from Hawkwing. It seems very likely that Bonwhin had been attempting to guide or control his decisions for some time, and considering her eventual fate (deposed by the Hall of the Tower in FY 992, stilled, and, until her death in FY 996, kept working among the scullions, though this last is known only from sources outside the Tower), it is possible that she may have overstepped whatever bounds Aes Sedai put on such manipulations. But that is only speculation.

Several sources say that Hawkwing discovered proof that the Tower had been behind some or all of the revolts he had faced to that time, though by then he must have been dealing with Tar Valon long enough for such machinations to come as no real surprise. Some sources claim that he discovered that Bonwhin herself had been involved in the deaths of Amaline and their children. That

last, at least, would explain the ferocity with which he turned on Tar Valon. And it was war to the knife, without truce to the end. On his deathbed, Hawkwing refused an offer of Aes Sedai Healing that might have saved him.

The possible role of Tamika in relations with Tar Valon has been analyzed countless times; 'possible' because despite her evident power in the empire there is no evidence of any such role, whatever her relationship to Bonwhin and the Tower, yet that very relationship, with all its coolness and apparently deliberate distance on both sides, perhaps makes such speculation inevitable.

Other speculations range from the possible (Hawkwing simply deciding that he wanted all of the land) to the bizarre (a complicated plot by the White Tower – those who favor Aes Sedai conspiracies hidden under every bush favor this one, though the aims of the supposed plot vary wildly according to the scribe). The Jalwin Moerad theory is popular with those who reject obvious causes.

Very little is known of Moerad, though he appears in several sources, most notably in letters gathered in the Terhana Library in Bandar Eban. In FY 973 he appeared at Hawkwing's court, making his first entry into history. Many at the time wondered about his background, and some who inquired too closely into it may have suffered fatal accidents. It is noted that Tamika was icily cold toward Moerad, if always correct, yet although Hawkwing trusted her counsel, by the late summer of FY 974 Moerad was one of the High King's closest advisors. He maintained this position until Hawkwing's death despite frequent long absences, a volatile temper, and a temperament that more than one observer recorded as 'more than half insane.'

It is on that proximity of dates (late summer, Moerad became a counselor; early autumn, Hawkwing dismissed Aes Sedai from his service) and the startling fact that Moerad seemed openly contemptuous of Aes Sedai that all theories concerning him rest. Contempt is an odd stance toward Aes Sedai, and even those who hate Aes Sedai are wise enough to be discreet; yet such feelings are hardly enough to condemn him.

A partial manuscript (private collection in Andor), dated some twenty-three years after Hawkwing's death, builds on these shaky facts. According to the writer, within days of Hawkwing's demise Moerad was advising Marithelle Camaelaine. When she was assassinated, he supposedly began advising Norodim Nosokawa (again within days), and immediately after Nosokawa's death in battle, Moerad appeared at Elfraed Guitama's side. As these three came the closest to seizing the whole of Hawkwing's empire in the twenty years after his death, Moerad obviously either was an advisor of great skill or a man with a keen eye for a winner. How these things are supposed to tie into responsibility for Hawkwing turning against Aes Sedai is unfortunately among the missing portions of the manuscript. An odd note: The writer claims that Moerad never aged from the day he first appeared to the day he vanished, abruptly, some forty years later. What that says of the source's veracity is left to the reader.

Thus the life of Artur Hawkwing, Artur the High King. What might he have accomplished had he not turned against the Aes Sedai? The unification of the entire world? It has been suggested that had he not expended so much energy against Tar Valon, he might have launched his invasions of Seanchan and Shara sooner, and that with

his personal involvement the Shara and Seanchan expeditions would never have been lost. At whose feet do we lay the blame? Hawkwing? Bonwhin? Persons whose names are lost forever in the mists of history? Some account him a failure because what he built did not survive him, but if so, it was failure such as other men dream of achieving. Few successes achieve a tenth part so much.

Chapter 13

The War of the Hundred Years

ARTUR HAWKWING'S DEATH left a great void. With no living heirs to inherit the empire – none at least who dared announce themselves – any strong leader had a valid chance to rule the land. The strongest nobles began immediately vying for control of the empire, while others used the opportunity to attempt carving out smaller holdings. Almost at once war broke out over the scraps of the High King's legacy. This struggle, which depopulated large parts of the lands between the Aryth Ocean and the Aiel Waste, from the Sea of Storms to the Great Blight, lasted over a century and would be later known as the War of the Hundred Years. At its end, Artur Hawkwing's empire had been shattered, and the nations of the present day had risen from the wreckage, along with others that no longer survive.

The White Tower survived the chaos, though this time only through outside intervention. Despite Hawkwing's death, Souran Maravaile, a general under Hawkwing, continued the siege of the White Tower, determined to finish what the High King had begun. With a good portion of the dead king's military force at his disposal, it is possible that Souran would have succeeded in bringing down the Tower, but many histories credit Deane Aryman, raised to the Amyrlin Seat when Bonwhin was deposed, with saving the Tower by convincing Souran to raise the siege. It is certain Deane met with him and made serious attempts to undo the damage Bonwhin had done by attempting to control Artur Hawkwing, but new evidence now proves that it was actually Ishara, his lover and the daughter of Hawkwing's provincial governor of Andor, who convinced Souran to release the Tower. Deane did, however, manage to restore the prestige of the Tower, and was believed to be convincing the warring nobles to accept the leadership of the Tower and thus restore unity to the land when she was killed in a fall from her horse. The wars between nobles and factions continued until individual nations were strong enough to stand against them.

Some provinces made the transition to nationhood relatively intact, providing the governing family was strong enough to hold and defend it. Andor was one such: Ishara declared Andor a sovereign nation and took the title as Queen, but she was no stranger to royalty; the former governor, Ishara's mother, had been the daughter of the last King of Aldeshar before Hawkwing conquered it.

After Souran withdrew his army from Tar Valon he joined Ishara in Caemlyn, capital city of Andor. Many

believe that Ishara convinced him to break the siege because she knew she would need the Tower's support to hold Andor through the coming wars. This notion is further supported by the fact that she promised to send her first daughter to train in the Tower, channeler or not. To cement the support of the Tower, she made it law that the eldest daughter of the ruler of Andor would train in the Tower, and that the ruler would have an Aes Sedai advisor. At this time it was not yet established that Andor would always have a female ruler.

Souran was killed by assassins twenty-three years into the war, and Ishara would have had a son succeed her had not all her sons fallen as well. To keep the line in control of Andor, her daughter Alesinde took the throne. Alesinde's sons also died in battle, leaving a daughter to ascend the Lion Throne. Andor was one of the few nations to manage to hold both sovereignty and stability throughout the War of the Hundred Years. Much of the credit goes to the first nine Queens of Andor, those who held the nation together during the War of the Hundred Years (dates given are considered the most reliable):

1) Ishara; reigned FY 994 to FY 1020
2) Alesinde; reigned FY 1020 to FY 1035
3) Melasune; reigned FY 1035 to FY 1046
4) Termylle; reigned FY 1046 to FY 1054
5) Maragaine; reigned FY 1054 to FY 1073
6) Astara; reigned FY 1073 to FY 1085
7) Telaisien; reigned FY 1085 to FY 1103
8) Morrigan; reigned FY 1103 to FY 1114
9) Lyndelle ascended the throne in FY 1114 and ruled for fifty-one years.

By the war's end, the tradition was firmly established that only a queen would rule, that sons were to be soldiers, and the eldest son the leader of the armies. Because of Ishara's prudence, Andor was one of the first nations formed from Hawkwing's broken empire, as well as one of the strongest.

Over the course of the war many nations formed, re-formed, broke, and formed again. Eventually, after over a century of strife, the fighting trailed off, ceasing entirely in approximately FY 1117.

Not only nations grew from the chaos. Another blossom of those years was the Children of the Light; founded in FY 1021 by Lothair Mantelar to preach against Darkfriends. They too were changed by the violent nature of the times. Over the next odd ninety years they evolved from ascetic preachers who could fight at need to a well-armed and disciplined military organization dedicated to the eradication of Darkfriends everywhere. No one knows when they were given the name Whitecloaks, but it is to be doubted anyone has ever used it except disparagingly, a fact the Children are well aware of.

Of the war years as a whole only fragmentary records remain. FY 994 to FY 1117 are the generally accepted dates, but no competent historian lets them go entirely without question. The present-day calendar was adopted in large part because so much was lost that at the war's end there was considerable argument about what year it truly was. While records fix the beginning of the war firmly, by its end the actual year could have been anything from FY 1115 to FY 1119. And that span depends on the belief that some writers did in fact record the true year.

As to when the errors began, no one can be certain. As early as the third decade of the war different sources report different dates for the same event, though most likely these are simply errors in reporting or copying. Toward the end of the war, however, writers in the same country recorded widely varying dates for their local royal successions. Reasonable historians have adopted an admittedly arbitrary protocol that dates in the first third of the war are reasonably accurate, dates in the second third are subject to question, and dates in the final third must be based on the best estimates. It is because of these discrepancies that the Farede Calendar was presented and adopted after the war, making FY 1135 (as we believe) into Year 1 of the New Era.

Twenty-four nations rose during and just after the war, including the fourteen currently surviving lands. Those nations were Almoth, Altara, Amadicia, Andor, Arad Doman, Arafel, Cairhien, Caralain, Ghealdan, Goaban, Hardan, Illian, Irenvelle, Kandor, Kintara, Mar Haddon, Maredo, Malkier, Mosara, Murandy, Saldaea, Shienar, Tear, and Tarabon.

Malkier, whose sign was a golden crane in flight, was overrun by Trollocs in the autumn of 955 NE, and by 957 NE the Blight had completely covered the land that had been known as the Kingdom of the Seven Towers.

Though Malkier was the only nation during this period to fall to the Blight it was certainly not the only nation to disappear. Almoth, Caralain, Goaban, Hardan, Irenvelle, Kintara, Mar Haddon, Maredo, and Mosara all simply faded away, until by 600 NE only a few remnants of their people survived, claiming what was obviously gone. Some parts of these lands were claimed by other nations at various times, and by 800 NE even the ghosts

of the fallen nations had dissipated, perhaps leaving a name to mark the grasslands where their people once thrived. Far Madding was the only settlement larger than a small town or village remaining in any of those fallen nations.

Chapter 14

The New Era

 WITH THE END of the War of the Hundred Years came a relative peace for almost a thousand years. There were still squabbles between nations, but population levels had dropped so low that these squabbles seldom concerned national expansion. Most rulers concentrated on simply trying to hold all the land they claimed. Society as a whole began once again to rebuild itself from the ashes of war. Commerce and trade took the place of conquest.

In 509 NE, the Aiel, known only as a mysterious and deadly people who kept to themselves, granted to the nation of Cairhien the right to cross the Aiel Waste, a right formerly denied to all but Tinkers and peddlers. They gave the Cairhienin a sapling called *Avendoraldera*, an offshoot of the fabled *Avendesora* (which is a descendant of the

chora trees, it has since been learned), to seal the grant. The Aiel told them to carry a banner bearing the trefoil leaf of *Avendesora* and no more weapons than those needed for self-defense; free passage in the Waste gave Cairhienin merchants access to silks and other rare goods available only in lands beyond the Waste.

In recent years, it has been discovered that the Aiel had a very clear reason for their gift of *Avendoraldera*. During the Breaking of the World, the ancestors of the Cairhienin aided the Aiel's ancestors by allowing them water, and now that they had discovered who the Cairhienin were they were repaying a debt of honor. The Aiel simply did not feel it necessary to explain themselves to the 'wetlanders' they were rewarding.

The influx of Shara goods not only made Cairhien a wealthy nation, but enriched its neighbors as well. For the first time the land had a source for goods that would compete with the Sea Folk merchants'. Such good fortune seemed, at least to the Cairhienin, to herald a new era of prosperity. No one knew that the Aiel's gift contained the seed for yet another bloody war.

Nations did fight wars, but few lasted more than a year or two. The nations along the Blightborder seldom entered these; they had the Blight, and Trollocs, to fight. Others, however, have long histories of these 'small' wars between them, most notably Andor and Cairhien, Tear and Illian, Tear and Cairhien, and Arad Doman and Tarabon.

Over the years, the Children of the Light gained control of Amadicia, ruling in all but name; kings and queens still sat on the throne of Amadicia, but they did nothing without the approval of the Lord Captain Commander of the Children of the Light. In 957, the Children cast their

eyes on Altara, and whether or not they looked beyond, to Murandy and even Illian, Murandy and Illian believed that they did. The result is known to the Children as 'the Troubles,' to the rest of the world as the Whitecloak War. Lord Captain Pedron Niall (later to be chosen Lord Captain Commander) took the lead for the Children of the Light, while Mattin Stepaneos, King of Illian, headed the opposition. While it is true that Niall won the great majority of the battles, indeed capturing Mattin Stepaneos at the Battle of Soremaine (where only the bravery of the Illianer Companions enabled the bulk of the Illianer army to escape the trap), in the end the Children could not swallow so much at once. Mattin Stepaneos, who had been ransomed back to the Council of Nine in Illian, finally forced the Children to accept a treaty reaffirming the prewar borders between Amadicia and Altara.

The year 965 NE saw Laman Damodred take the throne of Cairhien. War resumed between Andor and Cairhien to continue with only a minor break until 968.

Other nations also had their problems as the millennium drew toward a close. Illian and Tear went to war once more in 970, and the hostilities lasted almost six years although some writers divide the intermittent fighting into three separate wars; in addition, the enmity between Cairhien and Andor had become constant. Even the marriage of Taringail Damodred of Cairhien, nephew of King Laman, to Tigraine, the Daughter-Heir of Andor, only granted a temporary peace. The political marriage was reportedly not a happy one, especially for Tigraine. In 972 she disappeared, and the reigning Queen, Mordrellen, died with no heir, triggering an internal struggle for succession that ended in Morgase Trakand taking the throne. In an attempt to prevent another war with Cairhien,

Morgase married Tigraine's widower, Taringail, but unlike Tigraine she was not above reminding Taringail that he was not and never could be co-ruler of Andor.

A pebble slipping on a mountaintop can begin an avalanche, even when it was right and necessary that the pebble slip. Morgase's failure to soothe Taringail's ego was such a pebble. In Cairhien, Laman's desire to see his nephew not merely co-ruler, but sole ruler, of Andor was well known; such things are difficult to hide in Cairhien, where children play the Game of Houses with their dolls and toy soldiers. That Taringail was in no way Morgase's equal in rule quickly became public knowledge in Cairhien, and among those who play the Game of Houses as Cairhienin do, such a small, possibly even temporary, failure is seen as a weakness. Plots were born to unseat Laman, and he hatched his own schemes to counter them. As a minor part of one of his schemes, Laman cut down *Avendoraldera* to make a throne which could never be duplicated, it was thought. The tree was cut down, and the avalanche began.

THE AIEL WAR

The destruction of *Avendoraldera* brought a war beyond anyone's nightmares. In the late spring of 976, tens of thousands of Aiel came sweeping over the Dragonwall to descend upon Cairhien. To the people of Cairhien, it seemed as if the entire Aiel nation had fallen upon them. In actuality it was only four clans, the Nakai, the Reyn, the Taardad, and the Shaarad; all under the leadership of Janduin, an Iron Mountain Taardad and clan chief of the Taardad Aiel. They had heard of Laman's deed, and

wanted the 'Treekiller' punished for his crime, though this was not known until many years later. The 'Aiel invasion' swept through Cairhien, capturing the capital city and putting it to the torch just months after the invaders crossed the Dragonwall. Only the library was spared. From Cairhien, the Aiel War, as it was quickly called, spread down through Tear, back up the River Erinin to Andor, and finally, three years after the Aiel had crossed the Dragonwall, to Tar Valon itself. By this time, almost every nation had sent soldiers against the invaders, lest the onslaught eventually reach their own lands. Only much later was it discovered that the Aiel were actually following Laman 'Treekiller.' To the people and rulers of the wetlands, it seemed the Aiel must be intent only on loot. Many towns and cities indeed were looted, though only one-fifth of everything was taken, in accordance with Aiel law. Of course, those who lost goods or loved ones only knew that they were victims of deadly savages; they did not consider how much more could have been taken by the victors had they chosen.

The Battle of Tar Valon, also called the Battle of the Shining Walls, the Battle of the Nations, the Battle of the Red Snows, and the Battle of the Blood Snow, began on the morning of the day before Danshu in the Year of Grace 978 of the New Era, when the Aiel were brought to battle by a loose coalition generally called 'the Grand Coalition,' or 'the Grand Alliance,' although a few have called it 'the Third Compact,' a term for which there is no basis in fact.

In addition to the surviving forces of Cairhien, the very temporary Alliance consisted of an army raised by Tar Valon and ten other nations as well as the Children of the Light. Though the Children of the Light were disgruntled

that the war to save civilization had become a battle to protect the Tar Valon 'witches,' they fought alongside the rest. Aes Sedai took part in the battle, but, bound by the Three Oaths, they were largely limited to defending against any thrust at Tar Valon itself; the Aiel were, after all, neither Shadowspawn nor Darkfriends, though the claim was made, of course. This was by far the closest cooperation between nations since Artur Hawkwing's empire had collapsed, but it fell apart upon the end of the Aiel War.

The Alliance had raised an immense force, approximately one hundred and seventy thousand men, an army of a size certainly not seen since Artur Hawkwing's day. The Aiel force is often claimed to have been twice as large as the Alliance army, but more reliable estimates put the actual number at one hundred thousand, and possibly less. Recently it has been possible to question the Aiel; they claim that at no time did the four clans have as many as one hundred thousand spears west of the Dragonwall. They put the number in front of Tar Valon at seventy to eighty thousand, half the size of the Alliance army or less. Given the proven reputation of the Aiel as soldiers and their unified command under Janduin, two-to-one odds in favor of the Alliance in no way contradicts the actual outcome of the battle.

It is said that participating in the temporary Grand Alliance were: Shienar with twenty-nine thousand men, Andor with twenty-eight thousand, Illian with twenty-six thousand, Tear with twenty-four thousand, Arafel with twenty-one thousand, Cairhien with six to seven thousand, Ghealdan with five thousand, Amadicia with four thousand, Murandy with three to four thousand, and Altara with roughly thirty-five hundred. Tar Valon

contributed twelve thousand men, while the Children of the Light had four thousand present. Each nation's force had its own leader: the ruler, or a lord considered that nation's best general.

In the beginning, at least some nations would have been willing to accept one captain-general – Agelmar of Shienar – but King Laman of Cairhien insisted on his right to command, as if the unbroken string of disasters suffered by Cairhienin arms was a recommendation. The Amyrlin Seat, Tamra Ospenya, wanted the reins in the hands of the White Tower. The Tairens (among others) opposed that as hotly as the Children of the Light, who were adamant. Mattin Stepaneos put himself forward, and so did Pedron Niall. Quickly other nations began to claim the position as a matter of national pride, until it became clear that no one leader could be chosen.

As a result each nation had one seat on a decision-making council, whatever the size of their contingent. The Children of the Light had one as well. Marya Somares, a Gray sister of great experience in negotiations, held a seat for the Tower, advised by Azil Mareed, a Domani captain in long service to the Tower, who commanded the Tower Guard. Field command of the armies was to rotate on a daily basis among the members of the council, excluding Marya Sedai, and of course, Mareed, who was not a member. The council held its first meeting twelve days before Danshu in 978 NE.

The council was perhaps lucky in the order in which they decided to rotate command – or perhaps they purposely gave the best generals the first chance, whether they voiced this or not. The order of command was: 1. Lord Agelmar Jagad of Shienar. 2. Pedron Niall, Lord Captain Commander of the Children of the Light. 3. Lord

Aranvor Naldwinn, Captain-General of the Queen's Guard of Andor (killed on the third day of fighting). 4. Lord Hirare Nachiman of Arafel (killed in a skirmish during the pursuit after the battle). 5. King Mattin Stepaneos of Illian. 6. The High Lord Astoril of Tear. 7. Lord Aleshin Talvaen of Ghealdan. 8. Lord Aeman Senhold of Amadicia. 9. King Laman Damodred of Cairhien (killed on the third day). 10. An Altaran to be selected. 11. A Murandian to be selected.

No Altaran or Murandian ever did command. Altara and Murandy each provided a gaggle of lords, and sometimes ladies, at the head of their own retainers; neither nation had an overall leader. Supposedly these nobles had worked out a rotation among themselves, with one to meet in council each day with full authority to speak for the rest. In actuality, as many as nine or ten nobles from each nation appeared at every meeting, all claiming that it was in fact their day to sit in the council. None made any real contribution to the council, since all who showed up spent their time squabbling. A number died fighting duels that arose from these arguments; it was even rumored that several duels were fought between Altaran noblewomen, at least one resulting in a fatality. The Altarans and Murandians were ineffective in the battle, as each noble chose where and when to fight. This is why their casualties were so high. It was not, as they claim, because they were always in the hottest fighting.

The duration of the battle is a matter of some dispute. First it must be noted that battles of this magnitude inevitably can be broken down into a number of smaller battles – each more akin in size to battles fought in the general run of wars. Each of these separate engagements, often overlapping in time, affect the outcome of the others.

The day before Danshu (the twenty-seventh day of Nesan) was the first of three days of heavy fighting on both sides of the Erinin to stop the Aiel overrunning Tar Valon. Some fighting occurred around the bridges across the Alindrelle Erinin, and there was fierce skirmishing on the first two nights. The first snows had long since fallen, and both sides were hampered not only by thick snow on the ground but by several brief snowstorms through the first two days of fighting. The Aiel had never seen or dealt with snow before crossing the Dragonwall, yet this was in no way evident in the ferocity of their fighting. Their flanking attacks and intermittent pricking strikes kept the Alliance on the defensive. The snowstorms were heavy on the morning of the second day, but by the late afternoon of that day the weather cleared, and the rest of the battle took place in deep snow but under bright, clear skies.

Late on the third day, the Aiel finally carried out their purpose of killing Laman of Cairhien, and during that night managed to concentrate their forces on the east side of the Erinin. Had the battle been between the armies of any two nations, vessels attempting to sail through the battle area would certainly have been fired upon by catapults and fire-arrows. For this reason merchant ships always stayed well clear of battles, and large numbers of riverships had collected above and below Tar Valon, waiting for the battle to end. Using rowboats taken from the shore, and even logs, Aiel managed to reach those vessels and capture them without raising any alarm on the shore. By means of ropes pulled by huge teams of men, they then hauled these craft back and forth between the riverbanks like barges, on every trip loaded almost to sinking. A remarkable feat, even more so considering the Aiel's

complete lack of familiarity with rivers, much less ships. By sunrise on the fourth day, the Aiel were already moving eastward.

This move caught the allied armies by surprise, but assuming that the Aiel were retreating in defeat, they quickly began a mounted pursuit, and engaged the Aiel rear guard in a number of skirmishes beginning late on the second day after Danshu. Some of these actions were in truth quite large, and they recurred at irregular intervals for twenty days, until just six days before the Feast of Lights, when the Aiel withdrew into Kinslayer's Dagger and the Alliance forces abandoned the pursuit, though some large forces did move into Cairhien south of Kinslayer's Dagger to guard against possible Aiel reemergence there.

Most historians record that the Battle of the Shining Walls lasted three days, but some include the first day of pursuit, making the total four. A few (writers with no understanding of war or battle) actually claim that the battle lasted until the Aiel 'were chased' into Kinslayer's Dagger. The worth of these last can be measured by the fact that they also claim that the Aiel barely managed to escape before an Alliance attack in great force would have annihilated them. Any competent military historian will see immediately that had the Alliance truly been able to launch such an attack, they would have done so during the first days of pursuit, before their infantry was outpaced by both their own cavalry and the Aiel. Skirmishes involving a thousand men or more on each side, and sometimes ten times that, occurred during the entire pursuit, and it must be taken that all the Alliance commanders truly wanted was to harry the Aiel back across the Spine of the World.

By spring of 979, Cairhien, having lost its King and much of its military might to the Aiel War, underwent an internal political realignment of Houses, also known as the Fourth War of Cairhienin Succession, which resulted in House Damodred losing the throne to House Riatin. The conflict was played out primarily through the great Game of Houses and never quite broke into a civil war, which is not to say, of course, that there was no bloodletting, but none of the many battles involved more than a few hundred men on either side. This political reorganization seemed to bring with it an end of hostilities with Andor, but it also meant that Taringail Damodred would no longer be able to fulfill his dream of having a son on the throne of Cairhien and a daughter on the throne of Andor. Those close to him have said that this embittered him, and some believe that he may have planned to take the Lion Throne of Andor for himself. He was assassinated in 984, leaving all plans unexecuted. Most sources believe the assassination was ordered by House Riatin of Cairhien as a means of preventing any coup by the heir to House Damodred, but there were rumors that it was done by someone loyal to Morgase, to protect her from Taringail's ambition.

In Autumn of 997, in Ghealdan, a man known as Logain Ablar proclaimed himself the Dragon Reborn. He could channel, and stories of Guaire Amalasan haunted the population as word of this new 'Dragon' spread. It had taken Artur Hawkwing's tactical brilliance to stop Amalasan. Who could contain or capture the new false Dragon? After carrying war across Ghealdan, Altara, and Murandy, though, Ablar was finally captured by a loose alliance of southern nations and taken to the White Tower, where he was gentled.

The appearance of a false Dragon who could channel seemed to the credulous a warning of strange things to come, for in 998, Trollocs, not seen outside of the Borderlands since the Trolloc Wars, suddenly appeared in Emond's Field, a small farming village in Andor, once in Manetheren. In the words of one commentator, 'All that came before was dust sliding down the mountainside. The avalanche was about to descend.'

The World of
the Wheel

Chapter 15

The World After
the Breaking

 STUDENTS OF GEOGRAPHY know that wind, weather, and time can change the shape of any continent or ocean. These changes are natural. Our world, however, because of the Breaking, has actually had two drastically different geographies.

No surviving maps tell exactly what the world was like before its continents were torn apart by the One Power, but there is no doubt it was very different from the world of today. The destruction seems to have radiated outward from Shayol Ghul – understandably, since that is where the Hundred Companions originally went mad – and the Breaking may not have been as cataclysmic in far distant parts of the world. Our present knowledge is limited to occasional clues discovered by explorers and students of historical geography: ruins that have obviously been far

removed from their original environment, or artifacts that give little clue to their origin.

Weights and measures

mile   A measure of distance equal to one thousand spans. Four miles make one league.

hide   A unit of area for measuring land, equal to 100 paces by 100 paces.

span   A measure of distance equal to two paces. A thousand spans make a mile.

units of weight
10 ounces = 1 pound;
10 pounds = 1 stone;
10 stone = 1 hundredweight;
10 hundredweight = 1 ton.

THE WORLD

Geographers of the modern world are only beginning to understand its true dimensions and features. Explorers and merchants bring back knowledge of lands beyond the sea and the Waste, but a great deal of territory is still uncharted.

There are three major continents, and an area of ice in each polar region. Our land, the Aiel Waste, and the land called Shara occupy one continent, and the Seanchan the second, much larger, which lies to the west far over the

Aryth Ocean. An unnamed continent, known only from
Sea Folk explorations, lies far to the south. A fourth continent may lie hidden beneath the massive ice of the
southern polar regions, but it is unknown and likely to
remain so.

THE MAIN CONTINENT

The only part of this continent which has been completely mapped is that containing our lands, bordered by
the Mountains of Dhoom to the north, the Aryth Ocean
to the west, the Sea of Storms to the south, and the mountains of the Spine of the World (also known as the
Dragonwall) to the east.

The Mountains of Dhoom rise from the eastern sea to
run through the Aiel Waste and Shara right into the sea in
the west, and may even continue beneath its waters if
they are, as suspected, a planetwide upheaval caused
during the Breaking. Extending both north and south of
the Mountains of Dhoom is the wasteland known as the
Great Blight, a region entirely corrupted by the Dark One
where Trollocs, Myrddraal, and other malignant shadow-
creatures thrive. Deep within the Blight lies the dark
volcanic mountain Shayol Ghul, the site of the Dark One's
prison. Some ancient records hint that the mountain may
once have been an island in a cool sea. Below the forbidding slopes of Shayol Ghul is a fog-shrouded valley
known as Thakan'dar. Despite the fog and the presence of
ice only a few hundred leagues to the north, this winter-
cold valley is as dry as any desert.

All around Shayol Ghul and north of the Blight
extends the waste known as the Blasted Lands. Devoid of

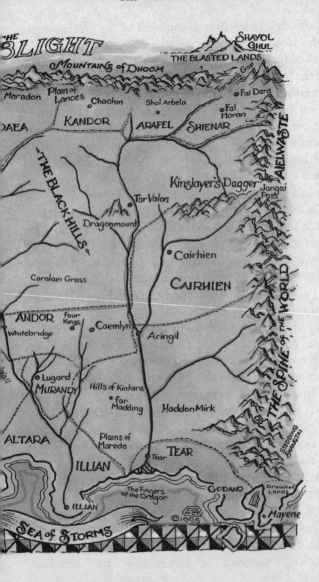

life, this desolation is even shunned by the foul creatures of the Blight. Historians believe that the area bore the brunt of the War of Power, which rendered it completely barren. Its proximity to Shayol Ghul and the corrupting influence of the Shadow no doubt keep it so. No one knows if anything lies north of the Blasted Lands other than the frozen ice of the northern ocean. Jain Farstrider was said to have willingly traveled there; however, whatever knowledge he gained was lost when he vanished within its trackless depths.

To the west lies the great Aryth Ocean.

To the south is the Sea of Storms and, some distance off the southern coast, the Isles of the Sea Folk. Roughly south of Illian and Mayene, these islands are scattered throughout the Sea of Storms. One is large, and there is an unknown number of medium-to-small islands. Only the Sea Folk themselves know the exact number and location of all their island homes.

To the east of the land lies the towering mountain range of the Spine of the World, also called the Dragonwall, separating the land from the Aiel Waste. There are only four usable passes through and one southern route around these mountains. The northernmost pass, Tarwin's Gap, lies in the valley between the Mountains of Dhoom and the Dragonwall, at the edge of what used to be the Kingdom of Malkier. It is now part of the Blight. Farther south, at the edge of Shienar, the mountains are breached by the Niamh Passes, actually a series of footpaths that traverse the range into the Aiel Waste.

The best known crossing, the Jangai Pass, lies just south of Kinslayer's Dagger, the dominant peak of the range, in Cairhien. The Aiel crossed the Jangai into

Cairhien during the Aiel War. Before that war it began the major trade route between Cairhien and Shara. It is still used by Tinkers and those merchants that wish to trade with the Aiel.

There is another, nameless breach in the mountains, at the eastern edge of Haddon Mirk, south of where the River Iralell originates, leading only to the Ogier *Stedding* Shangtai.

Passage by land to the south of the Dragonwall is possible, but requires traversing the hazardous Drowned Lands just north of Mayene, and leads only to the Waterless Sand in the southern part of the Aiel Waste.

The Drowned Lands are a huge treacherous saltwater swamp, a thick jungle of foliage interspersed with large shallows clogged by tall grasses. There are few open waterways, and even less dry land. Any piece of solid land a hundred paces long is considered huge.

The swamp is populated by a wide variety of flying and swimming creatures. Among the more hazardous swimmers are the water lizards, which can grow to twenty feet in length and have very sharp teeth in powerful jaws. Several varieties of snake are exceedingly venomous. Some of the less dangerous creatures include a multitude of brightly colored birds; the *nedar*, or tusked water-pig that can grow to three hundred pounds; the *soetam*, or great rat, that weighs ten stone; and the swamp cat, which weighs on average one and a half hundredweight. Mottled greenish-gray, the swamp cat, unlike its land-bound cousins loves to swim. There are two types of very small deer: the spikehorn, which is little more than knee-high to a man, and the forkhorn, which grows to waist height. Like every other mammal of the Drowned Lands, they swim very well.

East of the Drowned lands and bordering the coast is the *Termool*, or Waterless Sand. South of the Aiel Waste, it is a place where even the hardy Aiel cannot find water. This sand desert of drifting dunes that can be two or three hundred feet high contains no oases, no springs, and no known life. Fearsome windstorms arise suddenly and blow unabated for several days. Their passing leaves vast areas of the harsh landscape completely changed. Even the Aiel do not travel here.

North of the Waterless Sands is the Aiel Waste, home to the vast clans of Aiel who call it the Three-Fold Land. Very little is known about this land, save by the Aiel. The majority of the Waste is trackless badlands and baked flats, with the occasional oasis or mountain range. Three small ranges are known to branch off from the Spine itself into the waste.

Somewhere deep within the Waste lies the ancient city of Rhuidean, but only the Aiel know its exact location.

Along the northeast edge of the Waste rise cliffs one hundred to five hundred feet in height. Named the Cliffs of Dawn by the Aiel, this great land shift (no doubt dating from the Breaking) extends southward for approximately two hundred and fifty leagues from the Mountains of Dhoom and is topped by a series of mountain ranges of varying height. The rest of the eastern edge of the Waste is bordered by a massive split in the earth that ranges from one to three miles in depth. The Great Rift runs over four hundred and fifty leagues from the end of the Cliffs of Dawn into the Sea of Storms. It is bordered on both sides by badlands and mountains, but the eastern side of the rift, away from the Waste, appears to have much more water.

How far these badlands extend to the east is unknown, as is most other information concerning the east. Shara, as it is called (among other names) by the inhabitants who zealously protect their privacy, is bordered by the Sea of Storms to the south and the Morenal Ocean to the east. It is known to have five walled seaports along the southern shore, in which all foreign seaborne trading is done. Only a few maps showing the Shara shoreline exist, and many are incomplete, for simply coming within sight of the eastern coast brings a fierce and often deadly response from the natives. The five walled ports in the south are the only allowed landfall for foreign vessels, and the Sea Folk (at least) are wise enough to avoid the chance of shipwreck anywhere else along that coastline.

CONTINENT OF THE SEANCHAN

Far across the Aryth lies the continent of the Seanchan. Bordered by the Morenal Ocean to the west and the Aryth to the east, it is known to be approximately fifteen hundred leagues wide at its greatest breadth in the southern hemisphere. From the Mountains of Dhoom in the north to the southernmost point of the continent is a distance of approximately four thousand leagues.

Crisscrossed by rivers and mountain ranges, the continent also has four major islands to the south, east, and west, as well as three islands located in the dividing channel.

The Mountains of Dhoom in Seanchan were named by the men in Artur Hawkwing's invading armies, who immediately saw a resemblance between these mountains and ours of the same name. Seanchan also shares the

Blight, though it is less dangerous there, as Trollocs and Myrddraal were completely wiped out in this part of the world during the millennium after the Breaking. Despite the Seanchan claims of having destroyed *all* Shadowspawn, a few creatures, such as Draghkar, can still be found within their Blight. The corruption of the place is the same as within our own Blight, but in a less virulent form.

Hawkwing's invaders apparently recognized the comparative 'safety' of this place, for they named it the 'Lesser Blight,' despite the fact that it could – and can – kill a person twenty times faster than any other environment in the Empire of Seanchan. The Seanchan themselves generally refer to it simply as the Blight.

LAND OF THE MADMEN

Approximately equidistant from Seanchan's borders and roughly south of our land across the Sea of Storms is the third continent. Nameless, except to its inhabitants, it was discovered by the Sea Folk, who call it 'the Land of the Madmen' and do their best to avoid it. Until this publication, they were the only ones even aware of its existence. The Sea Folk have not even tried to chart its shoreline, though they do state that the continent is approximately seven hundred and fifty leagues across and five hundred leagues from north to south, with its southern coast extending to within five hundred miles of the southern icecap.

Many active volcanoes are located along the coastline, easily visible from the sea. Earthquakes and large storms are common in these seas, and icebergs are a constant

danger to any ships that travel far south of the northern edge of the continent, possibly owing to the numerous earthquakes cracking the edge of the icecap.

The Sea Folk tell fearsome tales of those who chanced to go ashore on the Land of the Madmen and made it back to their ships. The natives apparently never recovered from the Breaking, and never managed to reestablish order of any kind. The people are reported to live in wretched hovels in small, primitive villages. Any foreigner runs the risk of encountering channelers of *either* sex. The male channelers are frequently insane, of course, due to the taint, but the women are just as dangerous and unpredictable. If the stranger meets no channelers, he is simply overwhelmed by a mob of villagers who attempt to kill on sight anyone unknown to them. There seems no possibility of peaceful contact.

Chapter 16

Shara

'Only the wary dare trade with the ever-shifting sands.'
— A SEA FOLK SAYING CONCERNING SHARA

 THE LAND OF Shara has been an enigma for all of history since the Breaking. Cut off from the view of outsiders by their land's steep cliffs or the walls of the coastal cities, the people of Shara seem determined to protect their land and culture from any possible interaction with foreigners. It is unknown whether Shara feared contamination, or wished to prevent their own people, other than merchants, from learning about the outside world. Most of what has been known of Shara up to this time comes from the writings of Jain Farstrider, the Sea Folk, and the Aiel. These three sources often contradict themselves, sometimes even within the scope of a single document, yet what emerges is a portrait of a people who are, at times, deliberately duplicitous. Farstrider's *Travels* states flatly that lying to foreigners appears to be endemic to the

culture. Little concerning the people of Shara can be stated as absolute fact, save the experiences of the traders and explorers who have attempted to deal with them. Even the name of their land seems to change from moment to moment. For the purposes of this record, however, we will use Shara as the most common and easily pronounced of the many used.

LAND OF BARRIERS

With the Ocean on two sides and mountains, cliffs, and a chasm on the other two, Shara has had little difficulty in limiting foreigners' access. All outsider trade is strictly confined to the six specially designated trading towns scattered along the Cliffs of Dawn and the five trading ports on the southern coast.

These ports and towns are stoutly walled in such a way as to prevent any view from without, or within. In the port cities these massive walls stretch all the way into the harbor itself. None of the buildings behind these walls are tall enough to be visible above them, and foreigners are not allowed behind or on top of the walls on pain of death. There are no trading ports along the eastern coast. Any ships foolhardy enough to travel within sight of that coast are dealt with harshly by the native channelers. Those unlucky folk who have made landfall at any site outside the designated areas, whether deliberately or by shipwreck, have vanished completely – either enslaved, or killed immediately upon discovery.

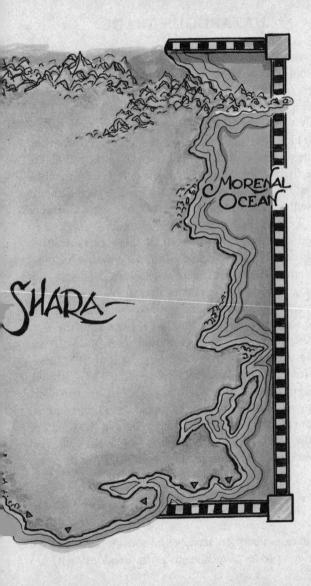

MORENAL
OCEAN

SHARA

HAZARDOUS TRADE

Even within the designated safe trading areas of these ports and towns, the Sharans do not believe that foreigners deserve to be told the truth about anything, often including the very goods they are buying. Traders learn quickly to check their purchases very carefully. When buying cloth, even in large quantities, each and every bolt must be unwound and checked from beginning to end to insure that full measure has been given, and that the material is the same throughout. The Sharan merchants are unwilling even to allow the truth of their appearance to be known, walking among outsiders only when cloaked and veiled. As a result of these eccentricities, trade is so difficult that no one would conduct business with Shara if their goods were not so very profitable. But the silk and ivory they export is unavailable anyplace else (save perhaps Seanchan) and is always in great demand.

The Sea Folk conduct most of the trade in the port cities, though there are occasional ships from Illian, Mayene, and some of the other seagoing countries. Land-based trade used to be largely monopolized by Cairhien, because of the Aiel gift of safe passage, but since the Aiel War, however, most overland trade has been limited to the Aiel, and an occasional merchant friendly to the Aiel. For the most part, people are content to let the Sea Folk deal with Shara, even if it means they must pay a higher price.

RULERS AND GOVERNMENT

The Sharans claim to have a monolithic empire, one nation completely at peace since the Breaking, with no

wars or rebellions of any kind. They often claim that even the Trolloc Wars did not touch them, despite Aiel statements that it did, and the fact that the Mountains of Dhoom and the Great Blight cut across the northern part of their land in much the same way as they do our own. Occasionally a Sharan will admit that the Trollocs were a problem, but only a minor one. They consistently deny any knowledge of Artur Hawkwing's invasion fleet, insisting, despite the Sea Folk's eyewitness accounts, that it never existed.

Some documents were recently discovered that, if authentic, contain some revealing information on the heretofore secret land of Shara. It is unknown whether these documents were written by a native, or a foreigner who managed to infiltrate the immensely tight national security. If a native, it was someone very highly placed acting at great risk.

According to these documents, the land is ruled by a single absolute monarch called Sh'boan if female and Sh'botay if male. This monarch, which was a Sh'boan at the time of writing, selects a mate, in this case a Sh'botay, then rules absolutely for seven years. At the end of the seventh year the reigning monarch dies, and the rule passes to her mate, who then chooses a new mate and reigns until his death in seven years. This pattern has apparently continued virtually unchanged since the time of the Breaking, three thousand years ago. The people believe the deaths are simply the 'Will of the Pattern,' but the unknown writer apparently believes otherwise.

THE AYYAD

The document states that there are channelers in Shara, both men and women, called the Ayyad. They live in villages cut off from the outside world, surrounded by high walls. No one except the Ayyad are allowed to enter, and supposedly no Ayyad leaves without permission, though the source of this permission is somewhat vague, something the writer apparently believes is deliberate. Any non-Ayyad managing to gain access to one of these villages is killed on sight. All Sharans know that no Ayyad will channel without instructions from or the permission of the currently ruling Sh'boan or Sh'botay. They therefore believe that any Ayyad who is outside the villages has such permission.

The Ayyad are tattooed on their faces at birth. Someone who is discovered to be able to channel later in life, presumed to be the result of a union between one of their ancestors and an Ayyad, is seized, tattooed, and confined to an Ayyad village for the rest of his or her life.

Sexual congress between Ayyad and non-Ayyad is punishable by death for the non-Ayyad, and for the Ayyad if it can be proven the Ayyad forced the other. Any child of such a union is killed by exposure to the elements.

Normally only female Ayyad ever leave the villages, though there are two exceptions to this rule. Male Ayyad are kept completely cloistered. It is forbidden to teach a male Ayyad to read, write, or do much of anything else beyond feeding and dressing himself and simple chores. Male Ayyad are considered breeding stock for female Ayyad. The Ayyad maintain detailed records of each bloodline in much the way the Cairhienin record the pedigrees of their pure-blooded horses.

Daughters are raised by their mothers, but sons are raised communally. Apparently these boys are never called 'sons' among the Ayyad, only 'the male.' When the boy reaches the age of approximately sixteen, he is taken from his confinement, hooded, and transported inside a closed wagon to a distant village, thus never seeing anything outside the villages. Once in his new village he will be matched with one or more women who wish children, Around his twenty-first year – or sooner if he shows signs of beginning to channel – he is once more hooded and taken away, as if on his way to another village. Instead he is killed and the body cremated.

MANIFEST DESTINY

The writer goes on to make some amazing charges, claiming that, instead of the Will of the Pattern being responsible for the monarchs' deaths every seven years, they are actually killed by the Ayyad. Indeed, this document states that, unbeknownst to the people, the Ayyad are the real power in Shara.

The ruler is surrounded with Ayyad women as servants. The only way to approach Sh'boan or Sh'botay, especially for a favor or ruling, is through these women, and the reply is usually delivered by these same women. Actual speech with the Sh'boan or Sh'botay is reckoned a very great honor, rarely bestowed.

Some rulers have failed to live the full measure of their seven years – a failure taken as a sign of the Creator's displeasure, causing penances served across the land by high and low alike. The writer states that it is more likely that these rulers discovered that, despite their great power,

the real control of the land was in the hands of the Ayyad through the apparent 'servant women' surrounding the ruler.

SLAVERY

With such a convoluted power structure it is not a surprise to discover that the Sharan also practice chattel slavery. Their culture seems entirely based on misdirection and the enslavement of the many by the few. If any part of this new document is accurate, it paints a very grim picture. Perhaps there is reason to be grateful that they are content to keep their secrets behind their walls rather than attempting to inflict them on their neighbors.

Chapter 17

Seanchan

'On the heights, the paths are paved with daggers.'
— SEANCHAN SAYING

 THOUGH THEIR LAND is much farther distant from ours than is Shara, nearly three thousand leagues across the Aryth Ocean, the people of Seanchan must, in the light of recent events, be taken seriously. To understand the Seanchan, it is necessary to first understand their history, as well as our ancestors' part in it. For just as Artur Hawkwing is largely responsible for many of our current nations and customs, so to an even greater degree his son Luthair Paendrag Mondwin is responsible for Seanchan. To a greater degree, because unlike his father's empire, Luthair's legacy still stands whole and strong to honor him.

The Seanchan Imperial Sigil is a golden hawk in flight, clutching three lightning bolts in its claws. The Imperial Banner is a wide border of royal blue around a white box inside which a golden hawk in flight clutches

three lightning bolts in its claws. If the Empress (or Emperor) is present, it is fringed in gold; if the heir to the throne is present, it is fringed in blue. This is the same banner Hawkwing's son, Luthair Paendrag, carried in his conquest of Seanchan. It has remained unchanged since his victory.

Before Hawkwing sent Luthair and his armies across the ocean, Seanchan was a constantly shifting quilt of nations of various sizes, most ruled by Aes Sedai. Any attempt to map the history of Seanchan would drive a cartographer to madness, for borders shifted with frequent wars as countries were swallowed whole or divided, and rebellions split off parts of others that sometimes grew into nationhood and sometimes were consumed. Today both the Tower of Ravens and the Court of the Nine Moons are located in Seandar, the Imperial capital, located in the northeast of the Seanchan continent. Seandar is the largest city in the Empire. The other major cities in descending order of size are: Kirendad, Noren M'Shar, Asinbayar, Qirat, Imfaral (location of the Towers of Midnight), Sohima, T'zura, Anangore, Shon Kifar, and Rampore.

Aes Sedai, who made open use of their power, formed temporary alliances with one another, as when following one of their number who had achieved a throne, but in reality it was every woman for herself, all scheming and plotting for advancement. Indeed, this was the way of everyone, not just Aes Sedai, throughout Seanchan. Those few who were truly faithful to their word were considered fools. Assassination was the most common cause of death among Aes Sedai, and among all who achieved power.

Almost since the Breaking Seanchan had been a land of intrigue and nearly constant warfare. Alliances were

always temporary, usually for the space of a war and often not lasting the length of it. It was not uncommon for a nation allied to one side at the beginning of a war to be allied to the other at the end, and in more than a few instances nations shifted allegiance more than once in the course of a war. No nation trusted another.

That suspicious, scheming division was the primary reason that Luthair Paendrag and his descendants were able to conquer all of Seanchan. Some nations allied themselves with him against others, but none remained constant. Eventually Luthair Paendrag, whom the Seanchan had begun to call the Hammer, no longer trusted any of the native-born, nor did his descendants, or the descendants of his soldiers and retainers. Luthair had brought with him, inherited from his father's difficulties, a profound distrust for all things Aes Sedai. When he discovered the cutthroat nature of the Aes Sedai who ruled Seanchan, that distrust grew into outright hatred.

ONE NATION

Eventually those who allied themselves with Luthair's descendants did remain constant, because it was clear by then that Luthair's dynasty was the great power in Seanchan. The first nobility of the Empire of Seanchan would all be descended from Luthair Paendrag's followers, and it would be centuries before others began being raised to 'the Blood.'

The Conquest, however, also called the Consolidation, required nearly three hundred years, and another two centuries passed before the last resistance was expunged and Luthair's descendants reigned over a land totally at peace. So far as any empire can be at peace.

The second thing that enabled Luthair Paendrag to conquer such a vast land, and one with so many unruly Aes Sedai, was the discovery of the *a'dam*, which enabled him to force captured Aes Sedai to serve him, and later

the discovery of *sul'dam*, which meant that he no longer needed Aes Sedai allies at all.

The *a'dam* is a *ter'angreal*, believed to be unique to Seanchan, used to control a woman who can channel. The most common is usually in the form of a silvery metal collar and bracelet linked by a leash of the same material. The *a'dam* can only be used by a woman who has at least the potential to channel, and it has no effect on any woman who cannot channel. The *ter'angreal* creates a link between the two women so that the wearer of the bracelet can inflict her wishes and desires upon the collared woman. If a man who can channel is linked to a woman by an *a'dam*, the result is usually an excruciating death for both. Simply touching an *a'dam* can result in pain for a man who can channel when the *a'dam* is being worn by a woman who can channel.

The first *a'dam* was made by an Aes Sedai, Deain, who brought it to Luthair Paendrag in an attempt to curry favor with him. She knew he had no Aes Sedai in his armies, and for the most part the Aes Sedai hated him. Deain believed that Luthair would eventually win and felt that she would be richly rewarded for bringing him a gift that could hand him the Power of the Aes Sedai, willing or not. Several years after that, the first *sul'dam* were found – women who could learn to channel and had the spark, but could not actually channel without training. These women were considered ideal controllers of the *damane*, the Leashed Ones. For her trouble Deain was rewarded with imprisonment by her own device. She was, after all, Aes Sedai and thus not to be trusted. It is said her screams 'shook the Towers of Midnight.'

Once the *a'dam* gained regular use, the title Aes Sedai disappeared completely from Seanchan, and those who

could channel were renamed *marath'damane*, or Those Who Must Be Leashed.

There is no doubt that the current power of the Imperial family over an entire continent is directly linked to their subjugation and control of all Seanchan Aes Sedai. It is fairly certain that in the beginning Luthair knew that *sul'dam* were women who could be trained to use the One Power, but with his antipathy toward Aes Sedai this information was likely suppressed. Certainly it was lost within a hundred years.

LEASHING THE POWER

In modern Seanchan young women are tested for the ability to channel or the ability to wear the bracelet each year until they pass the age of manifestation. Those who have the ability inborn become *damane* and are immediately leashed and put into service. They are completely written out of all family records and from the citizen rolls, for to be *damane* is to be less than human. Becoming valued slaves, the *damane* are seldom killed, even for infractions that would result in death for any lesser slave. They are sometimes horribly mutilated for punishment, as it is possible to channel without hands, feet, or tongue.

Young women who show the ability to use the *a'dam* but who cannot channel are made *sul'dam*, or 'leash-holder,' and honored for their abilities, often gaining prestige for their families as well. They are trained in the care and handling of *damane* in much the same way a huntsman is trained to control his hounds, save that the link is far more personal. Recognizable by the red panels

and silver forked lightning on the breast and sides of their dark blue dresses, *sul'dam* are responsible for every action of the *damane* under their control. In the course of nature there are always many more *sul'dam* than *damane*. Because of this it is not unusual for a *damane* to have many different *sul'dams* over the course of her lifetime.

The *damane* are not only used as weapons but also aid in construction of large bridges or any structures that would be difficult or impossible without the One Power. The few *damane* that are strong in Earth (predominantly a male strength) locate and refine metals and rare ores, and are highly valued. Some *damane* are also used to heal the sick and injured, though only those who are wealthy or among the upper classes. Frequently, however, their healing use is rejected because of the belief that Aes Sedai are not human – roughly the equivalent of allowing a dog to be one's healer. This may be the reason that the ability itself is rare. The abilities shown by *damane* differ widely from those displayed by Aes Sedai in many areas.

Men who are able to channel are executed and expunged from all records.

CLASS STRUCTURE

Since Luthair's conquest, Seanchan has evolved into a nation that is stratified and has very little movement between the ranks. That is not to say that there are no power struggles, only that almost all of them are between members of the same class. The society is based on the concept that everyone has a place in which to serve, and everyone should be in their place.

The lowest class in Seanchan is usually the *da'covale*, or 'those who are property,' or simply *covale*, 'property.' No doubt Luthair was surprised at a culture that allowed people to be bought and sold along with animals and household goods, but if the conquerors ever attempted to eradicate the institution, they failed. In fact, most of the underlying culture and customs of Seanchan seem to have survived the invasion intact. One might say Seanchan simply absorbed its invaders.

Ironically, perhaps because of the widespread slavery, Seanchan honor and power do not necessarily equate with freedom, as they do in most other lands. Commoners and merchants rank just above lowly slaves, but many upper-class slaves, such as the *so'jhin*, the hereditary upper servants of the Blood, outrank free men and women. Some of the most honored and powerful members of Seanchan society are actually the property of the Imperial family. It is a rare honor for a commoner of free birth to be chosen as a high-level servant, but one that is eagerly sought, for it is one of the few ways to advance beyond one's station of birth. The loss of freedom, even for future generations, is believed a very small price to pay for such advancement.

The highest place in Seanchan society is unquestionably held by the nobility, limited to those who are 'of the Blood.' Originally only descendants of either Luthair Paendrag himself or members of his armies, over the years the nobility has changed. Today it is possible, though rare, for even a common soldier to be raised as a reward. That soldier's children and descendants also will be members of the Blood.

The Empire is currently ruled by the Empress from the Court of the Nine Moons, where she reigns upon the

famed Crystal Throne. Believed to be a direct descendant of Luthair Paendrag, she is the absolute monarch of all Seanchan and is considered the Empire made flesh.

Succession to the throne is not controlled by sex or passed on to the firstborn child as in many other kingdoms; the Empress will choose her successor from among the immediate royal family. As may be imagined, the family members vie furiously for the Empress's favor. Plotting and intrigue between the contenders are not only expected, they are actually encouraged. The Seanchan believe that such behavior, when successful, shows strength and leadership – at least of the type the Seanchan value. In a sense, all the power struggles between rival countries and rulers in the pre-Paendrag Seanchan now occur between rivals of the ruling class.

Appearances and etiquette are supremely important to the Seanchan, and physical manifestations of rank are essential. The ways in which Seanchan shave their heads illustrate this point.

Members of the Blood shave the sides of the head, leaving a crest of hair on top that often flows down the back. A Voice of the Blood will wear the left side of the head shaved and the right side braided. A Voice of the Throne will shave the right side and wear the left side braided. Members of the Imperial family shave their heads completely. Commoners do not shave any part of their heads. Among the Seanchan no one displays baldness publicly. Men who go bald usually wear a wig, and must at least cover their heads with a cap.

Long lacquered fingernails are another visible sign of rank. The more lacquered fingernails, the higher the rank of the noble. All nobles, beginning with the lowest, wear long exaggerated nails, lacquering at least their

little fingers. High Lords or Ladies paint the nails on their ring fingers as well. Members of the royal family have three painted long nails, on the little finger, the ring finger, and the middle finger, leaving only the index finger and thumb free. The ruler will have all five nails painted. Each lord or lady's nails are lacquered in colors indicative of their house.

IMPERIAL CONTROL

The Imperial family holds its power through intimidation as well as manipulation. The Crystal Throne itself is a great *ter'angreal* that causes anyone who approaches it to feel immense awe and wonder. Of course, only the reigning monarch is ever allowed to use it.

The members of the Imperial family and of the Blood also seldom speak directly to anyone of lesser rank than themselves, save to bestow an immense honor upon them. Most communication is done through a 'Voice,' a servant, usually hereditary, who actually speaks for his/her master or mistress. The Voice receives instructions through a variety of subtle nonverbal gestures from the master. It is forbidden for a person of lesser rank to make eye contact with one of greater. Even the Voice must never look the master directly in the eye while watching for signals or commands.

SEANCHAN HONOR

Despite the political machinations of Seanchan life, honor is supremely important to them. They practice an idealized

form of chivalry based on the value of their word. To them, a word of honor, once given, is considered absolute. This is true for all – man, woman, slave or noble.

For the Seanchan, honor and status are directly linked with the ability to look someone in the eyes. The word *sei'taer* literally means 'straight eyes' or 'level eyes' in the Old Tongue. Among the Seanchan, to say that someone 'has *sei'taer*' or 'is *sei'taer*' means that they have 'face' or honor. 'Face' can be lowered or earned. It can also be lost. The Seanchan say that one 'is *sei'mosiev*,' or 'has become *sei'mosiev*,' to mean 'has lost face.' In the Old Tongue *sei'-mosiev* literally means 'lowered eyes' or 'downcast eyes.' One can become *sei'mosiev* either by one's own actions or inactions, or by the actions or inactions of another.

IMPERIAL SECURITY

Among the most honored Imperial servants are the Deathwatch Guards, the personal guard of the Imperial family. They are noted for their equal willingness to kill or die, whichever is necessary, and are easily recognized by their black-tasseled spears and black-lacquered shields. Though the guard are actually the property of the Imperial Personage, they are often loaned to others as a sign of Imperial favor. The most elite section of the Deathwatch Guards is charged with the personal safety of the Empress and her immediate family. These guards are never loaned. Nor are they all human. Ogier make up a portion of the Deathwatch, although they are the only ones not property, and are considered incredibly fierce and more deadly than their human counterparts. The Ogier of the Deathwatch are grim in demeanor and

action compared to their brothers and sisters across the ocean.

Also charged with Imperial security are the Seekers for Truth, a police and spy organization belonging to the Imperial Throne. The wide powers granted to the Seekers make them highly respected and greatly feared. Chosen from all strata of society, though usually not of the Blood, Seekers are granted almost unlimited powers. To be made a Seeker is a great honor and a path to great status. Though Seekers are property, they may arrest anyone who does not answer their questions or cooperate fully with them. Even those of the Blood are not exempt. To fail to cooperate with them is treason. The Seekers themselves define the level of cooperation required, subject only to review by the Empress. They are loyal exclusively to the Empress herself.

The Seekers for Truth hunt Darkfriends and act as secret police. The use of Seekers has allowed the hunt for Darkfriends to be more organized than in other realms, yet the proportion of Darkfriends does not seem to be any less than before the Seekers began their hunt. As secret police, they root out treasonous behavior and often also function as torturers.

Most prisoners of the Seekers are held within the forbidding Tower of Ravens, the central imperial prison. Many of the prisoners held there are of the Blood. Since no one may spill a drop of blood from one who is of the Blood, the torturers have been forced to devise noninvasive but excruciatingly painful methods of questioning the nobles housed there. The challenge is to break the subject without allowing him to shed any blood. Most prisoners who know they are destined for the Tower of Ravens attempt suicide.

Seanchan warriors' and nobles' swords have thick curved blades with a back edge one-quarter to one-third the length of the blade, a two-handed hilt, and quillons shaped like a C or a crescent moon. The sword pommel is a cap. Among nobles the cap is usually formed in the shape of an animal's head, the hilt itself is sometimes worked in the figure of a woman, say, or a fanciful creature, and the sword and scabbard are ornate with gold and gems.

Seanchan warriors also use spears, which are decorated with tassels in the house colors, and shields, which are lacquered, also in the house colors, except for the Deathwatch Guards, whose color on both spear and shield is black.

THE RETURN

In the early days of conquest, Luthair Paendrag made no secret of the fact that he planned to add Seanchan to his father's empire across the sea. When the message came of Hawkwing's death, followed by no others, Luthair reached the obvious conclusion: something had happened to that empire. Luthair's goal changed from simply adding Seanchan to Hawkwing's empire, to using Seanchan to insure its strength, and, if necessary, to take it back and avenge Hawkwing's death. Seanchan was set out in the *Corenne*, the Return.

It was long after Luthair's death that the first ships were finally able to sail back across the Aryth Ocean to Falme. The Seanchan in the more than five hundred ships of all sizes called themselves *Hailene*, or in the Old Tongue, 'Those Who Come Before,' or 'Forerunners.'

They were the advance scouts for the Seanchan invasion force. If they found the empire whole, they were to enjoy the welcome they were due and send word back. If they found it, as they did, much changed from Hawkwing's day, they were to prepare the way for the Return, through military invasion if necessary.

The invasion force, made up of different fleets, and all sizes of vessel from the Great Ships down, has been gathering for many years now in every port and inlet on the eastern seaboard of Seanchan. It consists of thousands of ships and hundreds of thousands of people. The *Corenne*'s invasion fleet has been in the planning for over a century, awaiting only the command of the Empress to journey across the Aryth and retake the homeland of Seanchan's first Emperor.

Chapter 18

The Exotic Animals of Seanchan

WHEN LUTHAIR PAENDRAG's armies began their conquest of Seanchan, they confronted not only the terrifying Aes Sedai who freely used the Power as a military weapon, but strange beasts out of nightmare that flew at them from above or attacked them with claws and teeth, often tearing men from their saddles to devour them on the spot. From horned frog-creatures the size of large bears to horse-sized catlike animals, these creatures seemed as if they could only have come from the evil of Shadow. It was thus, between the Aes Sedai and the creatures believed to be some new kind of Shadowspawn, that the defenders of this new continent came to be known as the Armies of the Night.

These strange new creatures were not Shadowspawn at all, but the descendants of beasts brought back from

parallel worlds, via Portal Stones, during the first thousand years after the Breaking, probably in an attempt to find aid against the real Shadowspawn. While the creatures' effectiveness was not recorded, it was during this same period that all remaining Shadowspawn on the continent were eradicated. The creatures remained, their care and training surviving through all the political upheavals until Luthair's arrival. The knowledge that allowed their procurement by way of the Portal Stones, however, was lost.

By the time Luthair invaded, such creatures as the *grolm*, *torm*, *lopar*, *corlm*, *raken*, and *to'raken* were used throughout the armies of the area. After his successful conquest, Luthair adopted them into his own armies, like his newly leashed *damane*. His descendants continue the tradition. The animals are currently maintained as an essential part of the military, with their handlers and trainers assured an honored place in the hierarchy.

Animal handlers or riders in Seanchan are known as *morat*, or 'one who handles.' A *morat'grolm*, for example, is a *grolm* handler. A trainer is called *der'morat*, as in *der'-morat'grolm*. The word *der* means 'experienced' or 'master,' and often denotes rank.

To become an animal master, and thus earn the prefix *der*, requires a certain level of seniority. This seniority counts within each specific discipline and the overall social ranking. For example, the most senior *der'morat'-corlm* will never be the social equal of a *morat'lopar*, much less a *der'suldam*. Handlers or *morat* for more ordinary beasts, such as *s'redits* or horses, rank below those for 'exotics.'

Note that the *der'sul'dam* and *sul'dam*, while the highest ranked of the exotic animal handlers, are definitely

included in this group, indicating once again the Seanchan belief that *damane* are not people but dangerous animals.

The social order among handlers of 'exotics' is as follows:

> *der'sul'dam*
> *sul'dam*
> *der'morat'raken*
> *der'morat'to'raken*
> *morat'raken*
> *der'morat'torm*
> *morat'to'raken*
> *der'morat'lopar*
> *morat'torm*
> *der'morat'grolm*
> *morat'lopar*
> *der'morat'corlm*
> *morat'grolm*
> *morat'corlm*

TORM

The most intelligent of the Seanchan 'exotics' (after *damane*, of course) are the *torm*. Resembling a cross between a horse-sized cat and a lizard, *torm* have bronze scales, six-clawed feet that can grip the stones of the road; and three eyes. The *torm* is primarily a carnivore but will subsist on a plant diet for as much as three or four days if it must. If deprived of meat longer, the *torm* becomes increasingly hard to control as it seeks to hunt.

Despite their reptilian appearance, they bear live young and nurse them, always in single births. They are not widely available, at least partly due to high mortality before reaching adulthood. Before they are trained they often fight fiercely with each other to establish dominance, and such fights often continue to the death.

Many who have seen a *torm* find its gaze very disturbing, quite apart from the number of its eyes. This is in part due to its very high intelligence quotient, well above that of a very bright dog. Though far below humans in any overall sense, they can come close to our level in certain areas of problem solving, such as maze tests.

Because of their excellent hunting abilities, early handlers tried to use *torm* as trackers and hunters, but they discovered that a *torm* hunts what it chooses and cannot be put to hunt. Some have taken this fact as one indication of the animal's intelligence.

As riding animals, their speed and endurance are superior to that of a horse, but they are particular about their riders. Not everyone can ride a *torm*; in fact, it is harder to find someone suitable to be a *morat'torm* than to find *morat* for any of the other 'exotics.' For no perceptible reason it will turn on one potential rider after another before finally accepting one. Once it has found that one rider, the *torm* will not allow another to mount. If that rider dies, it takes some time to get a *torm* to accept another.

Like horses, *torm* are controlled with rein and leg pressure.

They are primarily ridden by scout units, despite the fact that they are ferocious fighters. Though their claws and scales might seem to make them much better battle

mounts than horses, they are unsuitable for protracted
fighting. There are relatively few of them compared to
horses, of course, and they are harder to replace, both
because of the low survival rate to adulthood and the
length of training time required. Perhaps the greatest
unsuitability, however, is the *torm*'s susceptibility to fighting frenzy if exposed to battle for too long a time. Even
the best trained *torm* can be overcome. When frenzy
occurs the *morat* can only hang on, because the *torm*
becomes uncontrollable, moving and killing as it
chooses, pausing only to savage corpses or feed. It may
not regain calm for hours after the battle is done.
Strangely, the *torm* rarely turns on its rider during one of
these frenzies, but it will strike at anyone else within
reach.

A *torm* will always strike at any *corlm* in reach, and
while *morat* can keep the attack from coming to actual
combat, they are simply never used together.

CORLM

At first glance, the *corlm* appears to be a flightless bird,
sometimes as much as eight feet tall, with a long neck and
a sort of double crest on its head, but instead of feathers
it is covered with long striped or mottled hair resembling
the color pattern of some house cats. This fur, usually
gray, black, or brown, extends to the tail, which it flattens
out for stability while running. The double crest is really
a pair of upstanding ears, which are quite mobile.
Averaging three hundred pounds at maturity, the *corlm* is
equipped with four-toed small-clawed hind feet and tiny
forearms usually held close to its body. The forepaws are

seldom used save in nest building and feeding, despite the long clawed 'fingers.' The beak is large, appearing over-sized for the long and oblong head, and is hooked like the beak of a bird of prey. Like a bird of prey, the *corlm* uses its beak for killing. Unlike the *torm*, it has only two eyes, set on the sides of its head.

The *corlm* is a carnivore, and an extremely efficient predator, able to track prey with both scent and hearing. It is unmatched as a tracker, can outrun a man in short sprints, and can equal a man over long distances. The *corlm* responds to both spoken commands and whistles pitched above human hearing.

Appearing to be solitary animals in their own environment, they are always used singly, as they do not tolerate each other well except at mating time. The female lays her eggs one at a time, and often they do not hatch.

LOPAR

The premier fighter of the 'exotics,' the *lopar* is a hulking animal weighing between fifteen hundred and two thousand pounds when full grown. It has only two eyes, large and dark, surrounded by horny ridges and set into a large round head with no external ears. Its legs are longer than those of a bear in proportion to size, but still look short because of their thickness and the size of the rest of the animal, appearing bowed when the animal is on all fours. The *lopar* has a leathery, hairless hide, in colors that range from dark brown to a pale reddish hue. It has six toes on both front and rear paws, all with very large retractable claws. It uses both forepaws for grasping and handling. *Lopar* will sometimes rear upon their hind legs, when

fighting, to a height of as much as ten feet; they can easily snatch a man from horseback.

A *lopar*'s intelligence is higher than that of a dog, probably equal to that of a *torm*. As with *torm*, some people find their gaze disturbing, but there is not the cold malevolence in the gaze of a *lopar* that there is with a *torm*. Able to sprint as fast or faster than a horse, it tires easily at longer distances.

Despite its fearsome appearance, the *lopar* can be handled by anyone properly trained and is usually placid, and even friendly, unless commanded to fight. *Lopar* mating, however, resembles a battle and usually results in wounds to both male and female. Births are always in pairs, though with a very high mortality rate as with all the 'exotics.' Both males and females sometimes engage in a sort of dominance display, with each animal rearing to its full height and roaring loudly. The shorter of the two then backs down, dropping flat on its belly almost immediately. If the two animals are the same size, combat can result unless they are properly controlled by *morat*.

The *lopar* is used as a guard animal and as a ferocious fighter in battle. For battle it is normally fitted with a sort of leather coat or barding covered with overlapping metal plates to protect the spine, central chest, and belly. Because of its usually placid nature and excellent fighting ability, the Blood frequently use *lopar* to protect their children. *Lopar* used as bodyguards often become attached and fiercely protective. Animals that form this attachment are usually reluctant to leave the one they serve and frequently refuse to eat for some time afterward.

GROLM

Weighing in at three hundred to five hundred pounds, *grolm* are the size of large bears, but with the gray-green coloration and skin texture of very tough frogs. Like the *torm*, they have three eyes, but the eyes are small and fierce, lacking the *torm*'s intelligence, and are ringed by hard ridges. Their horny-lipped beaks are hooked for ripping flesh.

When walking, *grolm* appear almost awkward, moving with a waddling motion, but all traces of awkwardness vanish when they run, taking great leaps and bounds that propel them over the ground at great speed. They also have very good vision, a keen sense of smell, and are extremely territorial. Because of these characteristics they make excellent guard animals. They rapidly learn who is allowed in a given area, and will use their sense of smell to distinguish anyone who is nervous or afraid.

Grolm are used in battle, though only against lightly armored opponents, to break holes in an enemy line which will be quickly exploited by human soldiers. They can also be used against cavalry, as horses often panic in their presence unless trained to tolerate them. Fortunately they are very hard to kill. *Grolm* hides are thick enough to turn most blows from swords, axes, or spears. Arrows even fail to penetrate those hides unless aimed at a vulnerable spot such as an eye. Even when they are injured, nonfatal wounds seldom incapacitate them. It takes ferocious wounds to even slow one significantly, and they heal rapidly. This is fortunate, since their young, born in multiple births, have a very high mortality rate. It is rare for more than one offspring of a 'litter' to survive.

In their natural environment they are apparently pack animals, though in captivity they can turn on one another if not properly controlled. They will often rip apart and eat one of their own that has been injured, and they even consume their own dead.

Grolm are controlled with spoken commands, hand signals, and the use of a small, piercing whistle-like flute. Among *morat'grolm* it is a matter of pride to use only the hand signals and the flute, perhaps in distant imitation of the way the Blood communicate.

RAKEN

A large flying animal, the *raken* has a body considerably longer than a horse's and about equal in girth, with leathery gray skin and large, powerful wings much like those of a bat. Its intelligence is roughly equivalent to that of a horse. The animal's head sports a long horny snout with hard ridges that serve both as lips and teeth as well as powerful jaws that are easily capable of shearing through a branch or an arm. Two eyes set on the front of the head give the *raken* superior vision. The head is supported by a long, graceful neck. It has a very long, thin tail, quite frail-looking in comparison with the rest of the animal, which usually appears simply to trail behind in flight. That tail is actually very strong. While it is not used as a weapon, the *raken* often lashes the tail in anger when perched or on the ground, and has been known to accidentally break the arm or leg of a *morat* careless enough to come too close. In flight, the tail is used with great dexterity to aid in balance and control. The *raken* has two legs, relatively thin for the

size of its body, which end in feet with six long, and very strong, taloned toes arranged four before and two behind.

On the ground, it normally crouches rather than standing erect, and raises its head on its long neck to look around. It stands erect only when alarmed or preparing to fly. When a *raken* is crouched, it is quite possible to simply throw a leg over the saddle.

While the *raken* is slow and awkward on the ground, it is an extremely agile flier, and very quick when it needs to be. Maximum flight speed is three to four times the speed of a horse. It can maintain this speed over short distances, but can fly fairly long distances at lower speeds without rest.

Primarily used for scouting and carrying messages, the *raken* can carry two people, if they are small, and is controlled by reins, attached to rings fixed permanently in the animal's horny nostrils, and leg pressure. The riders, *morat'raken*, sometimes called 'fliers,' are all either women or smaller than average men, and often ride double, one behind the other, in a specially constructed lightweight saddle that seats two. Paired *morat* are used in situations where extra eyes are wanted, as on most scouting missions, but when great speed is required, or long distances, only one *morat* rides. Long distance for a *raken* is three to four hundred miles.

A *raken* will fly even if injured or ill, although not as far or as fast, of course, and may be, like some horses, ridden to the point of its death.

It can perch comfortably even on vertical surfaces if there is any purchase for its claws. In some cases when perching on such precipices it will spread its wings across the surface, in effect clutching with them. The *raken* will

perch in large trees where the branches can support it, but it prefers open ground or cliffs.

It is an omnivore, though apparently perfectly content with an all-plant diet. An egg layer, the female *raken* lay one egg at a time.

TO'RAKEN

The *to'raken* is probably related to the *raken* and looks in general appearance much like the *raken* except that it is much larger and is mottled brown in color rather than gray. Like the *raken*, it crouches when on the ground, rather than standing erect, raising its head to look around. Yet because of its much larger size, the *to'raken*'s crouched back can be nine feet or more above the ground. It has the intelligence level of a horse and is an herbivore. Like the female *raken*, the female lays her eggs one at a time. It does not perch in trees, however large, no doubt due to its great size and weight. It much prefers the tops of cliffs or hills. Unlike the *raken*, which can simply throw itself into the air, a *to'raken* must run as much as one hundred paces while flapping its wings before launching itself from level ground.

At least as awkward on the ground as *raken*, the *to'raken* is neither as agile in the air nor as fast as *raken*. Its maximum speed is little more than twice that of a horse. It also does not perch on vertical surfaces, but on surfaces that are steep for it, it uses the same spread-wing clutching as its cousin.

The value of a *to'raken* lies in its strength and endurance. A *to'raken* has the ability to fly much farther than a *raken* without rest. They have been known to fly

over a thousand miles at moderate speed when carrying only one *morat* in the saddle. They can also carry much larger loads. With one *morat* up, a *to'raken* can carry an additional one thousand pounds or more of cargo as far as two hundred miles.

They are primarily used for transporting people who must be moved quickly or urgent cargo. While they have occasionally been used in battle, with archers or cross-bowmen behind a single *morat*, the bowmen are not low enough and slow enough to be effective until the *to'raken* is in range of arrows and crossbow bolts from the ground. An injured *to'raken* does not fly well. Unlike the *raken*, when injured they often refuse to fly farther than a safe landing point. Of course that usually means safe from the point of view of the *to'raken*, not necessarily of the *morat*. As a result, this extremely valuable animal is seldom used in battle.

A *morat* who can handle *raken* can handle *to'raken*, and vice versa, but *morat'raken* are considered superior to *morat'to'raken*. To order a *morat'raken* to fly a *to'raken* would entail a loss of face for the flier, a fact which even the Blood recognizes.

Chapter 19

The Sea Folk Islands

*'A ship is alive . . . treat him well and care for him
properly and he will fight for you against the worst
sea.'*

— SEA FOLK SAYING

 MOST OF THE islands in the Aryth Ocean and
the Sea of Storms are home port to the
Atha'an Miere, known to most as the Sea
Folk. Only a few of these island groups are
known to outsiders, and fewer still have been seen by
them, since the Atha'an Miere do not usually allow visitors or traders, though they are certainly not as cruel to
intruders as are the people of Shara or Seanchan. The Sea
Folk perform most sea trade, and nearly all of the trade in
silk and ivory from Shara, yet few people know them save
through stories and legend.

The best known and largest of the Sea Folk islands is
Tremalking, located southwest of Tarabon and Amadicia.
Much smaller in size are the island groups that make up
the Aile Jafar, approximately due west of Tarabon, and the
Aile Somera; due west of Toman Head. Many other small

to medium islands sprinkled throughout the ocean remain known only to the Sea Folk themselves.

To understand the Atha'an Miere, one must study not their islands, but their ships and the waters they sail, for the People of the Sea prefer to live out most of their lives aboard their ships. They are born on the water – even if the mother must row out from shore in a borrowed boat to bear her child – and they die on the water if at all possible. Any time spent away from the sea is that spent awaiting another ship, another voyage.

At the Breaking of the World, when their ancestors fled the heaving land for the safety of the sea, the Atha'an Miere knew nothing of the ships they took, or of the seas on which they drifted, only that no land-bound place was safe. Over the course of many years they learned the ways of storm and tide, and became as one with their vessels. The Jendai Prophecy, first spoken during those early years, held that the People of the Sea were fated to wander the waters until the Coramoor should return. Indeed, the vast reaches of the open sea are their true kingdom.

THE ATHA'AN MIERE

With brightly colored tattoos upon their hands, some of which denote clan, equally brilliant sashes on their waists, gold and silver jewelry, and a distinct style of dress, the Atha'an Miere are as exotic in appearance as they are mysterious. Throughout the known world tales relate the almost irresistible allure of the Sea Folk women, the epitome of beauty and temptation. The deep chocolate coloration of their skin and their unequaled grace, born of years balancing on wind-lashed rigging on the

high seas, contribute to their allure; the Sea Folk custom of wearing nothing above the waist except jewelry once beyond sight of land has enhanced the legends. The well-muscled men, clean-shaven and bare-chested, are also considered dangerously handsome.

Men and women both wear baggy breeches held at the waist by brightly colored sashes, multiple earrings, neck chains and bracelets, and bare feet, though the quality of the breeches and scarf fabrics is directly related to the status and financial state of the wearer. The women also wear brightly colored, loose-fitting blouses, though only while in port – probably in an attempt to avoid shocking the locals. The women also often wear a ring in the left side of their nose. Women of rank wear a fine chain, hung with medallions, connecting the nose ring with one of their earrings. The quantity of medallions is directly related to rank, with high-ranking women wearing more medallions than those of lower rank. The men do not wear nose chains or nose rings.

CHAIN OF COMMAND

The Sailmistress is the commander of the ship and crew. She controls where and when the ship travels, as well as who may board him. She is also regarded as the head of the family that is the ship's crew, whether or not the relationship is actually one of blood. The Sailmistress always wears a nose-to-ear chain; the medallions on it denote clan, sept, and rank.

The Sailmistress is aided in her task by the Windfinder, also always a woman, who is second officer and chief navigator. It is the great secret of the Atha'an Miere that

the Windfinders are often women who can channel. All female channelers among the Sea Folk, save the few girls sent as tokens to the White Tower to allay suspicion, become Windfinders, though not all Windfinders are able to channel. The Windfinder uses her gifts and skills to aid her ship, and, if able to channel, to defend it from storms as well as hostile forces.

Defense, as well as all trade, is managed by the Cargomaster. Often married to the Sailmistress, his is the first and final word in all trade negotiations and matters of defense. He cannot tell the Sailmistress where to sail, and she cannot tell him what goods to trade for. Needless to say, however, the ship's ultimate profitability, indeed its survival, depends upon the Sailmistress and the Cargomaster working smoothly together.

The Sea Folk are divided into clans and septs, with each clan or sept operating its own dry dock at most of the various island ports. These docks are as close to a land-based home as the Atha'an Miere allow themselves. Each clan is headed by a Wavemistress, the equivalent of a clan chieftain, chosen for life by the Sailmistresses within the clan from among themselves. In turn the Wavemistress appoints a Swordmaster, usually her former Cargomaster, and often her husband. The Swordmaster has authority over the other Cargomasters of the clan, and can direct them in matters of trade and defense to benefit the clan as a whole. The Wavemistress also has a Windfinder as an advisor, usually the woman who served in that capacity before her promotion. Her Windfinder has authority over other clan Windfinders. A Sailmistress's crew is often kept intact after she is named Wavemistress (she adds whatever personnel are necessary to her increased duties), though sometimes it is

necessary to turn the ship temporarily over to another while she handles clan duties elsewhere. A Wavemistress can be recognized by the greater number of medallions on her nose chain – usually they almost touch each other in a solid line from nose to ear – and by a two-tiered red parasol, fringed in gold, that her attendants carry.

All the clans and septs, as well as the islands themselves, are ruled by a woman known as the Mistress of the Ships. She holds the same authority as any land-based queen, but is chosen not by birth or lineage, but by selection from among the Wavemistresses. She in turn appoints a Master of the Blades, usually her former Swordmaster, and a Windfinder advisor who has authority over all Windfinders. The Master of the Blades has authority over all the Swordmasters, and is responsible for the defense and security of the Atha'an Miere. The Mistress of the Ships can be recognized by her three-tiered blue parasol trimmed in gold fringe as well as a nose chain so thick with medallions that they overlap one another. Her Master of the Blades has a two-tiered parasol in the same colors. Though her heart and soul are with her ship, the Mistress of the Ships is usually forced to spend a great deal of time ashore in order to be easily accessible to her people. Nevertheless, her primary residence is always her ship.

THE SHIPS

To the Atha'an Miere, each ship is a living spirit, gifted with a man's heart and a man's courage. These ships are as much a part of the Sea Folk family as any human. The new crew themselves oversee the construction of their

ship, doing most of the skilled labor themselves. The result is that every ship leaving the Atha'an Miere ship-yards has been lovingly made, from the laying of the keel to the final rigging and caulking, by the very folk that will sail him.

The ship is usually owned by the clan of the Sailmistress who captains him, if not by the Sailmistress herself, though occasionally a ship belongs to a clan different from those who sail him. This only occurs if a ship incurs debt beyond the ability of its own crew and clan to pay. Then the ship and crew sail for their benefactors until the debt and all additional interest are repaid in full.

The Atha'an Miere ships fall into four general classes. From smallest to largest they are the darter, soarer, skimmer, and raker. Anything smaller than a darter is considered a boat, not a ship. The fastest class of ship is the raker. Lean, long, and incredibly swift over the water, rakers always carry three masts and are square-rigged. The skimmer is also three-masted and is as long as a raker, but it is broader in the beam and of a greater displacement, which makes it slower than a raker, though still usually much faster than any mainland ship of comparable displacement. The soarer, a two-masted vessel, while smaller than a skimmer, is faster and usually quite agile. The smallest of the Sea Folk vessels, the darter, can have one or two masts.

The ships vary in their rigging. 'High-rigged' means that the major sails on every mast are square sails. 'Half-rigged' means that at least one, but not all, masts carry no major square sails, but rather gaff sails. 'Low-rigged' means that all masts carry gaff sails as the major, or only, sails. Thus 'a half-rigged skimmer' is a skimmer-class vessel in which one or more, but not all, of the masts

have square sails for the majors. A raker is always high-rigged, and it goes without saying.

These ships, far superior to any other oceangoing vessels in both speed and manageability, are the key to the Atha'an Miere's unquestioned dominance of the sea trade. Spared the ravages of both the Trolloc Wars and the War of the Hundred Years, they were able to develop their seafaring technology undisturbed. Now that technology, coupled with the paralyzing conservatism of the mainlanders, maintains their edge.

THE AMAYAR

Unknown to most mainlanders, there are people inhabiting and thriving on the islands who are as uncomfortable away from land as the Sea Folk are upon it. It is from these almost unknown people that goods such as the famed 'Sea Folk porcelain' and fine glassware actually originate. These land-dwelling inhabitants of the islands are called the Amayar.

Physically, the Amayar are shorter and much fairer than the Atha'an Miere, with a high percentage of yellow or light brown hair and blue or hazel eyes. Although short, on the average about equal to the people of Cairhien in height, men and women are usually rather stockily built. They follow what they call the Water Way, which, while not as pacifistic as the Way of the Leaf, still prizes acceptance of what is rather than what might be wished for. There is a strong strain of belief among them that what we call 'reality' is not truly real, but only a way-post on the path to another existence. Violence is frowned upon. While young men might get into a fistfight or

wrestling match, they would be held up to public shame for it. Murder and other violent crimes are extremely rare; a murder is a thing remembered, and considered a point of shame, for generations.

Intermarriage between the Atha'an Miere and the Amayar is unknown. Frankly, they would be shocked by the very notion; each finds the other's ways and customs faintly unpleasant. The general feeling of the poorest of one toward the richest of the other is 'Thank the Light I am not him.' Despite this they get on well, partly because of the Sea Folk's benign rule and fair dealings, and partly because, aside from the things they trade for, neither has one single thing the other wants.

The Amayar raise sheep, goats, and small cattle, which are either black or spotted white and black. Their horses are small, the size of mainland ponies. Small oxen are used for most hauling. They make incomparably delicate porcelain and glass of renown throughout the mainland nations. The Atha'an Miere generally receive credit for their craftsmanship, but the Amayar do not care. They are aware of the mainland, know the prices charged by the Atha'an Miere, and are satisfied with the prices they receive, which is all that matters to them. They neither desire to travel across the water and try selling these things on the mainland themselves, nor wish to have strangers disturb the tranquility of their lives. They have no reason to fear or dislike the mainlanders, nor do they; they just don't want strangers mucking about. They know and, for the most part, trust the Sea Folk.

By Sea Folk law, any Amayar who wishes it must be granted the gift of passage, and no gift may be accepted in return. Yet they seldom travel even between the Sea Folk islands, and never to the mainland. The only boats they

own themselves are fairly small, used for fishing in the coastal waters of the islands. Even among the Amayar fishermen few know how to swim. Some of the Amayar work in the Sea Folk's shipyards, ropewalks, and dry docks, but they stay only long enough to earn whatever sum they are seeking and then move on.

Even though the majority of the land-based population of the islands is Amayar, the governors are appointed from among the Atha'an Miere, never the Amayar. Sea Folk consider this duty off ship to be onerous, but take a view that an island must be treated like a ship; the 'vessel' tended and the 'crew' cared for. Because Sea Folk want to remain with their ships, the governors rarely venture away from the ports and shipbuilding facilities except on tours to make sure that all is well. The result is a benign neglect: the Amayar are, in effect, left to govern themselves in their villages. There is no record or even rumor of any sort of rebellion or protest against their rulers.

Chapter 20

The Aiel

'Till shade is gone, till water is gone,
into the Shadow with teeth bared,
screaming defiance with the last breath,
to spit in Sightblinder's eye on the last Day.'
— Aiel Oath

THE WASTE

 East of the Dragonwall and west of the cliffs and chasms of Shara lies the Aiel Waste. Called *Djevik K'Shar*, 'The Dying Ground' in the Trolloc tongue, it is a harsh, rugged, and all but waterless land that appears uninhabitable. Yet this Waste is home to the Aiel, a race of people as fierce and hardy as their rugged environment. These tall and fair-haired people are lethal fighters and skilled trackers, with both men and women serving as warriors. Believed to be the most deadly fighters on the continent, if not in the world, they veil their faces before they kill and have established a well-earned reputation for defending their land from outsiders. They call the Waste the Three-Fold Land, for they believe it is first a shaping stone to make them; second, a testing ground to prove their worth; and

third, a punishment for their sin – though the exact sin is apparently unknown. Only those select few on friendly terms with the Aiel dare to enter the Waste: peddlers, gleemen, and the Tuatha'an Tinkers. At one time the merchants of Cairhien were also welcomed, but that welcome was revoked when Laman destroyed *Avendoraldera*. Everyone else is considered an enemy.

The Aiel were not always a warrior people. Recently discovered historical information reveals that the Aiel not only evolved their warlike tendencies after the Breaking, but are actually related to the peaceful Tuatha'an, whom they avoid, but never harm.

HISTORY OF THE AIEL

During the Age of Legends a pacifistic people known as the Da'shain Aiel had sworn the Covenant to serve the Aes Sedai and follow a nonviolent code known as the Way of the Leaf. Within this code all trials were to be accepted and endured. There was no excuse for violence. All who lived in that time knew of the Covenant and the Aiel's code, and honored them for it. Their service was highly valued, their songs a treasure to all who heard them sing. When the war came, and after it the Breaking of the World, they would not betray their code by fighting. This was not for any lack of courage, for there are stories that tell of the Da'shain standing against danger unto death, without raising a hand, in order to buy time so that others might live.

When the Breaking began, the Aes Sedai apparently realized that the Da'shain would be slaughtered uselessly if they remained in the cities. There may also have been a

Foretelling that the Aiel would eventually produce a man who would stand against the Dark One. The Aes Sedai must have known that the Da'shain were too proud to leave the cities simply for their own safety, or even for a possible future salvation, and therefore devised a great task worthy of the Da'shain. They were given precious *angreal* and *ter'angreal* and told to take them all to a place of safety. With insane male Aes Sedai rampaging through the world, it was important to keep these powerful tools out of their reach. The Da'shain never knew that this task was also meant to get the Aiel themselves out of harm's way because the Aes Sedai could no longer protect them. The second covenant, occasionally spoken of by Aiel and Tinkers, probably refers to this last duty the Aes Sedai laid upon the Aiel.

THE FIRST DIVISION

Before the Breaking it was unheard of to harm or even threaten the Da'shain Aiel. Everyone knew they had sworn to the Covenant and followed the Way of the Leaf. But the Da'shain's pacifism was no longer respected in the Breaking's all-out struggle for survival. Eventually as the years passed some of the Da'shain decided to leave the rest, convinced that the guardianship of the Aes Sedai relics was a hopeless mission. They decided to go in search of the Old Song, perhaps in hope of rekindling a better time when the Way of the Leaf was all and life was not so hard. They abandoned their vow of service in favor of their own future, and so were considered 'lost' by the rest of the Aiel. This splinter group was the beginning of the Tuatha'an, who to this

day dedicate themselves to the Way of the Leaf and the search for the Old Song.

THE SECOND DIVISION

Those Aiel that remained continued to keep the Covenant, and to protect the relics, but they could not protect their own children and families against the lawless hordes that roamed the broken world. Children were stolen, women raped, men killed, and they could not defend against or avenge these wrongs without betraying their code. At some point, however, some of the younger men found the Way unbearable in the face of such losses. One by one they decided to fight back. This resulted in the first kill by an Aiel, and in the casting out of that Aiel, and all after him, for betraying their beliefs. At this time it was understood that it was the Covenant and the Way of the Leaf that made one Aiel. When the first young man turned to his family for support, he was reputed to have been told to 'hide your face . . . I had a son, once, with a face like that. I do not wish to see it on a stranger.' This is the legendary origin of the Aiel face-veiling before a kill.

None of these disowned young men were willing to abandon the wagons entirely, and instead followed in their wake. They still thought of themselves as Aiel and kept the name, refusing to accept the idea that a willingness to defend their families could completely eradicate their heritage. They lived in tents and survived off the land, providing protection for those who would not protect themselves, despite the latter's insistence that they did not exist.

THE MAIDENS OF THE SPEAR

The fighting men had established a fairly sizable group by the time the first woman joined them. Named Morin, she was a mother whose young daughter had been stolen from her. She came to the warriors for help, but insisted on joining them for the rescue, fully aware that it would mean permanent exile from the wagons and her family. Up to this point no woman of the Aiel had ever participated in battle, though several had come to the warriors for aid. The legend tells that a spear was shortened to fit her, becoming the prototype for the now famous Aiel stabbing spears used by men and women alike.

Morin is said to have sworn that she had left her old life and husband behind and was now married only to her spear. She proved herself in battle and became the first of the Maidens of the Spear. Even today no Maiden may marry and remain in the society, nor may she fight while carrying a child, though apparently nonmarital relationships are quite common. Any child born to a Maiden is given to a family to raise, with no one knowing the true identity of the mother or her child. The current ultimatum recited to a woman becoming a Maiden is: 'You may belong to no man, nor any man belong to you, nor any child. The spear is your lover, your child, and your life.' It is interesting to note that none of the male warrior societies has restrictions nearly so stringent as those Morin helped create.

There are indications that Morin had had a foretelling that she would bear a child to the warrior chief, Jeordam, which she did, thus beginning the process that allowed the tent-dwelling Aiel to sustain a self-reproducing culture

on their own. By this time they had already begun to call the pacifists 'Jenn Aiel' – a derisive term for the 'Only True Aiel' – while the warriors were simply 'Aiel.' They had abandoned the use of the 'Da'shain' prefix, and it was forgotten entirely by the next generation. Of course the wagon-dwellers still pretended their protectors did not exist. If they had any name at all for their outcasts, it is unknown.

There were still some aspects of their original beliefs the warriors would not abandon. They would not use swords, since a sword existed only to kill a human. All their weapons, such as spears, knives, and bows, could be used in hunting, building, or farming, as well as in defense. In this manner they could still claim to be true to the Way, and thus to the name Aiel.

Over time the warrior Aiel grew and the Jenn Aiel, who eventually adopted that derisive name, began to dwindle. The warriors started to develop their own culture and skills, with less and less direct contact with the folk in the wagons. Their numbers were now increasing by births without the need for recruitment from the Jenn. The protection they had provided the Jenn through the years had also reduced the need for the wagon folk to seek the warriors' path. Yet the Jenn Aiel's birth rate had dropped, and they were losing folk to the droughts and hardships of the trail that seemed to barely affect their more hardy tent-living relatives. The few Aes Sedai the Jenn Aiel had picked up along the way probably helped to reduce the losses, but not the overall trend. These ancient Aes Sedai kept to the wagons and avoided all contact with the warrior Aiel, probably as appalled as the Jenn at what those outcasts had become. Survivors of the Breaking, they were certain that it was the Jenn Aiel, closest in

thought and culture to the Da'shain Aiel they remembered, who needed their aid and protection.

THE WATER GIFT

We have no clear picture of elapsed time for the Aiel nomads, but it is known that their wanderings eventually took them along the Spine of the World and through the land that is now Cairhien. There they discovered that some people were still capable of generosity, a fact so unusual to their experience with those not Aiel that it became a part of their folklore. The story survives to this day of how the leader of a palisaded town agreed to allow the Aiel to take whatever water they wanted if the Aiel would dig the wells to get it. In retrospect this was only common sense, as the wells would serve the local populace long after the travelers had moved on, but to the Aiel it was the first time in remembrance that they had not had to fight for what they needed. It was this act that, hundreds of years later, led to the gift of *Avendoraldera*, a sapling of the one surviving chora tree, to the Cairhienin when they discovered them to be the descendants of those who gave water to the Aiel.

From the Spine of the World the Aiel, guided by the Aes Sedai, traversed one of the few passes to head east into the desolate land beyond, perhaps in an Aes Sedai attempt to protect the Jenn Aiel from contamination by other cultures so that the prophecy told during the Breaking could come true. The tent-dwellers followed, still prepared to defend the Jenn if necessary, though by this time they did so more out of habit and tradition than necessity.

It was sometime just after crossing into the waste that the tent-dwellers began to divide into clans and septs, though the Jenn apparently maintained their conventional family groupings and social structure.

RHUIDEAN

Deep in the waste, in the valley beneath a mountain later named Chaendaer, the wagons finally stopped, and the Jenn Aiel, aided by the Aes Sedai, began to build a city. They named it Rhuidean. The design was probably inspired by Aes Sedai memories of cities before the Breaking, with tall buildings of many-colored shining glass reaching into the sky, exquisite statues, and wide avenues. The last surviving chora tree, called *Avendesora* by wetlanders, was planted in the central square.

Outside the city the tent-dwellers spread out over the all but barren land and made it their own. Eventually their numbers grew great enough that individual groups began to contest with one another until all vestiges of their original unity was lost. They forgot that they were ever part of the Way of the Leaf, they forgot that they were ever kin to the Jenn; they forgot everything of their heritage save the conquest of their harsh new homeland and their wars with one another.

Within the great unfinished city, however, the Jenn were dying out. Despite the best efforts of the Aes Sedai, their plans and the prophecy were unraveling. The Aes Sedai realized that they had made a mistake. If a child was to be born of the Aiel to fight the Dark One, he would not be born of the Jenn. But the Aes Sedai had no ties with the nomadic Aiel warriors. In order to save the prophecy, and

perhaps Aes Sedai control of it, they had to find a way to share the truth with the warriors in a way that would not destroy them as well.

LEGACY OF RHUIDEAN

The Aes Sedai contacted the Wise Ones of the Aiel through their dreams, sending a message that all clan chiefs must come to Rhuidean or face complete dissolution of themselves and their clans. Those that came would have a chance to unify the Aiel, but those who refused would watch their people vanish over time. For those who came a permanent truce was declared – the Peace of Rhuidean – which could not be broken. All fighting was prohibited within sight of Chaendaer. Within the heart of Rhuidean the Aes Sedai prepared a great *ter'angreal* that contained within it all the history of the Aiel. Each clan chief was required to enter the city and face its terrible glass columns. Those who returned, only one in three, had demonstrated the strength to face the truth of their heritage, and the knowledge of the prophecy that must be fulfilled through them. Those who lacked the strength to face those truths never returned at all.

In this way the Aes Sedai managed to insure that the history of the Aiel would not be lost, and the prophecy might still be fulfilled. From that time forward all clan chiefs have been required to enter Rhuidean and pass through the *ter'angreal* before being accepted as chief. The men could only enter Rhuidean once.

Women who would be Wise Ones also were required to enter the glass columns, though only on their second visit to the city; they had a much higher survival rate

than the men. (On their first visit they had to enter a three-ringed *ter'angreal* much like the one used for the Accepted in the White Tower of Tar Valon.)

Thus for almost three thousand years the chiefs and the Wise Ones kept secret the history of the Aiel, guiding their people from its perspective while protecting them from its truth.

Eventually the last of the Jenn and the Aes Sedai died, but not before the Aes Sedai placed machinery of Power to protect Rhuidean from outsiders and preserve it for the Aiel. Those outside the Waste knew nothing of its existence, for the prescribed penalty for a non-Aiel entering the valley of Rhuidean was death. Even among the Aiel, only chiefs and Wise Ones ever saw the inner city itself – until it was recently reopened for habitation.

The unveiling of Rhuidean by Rand al'Thor has revealed that ancient city to the world. The city now sits above a newly formed lake fed by an underground ocean of fresh water. This lake in turn feeds the only known river in the Waste, which brings water to lands that have known only drought since the time of the Breaking. As a result of these changes, Aiel now inhabit the city the Jenn could not finish.

Rand al'Thor, however, revealed more than Rhuidean's landscape. He also revealed the secrets of the Aiel's history to the entirety of the Aiel, something the Aes Sedai had carefully avoided. The belief that the Aiel had once failed the Aes Sedai had long been a part of Aiel history, along with the belief that a second failure would end in their destruction, but the knowledge that their entire way of life might itself comprise the betrayal was more than many could bear. They began to suffer from 'the Bleakness,' a malaise that causes Aiel to abandon their

warrior's ways or deny the truths and refuse to follow the man most believe to be the *Car'a'carn*, or chief of chiefs.

GROWTH OF THE AIEL CLANS

The warrior Aiel continued to spread over the length and breadth of the Waste. The clans came to number twelve, and grew to be as large as nations, fighting with each other, and raiding each other, as many nations do. Most of all, they all fought anyone who dared to enter the Waste uninvited. Some outsiders, dubbed 'wetlanders' by the Aiel, dared the Waste despite the threat, drawn by the promise of the silks and ivory that lay just beyond its borders. Those few who survived the attempt brought back stories of vicious fair-haired warriors with veiled faces who sprang from the very ground to kill trespassers with merciless ease. Even Artur Hawkwing was unable to conquer the proud people of the Waste; their ferocity and unorthodox fighting style were more than a match for even *his* highly skilled army.

Tempered over time by the unforgiving hardships of their land, the Aiel deserve much of their fearsome reputation. They still veil their faces before they kill and are equally deadly with weapons or bare hands. Echoes of their ancestors' love of music and dance can now be heard only as their pipers play the waiting clans into battle. To them battle has become 'the dance of spears,' in which the steps are lethal. Yet even today no Aiel will willingly touch a sword even on point of death, or ride a horse unless pressed.

The twelve clans of the Aiel – the Chareen, the Codarra, the Daryne, the Goshien, the Miagoma, the Nakai, the

Reyn, the Shaarad, the Shaido, the Shiande, the Taardad, and the Tomanelle – have a thirteenth fellow, the extinct Jenn, also called the 'Clan That Is Not.' Each clan is made up of many septs, such as the Jaern Rift sept of the Codarra and the White Mountain sept of the Chareen, with no set number for the septs that comprise a clan.

In addition, the warriors themselves are divided into twelve separate societies. These are the *Seia Doon* (Black Eyes), *Far Aldazar Din* (Brothers of the Eagle), *Rahien Sorei* (Dawn Runners), *Sovin Nai* (Knife Hands), *Far Dareis Mai* (Maidens of the Spear), *Hama N'dore* (Mountain Dancers), *Cor Darei* (Night Spears), *Aethan Dor* (Red Shields), *Shae'en M'taal* (Stone Dogs), *Sha'mad Conde* (Thunder Walkers), *Tain Shari* (True Bloods), and *Duadhe Mahdi'in* (Water Seekers). Each has its own customs, and sometimes it has specific duties. For example, Red Shields act as police, and Stone Dogs are often used as rear guards during retreats, while Maidens of the Spear are often scouts. Raids and battles between clans have been commonplace since the first clans were formed, but the members of the same society will not fight each other even when their clans do so. Because of this there are always lines of contact between the clans, even during open warfare.

THE CODE OF HONOR AND OBLIGATION

The Aiel have replaced the code of passive acceptance with a complex code of honor and obligation called *ji'e'-toh*. By this code there are many paths to honor, each with its own measure and price, and each facet of life has

its own paths. In battle, for example, the smallest honor is that gained by killing, for anyone can kill, while the greatest is to touch an armed living enemy without causing harm. To take an enemy and make him *gai'shain* falls somewhere between the two extremes. All must seek their own honor through the code, and honor is valued above all else in Aiel society.

Shame also has many levels within the code, and is considered on many of those levels to be worse than pain, injury, or even death. The facet of the code that outweighs all others in all its various degrees is *toh*, or obligation: any obligation, no matter how small or insignificant, *must* be met in full. *Toh* is so important to these people that an Aiel will accept even shame, if necessary, to fulfill an obligation that might appear minor to one not tied to the code.

Consider the role of the *gai'shain*. The name means 'pledged to peace in battle' in the Old Tongue and is used to refer to those Aiel taken prisoner by other Aiel during a raid or battle. These prisoners are required by *ji'e'toh* to serve their captor for one year and a day, touching no weapon and doing no violence in that time. They must complete this service humbly and obediently with no complaint or thought of escape. They wear white robes to clearly distinguish them from other Aiel during their service. Even if they are somehow returned to their own people, that period of service must be completed. Perhaps the *gai'shain* are a throwback to the obedient and nonviolent service the original Da'shain Aiel used to give to the Aes Sedai. Also according to the code, Wise Ones, a blacksmith, a child under the age of fifteen, and a woman with a child under the age of ten are all exempted from service as *gai'shain*.

THE WISE ONES

As in most cultures of the world, the Aiel have those who can channel and who can be taught. Women with the spark are all found by the Wise Ones and trained to become Wise Ones. All channelers are Wise Ones, but not all Wise Ones can channel. The fact that many Wise Ones can channel is not spoken of among the Aiel. All Wise Ones are trained in healing, herbs, and other lore, much like Wisdoms. The Wise Ones have great authority and influence with sept and clan chiefs, and carry great responsibility as well. They stand outside all feuds and battle, and according to *ji'e'toh* may not be harmed or impeded in any way. For a Wise One to take part in a battle would be a great violation of custom and tradition. Recently, this has happened, and its ultimate effect is yet to be seen.

By custom these women avoid all contact with Aes Sedai, probably to prevent the Aes Sedai from recognizing the channelers among them. Some Wise Ones are also Dreamwalkers, able to enter the World of Dreams, *Tel'aran'rhiod*, and to speak to others in their dreams.

The young men who discover they can channel leave their clans to face the Dark One on the slopes of Shayol Ghul and die.

AIEL CULTURE

The Aiel begin learning survival skills and the handling of the spear at a very young age, with games designed to enhance skill, speed, and accuracy. But they are also taught the intricacies of *ji'e'toh* and politics, as well as

basic arithmetic and reading. Though the Aiel appear to live a barbaric life, they value books and literature highly and are usually well educated. Any peddler carrying books is certain to find a welcome among them.

No longer nomadic, the Aiel have carved out strongholds among the cliffs, hills, and canyons of the Waste. Each sept has its own hold and within it the Roofmistress, the wife of the chief, reigns supreme, having the right to welcome or turn away even her own husband from water and shade. In most holds the dwellings are clay and brick on the surface, with flat roofs for growing plants, but usually burrowed deep into the stone to form spacious and comfortable rooms well insulated from the heat. Aiel rooms are carpeted with rugs, hung with tapestries, and furnished with comfortable mats and cushions, shelves, and tables, but no chairs. The chief alone owns a chair among the Aiel. Though the Aiel dress plainly, their homes are usually draped in bright colors and a variety of textures. Fine statuary, porcelains, and a wide variety of books line the niches of many, making them as brilliant and elegant inside as they are drab on the outside. The Aiel tradition of looting a fifth of the goods in any raid or war has allowed most of them to acquire many rare items, especially in the Aiel War when they crossed the Dragonwall. Their trade with Shara has brought them silks and ivory as well. With such pleasant environments hewn from the rugged land, the Aiel live as nomads only when following the herds in a search for grazing land or when traveling to battle.

Within each of these holds a wide variety of crops are grown on terraced ledges and the flat roofs of houses, though they must usually be hand-watered in the harsh climate. This daily chore is usually done by the children

and the *gai'shain*. Careful cultivation produces fruits and vegetables for a highly varied diet.

Weaving and jewelry making are the primary crafts, with metalsmithing close behind. The Aiel mine their own gold and silver, as well as many less precious ores. They also mine rubies, sapphires, moonstones, and fire-drops, though do not facet-cut any of these gems in their work. Metalworking of any kind is highly valued by the Aiel; smiths may not be made *gai'shain*, as that service would deprive the hold of their skills for a year and a day. Textiles such as wool and *algode* are woven into a variety of fabrics. The wool comes from the sheep and goats that graze on the sparse land, and the *algode* from intensely irrigated plots within each hold. There is very little usable wood in the Waste, and as a result there are no wood-workers. The few wooden items brought into the Waste are highly prized.

The code of dress among the Aiel has changed very little since the Age of Legends and the Da'shain Aiel. The *cadin'sor*, worn by all men and by all Maidens of the Spear, is an adaptation of the ancient Da'shain working clothes. The word even roughly translates as 'working clothes' in the Old Tongue. The classic coat and breeches are colored in browns or grays that fade into rock, sand, or shadow. The Aiel have added soft, laced knee-high boots practical for desert wear, as well as a *shoufa*, a scarflike garment, usually the color of sand or rock, that is wrapped around the head and neck, leaving only the face bare. When preparing to kill, they pull the *shoufa* over the nose and mouth as well, veiling the face according to tradition. The only difference between the garb of male warriors and that of other Aiel men is that the warriors carry a larger knife. The cut of the *cadin'sor* coat is different for

each clan and has slight variations according to sept, though the differences, clear to any Aiel, are subtle and difficult for an outsider to see.

All Aiel men, and the women who are Maidens of the Spear, wear their hair cut short except for a tail on the nape of the neck. Women who are not Maidens wear their hair shoulder length and longer, but rarely braid it or gather it up. They frequently pull it away from the face with a scarf. Their long skirts, blouses, and shawls are in drab desert colors, and they adorn themselves with many bracelets and necklaces, often carved ivory or precious metals. High-ranking women are likely to display an abundance of valuable jewelry. Maidens of the Spear often possess jewelry, but rarely wear more than an occasional piece at a special event. The men wear no jewelry at all, though the mark of a chief, placed in his skin at Rhuidean, often has the metallic look of a strange bracelet.

AIEL KINSHIP

Relationships within the Aiel are both precise and complex. There is a specific term for every relationship of blood and marriage. First-brothers and first-sisters are those who have the same mother, but not necessarily the same father. (Among the Aiel, having the same mother means a closer relationship than having the same father.) Second-brothers and second-sisters are the children of one's mother's first-brother or first-sister, and sister-mothers and sister-fathers are first-sisters and first-brothers of one's mother. A greatfather or greatmother is the father or mother of one's own mother, while the parents of one's

father are second greatfather or second greatmother. Kinship terms include some relationships not bound by blood. Friends who are as close as first-sisters or first-brothers are called near-sisters or near-brothers. Near-sisters often adopt one another formally as first-sisters. Near-brothers almost never do.

Marriage among the Aiel is not always monogamous. Within the Aiel it is perfectly acceptable for a man and two women to marry, though all must be in agreement. The women are usually near-sisters or first-sisters, who then become sister-wives. Once joined, they are considered married to each other as well as to the man. There are, however, no records of one woman marrying two men.

There are as many terms as there are blood ties, but only a born Aiel is likely to avoid hopeless confusion beyond the terms for immediate family relationships.

THE LOST ONES

But what of those Aiel that left the wagons so long ago to seek the Old Song? The Tuatha'an alone among the descendants of the original Da'shain Aiel still follow the Way of the Leaf. By the Tuatha'an Way of the Leaf, all people should live their lives with the leaves as an example. 'For the leaf lives its appointed time, and does not struggle against the wind that carries it away. The leaf does no harm, and finally falls to nourish new leaves.' The Tuatha'an believe that no man should harm another for any reason whatsoever.

Known by most as the Traveling People, the Tuatha'an now roam the land, both in and out of the Waste, in caravans of brightly colored wagons. Led by a man called a

Mahdi, each caravan continues its search for the lost dream of peace. Clothed in equally bright coats and dresses, they move as if always listening to a tune, always ready for a dance. Unlike the Aiel, who only sing battle chants or a dirge for the slain, the Tuatha'an sing or play at any opportunity. Where they go, music is always near.

The Tuatha'an are known also as the Tinkers, though they occasionally do other work. Their craftsmanship is superb, usually mending items better than new. Yet they are shunned and distrusted by folk in villages and small towns who do not understand them. Stories, usually false, say that the Tinkers steal young children and try to convert young people to their beliefs. The fact that the Tinkers will not defend themselves against such attacks simply lends credence to those wanting to hate. In actuality, most who convert to the Tinker way are simply drawn to follow them by the simplicity of their beliefs.

The Tinkers are one of the few peoples traditionally allowed to cross the Waste unmolested, undoubtedly because the chiefs of the Aiel clans know their history. The Tuatha'an themselves almost certainly do not know of their origins, or of their relationship to the Aiel.

Chapter 21

The Ogier

'Clear the field, smooth it low,
Let no weed or stubble stand,
Here we labor, here we toil,
Here the towering trees will
grow.'

— FROM AN OGIER SONG

 UNLIKE THE OTHER races so far chronicled, the Ogier do not have a specific country to call their own but rather live in secluded *stedding* scattered throughout the world. They are also the only natural nonhuman sentient race known. (Creatures such as Nym and Trollocs are constructs and therefore artificial, not natural.) Ogier resemble humans in general build and dress, but are a genetically separate species with long tufted ears and broad, vaguely snoutlike noses. Much larger than humans, the men average ten feet in height or better with the women standing only slightly shorter. They are also much longer-lived. A typical Ogier life span is at least three to four times that of a human, and they are not considered mature enough to leave the *stedding* until they have reached the age of at least one hundred. This

longer life may also be the cause of their deliberately slow and certain behavior. They consider humans to be much too hasty and impatient.

STEDDING

Ogier *stedding* seem to be shielded in some unknown way that completely prevents the One Power from being channeled, or even sensed, within their boundaries; attempts to wield the One Power from outside a *stedding* have no effect inside it. The very air within a *stedding* seems somehow different from that outside, fresher or more peaceful, causing most visitors to shiver in surprise upon entering. No Trolloc will enter a *stedding* unless driven, and even Myrddraal will do so only at the greatest need and with the greatest reluctance. It is said that Darkfriends, if truly dedicated, also feel uncomfortable and unwelcome there. The exact properties of a *stedding* are unknown.

There are forty-one inhabited *stedding* in the 'known world' – that is, between the Aryth Ocean and the Aiel Waste. While populations vary considerably, and Ogier seem to consider such numbers not worth gathering (if they do, they have never made them known to humankind), it has been estimated that the average *stedding* has a population of something over six thousand. The total Ogier population between the Aryth Ocean and the Spine of the World is perhaps slightly in excess of two hundred fifty thousand.

With the Breaking behind them – and, when Ogier life span is taken into account, with memories of human strife fresh – the Ogier who resettled the lost *stedding*

often chose those in rugged mountains or deep forests. *Stedding* Tsofu, in Cairhien, is the least isolated from humankind, and it lies a full day's travel from the nearest human village. Several *stedding* known to the Ogier have never been resettled, because they are too close to human habitation. Given the general Ogier preference to remain apart from humanity, exact locations cannot be revealed.

The Spine of the World contains the largest regional concentration of Ogier *stedding*, with twelve hidden in its rugged peaks and valleys. From north to south they are: *Stedding* Qichen, *Stedding* Sanshen, *Stedding* Handu, *Stedding* Chanti, *Stedding* Lantoine, *Stedding* Yongen, *Stedding* Mashong, *Stedding* Sintiang, *Stedding* Taijing (east of Cantoine), *Stedding* Kolomon, *Stedding* Daiting, and *Stedding* Shangtai, where Loial was born.

In Kinslayer's Dagger, separate from the range that makes up the Spine of the World, there is only one: *Stedding* Yontiang.

There are four *stedding* west of the Dragonwall and east of the River Erinin: *Stedding* Nurshang, between Kinslayer's Dagger and Shienar, *Stedding* Tsofu in Cairhien, *Stedding* Cantoine just north of the River Iralell, and *Stedding* Jenshin in Haddon Mirk.

The Borderlands hold seven *stedding*, the second largest regional concentration: *Stedding* Chosium, Jongai, and Saishen in Saldaea, *Stedding* Chiantal in Kandor, *Stedding* Shanjing and Tanhal in Arafel, and *Stedding* Sholoon in Shienar.

In the Black Hills there are three: *Stedding* Feindu, Shajin and Jentoine. *Stedding* Shamendar, Taishin, Leitiang, and Tsochan are located in the forests north of the River Ivo.

Six lie in the Mountains of Mist: From north to south they are: *Stedding* Chinden, *Stedding* Tsofan, *Stedding* Yandar, *Stedding* Madan, *Stedding* Jinsiun, and *Stedding* Shangloon.

In contrast there are only two in the Mountains north of the River Dhagon: *Stedding* Mintai and Wenchen; and two more along the Shadow Coast: *Stedding* Shadoon and *Stedding* Mardoon.

HISTORY

In the Age of Legends, Ogier lived and worked among humans, and traveled widely outside their *stedding*. They had a special gift for growing things, and worked closely with the Nym. Though unrelated to the One Power, many of them had the ability to affect living things, especially plants, with their songs. These gifted Ogier could cause plants to respond to sound, bending to any desired formation. The songs could also encourage a plant to grow stronger and taller. Those few Ogier who have the gift now are known as Treesingers. The marvelous items they create without damage to the parent plant – those made of sung wood – are highly prized. In the Age of Legends the ability and hence sung wood itself was very common.

The Ogier were also reputed to have served among that Age's law enforcement. Although considered a pacific people and extremely slow to anger, some old stories say they fought alongside humans in the Trolloc Wars, and call them implacable enemies.

During the Breaking the land and sea shifted so dramatically that the *stedding* were lost or swallowed

entirely. Those Ogier that survived the upheaval of land and sea found themselves homeless and adrift, wandering in search of their lost sanctuaries. Among Ogier this time is known as the Exile. After many years their Longing for the peace and beauty that only existed within the *stedding* became so strong that they began to sicken and die. Many more died than did not. Since that time the Ogier do not leave the *stedding* for extensive periods. If an Ogier stays Outside for too long, the Longing takes him and he begins to weaken. If he does not return, he dies. Though this was not true during the Age of Legends, the long Exile apparently sensitized the Survivors and their descendants so that all Ogier are now bound to the *stedding*.

LIFESTYLE

Widely known as wondrous stonemasons, the Ogier much prefer to work with living and growing things, as they did in ages past. An Ogier was known in the Old Tongue as *tia avende alantin* or Brother to the Trees. They only took up stonework during the Exile, quickly revealing almost as great a talent for the stone as for plants. Because of their love for living things most of their stonework is amazingly organic in design. When given free rein, as in the construction of much of the city of Tar Valon, they can create buildings that almost give the illusion of life. Many of the great human cities still boast buildings built by Ogier. Though most Ogier believe stonework is beneath their skills, it is the stonemasonry that brings money for trade goods into the *stedding*.

Once the *stedding* were rediscovered, the Ogier settled in determined to stay. The long Exile's scars are now engraved into the entire race. They have little contact with humans, only leaving their homes to travel to other *stedding* or to do stonework. Ogier appearances outside the *stedding* are so rare that most people no longer believe in them, thinking them a fantasy.

Within the *stedding* Ogier live in houses built into the earth. They spend much of the time tending living things, especially the Great Trees. These mammoth hardwoods tower hundreds of feet into the air with trunks as much as one hundred paces across. Before the Breaking such trees were common, but now they are quite rare and zealously prized by the Ogier. Many *stedding* use the polished stump of one of these trees for meetings.

The second greatest love of all Ogier is knowledge. They love to read and write, and value books and records very highly. Because of their longer life span, their tradition of history-telling, and their literacy, many of their stories contain information lost to humans. Ogier have their own written language, known to humans as Ogier script, though they usually speak the common tongue when humans are about.

Each *stedding* is governed by a Council of Elders, who hold public meetings within and between *stedding*. These meetings are traditionally held at the great stump of the *stedding*. The Elders preside, but any adult Ogier may speak before the stump, though they often choose an advocate to present their case to the Council. These advocates are not hired, but act because they believe in the Ogier they represent and the truth of his or her case.

The Council, which is the only full-time government within a *stedding*, is aided by other Ogier on particular projects at one time or another as their skills are needed. The Ogier also use a system of apprenticeship to train younger Ogier in responsibility as well as work skills. These youngsters get the more menial jobs while training for greater skills and responsibilities. Ogier believe that such labor builds character.

In many ways the Ogier are an almost matriarchal society. The Head of the Council of Elders is often a woman, and mothers and wives have more authority than their husbands. Marriages are arranged by mothers, with the consent of the bride-to-be, but the groom-to-be has no real say-so. Many a young Ogier has gone to work a bachelor and returned home to find that he will be a groom tomorrow.

Besides tending plants and working stone, the Ogier raise sheep, make cloth, and create fine metalwork and jewelry. Their clothes are often heavily embroidered, with women wearing embroidered flowers in a quantity to suit their station. Girls wear flowered trim only on their cloaks, while women Elders' dresses are embroidered from throat to ankle. Necklaces and bracelets, in the distinctive patterns reminiscent of vines and plants, are also worn, but earrings are not. Ogier ears are a secondary erogenous zone, and are therefore kept partially covered by hair. To bare them enough for earrings would be much too shocking for Ogier sensibilities. All women wear their hair loose and long. Men wear their hair shorter than that of women.

Men's coats are of various lengths, and their shirts and trousers are plain. Every aspect of clothing and jewelry for both men and women reflects the profound Ogier

respect for nature, and indeed, all living things. Perhaps their withdrawal from humanity is a reminder that humanity is losing that quality.

Chapter 22

The Ways

THE GIFT

 DURING THE BREAKING those few Ogier who remained in their *stedding* found that they were all but trapped there – turmoil had made travel between *stedding* dangerous almost to the point of impossibility – so that the Ogier who kept their sanctuary faced a different kind of exile, the loss of contact with their brothers and sisters in other *stedding*.

At this time many male Aes Sedai who had not yet succumbed to the madness were offered refuge within the *stedding*. Only there could they be free of the taint the Dark One had placed on *saidin*. In gratitude for this protection, one group of Aes Sedai made a gift for the Ogier, a gift that would allow the Ogier to pass from one *stedding* to another in safety: this gift was the 'Ways,' pathways from one *stedding* to another, grown from the One Power. The Ways were a world apart, for even if the land between

two *stedding* was shattered or twisted, the Ways joining them remained unchanged, free of the Breaking.

Eventually all the male Aes Sedai left the *stedding* driven by the need to feel the True Source and the forlorn hope that the taint on *saidin* was gone. Before they left they gave the Ogier another gift, the Talisman of Growing.

THE WAYGATE

The Talisman of Growing is a *ter'angreal* which is triggered by certain kinds of singing, such as Ogier Treesinging. It allowed the Ogier to expand the Ways after the Aes Sedai had gone. As lost *stedding* were found, the Ogier grew Ways to them. The Talisman cannot create an entirely new Way between two spots, but it can make a branch 'grow' from an existing Way, and the Ogier can sing this growing into a 'flower,' the 'flower' of the Waygate, the only part of the Ways that is actually in the world. Waygates are worked in such intricate organic detail that they resemble a wall of living vines and flowers covered over with very fine stone dust. When activated, usually by moving the 'key' sculpted as a removable *Avendesora* leaf, the carved foliage changes slowly to living shrubbery, and the gate's double doors swing outward to reveal a glassy, mirrorlike permeable barrier.

Each Waygate has two of the *Avendesora* leaf keys, one on the outside and one within. The gates can be locked by placing both leaves on the same side, thus preventing normal opening from the other side.

Because the Ways are built from the One Power, which will not function within a *stedding*, the Waygates were

always located just outside the *stedding*. As the network of Ways grew, it eventually connected not only the *stedding*, but the great Ogier-built cities as well, allowing the Ogier easy access. The Ogier planted groves filled with a wide assortment of plants and trees, including the Great Trees, outside these cities to comfort the Ogier who worked there, so that the Longing would not overtake them. The Ways were grown to these groves. Many of these groves have since disappeared. The grove in Caemlyn has been swallowed up by the expansion of the city; that in Cairhien has been left untended until it is indistinguishable from any other forest. The grove outside Tear is now an empty pasture, and Illian's has been tamed into a royal park for the king and his favorites; yet in each case the Waygates themselves still exist, though now they may stand in a courtyard or even the basement of a modern building.

WITHIN THE WAYS

The Ways themselves are alive in some manner that even the Ogier do not understand and Aes Sedai have forgotten. They exist outside the normal confines of time and space through the One Power. Many Ogier believe they are actually a world unto themselves, connected only by the Pattern. In any case, normal physical rules do not apply to the network of the Ways. Ramps, islands, and bridges seem to hang free within a vast emptiness, sometimes one over another, with no apparent means of support. Directions such as north or south, up or down, have no real meaning in the Ways, and paths often spiral above or below for no obvious reason. A day's walk may bring a traveler to a destination more than a hundred or

even five hundred miles distant from his starting point, depending on the path taken. Guidings – tall slabs of stone inlaid with Ogier script in metal – stand at every juncture of multiple Ways. Signpost columns of stone, also in Ogier script, mark the entrance of each bridge and ramp.

According to Ogier journals, the Ways were originally well lighted, so that a traveler could see the myriad islands suspended in the vast openness. Day and night had no meaning. It was always day within the Ways. The islands themselves were lushly planted with carpets of thick grass and a variety of fruit trees. Ranging in size from fifty to well over one hundred paces in diameter, these islands varied in shape from long ovals to perfectly round circles. Each verdant isle had railings grown around the perimeter, perhaps to keep the unwary traveler or pack animal from accidentally falling off. The bridges also had railings, but the broad ramps joining islands and bridges did not, save a chest-high balustrade of white stone where bridges and ramps joined.

Ogier and Ogier-guided humans were the only ones who used the Ways. Some Aes Sedai documents suggest that the Aes Sedai who created the Ways may have placed traps for any Shadowspawn who might gain entrance. Evidence of those traps has been discovered, along with the Shadowspawn victims, but there is reason to believe such traps are no longer very effective.

DETERIORATION OF THE WAYS

For almost two thousand years, the Ways provided safe transit for Ogier and human alike. Then, during the War

of the Hundred Years, they began to change, growing gradually dank and dim. The change was so slow that few noticed it until darkness enveloped the bridges. Not all the travelers who went in came out again, and over time the numbers of travelers who vanished grew from a few to many. Some who did come out had been driven mad. Those who could speak raved about *Machin Shin*, the Black Wind, or of a presence that watched from the shadows. The Ways became completely dark.

Since the darkness descended upon the Ways, something has hunted within their depths. A cold wind that howls with voices of death and decay blows through the Ways where no wind should stir. Called *Machin Shin* by the Ogier, it haunts the Ways and feeds upon unwary travelers. Even the Ogier do not know what it is. Possibly, since the Ways were born of the tainted Power, the Black Wind was also born from the corruption. Some say that it may be a parasite, natural to the Ways but corrupted. Still others believe it was a remnant of the War of the Shadow that hid in the Ways and can no longer find a path out. Whatever its origin, it is indisputable fact that *Machin Shin* steals minds and souls, leaving the survivors as empty, living husks. There is little doubt that this creature has taken all travelers who have vanished throughout the years.

Ogier Elders now ban any Ogier or human from traveling the Ways, for the darkness, and the creature that roams the Ways, have made them deadly. The few who have dared travel them in recent years relate that the organic stone, once beautiful and smooth, is now pitted and broken, sometimes to the point of crumbling when touched. The trees and grass that once graced the islands are long gone, and the darkness is thick, deeper than night, and resistant to any light brought against it.

The Ways were grown from the One Power by male Aes Sedai, and therefore with *saidin*. The deterioration of the Ways is almost certainly a result of the taint from *saidin* seeping into that which was made from it, not from any touch of the Shadow itself, though this distinction scarcely makes them any less deadly.

Chapter 23

Tel'aran'rhiod

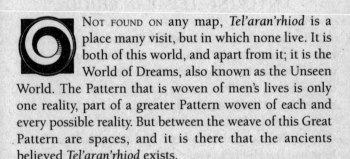 NOT FOUND ON any map, *Tel'aran'rhiod* is a place many visit, but in which none live. It is both of this world, and apart from it; it is the World of Dreams, also known as the Unseen World. The Pattern that is woven of men's lives is only one reality, part of a greater Pattern woven of each and every possible reality. But between the weave of this Great Pattern are spaces, and it is there that the ancients believed *Tel'aran'rhiod* exists.

THE WORLD OF DREAMS

Almost anyone may touch this world by accident; one need only dream to have a chance of entering it for a moment. Usually this visit, when it happens, is so brief

that those who glimpse it do not even know they have passed into a place beyond their normal dreams. Unlike personal dreamscapes, however, *Tel'aran'rhiod* is an actual place, with actual dangers. A wound taken while dreaming there will still exist on awakening, even though that body never actually entered the World of Dreams. Those who 'die' in normal dreams usually wake, but those who die in *Tel'aran'rhiod* never do. That fact is undoubtedly the source of the belief that those who die in their dreams will not wake.

This reciprocal action only affects living things, and the waking world is not affected in any way by actions taken within the World of Dreams, so long as they do not involve another living being.

ENTERING *TEL'ARAN'RHIOD*

While many glimpse this world by accident, very few have ever had the ability to enter it at will. Such people are known as dreamwalkers. Some Aiel dreamwalkers cannot touch the True Source, so this Talent is not connected to the ability to channel the One Power.

An individual's dreams form their own kind of world that can be touched by others. Aiel dreamwalkers have long had the ability to enter others' dreams, and use it to deliver messages, such as the ancient call that drew the clan chiefs to Rhuidean. Within such dreams the visitor is at a disadvantage, and can be trapped by the dreamer. While pulling others into one's own dream is quite possible, dreamwalkers never do so because they believe it is far too dangerous, and an evil act.

Though dreamwalkers can enter *Tel'aran'rhiod* unaided

from their normal dreams, certain *ter'angreal* allow the un-Talented user, even a nonchanneler, entry as well. There are rumors that the making of such *ter'angreal* may be reviving. One has only to fall asleep with the *ter'angreal* held against the skin to gain entrance to *Tel'aran'rhiod*.

One can enter the Unseen World physically, if one is a channeler with the ability to Travel, for Traveling opens the weave into *Tel'aran'rhiod* in much the same way it opens a hole to a given location in the waking world. The Aiel dreamwalkers, however, warn strongly against entering the World of Dreams physically. They believe that those who do so will lose a part of what makes them human. Whether or not that is so, those who journey there corporeally face a different challenge than do those who enter in their dreams. Dreamwalkers need not worry about food and rest, for they do not hunger in dreams and their bodies are already resting. A physical visitor within *Tel'aran'rhiod* will eventually find herself in need of both rest and nourishment.

A DIFFERENT REALITY

Tel'aran'rhiod is a nonpermanent reflection of the waking world. All the mountains, continents, oceans, plains, and forests exist there, as do buildings and roads, matching, for the most part, those within the waking world. These things are all solid, relatively permanent objects, and therefore appear solid and permanent within *Tel'aran'rhiod*. All movable objects, such as bowls on a table, workpapers, and food, are quite ephemeral, fading in and out or constantly changing. Perhaps they do not exist in

one place in the waking world long enough to make more than a transitory impression in the World of Dreams. Any food a physical visitor may manage to eat is likely to fade away before reaching the stomach, and as a result is unlikely to give much nourishment. Papers on a desk may change text and position right before the eyes of an observer, or jewelry appear and disappear from a jewel-box. Only items that have managed to remain unmoved long enough to make a solid impression, such as fruits or vegetables still on the vine, may exist long enough for the visitor to use them. Whatever the visitor uses, however, will not affect its counterpart in the waking world.

Humans are not the only living creatures that travel this world. Wild animals also journey here, but domestic animals are conspicuously absent. Some hold that domestic animals have been so greatly changed by their relationship with man that they have forever lost their connection to the permanence of nature, and therefore to the World of Dreams.

The World of Dreams, unlike the waking world, can be altered and affected by the thoughts of those within it. In this aspect it closely resembles an actual dream – what you think in essence can become reality for that world. It is possible to create almost anything that can be imagined. Unfortunately that creation will fade when the concentration of its creator wavers. Physics works differently here. One can fly from one place to another – or simply imagine another location and appear there. One can take on any appearance, and any mode of dress, whatsoever.

Tel'aran'rhiod's flexible character makes it very seductive, for there one can go anywhere and do almost anything. But it is also very dangerous. As a result the Aiel

dreamwalkers forbid any who are inexperienced from traveling its paths alone. The Aes Sedai have no such rule, perhaps because dreamwalkers have been rare among Aes Sedai in the last thousand years or so.

Over the last century, new abilities unrelated to the One Power have begun to appear; possibly old Talents that were lost throughout the turning of the Wheel have begun to reemerge. Among these new abilities are those of the Wolfbrothers, who often can be recognized by their golden, wolflike eyes. Wolfbrothers can communicate directly with wolves, mind to mind, over long distances, and have heightened senses more akin to a predatory animal's than a human's. They also have the ability to enter *Tel'aran'rhiod*, though they call it the wolf dream. The few known Wolfbrothers include Elyas Machera, once a warder, and Lord Perrin Aybara, known as 'Goldeneyes.'

The entrance to the wolf dream is different for Wolfbrothers than for dreamwalkers. Lord Perrin tells of a fleeting image of windows opening onto other events in other places. He believes that these 'window-visions' may be related to the dreamwalkers' occasional ability to see hints of future events, but there are too few data available for a detailed comparison. We are deeply grateful to Lord Perrin for his assistance, and to his gracious wife, the Lady Faile, for convincing him to give it.

Within the Land

IN THE AGE of Legends, the world was thickly populated, with no lands unclaimed. The disastrous upheavals of the Breaking decimated the population, but a gradual recovery meant that by the end of the reign of Artur Hawkwing, all the land between the Aiel Waste and the Aryth Ocean harbored some level of civilization. After Hawkwing's death, however, the population began a gradual decrease that the chaos of the War of the Hundred Years alone does not account for. Toward the end of the war rulers were claiming lands they lacked the manpower to hold. This decline has continued until the present, and there are now vast tracts of unpopulated land unclaimed by any nation, as well as areas that, though claimed in theory, are in practice autonomous and beyond the scope of their 'official'

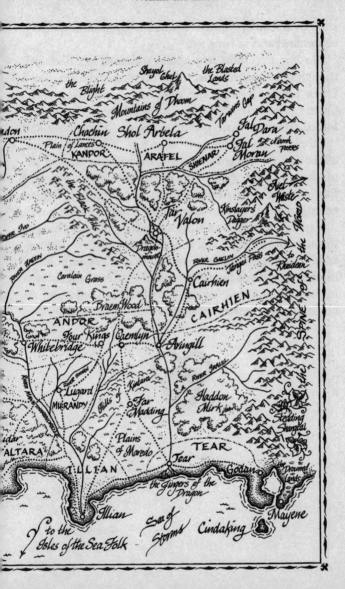

ruler to defend or control. Towns and even some cities lie abandoned and in ruin.

No one is certain why the population has declined, though some theorize that it has been caused by the Dark One's touch through the gradually weakening seals. Others believe it is simply a by-product of the world's forced return to more primitive ways as knowledge and the tools of civilization have been lost. Whatever reason, all nations are affected by it, from the vast too-empty halls of the powerful White Tower, to the little village of Emond's Field in Andor, which has forgotten it ever belonged to a Queen or was part of a larger nation.

Current unrest is causing rampant political changes throughout the land, and it is difficult – perhaps impossible – to obtain anything resembling accurate political information. Thus the names and statistics in the following section are those of the last official records, and do not necessarily portray matters as they are to date.

Chapter 24

The White Tower

'An Aes Sedai never lies,
but the truth she speaks
may not be the truth you think you hear.'
— Saying concerning sisters
of the White Tower

 Sigil of the White Tower   A stylized white flame; a white teardrop, point up; the White Flame; the Flame of Tar Valon.

Banner   The Flame of Tar Valon centered in a swirl or spiral of seven colors, running in order from the topmost center: blue, green, white, gray, yellow, red. Each element of the spiral circles the flame completely one time before its widest end reaches the edge of the banner.

AES SEDAI

Throughout the centuries of upheaval since the Breaking of the World, only the city of Tar Valon and the Aes Sedai within it have managed to retain both their sovereignty

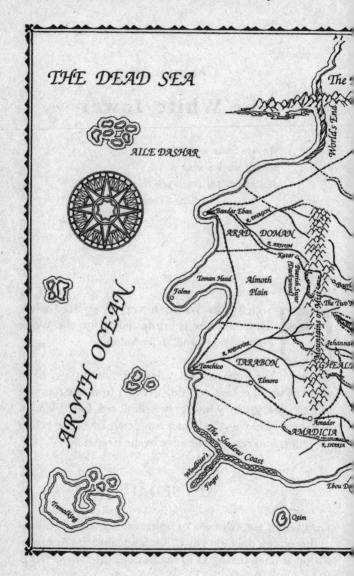

and traditions in an unbroken line since the White Tower was first established in 98 AB. No kingdom or people, save perhaps the Ogier, has managed to approach the longevity of the White Tower's reign in Tar Valon, much less attain the level of influence the Aes Sedai wield throughout the rest of the land, this despite the fact that no other kingdom claims to fully trust, or even understand them. Some still hold them responsible for the Breaking of the World. Of course, many of the Aes Sedai claim that their traditions are unchanged since before the Breaking, but the historical evidence indicates that modern Aes Sedai differ greatly in organization and level of knowledge from their predecessors during the Age of Legends.

Although Aes Sedai have the world think that the White Tower has a monopoly on wielding the One Power, at least among women – indeed, many believe it is so – the fact remains that there are women who can channel who are not part of the Tower, and their number is unknown. Few Aes Sedai recruit, normally, although when they *do* discover a girl who can learn to channel, they let nothing stand in the way of enrolling her as a novice in the Tower. (Historically most novices have been sixteen or younger when first enrolled, and the Tower usually has refused to accept any novice over the age of eighteen as too old to adapt to the discipline.) Rather than scouring the countryside, the preferred method is to allow the girl to come to an Aes Sedai and ask, and better yet, for her to come to the Tower itself. Women who can channel and are not part of the Tower include wilders, who develop the ability in themselves, and women who have been sent away from the Tower for one reason or another, and of late there have been

reports concerning Aiel Wise Ones and the Windfinders of the Sea Folk. Women who can channel but are not Aes Sedai almost inevitably maintain an extremely low profile, frequently hiding their abilities from everyone around them and even moving to another town or village if those abilities are suspected. The reason is quite simple: fear that Aes Sedai might believe they were claiming to be Aes Sedai. Aes Sedai punish such false claims with a severity the recipient remembers the rest of her life.

While women who channel without the White Tower's blessing walk warily and keep from sight, men who can wield the One Power have much more to fear. They are hunted, most particularly by the Red Ajah, and once captured they are, by Tower law, carried to Tar Valon to be tried and gentled, cut off from the ability. Historically, few of these men have remained at large long enough to cause any widespread damage, but they have been objects of fear and loathing since the Breaking. Frequently even a man's own family will betray his secret to the Aes Sedai. What changes may come now that such men are being gathered into the Asha'man, only time will tell.

An Aes Sedai, who prefers to remain anonymous, and one male channeler were asked to describe the feeling of channeling the One Power. The following are their answers:

Aes Sedai: 'When I reach out to touch the True Source, to let the One Power fill me, I feel whole and complete in a way that makes me realize how empty and shallow my life is when I am not channeling. There is great joy – almost a rapture – and a feeling of being completely

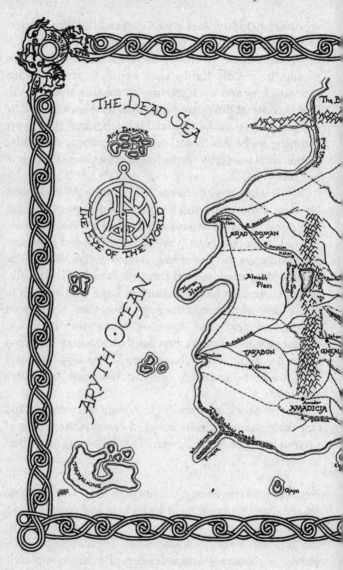

The earliest known map of the land

enveloped by the warmth and love of the Light. Only when I am channeling do I feel really alive. To release the Power is like shutting out the sunlight. I am empty without it, like a painting stripped of its color. I suspect that is why the training we receive as Aes Sedai is so demanding. If it were not, I doubt if any of us would have the strength of will to release the Power once we held it.'

Asha'man: 'I understand that the women feel a warmth of enveloping emotion. It is not like that for me. If anything, touching the source is like a retreat from all emotion, completely still and calm while at the same time aware of everything at once. The Power is not something that comes to you easily. Rather you must fight for it, struggle to grasp it and hold it, knowing that it will devour you if you lose that struggle. It is not unlike trying to balance upon the fury of a rushing avalanche: if you slip, it will pull you under and crush you without a moment's mercy, but if you can maintain that precarious balance, there is nothing you cannot do.

'And of course there is the taint, covering *saidin* like a poisonous slick on the surface of an otherwise fine wine. It is impossible to touch the Source without feeling the poison, but it doesn't matter, the Power is all-important . . .'

POLITICAL STRENGTH OF THE TOWER

The Aes Sedai claim that no one but a channeler can truly understand another channeler, and indeed fear, distrust, and hate are natural by-products of ignorance where

something as awesome as the One Power is concerned. Were they not backed by the political strength of the White Tower, the channelers would be prey to all manner of attacks from those who consider them witches. To avoid this, the Aes Sedai have seen to it that nearly all rulers have had an Aes Sedai advisor at one time or another. There are even those who say, though not within range of Aes Sedai, that the kings and queens are little more than puppets, serving the whims and dictates of the White Tower's hidden agendas. Though many rulers would certainly argue that point, none are likely to dispute the fact that the Aes Sedai meddle in many affairs that do not seem to concern them. It is said that Aes Sedai invented the Great Game – also known as the Game of Houses.

A BREED APART

The distrust with which Aes Sedai are often viewed is also caused by the fact that they *are* different. Channelling the One Power changes them. The ageless face of Aes Sedai is well known. One who is old enough to be a great-grandmother may have only a few gray hairs, and will have no lines or wrinkles. In addition, Aes Sedai live much longer than nonchannelers – though not so long as those Aes Sedai living during the Age of Legends – because channeling actually slows the aging process.

Before being raised to the level of Aes Sedai, each Accepted is required to swear three oaths while holding the Oath Rod, a *ter'angreal* that makes oaths binding. They are:

1) To speak no word that is not true.
2) To make no weapon with which one man may kill another.
3) Never to use the One Power as a weapon except against Shadowspawn, or in the last extreme defense of her own life or that of her Warder or another Aes Sedai.

The second oath was the first adopted, soon after the Tower's founding, at a time when the Breaking was a living memory to some Aes Sedai and stories of the War of the Shadow were well remembered. The first oath, while held to the letter, is often circumvented by careful speaking. It is believed that the last two are inviolable.

Of course the actual weaving of the threads of Power also serves to set Aes Sedai apart, for they accomplish works with the Power that are otherwise impossible, limited only by the Three Oaths, where nonchannelers must rely on their own brain, brawn, and man-made tools. Though Aes Sedai abilities certainly have limits, those limits are all but invisible to those who cannot channel.

TALENTS

Some Aes Sedai have a special ability in the use of the One Power called a Talent. These Talents manifest in specific areas and are seldom related to the strength of the individual's ability to channel. The most common Talent is Healing. Other major Talents include Cloud Dancing, the control of weather, and Earth Singing, which involves controlling movements of the Earth – for

example, preventing or causing earthquakes or avalanches. Minor Talents are seldom given a name, such as the ability to see *ta'veren* or to duplicate the chance-twisting effect of *ta'veren* (though in a very small area rarely covering more than a few square feet). Some major Talents, such as Traveling – the ability to shift from one place to another without crossing the intervening space – are only now being rediscovered. Others, such as Foretelling – the ability to foretell future events, but in a general way – and Delving – the locating of ores and occasionally their removal from the ground – are rare. Many Talents are now known only by their names and sometimes vague description, such as Aligning the Matrix, Spinning Earthfire, and Milking Tears.

One of the Talents until recently believed lost is that of Dreaming, thought to have vanished in 526 NE upon the death of Corianin Nedeal, the last acknowledged Dreamer. With the discovery of the Aiel dreamwalkers, and rumors of one among the Aes Sedai gifted with this Talent, it appears to have resurfaced in the Pattern.

Some Dreamers can dreamwalk, having the ability to enter *Tel'aran'rhiod*, as well as other people's dreams, but all Dreamers have visions within their dreams that go beyond anything they might see in either of these places, that seem to tell of future events in a fairly specific manner. Aes Sedai who have studied the phenomenon and written about it believe that these Dreamers' premonitions are not as certain to occur as those seen within a Foretelling, but concede that they are much more than mere dreams. The scholars believe these dreams indicate *possible* future events, and must therefore be carefully interpreted. Some say that these dreams are the Pattern's warning of what may happen

while there is still a chance to change the flow of the Pattern.

Those with the Foretelling, on the other hand, know that certain events *will* happen; that these events are firmly set into the fabric of the Pattern, although the Foretellers simply do not know when and how. Foretelling has often been erroneously considered a type of Dreaming, but it cannot be called at will, and some with the Talent only have one or two 'visions' in their entire lifetime. Foretelling is also linked to the Power (only those who can channel may have the Foretelling), but Dreaming and dreamwalking are not connected to the ability to channel. This may partially explain why there are more dreamwalkers among the Aiel Wise Ones than Dreamers among the Aes Sedai.

BECOMING AES SEDAI

Once a girl is discovered to have the ability to channel or learn to channel, she is brought to the White Tower for years of careful training.

Girls with the spark begin as novices, are given a course of study and chores designed to strengthen both mind and body as well as teach them the Aes Sedai way. They learn how to use their gift, and they learn the consequences of its misuse, for though the gift of channeling is given by nature, it can be taken away by a circle of thirteen Aes Sedai. This punishment is rarely executed except for the most extreme crimes against the Tower. As a warning, all novices are required to learn the name and crimes of all women who have suffered stilling within the White Tower's history. Until recently, no

woman had been judicially stilled in over one hundred years.

It normally takes five to ten years of study for a novice to be raised to the next level, that of Accepted. The rule and discipline during this time are very strict. On extremely rare occasions, wilders, women who already know how to channel, are allowed to bypass the novitiate level and move immediately to becoming Accepted, depending on their skills and maturity, but in the entire history of the White Tower this has been done only a handful of times, and it is more than controversial. All who wish to be raised to the level of Accepted must pass a final test utilizing a *ter'angreal* kept within a domed room in the bedrock beneath the White Tower. A candidate for Acceptance must strip naked and pass through the three silver arches of this *ter'angreal*, one at a time, and find her way back. Each candidate is allowed to refuse the test twice, but at the third refusal to enter, or if the novice cannot complete all three passes through the *ter'angreal* once begun, she is put out of the Tower, never to become Aes Sedai.

According to the Aes Sedai, this *ter'angreal* is said to present the worst fears of the candidate, allowing her to pass through her fears to gain Acceptance. The first passage is for what was, the second for what is, and the third for what will be. Some who enter never return. In each case the *ter'angreal* gives those being tested a compelling reason to stay within its grasp. To emerge they must want to be Aes Sedai more than anything else. Even the Aes Sedai who use it do not know if the worlds within the *ter'angreal* are real or illusion.

Upon completing this test, a successful candidate is Accepted among the Aes Sedai. As Accepted, she is

given a ring in the shape of the Great Serpent. The Great Serpent symbol was ancient before the Age of Legends began. It is a serpent eating its own tail, and has long symbolized time and eternity. The Serpent ring is a sign of sisterhood among the Aes Sedai. For an Accepted it is to be worn at all times on the third finger of the right hand. Full Aes Sedai may wear their ring on any finger or remove it completely as circumstances dictate. In addition, the successful candidate's plain white novice's dress is exchanged for one with seven narrow bands of color at both hem and cuffs. The Accepted are somewhat less confined by rules than the novices, and are allowed, within limits, to choose their own areas of study.

It usually takes many years for an Accepted to be raised to the level of a full Aes Sedai. The test for Aes Sedai involves demonstrating the ability to channel and maintain calm under 'extreme conditions,' but its exact nature is a closely guarded secret. To be raised Aes Sedai, the Accepted candidate must swear the Three Oaths on the Oath Rod. As a new Aes Sedai, she must declare which of the seven Ajahs she has chosen for her own; she now has the right to wear the shawl bearing the Flame of Tar Valon and fringed with the color of her Ajah.

Any woman who comes to the White Tower and can learn is taught, but obviously not all have the potential to become Aes Sedai. These are taught enough to be safe, to themselves and others, then sent away. For one who does have the potential, however, the Tower's patience seems endless. Slow learners, as opposed to those who attempt tests and fail, are encouraged to go on, and indeed, like other novices and Accepted, are not allowed to leave. Some reportedly have spent several decades in reaching

the Aes Sedai shawl. Reports of changes in these positions remain unconfirmed.

WARDERS

Once a woman has become a full Aes Sedai, she may bond a Warder. While most Ajahs hold that an Aes Sedai may have one Warder bonded to her at a time, there is no law concerning their number. Red sisters bond no Warders at all, while Greens bond as many as they wish.

The bonding is done with the One Power, and permanently links the Warder and the Aes Sedai. Ethically the Warder – also called *Gaidin*, Brother to Battle – must accede to the bonding voluntarily, but it has been known to be done against the Warder's will. The bond gives the Warder the gift of quick healing, the ability to go without food, water, or rest for long periods of time, and the ability to sense the taint of the Dark One at a distance. He can also sense certain things about his charge, including her death.

The bond allows the Aes Sedai to know if her Warder is alive, no matter how far away he might be, though it does not tell her the actual distance. When he dies she will know, through the bond, the moment and manner of his death. When a Warder dies, the surviving Aes Sedai often will bond another eventually, although rarely before the emotional upheaval caused by the death fades. Some Aes Sedai believe this upheaval is a result of the emotional control that is required for channeling, but no definitive proof has been offered. If the Warder lives but his Aes Sedai is killed, the Warder loses the will to live. Worse, he seems to seek death. Attempts to keep these Warders alive usually fail.

Many non-Aes Sedai believe that Warders' uncanny fighting ability must also be a product of the bond, for they are among the most fearsome warriors known, but the Aes Sedai deny this. They insist that Warders are chosen largely for their natural talent, which is then honed to a fine edge through rigorous training in the practice yards. Warders live wherever their Aes Sedai live, and have special quarters located at the White Tower. Their loyalties are completely linked to their Aes Sedai, and any disagreements are kept private between them. There have been cases of Aes Sedai marrying their Gaidin, primarily among the members of the Green Ajah, but for the most part, Aes Sedai–Warder relations are chaste. This chastity is not due to any particular rules or traditions, but rather to the fact that the pressures and demands of the Aes Sedai life preclude personal relationships beyond that of channeler and protector. There are indications that the Aes Sedai receive other benefits from the bond with their Gaidin, but their exact nature is a closely held secret.

THE HIERARCHY OF THE TOWER

Each Aes Sedai, except the Amyrlin Seat, belongs to one of the seven societies or Ajahs of the White Tower. These seven Ajahs are designated by color: Blue, Red, White, Green, Brown, Yellow, and Gray. Each follows a specific philosophy of the use of the One Power and the purposes of the Aes Sedai; each has its own agenda, its own internal style of rule, and its own traditions.

The White Tower is ruled by the Hall of the Tower, which consists of three representatives, called 'Sitters,'

from each Ajah; the Amyrlin Seat; and the Keeper of the Chronicles. This council creates all official policy.

The Amyrlin Seat rules over the Hall from a chair of the same name and is elected for life by the Hall of the Tower. She is the supreme head of the Tower, and is a member of *all* Ajahs, denoted by all seven colors upon her stole, regardless of the Ajah she was raised from. At the same time, she is considered to be of *no* Ajah, favoring none above another.

The Amyrlin is undoubtedly always one of the most, if not *the* most powerful single ruler within the Land. Elisane Tishar is generally believed to have been the first to hold the title of Amyrlin Seat of the Hall of the White Tower, over a hundred years before the Tower was actually finished. The exact date of her ascension has been lost, but it is known that she reigned as of the year 98 AB. Names of the Amyrlins who followed her until Artur Hawkwing's time have largely been lost (except perhaps in the secret files of the Tower). The following is a list of the Amyrlins from FY 939 (approximately) until the current two claimants were raised, in 999 NE. The dates of the first two are approximate, since all dates during the War of the Hundred Years are uncertain at best.

1) Bonwhin Meraighdin* (Red Ajah): FY 939(?) Stripped of staff and stole for trying to manipulate Artur Hawkwing to control the world. She was the last of the Red Ajah to be raised until Elaida a'Roihan deposed Siuan Sanche.

2) Deane Aryman (Blue Ajah): FY 992(?)–FY 1084(?).

3) Selame Necoine (Green Ajah): FY 1084(?)–5 NE.

4) Rabayn Marushta (White Ajah): 5–36 NE.

5)   Dalaine Ndaye (Gray Ajah): 36–64 NE.
6)   Edarna Noregovna (Blue Ajah): 64–115 NE.
7)   Balladare Arandaille (Brown Ajah): 115–142 NE.
8)   Medanor Eramandos (Gray Ajah): 142–171 NE.
9)   Kiyosa Natomo (Green Ajah): 171–197 NE.
10) Catala Lucanvalle (Yellow Ajah): 197–223 NE.
11) Elise Strang (Gray Ajah): 223–244 NE.
12) Comarra Zepava (Blue Ajah): 244–276 NE.
13) Serenia Latar (Gray Ajah): 276–306 NE.
14) Doniella Alievin (Brown Ajah): 306–332 NE.
15) Aliane Senican (White Ajah): 332–355 NE.
16) Suilin Escanda (Blue Ajah): 355–396 NE.
17) Nirelle Coidevwin (Green Ajah): 396–419 NE.
18) Ishara Nawan (Blue Ajah): 419–454 NE.
19) Cerilla Marodred (Gray Ajah): 454–476 NE.
20) Igaine Luin (Brown Ajah): 476–520 NE.
21) Beryl Marle (White Ajah): 520–533 NE.
22) Eldaya Tolen (Blue Ajah): 533–549 NE.
23) Alvera Ramosanya (Yellow Ajah): 549–578 NE.
24) Shein Chunla (Green Ajah): 578–601 NE.
25) Gerra Kishar (Gray Ajah): 601–638 NE.
26) Varuna Morrigan (Green Ajah): 638–681 NE.
27) Cemaile Sorenthaine (Gray Ajah): 681–705 NE.
28) Marasale Jureen (Yellow Ajah): 705–732 NE.
29) Feragaine Saralman (Blue Ajah): 732–754 NE.
30) Myriam Copan (Green Ajah): 754–797 NE.
31) Zeranda Tyrim (Brown Ajah): 797–817 NE.
32) Parenia Demalle (Gray Ajah): 817–866 NE.
33) Sereille Bagand (White Ajah): 866–890 NE.
34) Aleis Romlin (Green Ajah): 890–922 NE.
35) Kirin Melway (Brown Ajah) 922–950 NE.
36) Noane Masadim (Blue Ajah): 950–973 NE.
37) Tamra Ospenya (Blue Ajah): 973–979 NE.

38) Sierin Vayu (Gray Ajah): 979–984 NE.
39) Marith Jaen (Blue Ajah): 984–988 NE.
40) Siuan Sanche* (Blue Ajah): 988–999 NE. Stripped
    of staff and stole in a move still surrounded by con-
    troversy (some say it led to the division of the
    Tower), and stilled, along with her Keeper of the
    Chronicles.
41) Elaida a'Roihan (Red Ajah): 999 NE. Amyrlin of the
    Tower in Tar Valon.
41) Egwene al'Vere (none): 999 NE. Amyrlin of the
    Tower in Exile.

In 999 NE, open division occurred in the Tower for the
first time since its founding. Both 'Towers' claim the right
to name an Amyrlin. Only time will tell which may survive.

Considered equal, if not slightly superior, to any king
or queen, theoretically at least the Amyrlin Seat has
absolute power over all the Aes Sedai. In actuality, according to sources close to the Tower, the Amyrlin must
usually engage in fairly sophisticated political give and
take with the Hall to keep her reign strong. It has been
suggested that the fall of Amyrlin Siuan Sanche, the
youngest to assume stole and staff (until the Tower's split
in 999 NE), may have been caused by her failure to maintain this precarious balance, though only the Tower
knows for certain.

*Since the Breaking of the World only three Amyrlins have been
stripped of stole and staff. The first, Tetsuan, predates Bonwhin and
was rumored to have been involved in the betrayal of Manetheren
during the Trolloc Wars. Tetsuan was of the Red Ajah. Breakdown
by Ajah: 11 Blue, 9 Gray, 7 Green, 5 White, 3 Yellow, 2 Red.

Second in authority to the Amyrlin is the Keeper of the Chronicles. She is chosen by the Amyrlin, usually upon her own ascension to the Seat, and is traditionally from the same Ajah. Her badge of office also is a stole, about a hand wide, in the color of her Ajah, though the Keeper does not represent her Ajah. She speaks only for the Amyrlin, who represents all Aes Sedai. The Keeper also acts as secretary to the Amyrlin, and oversees the official business of the Tower.

THE SEVEN AJAHS

Each Ajah has its Sitters in the Hall to represent it, and each has its own internal ruler or ruling council, but the head of a given Ajah is not necessarily also a Sitter for that Ajah – if not, the Sitters are believed answerable to the head of their Ajah for their actions in the Hall. The Aes Sedai are loath to release information on the individual Ajahs, much less the actual identity of their leaders, who are known only within each Ajah.

It is known that the Red Ajah's primary goal is to protect the Land from all men who can touch the True Source. They hunt down men who can channel and bring them to the Tower to be gentled. They refuse to bond any Warders, possibly because their purpose makes it difficult for them to trust or work closely with any man. The Red Ajah, the largest, is led by a single woman, who wields a great deal of power.

The Blue Ajah is also run by a single very powerful woman, and is perhaps the most influential of the Ajahs, although one of the smaller ones. The primary focus of the Blue Ajah is to champion worthy causes (thought

worthy by Aes Sedai standards) and to promote justice. Skilled at political maneuvering, Blues are also able administrators. Since Artur Hawkwing's time, more Amyrlins have been raised from the Blue than from any other Ajah.

Forsaking mundane life in general, members of the Brown Ajah are dedicated to seeking and preserving knowledge. Unlike the Blue and Red Ajahs, the Brown Ajah is run by a ruling council. The Browns are primarily responsible for the procurement and preservation of the vast cache of books and scrolls which help make the Tower library the largest single repository of knowledge in the Land. Much that is known of artifacts or new Talents has been discovered by sisters of the Brown Ajah.

The Green Ajah is also known as the Battle Ajah. Their primary goal is to hold themselves ready for Tarmon Gai'don, the Last Battle with the Dark One. Fierce fighters of Shadowspawn, they are also known for their appreciation of men, a trait fairly rare among the other Ajahs. Green sisters do not believe in limiting themselves to only one Warder. Some have been known to bond three or more at one time. While this fact is a sometime source of humor among sisters of the other Ajahs, it is not entirely a frivolous practice. During the Trolloc Wars the Greens' additional Warders made a positive difference in battle.

Those Aes Sedai with an especially strong Talent for Healing join the Yellow Ajah. Yellow sisters are wholly devoted to Healing sickness and injury as well as finding new cures and new methods of using the One Power to restore health, though in truth, few believe any better method exists than the one known since the Breaking.

The Gray Ajah are mediators, seeking harmony and consensus. Many kingdoms use Gray sisters to insure that their treaties with one another will hold, though there is always the fear that these treaties, when concluded with Aes Sedai aid, may further the Tower's goals more than those of the original parties.

The White Ajah, unlike all the others, avoid both the world and worldly knowledge. Questions of philosophy engross them, and the search for truth is their all-consuming passion.

While neither the White Tower nor any Ajah has ever made their numbers known, rough approximations of size are possible with respect to the Ajahs. With a membership encompassing nearly one in five of Aes Sedai at the time of writing (an indication of the perceived importance of their avowed primary task), the Red Ajah is certainly the largest. Close behind comes the Green, followed in order by the Gray, the Brown, the Yellow, the Blue, and finally, the White Ajah. It seems that these sizes have remained roughly in the same proportions since the Breaking, with seldom a shift of more than one place in the ranking, but no one can say what effect current events will have.

There is an eighth Ajah, though it has no official Sitters in the Hall, and historically has never been mentioned to anyone outside the Aes Sedai save with vehement denial. Most Aes Sedai refuse to believe it exists. It is the Black Ajah. Its sisters are said to have forsworn all their oaths, and serve only the Shadow. They are rumored to walk the halls of the Tower disguised as members of the other seven Ajahs.

SPIES AND INFORMANTS

All Ajahs, except perhaps the White, have their own 'eyes-and-ears' that gather information and even spy for them. These informants are not themselves Aes Sedai, and are loyal only to the particular Ajah, and in some cases, the particular individual Aes Sedai, who arranged their service. There are rumored cases of 'double agents,' but few are brave enough to cross the Aes Sedai in that way. Informants for the Yellow Ajah look for outbreaks of disease; those loyal to the Browns look for caches of books and knowledge; those for the Greens relay information concerning military matters; and the Blue informants report on matters of political intrigue.

Each Ajah has one sister as the head of the Ajah's intelligence network whose job is to compile and coordinate the information gathered by the eyes-and-ears and bring it to the head or ruling council of that Ajah. Each Ajah then decides what, if any, of that information it is willing to share with the Tower as a whole through their Sitters. Knowledge they decide to share with the Amyrlin Seat traditionally is passed through the Keeper. There is no doubt that the Aes Sedai believe that knowledge is power. Perhaps because of this, no Ajah ever shares *all* its information with the Hall. Or with the Amyrlin.

The Amyrlin has her own vast intelligence network, and is therefore not totally dependent on the Ajahs. Her designated overseer is officially the head of intelligence for the entire Tower, but in actuality is answerable only to the Amyrlin herself.

The Amyrlin is not the only Aes Sedai with a personal information network. In fact, only the Whites and those Aes Sedai who spend their lives at study inside the Tower

are known to lack one. Individual Aes Sedai are not bound to share their information with either the Tower or their own Ajah, and in fact frequently share nothing. All these overlapping but unrelated networks give rise to a vast, tangled web of secrets and intrigue, with each Aes Sedai concentrating first and foremost on her own personal goals, and (similarly) each Ajah.

The system would never work at all except for the fact that the Aes Sedai work more on tradition than on rules, and according to tradition, one sister will not interfere in what another Aes Sedai is doing unless she honestly believes it is leading to certain disaster.

THE WHITE TOWER

Each Ajah occupies one of seven pie-shaped sections in the top half of the huge main Tower containing living quarters for its members as well as meeting rooms and workrooms reserved for that Ajah, though some members of the Brown have rooms in or near the huge library as well. These sections are equal in size, although the Ajahs are not, but even the largest Ajah, the Red, does not come anywhere near filling its allotted space. The main Hall of the Tower and all common rooms are located in the lower half of the building.

The Tower has never been fully occupied since it was originally built, and in fact seems to be losing rather than gaining inhabitants. Though they are careful never to say so near any sisters of the Red Ajah, some Aes Sedai believe that the removal of male channelers from the gene pool, coupled with the fact that female Aes Sedai rarely marry and have children themselves, is the cause of a

gradual purging of channelers from the population over
the last three thousand years.

THE LIBRARY

The largest structure next to the Tower itself within the
Aes Sedai compound is the Great Library. Containing
vast storage as well as offices and workrooms, it is
rumored to have as many secret rooms as it has open
sections, and innumerable objects of power no doubt lie
within it. Though only partially open to outsiders, there
is little doubt that it contains one of the greatest collec-
tions of knowledge, if not the greatest, in the world.
This library alone would guarantee Tar Valon's place as
a great city, even if the White Tower were not located
within it.

There have always been rumors of a closed section of
the White Tower library, supposedly open only to a
select few even among the Aes Sedai. The White Tower
has never issued a direct denial of its existence – so far
as can be determined by any public record – but then
again, given the widely known devious nature of Aes
Sedai, it is entirely possible for them to offer denials
which, on close study, prove to be no denials at all,
when in fact they could have made the statement quite
straightforward, all because they believed that pretending that they were hiding something, or that they were
doing what in actuality they were not, would aid in gaining a goal. Such actions have been documented many
times; such a list would be as large as this volume.
Another always whispered rumor, which, interestingly
enough, the White Tower has also never contradicted

straight out, holds that there is a Tower law covering the secret repository; by that law, unauthorized attempts to penetrate the records carry severe penalties, and revealing either the existence of the repository or its contents is on a level with treason or rebellion. Additionally, *this law itself* is supposed to be a part of the repository, thus completing the circle of secrecy in a manner that would be incredible among any except the Aes Sedai or the Seanchan.

TAR VALON

The city of Tar Valon is governed by a council of Aes Sedai chosen by the Hall of the Tower. This council oversees a staff of non-Aes Sedai clerks and bureaucrats that actually handles the day-to-day administration of the city. This job is complicated by the fact that Tar Valon and its White Tower attract people of all countries and all ranks. They cross the great Ogier-built bridges to the city on matters ranging from state visits to pilgrimages, or to conclude treaties or business deals. Though the island is only three or four miles across, with much of the land given over to parks and gardens, representatives of almost every race and country of the land live and work within its walls.

Tar Valon's centralized location between the Borderlands of the north and the kingdoms of the southeast and west make it ideal for trade; the River Erinin allows water-borne traffic, while the great bridges give land caravans easy access to many major roadways.

Since Tar Valon was first established, in 98 AB, the city has never fallen to invaders, and has only rarely suffered

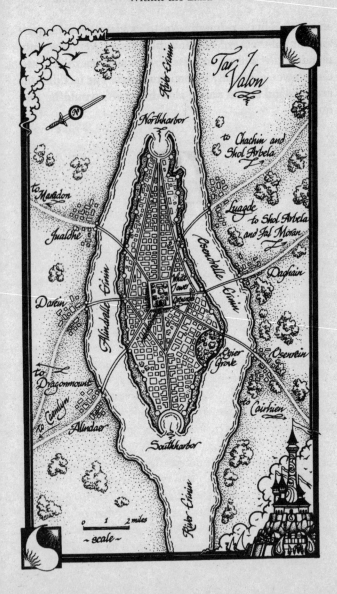

an attack. This is primarily due to its identity as the heart and soul of the Aes Sedai and their Tower. Very few commanders are willing to face women who can wield the One Power, especially in large numbers. The fact that the entire island city is walled also deters any would-be conquerors.

Chapter 25

The Children of the Light

Sigil of the Children of the Light   The Golden Sun; the Sunflare.

Banner   A golden flaring sun on a field of white; edged with gold.

HISTORY

The Children of the Light were founded in FY 1021, during the War of the Hundred Years, by Lothair Mantelar, as a priesthood dedicated to proselytizing against Darkfriends. Over the turbulent century that followed, the group evolved from preachers to fighters. At first they only fought as needed to defend themselves while preaching, but as the chaos of the war years grew, so

did the perceived need for military intervention against Darkfriends. The Children gradually turned from preaching against Darkfriends to actually fighting them, until by approximately FY 1111 the Children of the Light had become a full-fledged military society dedicated to the defeat of the Dark One and the destruction of all Darkfriends. Little has survived from these early formative years to tell how gentle preachers became the ruthless crusaders of the current day.

PURPOSE

Also known disparagingly as 'Whitecloaks,' because of their trademark white cloak, the Children of the Light believe they have been called by the Light to do battle with the Shadow. These men follow very strict ascetic beliefs, and usually give the impression that they alone know the truth and the path to righteousness. They seem determined to inflict their version of the Truth on any who disagree with either their philosophy or their methods.

Though they would be offended to hear it, the organization of the Children has some similarities to that of the Aes Sedai. Each society is controlled by one high-ranking individual; each owes allegiance to no nation, and is therefore not limited to one kingdom or region. The central headquarters of the Children, the Fortress of Light, is located in Amadicia's capital city of Amador, but only a small percentage of the total membership of the Children are ever in attendance at the Fortress at any one time. The majority are usually dispersed throughout the Land, constantly traveling in their search for Darkfriends.

Unlike the Aes Sedai, the Children have no oaths to prevent them from taking lives or harming ordinary people. Though they are sworn to do battle only against Darkfriends and creatures of Shadow, each individual captain or commander is left to decide what actually constitutes the difference between a Darkfriend and an innocent, and to determine the guilt and the punishment for the former. According to Whitecloak definitions, all Aes Sedai are Darkfriends, or at least evil, as are any who support them. Their claim is based on the belief that it was the Aes Sedai and the One Power that destroyed the world during the Breaking. There is no doubt that the Children and their attitudes are responsible for the intolerance of Aes Sedai in Amadicia. Anyone with the ability to channel is outlawed there. By law any channelers are to be imprisoned or exiled, but in actuality most are killed while 'resisting arrest.'

The Children do not openly rule a given city or province. Whereas no Amyrlin Seat has ever denied her rule of Tar Valon and its territory, the Children of the Light insist that Amadicia is a sovereign nation, answerable only to its reigning king or queen. However, while the monarch may rule the country in name, it is the Children and their Lord Captain Commander who rule it in fact, through their military and political might.

The Fortress of Light, in Amador, is the center of the Children's power and bureaucracy. It is there, in the great hall under the Dome of Truth, that the commanders of the Children gather to determine policy for the entire organization. Under the gilded dome lit by a thousand hanging lamps, or within his personal audience chamber (which has a solid gold sun inlaid into the wood floor), the head of the Whitecloaks, the Lord Captain

Commander, presides over the Council of the Anointed, which consists of approximately a dozen of the highest-ranking and most favored Lord Captains, as well as the High Inquisitor.

THE HAND OF THE LIGHT

The High Inquisitor – currently Rhadam Asunawa – ranks only slightly below the Lord Captain Commander. Though command for the military originates with the council, he alone issues the orders for the investigative Hand of the Light.

The majority of the Children, from the Lord Captains to the lowest trooper or recruit, are soldiers, dedicated to battle for the Light. They face death as a part of their duty. Members of the Hand of the Light, however, rarely if ever risk death in battle. They serve instead as interrogators or occupation forces. The fact that they rarely participate in the actual fighting, along with their morally superior attitude, frequently earns them the resentment of the regular troops.

Known among themselves as the Hand that digs out Truth, they are more often known to others as the Questioners. This nickname, however, is seldom used to their faces. Members often act as if they are a law unto themselves, entirely separate from the rest of the Children. Although technically under the command of the Lord Captain Commander, they usually answer only to the High Inquisitor. Ranks within the Hand of the Light are largely the same as in the regular order, with the exception of the Lord Inquisitors, who are equal in rank to the Lord Captains.

The avowed purpose of the Hand of the Light is to discover the truth in disputations and uncover Darkfriends. They are hampered by few rules, and torture is used extensively during most of their inquiries. According to their (anonymous) detractors, they have never had an innocent subject. In most cases they *know* the truth they seek; it is simply up to the Questioners involved to force their victim to confess it. Their methods, and the fact that anyone at all may be put to the question, including other Children of the Light, have made them deeply feared, within the Children and without.

THE SPYMASTERS

The intelligence branch of the Children consists of 'eyes-and-ears' spread throughout all kingdoms and provinces. All the gathered information is controlled and disseminated by a spymaster. In true espionage fashion, however, the 'official' spymaster and the man who is actually trusted with the delicate job of keeping the Lord Captain Commander well informed are not the same. It is not surprising in an organization as controversial as the Children that they believe even the true identity of the head of intelligence must be protected. Of course, the Lord Captain Commander is not the only Child to have access to intelligence information. According to high-level sources, many of the Lord Captains also have their own personal networks of eyes-and-ears.

ORGANIZATIONAL STRUCTURE

The Children of the Light are always deployed as mounted cavalry, usually in groups of about one hundred; they can move very quickly when necessary. The highest rank among the soldiery is Lord Captain. A Lord Captain usually commands a legion, which is officially two thousand men, though any given legion in the Children may actually be larger, and is often smaller. Below Lord Captain, the officers' ranks progress through Senior Lieutenant, Lieutenant, and Under-lieutenant. Below Under-lieutenant is the Hundredman, one who theoretically commands a hundred soldiers. In practice, the actual number varies widely.

The number of legions within the Children varies at any given time. Not all units are organized into legions, and not all are commanded by a Lord Captain. Some of the smaller units may be commanded by a Lieutenant or even an Under-Lieutenant; except when the Hundredman and his men are functioning alone, Lieutenant is usually the lowest rank to hold a position of command, though they usually act as support officers for the higher ranks. A Hundredman ranks below officers but above common soldiers and is usually a common soldier who has risen. When a Lord Captain commands a unit or legion, the Lieutenant chosen as second-in-command is given the temporary rank of Second Captain to differentiate him from any other Lieutenants within the unit.

Below the officer and Hundredman are Bannermen, with Second Bannermen below them, then Squadmen and Second Squadmen. Below these are the file leaders and the regular troopers. Within the Children the actual personnel assignments are as flexible as the size of the units,

and are changed often to suit the nature of the objective. There have even been times, though rare, when members of the soldiery have been 'loaned' to the Questioners. Though the Questioners have been known to fight, it is doubtful that they are ever 'loaned' as regular troops.

The Children of the Light always wear a pure white cloak or tabard over their clothes and armor. The left breast of each has a golden sunburst worked into it, a symbol of the Light they are sworn to follow. All officers' cloaks and tabards are further adorned with silver lightning bolts for under-officers, and golden stars or knots in increasing quantity to indicate rank for higher officers. Each Child is armored with a conical metal helm and plain breastplate. It is a matter of great pride to each member of the order to keep his white cloak spotless and his armor bright. Swords are worn by all Children, though never in the audience chambers of the Lord Captain Commander or beneath the Dome of Truth.

Members of the Hand of the Light order wear the same white cloak or tabard, but these 'Questioners' have a blood-red shepherd's crook emblazoned behind the sunburst. The High Inquisitor wears only the red crook, devoid of the flaring sun, as if to suggest his position allows him to stand outside the Children.

Chapter 26

The Military of the Land

'Time to dance with Jak o' the Shadows.'
— SAYING OF THE BAND OF THE RED HAND

NATIONAL ARMIES

PART OF THE reason the Children of the Light have thrived without serious challenge is the general lack of military organization and discipline throughout the nations of the land. Since the War of the Hundred Years, when most military science was lost, armed forces have lapsed into very casual arrangements.

The armies that do exist are in large part levied only when needed. Each levy is usually made up of a group of partially trained men who owe personal allegiance to the noble who gathers and finances them, rather than to any particular nation. This Lord or General uses his own rank and money not only to finance his unit, but to buy commissions or promotions as necessary.

The nearest thing to a standing army in most nations is a formation owing allegiance to that nation's throne.

These formations can run as large as five or six thousand men, which, while quite large by modern standards, pale beside the standing armies of tens of thousands commonplace during Hawkwing's time. The main military groups of the last centuries include: Amadicia's Guardians of the Gate; the Queen's Guard in Andor; the Legion of the Wall (now dispersed) in Ghealdan; the Companions in Illian; Mayene's Winged Guards; the King's Life Guard and the Panarch's Legion (both now dispersed) in Tarabon; the Defenders of the Stone in Tear; the Tower Guard of the White Tower; and, of course, the Children of the Light.

Perhaps because of the way the Game of Houses is played in Cairhien, there has never been such an army there, since even a monarch would want the power to remain centered in the House, not the throne. Altara's and Murandy's rulers are really not powerful enough to form them. Arad Doman has never had such a formation; the king there is elected by the Council of Merchants and can be removed by a three-quarters vote; such a body of soldiers would shift the balance of power unacceptably. Because of their proximity to the Blight, the Borderlands nations are organized for war as a whole, and therefore have no separate military formations.

ORDER OF COMMAND

Generally, aside from Captain-General or Lord Captain Commander or some other title indicating supreme command, the highest official rank is Captain. In the Queen's Guard of Andor and the Children of the Light

this is followed by Senior Lieutenant, Lieutenant, and Under-lieutenant. In general there is no set size for the formation commanded by any particular rank. The generic term for a unit of infantry of any size is a 'company' and of cavalry either a 'company' or a 'squadron,' and in any case it is usually given the name of the lord or officer commanding.

Among cavalry, NCO ranks are squadman and bannerman. The bannerman for a unit usually acts as the recruiting officer as well. Senior bannerman and senior squadman are 'floating' ranks, indicating that the individual is just that within his unit, whatever its size. Thus one could be the senior bannerman of Captain Selwin's company or the senior bannerman of the Queen's Guard or possibly both. In any case, the 'senior' designation is more than honorary; it conveys authority over others of that rank.

Among infantry, the NCO ranks are file leader (the equivalent of a squadman) and bannerman. There are also senior file leaders and senior bannermen. These designations are reached in the same way and carry the same sort of authority as their colleagues in the cavalry.

This rather simple organization has been sufficient for some centuries because most battles were between armies with five thousand to ten thousand men on either side. There have been battles with as many as twenty thousand to thirty thousand on either side, but these are rare. In these larger battles, higher command has almost always gone to the nobility and has depended in large part on how the nobles ranked themselves and their Houses.

WEAPONS AND ARMOR

Most infantry are armed with pikes, spears, bills, or (occasionally) axes, with the pikemen the most usual. Spear, bill, and axe troops are all considered more mobile than pikemen, yet pikes are preferred, since they stand the best chance against a mounted attack, and most in the present day think of battles primarily in terms of mounted conflict. In addition to these weapons most footmen carry knives, and sometimes even a short-sword. Longer swords are practically unknown among the infantry, as they are considered too unwieldy for close combat.

The average footman usually wears a jerkin of padded or studded leather, and some sort of helmet. Jerkins covered with metal discs or plates are not uncommon, and mail shirts are sometimes used, but actual plate armor is very rare.

Cavalry armament and armor vary widely from nation to nation, and within nations from one noble's retinue to the next. The armor ranges from full plate-and-mail for both horse and rider in the heavy cavalry, to a steel helmet, back and breast plates, and gauntlets in the light cavalry. Some mounted units have far less armor, relying on skill for their protection. Mounted units use various combinations of lance, sword, axe, mace, and horsebow.

Merchants' guards, even though usually mounted, have at most a helmet and a studded disc-sewn jerkin as armor. Swords are their most common weapons, though some carry bows or the occasional lance.

During the War of Power many weapons were made using the Power. Among these were very special swords

made so that they would not shatter or break, and would never lose their edge. Some, made for soldiers, bore no special mark. The sword of the Malkieri Kings was one of these. Others were made for lord-generals, and bore a heron or other mark deep within the metal. Today these heron-marked blades are very rare and are awarded only to those skilled enough to be given the title of blademaster. Because the number of blademasters exceeds the number of swords that survived the war, many of the current heron-marked swords are not Aes Sedai work. They are, however, the finest steel that men can temper.

THE BAND OF THE RED HAND

The huge battles of Hawkwing's rise, with armies of two hundred thousand men or more on either side, and of the Trolloc Wars, where reportedly as many as three hundred thousand men often engaged even larger numbers of Trollocs and Myrddraal, required a more detailed command structure than that currently in use in most nations. In those times a Banner was commanded by a Banner-General, a Legion by a Lieutenant-General, and a Great Legion by a Captain-General. The army itself was commanded by a Marshal-General, which was a 'temporary' title given to the Captain-General chosen for overall command. This halted any arguments over noble rank.

Only in the last few years has any current commander begun to attempt a return to that earlier, more efficient military structure. That commander is Matrim 'Mat' Cauthon; his command, the Band of the Red Hand. Cauthon, believed by many to be a Lord, is actually a

young farmer from the Two Rivers district of Andor. The son of Abell and Natti Cauthon, he is said to be *ta'veren* and is also extremely lucky. No one is certain where he gained his amazing knowledge of military strategy, or the unusual black raven-crested spear that serves as his personal weapon. He is known to be an associate of the Dragon Reborn.

The original Band of the Red Hand was a unit of legendary heroes during the Trolloc Wars. It is said they were the last to fall to the Trollocs, guarding King Aemon himself, when Manetheren died. Whether he knows the history behind the name of his group or not, Cauthon seems to be attempting to re-create the standardization of size, designation, and composition of units that has not been seen since before the War of the Hundred Years.

Though his final design is as yet unknown, Cauthon's organization of the Band in Maerone has already shown a sophistication currently lacking in most other levies or armies. At Maerone the Band's strength was approximately six thousand men, roughly divided into one half mounted and one half foot. The mounted units were divided into two equal groups of about fifteen hundred each, approximately the size of a banner (roughly fifteen hundred horse, or three thousand infantry), which was the basic military unit used at the highest point in military science of this Age, beginning a few centuries before the Trolloc Wars and lasting until the collapse of military science (as well as everything else) during the War of the Hundred Years.

The mounted units, commanded by Lord Talmanes Delovinde and Lord Nalesean Aldiaya, were further divided into six squadrons, each consisting of ten troops. It was the first troop of cavalry that led the unit and had

the bannerman bearing the unit's colors, the banner with the Red Hand.

The infantry, commanded by Captain Daerid Ondin, was divided into twelve companies, each consisting of five squads. Each squad mixed pikemen, billmen, and crossbowmen, with approximately one archer or crossbowman to four pike or billmen.

Those close to the Band suggest that Cauthon wants to increase the ratio of archers and crossbowmen. If this is indeed his plan, it would bring the ratio more into line with the numbers during the Trolloc Wars, when there was a preponderance of crossbowmen and archers.

Chapter 27

Andor

'Forward the White Lion of Andor!'
— BATTLE CRY OF THE QUEEN'S GUARD

 Sigil A rampant white lion; the White Lion.

Banner A white lion rampant on a field of red.

Capital city Caemlyn.

Symbols include the Lion Throne and the Rose Crown of Andor.

HISTORY

THE LARGEST NATION of the land, Andor is also one of the oldest. Its sovereignty dates from Artur Hawkwing's death, at the onset of the War of the Hundred Years,

before which it was a province under Hawkwing's governor Endara Casalain. The Royal Line can actually trace its rule of the area to a time before Hawkwing, for Endara was the daughter of Joal Ramedar, the last King of Aldeshar before Hawkwing's conquest. Upon the death of the High King, the governor's daughter Ishara joined with his greatest general, Souran Maravaile, to take control of the province from her mother and make it a nation. Ishara became the first Queen of Andor, and the blood of her line has been decisive in determining all subsequent successions.

Many traditions of Andor were established during Ishara's reign. Unlike most other rulers who emerged at the time of the High King's death, Ishara was wise enough to know that no one ruler would be able to take and hold the entire empire. Instead she set her sights on taking no larger a piece than she could actually defend. As a result the original boundaries of Andor included only the provincial capital of Caemlyn and a few surrounding villages. It took her five years to expand her control to the River Erinin, but the land she held was unquestionably hers; other rulers of the time were so greedy for new conquests that they seldom kept the lands they took. This tradition of cautious expansion continued throughout the reigns of all the Queens who followed.

Ishara knew that to survive as a nation Andor would need a strong military presence as well as powerful allies. Many historians believe that it was these needs that motivated her to marry Souran Maravaile, for he was Hawkwing's finest general and a brilliant military strategist. Others believe that love must have played at least a small role since, for all his abilities, Souran was only a commoner while she was of royal blood. They argue that

she would have had to love him to marry so far beneath her station. Souran was commanding the siege of Tar Valon at the time of Hawkwing's death and for almost a year after. Many believe that he had to love Ishara to be willing to break the siege at her request after having held it so long. Whether or not love was involved, Ishara knew she needed both Maravaile's army and the White Tower's goodwill. Marrying Souran gave her the first; sending her eldest daughter to study in the Tower gained her the second as well as an Aes Sedai advisor named Ballair. She was the first ruler to have an Aes Sedai advisor.

SUCCESSION

The most widely known tradition of Andor is that only a queen may sit upon the Lion Throne and wear the Rose Crown, never a king. (This initially arose when none of the royal sons survived the War of the Hundred Years, but eventually became law.) The eldest daughter is named Daughter-Heir. By law she is first sent to the Tower to study, then ascends the throne upon her mother's death or retirement. Her eldest brother, styled First Prince of the Sword, is sworn to protect and defend his sister with his life. The First Prince is trained from childhood to command the Queen's armies in times of war and to be her military advisor. If the Queen has no surviving brother, she appoints the First Prince.

When there is no surviving daughter, the throne is given to the nearest female blood relative. Succession is based not just on close relation to the former Queen, but on the degree of blood in matrilineal descent from Ishara. Such matters of lineage have become quite complex, since

all the Great Houses are related after years of intermarriage, and the question of succession has led to bloodshed when the Houses do not agree. These conflicts are known outside of Andor as the Andoran Wars of Succession. Andorans simply refer to them as 'disturbances,' refusing to acknowledge that their system for selecting an heir could possibly lead to war. There have been three wars for succession in Andor. The last of these 'disturbances' resulted in Morgase Trakand, By the Grace of the Light, Queen of Andor, Defender of the Realm, Protector of the People, High Seat of House Trakand, becoming ruler of Andor only after a long and bitter struggle. The Daughter-Heir, Tigraine, had disappeared under mysterious circumstances and was declared dead. Queen Mordrellen had died of grief with no available heirs, leaving a void which led to the Third Andoran War for Succession. Morgase eventually convinced the strongest Houses of Andor to support her claim as cousin and nearest blood relation to Tigraine. To solidify her position, Morgase went so far as to marry the former Daughter-Heir's widower, Prince Taringail Damodred of Cairhien, despite the fact that he was well known to have been a bad husband to Tigraine. Morgase bore two children by Taringail, the Daughter-Heir, Elayne, and the First Prince of the Sword, Gawyn, and adopted his and Tigraine's son Galadedrid.

Upon assuming the throne, Morgase immediately proved herself a shrewd and able leader by pardoning everyone who had opposed her. This action did much to prevent the festering animosities that have led to deadly scheming in so many other lands. She was determined that the Game of Houses, *Daes Dae'mar*, would take no root in Andor. Recently Morgase vanished and is believed dead.

The sign of House Trakand is a silver keystone. Morgase's personal sign is three golden keys.

NATIONAL STABILITY

Andor is a large and wealthy realm reaching from the Mountains of Mist to the River Erinin, though the decrease in population has prevented her Queens from exercising their control of lands west of the River Manetherendrelle for several generations.

The people of Andor are usually fair-skinned, often with blue eyes and blond hair, though dark hair and eyes are common. Andoran women usually wear dresses with square-cut necks showing little if any cleavage, and fitted sleeves. These dresses are occasionally embroidered with flowers and leaves, and are worn belted at the waist. Highborn ladies' dresses are usually made of silk, with the embroidery and belt in metallic threads. Commoners wear the same basic style of dress, but of wool, usually with higher necklines and with an apron.

Andoran men wear trousers and shirts with a coat over all. The coat is made with turned-back cuffs and an upstanding collar. Among the nobility the material is often silk or brocade, and the coat is often embroidered in metallic threads. Common men wear strong serviceable wool.

Men and women both wear cloaks over their clothes as needed.

Palace servants wear a livery of red with white collars and cuffs and the White Lion of Andor upon their chests.

Exports such as wool, precious metals and iron work, tabac, and grain give Andor a healthy economy; the

Andoran mark is more highly valued and has more weight in gold than 'equivalent' coins of other nations.

Andor's success is also due in large part to the strength of her army, made up primarily of the Queen's Guard. For the last three reigns the heart and soul of the Guard has been one man, Captain-General Gareth Bryne, now retired. His leadership was largely responsible for keeping Andor strong despite continued pressure from outside forces. Andor has always been subject to pressure from the Children of the Light, possibly due to Andor's relationship with the White Tower, and Andor and Cairhien have been at war more times than any two nations except Tear and Illian. Ironically, since the Aiel War Andor has also provided Cairhien with nearly as much grain as Tear, despite the animosity.

THE QUEEN'S GUARD

When Andor goes to war, the Guard and the army are commanded by the First Prince of the Sword, but the Queen often rides with them as well. There are many stories told of such courageous rulers as Queen Modrellein, who alone and unarmed, carried the Lion Banner into the midst of the Tairen army to rally her troops. In peacetime the guard is responsible for upholding the Queen's law and keeping the peace. In areas far distant from the capital, members of the local militia assume the livery and duties of the Queen's Guard, though they lack the polish of the guardsmen, and their uniforms are often threadbare.

The uniforms of the Queen's Guard include a red undercoat, gleaming mail and plate armor, and a brilliant

red cloak. Long white collars hang over the armor, and white cuffs gleam at the wrist. Their helmets are conical with barred visors, and they often carry lances with thin red streamers fluttering from their tips. High-ranking officers wear knots of rank on their shoulder. The Captain-General wears four golden knots and wide gold bands on his white cuffs.

CAEMLYN

The capital, Caemlyn, is one of the most beautiful cities in the land, second only to Tar Valon, though its natives may argue that ranking. Like a gleaming crown upon its gently rolling hills, the city is actually made up of two sections, the New City, built well under two thousand years ago by the hands of man alone, and the ancient Inner City, much of which bears the mark of Ogier stone-masons. A great fifty-foot wall of silver white stone surrounds most of the official perimeter of the city, broken by tall round towers that flank massive arched gates. Outside the wall, buildings cluster thickly like lichen to a log, spreading outward from the glittering mosaic of the city in a gradual dispersion. Within its outer walls the city is laid out in a crazy quilt of streets and byways, with towers and domes gleaming white and gold in the sun. On the highest hills at its center rests the glittering Inner City, encircled by its own shining white wall and bejeweled with even more beautiful towers and domes. The broad paved streets of the Inner City are carefully designed to follow the natural curves of the hills, spiraling ever upward to the crowning glory of Caemlyn, the Royal Palace.

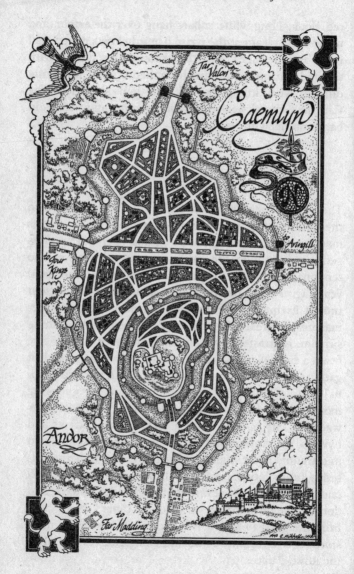

The Palace is both the seat of government for the nation of Andor, and the architectural rendering of her heart and soul. A shining example of Ogier craftsmanship, the Palace's snowy spires and stonework appear as delicate as lace, yet are as strong as iron. Within the Palace grounds extensive gardens bloom almost continuously, with many rare flowers and plants.

Caemlyn also has an excellent library, though it must be ranked far below the great repositories of the White Tower library, or the Royal Library in Cairhien.

WHITEBRIDGE

One of Andor's best known towns is Whitebridge, so named for the huge snow-white bridge that spans the River Arinelle. The town grew up around the large stone-paved square at the great bridge's eastern foot. The bridge is believed to date from the Age of Legends, and looks made of impossibly fragile white glass, yet is so strong even a chisel and hammer will not mar it. Despite its glasslike surface it never becomes slick, even in the hardest rain. The White Bridge is the only span crossing the Arinelle south of Maradon in Saldaea. As a result the town flourishes on trade.

Most buildings in the town are made of stone or brick, and the docks of wood. All classes of people are represented in Whitebridge, from merchants in their shiny lacquered carriages and velvet coats to farmers and peasants in rough wool.

Between Whitebridge and Caemlyn along the Caemlyn Road there are many towns and villages of varying sizes, including Four Kings, Market Sheran, and Carysford on

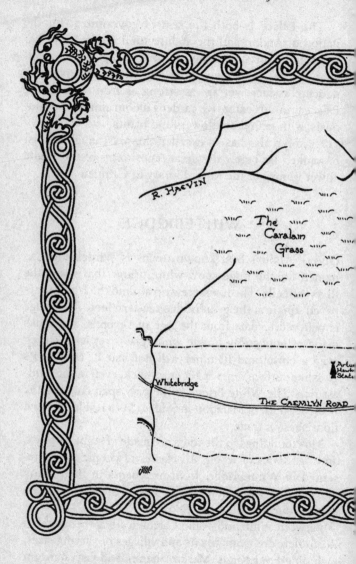

R. HAEVIN

The
Caralain
Grass

Whitebridge

Artur
Hawk
Statu

THE CAEMLYN ROAD

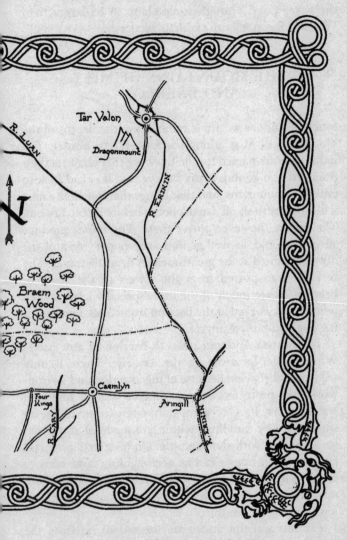

The earliest known map of Andor

the River Cary. Though some claim to be larger than Whitebridge, none can claim its scenery.

THE MOUNTAINS OF MIST AND BAERLON

Much of Andor's wealth is mined from the depths of the Mountains of Mist, along the far western border. The mountains are named for the thick fog that blankets their peaks all year round. Many believe that it is bad luck to enter the mountains, and that things that live in the mist will strip the flesh off a man's bones before he can cry out. The miners, however, thrive there. The mines produce silver and gold, as well as iron and copper. Most of the ores are refined at the great smelters near the mines. The rest are transported from the mines to the town of Baerlon, where much of the ore, especially iron, is then refined and worked at the Baerlon Ironworks, famous for the quality of its castings.

The nearest Andoran town to Baerlon of any size is Whitebridge, far away on the Arinelle. There is only wilderness between. Because of this, Baerlon and its ironworks are protected by a perimeter wall of logs and watchtowers, its City gates only open from sunrise to sundown. The buildings within are made of stone and wood, roofed with slate and tile. On its streets powerful Dhurran draft horses can be seen hauling large carts of ore to and from the ironworks. A large farming community extends to the north of the town, though there are a few farms to the south.

Baerlon and the mines are located so far from the center of Andoran power that the last several Queens

have had some difficulty maintaining their control over the area, saved only because there is no way for the miners to export the metals without going through the rest of Andor. As a result, many of Andor's other outlying communities have been almost completely ignored lest Andor lose the mines so essential to her economic health.

THE TWO RIVERS

One of these all but forgotten areas is the Two Rivers, so called because its villages lie in a triangle formed by the White River, the River Taren, and the Sand Hills below the greater boundary of the Mountains of Mist. Cut off as well by the Forest of Shadows to the south and the Mire to the east, these villages have little in common with the rest of Andor. In fact, most of the inhabitants of the area do not even know that they are part of a larger kingdom, much less that they are ruled by a Queen. They are content to export their valuable wool, tabac, and apple brandy without interference from or protection by the Queen or her Guard. Independent and stubborn almost to a man, their iron will sets them apart from those outside the area.

There are four villages in the Two Rivers, located along a single north-south road. In the largest of these, Taren Ferry, the ferry over the Taren provides the only public crossing into or out of the Two Rivers. The most remote village is Deven Ride, at the south end of the Old Road near the banks of the White River. In between are the villages of Watch Hill and Emond's Field.

Emond's Field sits at the juncture of the old Quarry Road, leading from a forgotten quarry somewhere in the

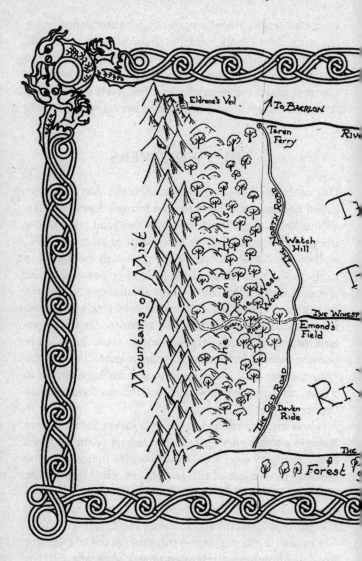

The earliest known map of the Two Rivers

mountains, and the North Road. It is the site of the fresh-water spring known as the Winespring.

Most of the small towns and villages in Andor, as in many of the other nations as well, are run by two groups, the Village Council headed by the Mayor, and the Women's Circle headed by the Village Wisdom, although there is some regional variation in these names. The members of the Village Council and the Women's Circle are elected by the townsmen and women respectively to represent them. The Mayor is usually elected by the people or by the Village Council. The Wisdom is chosen by the Women's Circle, for life, and is usually considered the equal of the Mayor. Wisdoms are selected for their knowledge of healing and herbs, their ability to foretell the weather, and their sensibility.

The Village Council rules on matters that affect the town as a whole, as well as negotiating with the councils of other towns and villages over matters of mutual inter-est. The Women's Circle handles matters that are considered solely women's responsibility, such as when to plant and when to harvest. Though their separate duties are well defined, the Village Council and the Women's Circle of most towns are at odds so often that this ongo-ing conflict, often just short of open warfare, is believed by most to be not only normal, but a traditional part of the dual council system.

Though they have little memory of it, most inhabi-tants of the Two Rivers are descendants of the lost nation of Manetheren. The White River is actually a part of the Manetherendrelle, the 'Waters of the Mountain Home.' The village of Emond's Field sits on the site originally called Aemon's Field, where King Aemon made his last, hopeless stand against the Shadow, two thousand years

ago. The site of the great capital city itself can be found in a valley on the eastern edge of the Mountains of Mist, though nothing remains of its ancient glory but the all-but-indestructible Waygate. Only broken glassy shards of melted rock and a few struggling plants stand on the place where the Red Eagle banner once flew, and Manetheren burned.

There are, however, rumors that the Red Eagle banner flies again in the Two Rivers, in the hands of Lord Perrin 'Goldeneyes' Aybara. It has been said that he has defended the land where the Queen could not and Whitecloaks would not. Those who have seen him claim that he has come to return the ancient glory to the land of King Aemon.

ANCIENT WONDERS

Much of the land claimed by Andor's Queen lies open and uninhabited. But there are many artifacts dating from a different time. Along the River Arinelle there are two such wonders. One is a canyon on the river whose high bluffs are carved for a distance of a half mile with statues a hundred feet tall. These statues appear to be the likenesses of forgotten kings and queens, some so old that their stone features have worn almost completely away. The second, set back from the river's edge, is a featureless tower of burnished steel standing two hundred feet tall and forty feet in diameter. Called the Tower of Ghenjei, it appears to be made of solid metal, for there are no windows and no doors. The builders of these wonders are unknown, as is their purpose. Travelers can only marvel at their ancient glory.

Chapter 28

The Borderlands: Shienar, Arafel, Kandor, and Saldaea

'Death is lighter than a feather,
duty heavier than a mountain.'
– SAYING IN SHIENAR

HOLDING BACK THE SHADOW

 IN THE FAR north of the land, the corruption of the Blight strives unceasingly to overwhelm the fragile human settlements along its edges. The creatures of Shadow were pushed back into the Blight at the end of the Trolloc Wars, but only the bravery and determination of the Borderland warriors have kept them there. Shienar, Saldaea, Arafel, and Kandor are separate nations, each sovereign and independent, but they share a single cause as guardians against the Shadow. Even when the rest of the land is at peace, their battle never ends. But the struggle to hold the border takes a heavy toll.

As little as a generation ago there were five nations instead of four. Now broken towers and infested lakes are all that remain of the lost Borderland nation Malkier, which once thrived under the banner of the Golden Crane. It was

known for its necklace of a thousand lakes and its seven great towers as well as its heroes. Now the only remnant of that nation outside the Blight is its Uncrowned King, al'Lan Mandragoran, son of the last reigning king, al'Akir Mandragoran, and heir to the lost throne. Malkier fell to the Blight in 953 NE, the year Lan was born. Though he was an infant, his parents anointed him *Dai Shan*, a Diademed Battle Lord, and consecrated him King. The ancient sword of the Malkieri Kings, a Power-wrought blade, was given to him. His life was sworn: 'to stand against the Shadow so long as iron is hard and stone abides. To defend the Malkieri while one drop of blood remains, and to avenge what cannot be defended.' They then sent him out of the doomed nation, with many buying his safety with their lives, while they faced their last battle.

The child was taken in and raised by the Shienarans. He never forgot his oath. At the age of sixteen he began a one-man war against the Blight and the Shadow. Called *Aan'allein* or 'Man Who Is an Entire People,' wielding his Power-wrought blade, Lan became a blademaster. He probably would have continued his hopeless fight unto death but for the intervention of Moiraine Sedai in 979 NE. Somehow she convinced him that his purpose would be better served as her Warder, and bonded him.

In an attempt to avoid the same fate as Malkier, the Borderlanders have erected signal towers all along the Blightborder at half-mile intervals. These tall stone towers afford good visibility, and are designed for ease of defense; they are equipped with a large mirror for sending signals by day, and a large iron brazier for signal fires to the darkness. When a potential threat is spotted by the watchers, they signal to a system of other towers farther from the border, who pass the message on into the heartland

fortresses. The fortresses then dispatch their lancers to drive the raiders back into the Blight. The same signal towers can be used to warn the population to move to safety within the fortresses.

The watchers are extremely vigilant, but Shadowspawn still get through the border. Fades are particularly difficult to spot because of their humanlike appearance and ability to travel from shadow to shadow. For this reason it is law in all the lands of the Blightborder that no one may hood his head or hide his face inside a town's walls. A Halfman can only pass among humans if his face is shadowed or hidden. In addition, each street and alley is always well lit at night, to eliminate shadows as much as possible. The battle against the Blight affects every citizen. Though only a few can be warriors, each citizen is well aware that he or she is a part of the struggle.

Despite their mutual cause, or perhaps because of it, the border nations take great pride in their differences. The battle is the same, the code of honor similar, but their customs and dress are often quite diverse.

THE EYE OF THE WORLD

Young men of the Borderlands often used to prove themselves by going on a great quest to find the Eye of the World, much as those in Illian hunt for the Horn of Valere. All that was known about the Eye was that it was a great object of the Power hidden somewhere deep within the Blight, guarded only by the Green Man within his enchanted grove. It was said to await those whose need was great enough. Among the legends of the grove one said that no one would be able to find it twice, for it

was constantly moving. Those few who have been there say that it is not the place that moves, but rather the location of the person who needs it.

The Eye is (or was) a pool of the pure essence of *saidin*, usable only by a man. It was made during the first days of the Breaking by one hundred Aes Sedai men and women working together. They died in the making of it, but they insured its purity despite the taint. The Green Man was given the task of guarding it against the need to come, for they knew that they would not survive to guard it.

News from Fal Dara states that the Eye no longer exists, that the need it was meant to fulfill has been met. If this is so, the young men of the Border will have to look elsewhere for a great quest in which to prove their mettle.

SHIENAR

> '*Peace favor your sword.*'
> — SHIENARAN WARRIOR'S BLESSING

Sigil   A swooping black hawk; the Black Hawk.

Banner   A black swooping hawk on a field of three blue and two white horizontal stripes.

Capital city   Fal Moran.

Symbols include the White Hart, personal sign of King Easar.

Shienar is a place of strong contrasts. In the far northeast, flanked by the Mountains of Dhoom and the Spine of the

World, it is a last bastion of civilization on the razor's edge of the bleak corruption of the Blight and the dangers of the Aiel Waste. Winters there are cold enough to cause trees to burst as their sap freezes, yet only a short distance away the Blight swelters in unnatural heat oppressive enough to drain a strong man's will.

The struggle to survive on the Blightborder affects every aspect of a Shienaran warrior's life and thoughts. Ask any what three things he values most, he will almost certainly answer the following: Peace – because he has known only war. Beauty – because the Blight is filled with ugliness. And most of all, life – because he has already sworn himself to death. For these men death is certain. Therefore it is the quality of life that matters, the honor gained, not the quantity of material wealth. Each lives his life prepared for battle, protected by heavy clothing and armor, but in death each is lowered unclothed into the welcoming dirt of the grave, with neither coffin nor shroud to protect his body. They believe all came from the earth, and they must return as they came, naked and unarmed, into the last embrace of the mother.

All mounted Shienaran warriors are known as lancers because of the fighting lances they carry. They are certainly the finest heavy cavalry in the land. They are also easily recognized, as each fighting man wears his hair in a topknot, with his head partially shaved around it. His weapons are always close at hand, with most fighters wearing one or two long-swords strapped to their backs and all wearing a broadsword, axe, or mace at their belt. Even in the safety of the fortresses, weapons are hung in readiness on every wall, or on stands near every bed. Armor is usually a combination of leather, mail, and plate,

often covered by a surcoat with the Black Hawk upon it.
Their powerful warhorses are armored as well, with steel
barding protecting the vulnerable head, neck and chest.
The loss of a horse can mean death to even a skilled warrior during a battle with Trollocs.

Every major Shienaran town is designed to be a defen-
sible fortress. Wherever possible the town is centered on
high ground to command the surrounding countryside.
The perimeter for a half-mile or more around each town
is clear-cut to prevent sneak attacks; nothing taller than
clipped grass is allowed to remain. This lack of cover, as
well as tall lookout towers built into the perimeter walls,
makes it impossible for anything to approach unseen.
The formidable town gates are reinforced with iron to
insure that any hostile forces that dare to cross the clear-
ing will find no easy entrance.

Shienar is ruled by King Easar of House Togita from
the capital city of Fal Moran, but like most borderland
rulers, Easar spends more time in the saddle defending
his lands with his sons than giving audiences. Fal Moran
is the heart and soul of Shienar, but it is the fortresses
closer to the Blightborder, such as Fal Dara, that embody
the true spirit of this land of eternal struggle.

FAL DARA

Fal Dara lies close to the Blightborder, part of the final
line of defense between it and the cities and farmsteads
farther incountry. Its wall, studded with towers, encloses
shops, inns, and homes around the central fortress. Only
farming communities lie outside its protection. Most of
the houses within and without the walls have sharp

peaked wooden shingled roofs that run almost to the ground. This angled design prevents the damaging buildup of snow and ice during the long winter. At the center of Fal Dara a dry moat, deep and wide with sharp spikes embedded in the bottom, and a second defensive wall studded with more towers, protect the inner keep, a massive fortress of stone built atop the highest point of the hill. The keep is the home of the Lord of Fal Dara, Agelmar Jagad, as well as his family, retainers, warriors, and servants. His fortress, as well as the walls that protect it and the town around it, are built for strength rather than beauty, yet there is a severe elegance in the stark lines of each wall and beauty in the massive stones.

In the years before the Trolloc Wars the city that stood on its site was called Mafal Dadaranell. It was Ogier-built, consisting of grand towers, graceful arching buildings, and intricate palaces joined by wide avenues. Yet nothing was strong enough to hold back the waves of Shadowspawn flooding from the Blight. When the Trolloc Wars finally ended, Mafal Dadaranell was gone, razed to the bare earth. Those who survived decided to build another city on the site of the old one, but the Ogier stonemasons were gone. Rather than make a poor imitation, they replaced its elaborate design with simplicity. A single rose placed just so instead of a garden; the simple fortress of Fal Dara in place of the city of Mafal Dadaranell.

Though not all Shienaran towns and fortresses have such interesting histories, all are linked more strongly by their shared threat than by their allegiance to the nation. Ankor Dail holds the eastern marches and guards the Spine of the World. Other fortresses such as Mos Shirare,

Fal Sion, and Camron Caan each provide an integral part of the defense of Shienar, and each has its own stories, and its own heroes.

ARAFEL

'The dancing is sweeter on the edge of a sword.'
— SAYING IN ARAFEL.

Sigil   A red rose and a white rose; the Roses.

Banner   Three white roses on a field of red quartered with three red roses on a field of white.

Capital city   Shol Arbela.

Arafel lies just west of Shienar and is made up of more rugged country than Shienar. The men are easily recognized by their distinctive hairstyle. They wear their hair in two long braids, usually with silver bells on the braid-ends. Most of the natives of Arafel are pale-skinned and appear to have unusually large eyes. Like all Borderlanders, the Arafellin maintain a strong military tradition for protection from creatures of the Blight. Arafellin warriors are skilled swordsmen. They always wear two swords, both strapped to their backs, one hilt over each shoulder, and are capable of using both at once, one in each hand. The nation is currently ruled by King Paitar Nachiman, whose sister Kiruna is an Aes Sedai of the Green Ajah.

KANDOR

Sigil   A rearing red horse; the Red Horse.

Banner   The Red Horse on a field of pale green.

Capital city   Chachin.

Kandor lies between the nations of Arafel and Saldaea, along the Blightborder. Though the martial arts are as highly developed here as in any border nation, the Kandori have also developed a skill for trade and alone of all the Border nations have established a highly respected guild for merchants. Though Chachin's nearness to the Blight prevents it from being a center of commerce, the merchants have established a strong reputation and have brought much wealth back with them. Kandori men are easily spotted by their distinctive forked beards, as well as one to three silver chains worn over their coats. Kandori also usually wear an earring, and the earrings of some successful merchants guilds are quite ostentatious. Members of the nobility also wear chains over their coats and earrings.

The current ruler of Kandor is Queen Ethenielle Kirukon Materasu.

SALDAEA

> *My heart rises with the sun.*
> *To the chime of swords*
> *I die at sunset . . .'*
> — SALDAEAN POEM

Sigil   Three silver fish, one above the other; the Silver Fish.

Banner   Three silver fish on a field of dark blue.

Capital city   Maradon.

Saldaea is the largest of the Border nations. Stretching from the unbroken cliffs on the Aryth Ocean known as World's End, to the River Arinelle and the northern edge of the Black Hills, it covers more area than Shienar and Arafel combined. Its ruler, the young Queen Tenobia, has single estates larger than the entire city-state of Mayene.

The people are known for their distinctively tilted almond-shaped eyes, as well as their military prowess. The Saldaeans' ferocity in battle is at least the equal of that of any other Border nation, and their equestrian skills are far superior. In fact, they are the finest light cavalry in the known world.

The Saldaean cavalry can perform mounted drills and maneuvers in units as large as nine thousand without a single horse or rider missing the mark. Seeming more at home in the saddle than on the ground, these men routinely perform stunts normally only done by gleemen, but all on the backs of galloping chargers. Standing in the saddle, on feet or on hands, riding two horses at once with one foot on the back of each, full-speed dismounts and remounts, and even crawling completely under and around the charging animal, are not unusual maneuvers.

The Marshal-General is responsible for defending Saldaea and commanding the military. The position is currently held by Lord Davram Bashere, who is also Queen Tenobia's uncle. Before Bashere, Muad Cheade was

Marshal-General. He was believed quite mad, and was always convinced someone was trying to kill him, yet every battle he commanded ended with a decisive victory. His madness was tolerated as a small price to pay for his brilliant strategies.

War for Saldaeans is a family event, for though the women do not actually participate in the fighting, the wives of most officers and all nobles traditionally accompany their husbands on all military campaigns except for those inside the Blight. Though girls are not taught the arts of the sword, many are quite skilled with knives or in hand-to-hand fighting, and many stories tell of women taking up the swords of their fallen husbands to lead the men back into battle. Whether or not these stories are true, it is true that a highborn lady of Saldaea is expected to be able to ride to the hunt all day while reciting poetry, then play the cittern at night while participating intelligently in discussions of how to counter Trolloc raids. The usual mode of dress for Saldaean women reflects their strength of will, consisting of a high-necked dress with long sleeves. Highborn women usually wear elaborate embroidery down the sleeves and on the collar, and the dress is often silk or brocade. Farmgirls wear the same basic style, but in wool. These farmgirls are just as fierce as their betters, known for shaving the head of any woman caught poaching another's chosen male. Men and women of all classes usually travel armed with at least a knife, though in Saldaea steel is never drawn except when the wearer intends to use it.

Despite their otherwise formidable virtue, Saldaean women can be extremely sensual. Ladies of the court are known for the subtlety of their seductions, using the language of fans to communicate their thoughts to potential

suitors. The infamous *sa'sara* is a dance outlawed by a number of Saldaean Queens for its indecency, and yet almost all noblewomen know how to dance it, though only a few may admit it publicly. The *sa'sara*, when danced by one who knows the moves, apparently has the ability to make men's blood boil. Saldaean history records three wars, two rebellions, and forty-seven unions and feuds between noble houses, as well as innumerable duels, sparked by women dancing the *sa'sara*. There is even a tale of a defeated queen who quelled a rebellion by dancing it for the victorious general. He is said to have married her and restored her throne, though the story has been denied by every Queen of Saldaea.

The economy of Saldaea is strong, with brisk trade in furs from the trappers, fine woods from the forests, and ice peppers from the farms. These goods are often shipped as far away as Mayene or Tear, where they command a good price from the nobility.

Chapter 29

Cairhien

'Take what you want, and pay for it.'
— SAYING IN CAIRHIEN

Sigil   A many-rayed golden rising sun; the Rising Sun.

Banner   A many-rayed golden sun rising on a field of blue.

Capital city   Cairhien.

Symbols include the Sun Throne.

HISTORY

CAIRHIEN BECAME AN independent nation at the end of the War of the Hundred Years. Her rulers at one time laid claim to a swath of land from Shienar to the River Erinin

to the Spine of the World. Now the land they control covers less than half that area.

In 566 NE, the Aiel granted Cairhienin merchants the exclusive right to travel the Silk Path from the Jangai Pass through the Aiel Waste. At the same time they gave her king *Avendoraldera*, the only known sapling of the lost Tree of Life. The nation grew fat on the trade that lay beyond the Aiel Waste, but the good fortune was short-lived. The Aiel War of 976–978 NE brought havoc to Cairhien and the rest of the land. The Aiel burned the city, only her libraries untouched, and took from Cairhien its right to use the Silk Path.

Cairhien's fertile farmland had produced more than enough to feed her people, but after the war the farmers and refugees from the land along the Dragonwall swarmed for protection to the walls of the larger cities, leaving their lands untended. With the farms lying fallow, the king was forced to rely on the goodwill of neighbors and their shipments of grain to feed the people.

In 998 NE the granaries burned and King Galldrian was assassinated, heralding a war of succession – and famine, for grain shipments were disrupted. A little over a year later, the Aiel again emerged from the Waste to attack Cairhien in what is known as the Shaido War. The city and nation survived only because of outside aid from the Dragon Reborn and his allies. At the end of the conflict, the Sun Throne remained empty, and Cairhien was forced to submit to the guardianship of a foreign regent. No other surviving nation has gone from such heights to such depths and still maintained its national identity and pride.

THE GAME OF HOUSES

The key to understanding Cairhien's volatile history lies in the nature of its people. As a whole they are stern and unyielding, preferring the world around them to adhere to strictly ordered aesthetics rather than natural chaos. Yet they thrive on the complexities of subtle political intrigue, using the art of misdirection and hidden meanings to gain power and status. For a Cairhienin, nothing is as it seems; everything has a deeper meaning, a hidden motive. It was the nobles of Cairhienin who took the style of intrigue created by the White Tower, gave it their own twist, and made it into what is now known as *Daes Dae'mar*, the dangerous and often deadly Game of Houses. The Great Game has gone on to infect all the southern nations at least to some extent.

It is *Daes Dae'mar* that is believed to be responsible for most of Cairhien's disastrous failures. It is now known that the First Aiel War, as the Cairhienin call it, was a direct result of King Laman Damodred's attempt to play the Game. He destroyed the Aiel gift to gain position by making a throne from the tree that would be unique in all the world, never guessing that it would ultimately cost him his life.

After the First Aiel War it was far easier for the last King of Cairhien, Galldrian su Riatin Rie, to placate the refugees and buy grain than to deal more directly with the problem and possibly risk losing prestige in the Game. Some say that Galldrian lost his life because the Game was more dear to him than the welfare of his people. What is known is that his assassination and the burning of the granaries plunged the nation into both a power

struggle and a struggle for survival. There is no doubt that *Daes Dae'mar* lay behind it all.

All members of noble Houses are involved in the politics of the Game from birth, and all must learn the art of misdirection and subtlety. As a result, every aspect of dress, behavior, and even architecture is very carefully ordered. Nothing about the Cairhienin nobility is ever spontaneous.

Before the Aiel War the Damodred kings of Cairhien owned one of the few Power-wrought heron-marked blades, despite the fact that few, if any of them, were blademasters. Set with a jeweled hilt and a very heavily worked jeweled scabbard, the sword was so gaudy it looked more like a ceremonial showpiece than the exceptional weapon it was. The last Damodred King, Laman, was wearing the sword when he fell to the Aiel during the Aiel War, but the sword disappeared from his body. It was only recently discovered that the Aiel took it, despite their dislike of swords, as proof of his death – swords being more easily transported than heads. It returned to Cairhien during the Shaido War, without its ornate scabbard or fittings, in the hands of Cairhien's rescuer, the Dragon Reborn.

THE CITY OF CAIRHIEN

In direct contrast to the convoluted maneuvering of their Great Game, the upper merchant classes prefer complete control and perfect order in their environment. Nowhere is this more obvious than in the capital city of Cairhien. It was built on the site of the ancient city of Al'cair'rahienallen, Hill of the Golden Dawn, but only the

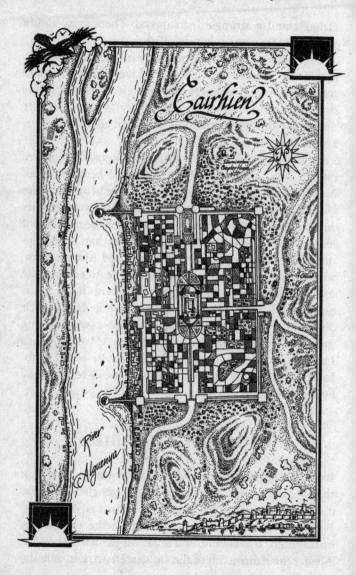

sunrise on the banners remains, and only the Ogier remember what it stood for. Al'cair'rahienallen had a great Ogier grove just beyond its boundaries, but the grove was not tended after the Trolloc Wars, the Great Trees are gone, and there remains only a forest where firewood is cut.

The modern city is laid out in a precise grid pattern within the perfect square formed by the high gray perimeter walls. The River Alguenya flows along one side of the city, yet the uncompromising perfection of the wall mocks the flowing curves of hills and river. Perhaps the Cairhienin architects wished to force nature to bend to their rigid control. The high walls are broken only by several well-guarded square gates. Within the walls, the famous Topless Towers of Cairhien stand in exact patterns, covered with scaffolding up to their jagged unfinished tops. Before the Aiel War, these towers were renowned as a wonder of the world, reaching almost to the clouds, it was said, but during the Aiel War they burned and fell. They were damaged again during the Shaido War.

Throughout the city wide paved streets run arrow-straight, despite any curves in the underlying terrain, meeting every crossing street at perfect right angles. Closed sedan chairs or curtained carriages travel the city among the pedestrians ostentatiously minding their own business. All the buildings and terraces are made of stone, decorated only with straight lines and sharp angles. The hills are so carved and terraced into straight lines that they look man-made.

Most of the structures have sustained some damage from the wars, except for the imposing bulk of the Royal Library of Cairhien. The Aiel spared it deliberately,

refusing to damage or destroy any book. Within its walls lies one of the greatest repositories of knowledge in the world, second only to that of Tar Valon. Though most Cairhienin do not know it, the Royal Library is probably the greatest treasure of their nation.

In recent times, under the regency, Cairhien has been enhanced by the formation of a school in the late Lord Barthanes' old manor to give inventors, philosophers, and those interested in science and thought a place to work. Some amazing works have already been produced there.

THE SUN PALACE

At the exact center of the city, on the highest hill, stands the massive square bulk of the Sun Palace of Cairhien, crowned with stepped towers precisely placed in concentric squares of increasing height. Tall narrow windows and lofty colonnaded walks enhance its stern command. Within its walls are many gardens, but even the plants, flowers, and trees are precisely pruned and strictly ordered into perfect square or rectangular beds.

Within the heart of the palace is the Grand Hall of the Sun, a great throne room with massive square columns of blue-streaked marble and a large golden mosaic Rising Sun set into the deep blue tiles of the floor. At the far end of the Hall, upon a wide dais, rests the soul of the palace, the Sun Throne. A model of Cairhienin restraint, the heavy armchair has simple straight lines despite the golden silk and gilding on its wood. The only curves are in the wavy-rayed golden sun set high on the throne's back, so made as to shine above the head of the occupant.

Even the artifacts and artwork displayed throughout the dark, heavy corridors of the Palace are chosen for their straight lines and sharp edges. Tapestries contain the only large concentrations of color, but even there the Cairhienin need for control is demonstrated through the rigid, tightly controlled groupings of the subjects depicted.

Outside the straight stone walls, the river is usually filled with ships, often carrying grain. During the time of the Silk Path, Cairhien became a major trade center, and the river a primary transport for imports and exports. The far bank used to bristle with tall granaries, but now there are only a few being reconstructed from the ashes of the civil war and the Shaido War.

CAIRHIENIN DRESS CODE

Cairhienin upper-class dress reflects their desire for control and order. The people are shorter and more pale-skinned than Andorans, though with darker hair, and the dark colors they prefer contrast with their fair skin. Men and women wear coats and dresses of black or dark blue or green. The darkness is relieved by narrow horizontal slashes of color across the chest and body, and dark ivory lace at the throat and wrists. The number of color slashes indicates the rank of the wearer, while their color indicates the House. A very high-ranking lord or lady might have slashes of color from collar to hem, while a lower-ranked noble might only have a few slashes across the chest.

The ladies wear their hair tightly coiffed into elaborate towers of curls carefully designed as unique to the wearer.

The men wear their hair long, with flat or bell-shaped velvet caps. Formal wear is much the same, equally dark, save that ladies' skirts are extremely wide and supported by hoops, and the materials used are finer. Even the liveried servants only have color in a few stripes on the cuffs and their house badge embroidered on the breast of coat or dress. Some liveries have house colors covering the collar or sleeves, but rarely the entire coat or dress. Upper servants show more color on their livery than lower attendants.

The lower classes are comparatively free from the restraints of the Great Game, and they are free to dress any way they wish. They often approach the extremes of flamboyance that their betters avoid. Their clothes may be ill-fitting and shabby, but they are extremely colorful. Bright skirts and shirts with coats and shawls of equally bright, though often clashing, colors are quite common.

Military dress follows the same dark colors as the nobles, but with a few embellishments. Officers wear slashes of rank across their coats much as nobles do, but they shave the front of the head and often dust it with white powder, leaving the hair hanging long in back. High-ranking officers wear ornately gilded cuirasses as well as large white plumes attached to their bell-shaped helmets and ornate gauntlets. Lesser officers and soldiers wear much plainer armor. Regular soldiers wear their hair cut short in a basic bowl cut. Until the Shaido War, the nobles who commanded the soldiers did not shave their heads, leaving that to the common-born, but after it many nobles who had 'seen the wolf' – as Cairhienin say of those who have seen action – took up the practice.

Cairhienin officers also wear small banners called 'con' on short staffs on their backs. These enable easy location of officers or a particular lord's personal retainers.

FOREGATE

Before the Shaido came, a secondary city lay outside the walls. Known as Foregate, this warren of gimcrack wood buildings and zigzag mud streets began as separate market villages for each of the city's gates, but over the years had grown into one vast hodgepodge of ramshackle buildings. After the Aiel War, when the refugee farmers from the east settled in Foregate, the then King Galldrian provided grain to feed them and all manner of parades and festivals to keep them from thoughts of uprising. As a result Foregate was a place of riotous color, with fireworks supplied by the Illuminators Guild many nights, horse races by the river, gleemen and musicians in every tavern and on every street corner, and abject poverty underlying everything.

When the Shaido attacked Cairhien, Foregate burned like tinder, nearly taking the city with it. Many outlying towns and cities were lost as well. Tein, a town on the Aiel side of the Jangai Pass, a remnant of the time the Silk Path was in use, had survived the Aiel War and the closing of the path, but fell to the Shaido. Selean, a similar, though larger, town on the Cairhien side of the pass, suffered the same fate. The few farmers in the area who had not fled to the capital also perished or were taken prisoner. There is no doubt that the Shaido would have destroyed the entire nation had Cairhien not received aid to stop them. If the Cairhienin have learned nothing else,

they have learned that their Great Game is a useless weapon against the Aiel.

FEAST OF LIGHTS

The only time the Cairhienin reserve breaks is during the celebration of the Feast of Lights. For two days all propriety is gone, as are all social barriers between nobles and commoners. The Cairhienin seem determined to make up for a year of careful etiquette with two days of wild abandon. One of the tenets of the holiday is that any man can kiss any woman, and any woman any man. As a result it is common to see nobles and commoners sporting together in various states of undress. Music and dancing fill the streets. Noblewomen are often seen with their hair piled high, bare to the waist beneath their cloaks; common women may abandon any covering above the waist except their hair.

At the end of the Feast, everyone returns to their own class and resumes the mask of reserve, with no repercussions for anything that might have occurred during the holiday, and no acknowledgment that anything did occur.

Chapter 30

The Other Nations

AMADICIA

Sigil   A red thistle leaf laid over a silver six-pointed star; the Thistle and Star.

Banner   The Thistle and Star on a field horizontally striped blue and gold, three of blue stripes and two gold.

Capital city   Amador.

AMADICIA

AMADICIA LIES SOUTH of the Mountains of Mist, between Tarabon and Altara. It is the home of the Children of the Light, who rule here more completely than the 'rightful' ruler. The appearance of a monarchy is maintained, if

only to free the Children from ceremonial duties, and the King, currently Ailron, does have some power, so long as he does not go against the wishes of the Children. His Serenda Palace is located only two miles from Amador and the Fortress of Light, the actual seat of power of the Children. As if to make up for his lack of real power, the King surrounds himself with much pomp and circumstance. His court is filled with fashionable ladies with their long curled hair, equally fashionable gentlemen in long colorful coats, and servants resplendent in red and gold livery.

As stated previously, channeling and channelers are outlawed in Amadicia. Thieves are also treated harshly. The thief is branded for the first offense, his or her right hand is cut off for the second, and he is hanged as punishment for the third, whether the stolen item was the King's crown or a loaf of bread. Both thieves and Aes Sedai avoid the nation entirely if possible.

ALTARA

'Lean back on your knife and let your tongue go free.'
— COMMON ALTARAN SAYING.

Sigil   Two golden leopards, one above the other; the Golden Leopards; the Leopards.

Banner   The Golden Leopards on a field checked four-by-four in red and blue; red is next to the staff on the topmost row.

Capital city   Ebou Dar.

Symbols include the Throne of the Winds.

Altara faces the Sea of Storms, wedged between the more
powerful nations of Illian and Amadicia, with northern
borders touching Murandy, Andor, and Ghealdan. It is
unified only in name. Most of the inhabitants prefer to
identify themselves as belonging to a particular town or
as being the subjects of a particular lord or lady, rather
than a subject of the Queen or a citizen of Altara. Even
the nobles seem to care little for their nation, seldom
paying taxes or offering more than lip service to the
Crown.

The Unsteady Throne

The Throne of the Winds is slightly more than a prize to
be taken by the most powerful noble, although many
powerful nobles have scorned to take it when given the
opportunity. In the thousand years since Hawkwing's
death, only one House, House Todande, has held the
throne for as much as five generations, and when they
lost it their fall was so complete that the House has
become subservient to all others. No other House has
ever been able to put more than two consecutive rulers on
the throne. The current ruler, Queen Tylin Quintara of
House Mitsobar, is the second of her House to hold the
throne. Her one surviving son, Beslan, is heir, but stands
only a marginal chance of actually taking it.

Mitsobar was not a powerful House when Tylin's father
first took the throne, and his control extended only
slightly beyond the palace walls. Due to his efforts and
her own, Tylin now controls the capital and the land
around it for a hundred miles, but little more. Altara is

under pressure from Amadicia; there is no doubt that the Children wish to control Altara, for its sovereignty is all that keeps them from controlling the river trade on the Eldar, or marching on Murandy and perhaps even Illian. If not for Illian's intervention during the Whitecloak War, they would have already succeeded. A weakly knit land such as Altara is an easy target for those with the power to take it.

Yet Altara does have a kind of national character. Her people, especially the women, are fierce and bold. They are extremely polite, yet quick to answer an insult with steel. Highborn or low, man or woman, all are equal on the dueling ground. This is most evident in the capital city Ebou Dar, center of Altaran culture and commerce.

In parts of Altara, especially Ebou Dar, it is the custom for a married or widowed woman to wear a 'Marriage Knife' hanging hilt-down from a choker around her neck. When a couple marries, the man gives the woman the knife as part of the ceremony. He then requests that she use it to kill him should he ever displease her.

The knife tells any who care to look a great deal about the wearer. A white sheath means the woman is widowed and does not intend to remarry. A blue sheath means she will consider offers. Jewels or glass beads set into the knife represent children of the wearer, white stones for sons and red for daughters. If a son died in a duel, the setting of the stone is enameled red; a daughter, the setting is enameled in white. If children die from a cause other than dueling, the settings are enameled in black. Red and white settings are a source of pride for Ebou Dari women. Many women remove their children's stones, effectively disowning them, if they refuse a duel once past the age of sixteen.

High Ladies and those with wealth wear a marriage knife of gold and jewels. Commoners wear one of brass set with colored glass. The materials do not matter as much as the content. Women who are engaged to be married wear a choker, to show all that they have been promised a knife.

Altarans can often be recognized by their dark hair, dark eyes, and olive complexion, but those from Ebou Dar are also easily recognizable by their distinctive attire. Women's dresses are often pale in color with snug bodices and full skirts over bright petticoats. The necklines of commoners are cut very narrow and deep, while for nobles the bodice has a round or oval cutout, allowing those with marriage knives to show them to best advantage, and those without to show that they are available. For commoners the skirt is always worn gathered above one knee to reveal the brilliantly colored petticoats beneath, while noblewomen wear it raised in the front. Large hoop earrings are worn by most women and some men. Men and women alike wear curved daggers through their belts or sashes, and often carry a work knife as well.

The trademark of an Ebou Dari man is his long, elaborate vest. These vests are often as brightly colored as a tinker's clothes, and are worn alone or over pale shirts with wide sleeves.

Sometimes the wealthy add a decorative silk coat slung about the shoulders, since it is deliberately too small to be worn conventionally. This 'cape' is held with a chain of silver or gold strung between the narrow embroidered lapels. When the cape is worn a long narrow sword is usually carried, in addition to the standard dagger. Both men and women adorn their hands with rings.

As in most cultures, the wealthy use silks and brocades

with embroidery, often set with jewels, while the poor and middle-class use wool, brass, and glass.

Ebou Dar

The city of Ebou Dar straddles the River Eldar, facing a large bay usually filled with ships. The river divides the city into two sections, one containing palaces and the homes and shops of the upper and middle classes, and one known as the Rahad, home to those of lower station and rougher demeanor.

The city is laced with canals as well as roads with all types of bridges. Barges and passenger boats are poled through the canals while carriages, wagons, and pedestrians crowd the roads and bridges. All the buildings are pale, either white stone or pale marble, or painted plastered brick. Many large buildings and palaces are set among the smaller ones, some enhanced with tall spires or domes in the shape of turnips or pears, decorated with colored bands of crimson, blue, or gold. A large wall surrounds the city proper, very thick and as white as the buildings within. It is broken by a series of gates with tall pointed archways over roads leading into the central city. Paved squares throughout the city contain a fountain bubbling water, a large statue, or both.

The Tarasin Palace

The largest of these squares is the Mol Hara, laid with very pale paving stones. At its center stands a heroic statue of a woman on a tall pedestal, with a fountain beneath, one arm raised to point toward the sea, the heart of Ebou Dari trade. One entire side of the square is dominated by

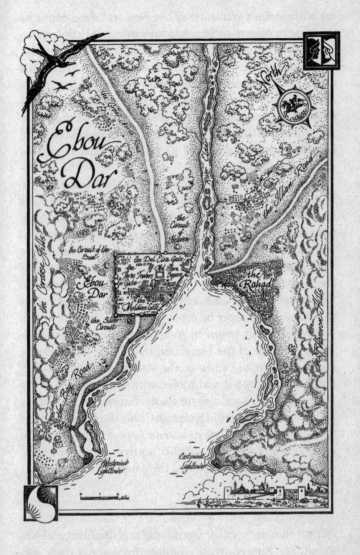

the white domes and spires of the Tarasin Palace, home to the Altaran monarch. Standing four stories tall, the palace is gleaming white except for the bands of gold and color on its domes. Inside, however, every room is filled with color. Subtle shades of blue, yellow, or rose adorn walls and ceilings, while the floors are tiled in offset diamonds of various colors. Most of the great houses and shops are also filled with color. Sea Folk porcelain, crystal, and bronze gleam from arched niches and most tapestries depict scenes of the sea.

The gardens are in courtyards in the center of the building. Most of the windows to the outside are kept shuttered, for the palace is surrounded on three sides by houses and shops. Unlike most cities, there is no particular order to the layout in Ebou Dar. Palaces are surrounded by inns and merchants' shops, great houses are flanked by hostelries, fishmongeries and cutleries. Shops and inns abound, with some shops even built onto the sides of the larger bridges.

Though many towns in Altara echo the preference for white masonry of the Ebou Dar, not all are as outwardly stark. The town of Remen on the Manetherendrelle River is built mostly of stone and roofed with bright tiles of every color. The streets are also unusual, running in chaos from a single central square. These roofs, plus the people's bright vests and petticoats, make Remen appear quite festive to outsiders. In general, the further north one goes in Altara, the more the architecture, and the people, look Andoran.

The Rahad

Across the river, even the dilapidated buildings of the Rahad are painted white, though the paint is dirty and

flaking. On many of the dwellings large chunks of plaster have come loose to reveal the coarse brick below. The streets in this quarter are often narrow alleys, shadowed by the looming five- and six-story buildings crowded along their length. The stench of decay fills the air as flies and vermin thrive on the refuse in the streets. It is here that the famed Ebou Dari ferocity is most apparent, for while duels are a normal part of Altaran life, in the Rahad they are an hourly occurrence. Many adversaries do not even bother with the formality of a duel, but simply kill their victim with a knife to the back. It is not unusual for someone to be killed simply because their clothes are fine. In such cases the thief uses a very narrow-bladed knife to avoid ruining the cloth.

Dueling

The Ebou Dari pride themselves on the ferocity of their women, and on their courage in a duel. Very few men or women reach adulthood without having fought in at least one duel, and these few are ostracized for being cowardly. While in many parts of the world men fight duels over women, only in Ebou Dar is it also common for women to fight duels over men. In both cases the 'prize' agrees to go with the winner. Married women are less likely to be challenged than unmarried ones, and widows who reject another marriage least of all. Most Ebou Dari women who survive to marry consider dueling scars to be a type of beauty mark. Altaran women claim that they will only harm a man if they are themselves harmed, threatened, or wronged, but by law the death of a man at the hands of a woman is justified unless proven otherwise. As a result men are very solicitous of women.

In general, outside the Rahad, most Altarans are extremely polite, lest they give cause for a challenge. Everything said is subject to challenge unless one of the parties formally states that the other may 'lean back on his dagger,' meaning that anything can be said and no insult will be taken. Most Altarans, and all who live in Ebou Dar, are armed with at least a curved dueling dagger at the waist, always in easy reach.

Salidar: The Tower in Exile

Ebou Dar is the political heart of Altara, but a town abandoned since the Whitecloak War and almost forgotten recently threatened the prominence of the capital. That town, Salidar, lies only a mile east of the River Eldar and Amadicia. Once known as the birthplace of Deane Aryman, the Aes Sedai who succeeded Bonwhin as Amyrlin and rescued the Tower from the destruction Bonwhin had poised it for, it was for a time the home of the White Tower in exile, most of those Aes Sedai who escaped from the apparent coup that split the Tower in Tar Valon. The sisters rebuilt the town, and made of it a Tower in purpose if not fact. It remains to be seen whether this 'Tower' will strengthen Queen Tylin's stand against her enemies, or further weaken the already fragile nation.

MURANDY

*'Trust no one but yourself,
and yourself not too much.'*
— Lugarder saying

Sigil   A red bull, the Red Bull.

Banner   The Red Bull on a field vertically striped blue and white; three blue and two white. Fringed in red when flown where the sovereign is present.

Capital city   Lugard.

Just north of Altara and south of Andor lies the nation of Murandy. As in Altara, the people of Murandy do not respect the political identity of their nation as much as they respect their local nobility. King Roedran officially rules Murandy, but the actual political power is divided between the all but independent lords and ladies who rule their own little patches of land. The king seldom has any real control over events in the capital city, much less the rest of the country. Many believe that the only reason Murandians tolerate a ruler at all is to provide a deterrent against annexation by neighboring nations, for their lack of national cohesion does not stop the people of Murandy from being extremely suspicious of outsiders. Most see every foreign action as part of a plot. Andorans are particularly despised, primarily due to a long history of disputes along their common border, although, close to the border the two people are almost indistinguishable except by dress.

Lugard

Located in the heart of Murandy, on the banks of the River Storn, the city of Lugard is both capital and trade center for the nation. Indeed, trade keeps Lugard alive. Regardless of political disagreements or distrust, freight wagons of every shape and size and nation crowd the large bare patches of

ground set aside for them within the city. Stables, horse lots, and inns outnumber houses and shops, and constant heavy traffic moves through the streets carrying goods to and from Andor, Illian, Ghealdan, Altara, and Arad Doman.

Lugard's commercial reputation, though well earned, is tarnished by its equally well-earned reputation for thievery and licentiousness. Lugarders view any outsider as a fair mark for theft or con game. The very appearance of the city gives off an aura of disrepute. Its tall gray perimeter walls have tumbled down in many places to no more than a small token fence and a pile of rubble. Most of the broad streets are unpaved, and even the paved streets are very dusty. The gray stone buildings with their bright-colored tile roofs are always covered with a dull haze of dirt. Jagged unkempt stone walls crisscross the haphazard layout of the city, marking divisions claimed by feuding nobles over the years. More than once Lugard has actually been divided among such nobles like a poorly carved roast.

ARAD DOMAN

*'A man who trades with a Domani
needs three sets of wits.'*
— WARNING AGAINST FOOLISHNESS

Sigil   A silver hand grasping a silver sword by the blade, point down; the Sword and Hand.

Banner   The Sword and Hand on a field of four green and three blue horizontal stripes.

Capital city   Bandar Eban.

Arad Doman lies between the Mountains of Mist and the Aryth Ocean, just north of the Almoth Plain. Though the plain is officially unclaimed, Arad Doman has long maneuvered for control of it against Tarabon. The Domani believe they are descendants of those who made the Tree of Life, but it is the Domani women that are legendary. Copper-skinned and exceedingly graceful, they are said to be able to twist a man around their wrist with a look, and imprison his heart with a single smile. The clothes they wear are considered scandalous by most other standards. Their dresses cover their bodies from neck to toes, but are barely opaque and cling to every curve, revealing nothing while hinting at everything. Only the women of the Sea Folk move with more sensual grace than the Domani, and no other woman can compare to a Domani when it comes to practicing the art of seduction, which mothers begin teaching daughters in girlhood. Most Domani merchants are women, and the nation owes its wealth to their success. Few men will come off the victor in trade with a Domani woman, but they often consider losing worth the experience.

The Domani are famous for their food, usually spiced meat slivers and vegetables in a variety of sauces. Their method of eating it, however, has been known to leave outlanders in fear of starvation. Rather than forks, or even knives, the Domani eat with nothing more than two thin sticks, used as a pair, called *sursa*. These sticks are held in one hand and deftly maneuvered to daintily pick up slivers of food from their various bowls.

Domani men are recognizable by their long, thin mustaches and earrings. Both men and women of nobility wear jewelry engraved or embossed with the symbols of their House. As much as the women are known for their

beauty, the men are known for their temper. It has been suggested that it is dealing with Domani women which gives them such a temper. Others say that it is eating with *sursa*.

The capital of Arad Doman is Bandar Eban, also their trade center. Though the Domani do not like to travel the sea, Domani merchants carry on major trade with the Sea Folk, and then disperse the goods to inland consumers. They also trade heavily with Tarabon, though that commerce may decline due to the outbreak of war, and with Saldaea. The nation is currently ruled by King Alsalam, who has been recently beset by civil war within, by the war with Tarabon, and by the rumored disappearance of several members of his family.

TARABON

> 'The best secret to reveal
> is the face behind a lady's veil,
> the most deadly
> is that of an Illuminator's spark.'
> — SAYING IN TANCHICO

Sigil   A golden tree with a thick bole and spreading branches balanced by roots below; the Tree; the Golden Tree.

Banner   The Golden Tree on a field vertically striped red and white; four red and three white.

Panarch's Banner and Sigil   Same but with the addition of a green staff behind the tree.

Capital city   Tanchico.

Symbols include the Throne of Light.

Tarabon, a sizable nation on the Aryth Ocean, lies just south of the disputed Almoth Plain. Taraboners call themselves the Tree of Man, and claim descent from rulers and nobles of the Age of Legends. In the years when Almoth lived, it was even rumored that Tarabon actually held either a branch or a living sapling of *Avendesora*. Their banner was designed originally to celebrate that fact and their claimed heritage, with its blue sky, black earth, and the spreading Tree of Life to join them.

Once a great trading nation, Tarabon was a major source of fine rugs, dyes, fireworks, and other luxury items, but the nation has recently fallen on hard times that threaten to destroy its commerce. Historically Tarabon has spent nearly three hundred years squabbling with Arad Doman over the Almoth Plain, but only in the last year has this conflict come to all-out war. Unfortunately, Tarabon has also been forced into conflict with the Dragonsworn, and the resulting dual conflict has strained the nation's resources and brought civil war to its cities.

In Tarabon it is considered impolite to completely reveal one's face except when eating or drinking. As a result, both men and women wear a transparent veil across the face. When anonymity is required, they may even don a mask to completely hide the features.

Taraboner men often sport facial hair under the veil in the form of a thick mustache, and wear a dark cylindrical cap on their thick dark hair. Both lords and commoners

wear baggy white trousers and coats embroidered with scrollwork on the shoulders, though the lords' coats are usually of finer material and their much more elaborate embroidery is often gold. Loose-fitting shirts with embroidered chests are worn under the coats. Occasionally the trousers are embroidered as well.

Noblewomen veil their faces, but they do not believe in hiding their figures. Most wear clinging gowns of thin silk that are almost as revealing as those worn by Domani women. Peasant women also prefer thin fabric, though their dresses are usually made of drab wool, quite coarse in comparison to their betters'.

Household servants wear wool, but of a finer quality than that available to most peasants, with the sigil of the House embroidered on the breast.

King, Panarch and Assembly

Tarabon is nominally ruled jointly by a king and a panarch, who are both elected by the Assembly of Lords. The King and the Panarch are equal in authority. The Panarch collects taxes, customs, and duties, controls the Civil Watch, and oversees the lower courts. Her personal guard is the Panarch's Legion. The King is responsible for spending the collected revenue properly, controls the army, and oversees the High Court. His personal guard is the King's Life Guard. The only major political duty of the Assembly of Lords is the election of both King and Panarch.

Guild of Illuminators

The Guild of Illuminators holds the secret to producing illuminations, or airborne fireworks displays. The group

founded their first chapter house in Tanchico, and later went on to establish one in Cairhien as well, though both have now been lost. They usually serve lords and kings by providing great entertainments of illuminations, but also sell lesser fireworks to others. These always include dire warnings of the disaster that can result from attempting to open them.

Illuminators protect their secrets at all cost, even unto murder. No one not born into the guild is allowed access to their knowledge. Each chapter house – none are known to exist at present – is run by a Mistress or Master of the House who is answerable to the guild for anything that happens within that house. There are rumors that the Guild is looking for a place to establish a new chapter house, possibly in Amadicia.

Tanchico

Tarabon's capital city may be one of the oldest surviving cities on the continent. Tarabon's historians claim that part of the Panarch's Palace was built as far back as the Age of Legends. They cite a wall bearing an ancient frieze depicting animals no living man has ever seen, as well as the numerous skeletons of these animals on display there. While doubtful, this antiquity would help substantiate their claim as descendants of that Age's nobility. There is no doubt that the Panarch's Palace, seated atop one of Tanchico's loftier hills, is a wondrous construct. Its central hall is lined with rows of white columns and lit from tiny carvings in the wall just below the ceiling and contains a grand display of all types of ancient artifacts, unmatched anywhere. The exhibit includes priceless *cuendillar* figures, rare sculptures, and even an *angreal*. It

is open to the public, noble and commoner alike, three days a month as well as on feastdays. Apply to the Panarch's Palace in writing for the precise dates.

Larger than Tear and possibly Caemlyn, Tanchico is spread over the steep hills embracing Tanchico Bay at the mouth of the River Andahar. This great harbor is usually crowded with ships of all kinds. Three separate peninsulas jut into the harbor, the Verana to the east, the Maseta in the center, and the Calpene nearest the sea. These peninsulas are guarded by a dozen fortresses that surround the harbor. Each of the peninsulas has a 'circle' or assembly arena among its buildings. The smallest of these, the Great Circle on the Calpene peninsula, can hold thousands of people to watch horse races or displays of illuminations. The largest arena is the King's Circle, located on the Maseta. The Panarch's Circle is slightly smaller than the King's Circle and is located on the Verana, as is the Panarch's Palace.

Hundreds of white palaces and other buildings cover the steep hills, their white stone or plaster glowing in the sun, highlighted by the sparkle of the occasional gilded tower or dome. Unfortunately the pristine appearance is an illusion. Over the years the buildings in Tanchico have been neglected to the point that the plaster on most is cracked and peeling to reveal shabby brick or wood beneath, and the stone of the palaces is chipped and cracked as well. The white façade is slipping to reveal a city rotting from within. Because of the recent trouble, the area on the Calpene near the Great Circle has become a haunt for homeless refugees. All the shops in the area have permanently closed. Cutthroats and thieves have always been a part of the city, but now they nearly rule the streets. Nobles' bodyguards have become a necessity.

Claimants to the throne are a constant threat to the fragile balance of power. The heads of those who are caught are placed on spikes above Traitors' Steps on the Maseta, but there is no certainty that such measures will help this old city, or Tarabon, survive.

GHEALDAN

'Blessed be the name of the Lord Dragon in the Light.'
– Benediction from the Prophet in Ghealdan

Sigil   Three silver stars arranged one above and two below; the Stars; the Silver Stars.

Banner   The Silver Stars on a field of red.

Capital city   Jehannah.

Symbols include the Light Blessed Throne.

Small Ghealdan lies between Amadicia and Altara with its back against Garen's Wall. Until recently Ghealdan was a relatively quiet and self-sufficient nation ruled by King Johanin from the Jheda Palace. His greatest worry was possible conquest from Amadicia. Then the Prophet of the Dragon Reborn came to Ghealdan, order vanished, and the man who sat the Light Blessed Throne fell. Four different rulers held the throne within the space of half a year, with only the latest, Alliandre Maritha Kigarin, managing to hold it for more than a few months. Johanin died suspiciously in a hunting accident. His successor Ellizelle ordered the army to disperse the crowds that came to see

the Prophet, only to have them routed by his followers. After the humiliating defeat she died of poison, a supposed suicide. Her successor Teresia lasted ten days, until she was forced to abdicate and marry a rich merchant. Marrying a commoner in Ghealdan means giving up all claim to the throne.

There is little doubt that the Lords of Ghealdan's High Crown Council had a hand in removing the failed rulers. With Whitecloaks waiting to move in for the kill, and chaos taking each town by turn, there were few good choices. Alliandre has survived only by allowing the Prophet to share her land, rather than trying to drive him out. Chaos still reigns in the towns and villages the Prophet visits, and whatever Ghealdan was before the Prophet came, it will be something far different after he is gone.

In each of the towns he visits, people give up their homes and families to follow him. These followers have grown until their numbers challenge the resources of even Ghealdan's largest towns. When they fill a town to bursting, they spill out to form a shantytown that sometimes rivals the main town, and sometimes dwarfs it. Ghealdan is still a nation, but it is a nation under internal siege from this man who claims to represent the Light, in the form of the Dragon Reborn.

Most of the towns in Ghealdan are walled and contain buildings made primarily of stone and roofed with slate. Buildings of several stories are not unusual in the larger towns, and some even contain palaces. Before the Prophet came, the Ghealdanin were wary of strangers. Now their land is all but overrun by strangers who claim to be following the Prophet. Some towns, such as Samara, have burned in the riots resulting from clashes between Whitecloaks and followers of the Prophet, both claiming

to be fighting in the name of the Light. As always, it is the natives that suffer.

ILLIAN

'You may have any palace you wish,
so long as it is not larger than mine.'
— FATEFUL WORDS OF THE
FIRST KING OF ILLIAN

Sigil   Nine golden bees arranged in a diamond, from top to bottom 1-2-3-2-1; the Golden Bees.

Banner   Nine Golden Bees on a field of dark green. Fringed in gold if flown where the sovereign is present.

Capital city   Illian.

Symbols include the Laurel Crown.

Illian is a powerful nation on the Sea of Storms bordering the weaker nations of Altara and Murandy. Wealthy from sea-, land-, and riverborne trade, Illian protected the weaker Altara during the Whitecloak War to insure that the nation would remain a buffer between Illian and Amadicia. The current ruler is Mattin Stepaneos, who also reigned during the Whitecloak War. His standard is Three Leopards, silver on black, and he is rumored to have an Aes Sedai advisor, though few claim to have ever seen her. Since Illian fell to the Dragon Reborn, the whereabouts of Mattin Stepaneos are not known, nor, despite rumors, even whether he is alive.

Most men of Illian wear long coats with raised collars and beards that leave their upper lip bare. Many lords also wear boots fringed with gold or silver. Women, both high and low, favor wide-brimmed hats held in place by long scarves that are wound around the neck in a utilitarian and decorative fashion. High ladies adorn themselves with decorative slippers heavily worked with gold and silver. Their dresses are cut high at the hem to show these slippers to best advantage. The dresses usually also have low-cut necklines to show the lady's natural assets to best advantage as well.

Rule of Three

In Illian the King is not the sole political leader of the nation. He is 'advised' by a council of lords, known as the Council of Nine. Historically these nine lords usually end up contending with the ruler for power. The King's power is further weakened by the presence of a second 'advisory' body, known as the Assemblage. Chosen by and from Illian's merchants and ship owners, they too end up contending for power more often than giving useful advice to either the Council of Nine or the King. The result is that no one group or person actually controls Illian's destiny. There is always a three-way battle over any task or legislation. According to many this provides needed checks and balances to prevent tyranny. According to others it creates needless confusion and delays any useful action.

Within the capital city of Illian the King's Palace and the Great Hall of the Council, both Ogier-built, bear witness to this struggle that is as old as Illian. The two huge white palaces are built at either end of the marble-columned Square of Tammaz, Illian's great central square,

and each appears identical to the other in every way, with columned walks, airy balconies, slender towers and purple roofs. But there is one subtle difference. The first king of Illian told the first Council that they could have any palace they wished, so long as it was not larger than his. (Even then the Council was contending for a bigger share of the power.) The result: their palace was built as a precise copy of the King's, but two feet smaller in every measurement.

To this day the Council of Nine and the King duel with each other, and the Assemblage contends with both. Fortunately this leaves most Illianers free to live their lives as they wish.

The City of Illian

Unlike the capitals of most other nations, Illian has no massive defensive wall around its perimeter; rather, its pale stone towers and palaces rise out of the huge marshy grassland that covers the southernmost edge of the country. From a little distance the city seems to be made of nothing but towers and palaces, many marked by the unmistakable artistry of Ogier craftsmanship, dwarfing the multitude of smaller buildings that make up Illian's bulk. Canals crisscross the width and breadth of the city, passing under bridges of all shapes and sizes, some even built by Ogier. Wagons, lacquered coaches with House sigils, and sedan chairs hurry overland while passenger boats and cargo barges fill the canals below.

As large as Cairhien or Caemlyn, Illian is a major seaport and a manufacturing center for fine rugs, textiles, and leather goods. Illian's production of finished leather is the largest in the land. Vast tanneries cover a number of

small islands among the marsh grass, producing more finished leather in a day than most village tanneries prepare in months, and adding their own distinctive aroma to the pungent smells of the marshland.

The port houses a large fishing fleet, which provides enough seafood to feed Illian and still export to neighboring nations. The small craft of the fishermen, the larger cargo ships, and the sleek Sea Folk rakers keep the bay crowded. Illian's great shipyards produce many of the ships that dock within her harbor, though their finest work can never match that of the Sea Folk.

Illian's port district is quite large. Named the Perfumed Quarter – its 'perfume' is the stench of hemp and pitch and sour harbor mud – it is all but cut off from the rest of the city. So long as they do nothing to affront a high lord or lady, its citizens are left to fend for themselves. Even magistrates seldom concern themselves with events in the Perfumed Quarter.

The Companions

Though Illian's military might is formidable, its finest soldiers are those within the elite unit called the Illianer Companions. These crack troops traditionally ride with the commanding general during any military action, to be deployed wherever their extraordinary abilities are needed, usually in the hottest fighting. During the Whitecloak War the Children of the Light set a trap at Soremaine that caught King Stepaneos and would have destroyed his entire army if it were not for the valor of the Companions. They held the field long enough to allow the rest of the army to escape to safety, and thus prevented Altara, as well as Murandy and Illian, from falling

under the sway of the Whitecloaks. Without their intervention Stepaneos would probably not have been able to wrest victory from the Soremaine defeat.

The Great Hunt of the Horn

Long ago, according to legend, the Horn of Valere was hidden to keep it safe until it was needed in the Last Battle. The Horn is much more than a musical instrument, for it can call back dead heroes from the grave to fight against the Shadow. On it is the inscription *Tia mi aven Moridin isainde vadin*, in the Old Tongue: The grave is no bar to my call. Prophecy states that it will be found in time for the Last Battle. Between the end of the Trolloc Wars and the beginning of the War of the Hundred Years, a Hunt was called. Many heroes searched for the Horn, and though none found it, their stories became legends that are now a part of the Great Hunt of the Horn, a bardic cycle that takes several days to tell in its entirety.

Almost four hundred years after the last hunt, a new hunt was called in Illian on the Feast of Teven. Hunters gathered from every nation of the world to seek the Horn, or at least immortality in story and song. The city celebrated their coming adventures with a grand carnival of costumes and fireworks, song, dance, and the telling of legends. Prizes were given to gleemen, the greatest prize going for the best telling of the Hunt cycle. The Hunters were sworn to their quest and sent forth from Illian with much pomp and circumstance.

Since the heroes' departure there have been rumors of the Horn appearing in Shienar, and in Falme some said they saw an army of heroes from legend charging to the

song of a triumphant Horn, but no one has yet returned the Horn to Illian.

TEAR

'Whoever holds the Stone of Tear
is Lord of Tear, city and nation.'
— TAIREN SAYING

Sigil   Three white crescent moons arranged diagonally; the Moons; the Crescent Moons.

Banner   Three white Crescent Moons slanting across a field half red, half gold.

Capital city   Tear.

Symbols include the Stone of Tear.

The nation of Tear lies just east of Illian and contains the greatest port on the Sea of Storms. This port is located well above the mouth of the River Erinin, and is guarded by the ancient fortress known as the Stone of Tear. Unlike other major ports, however, Tear's is not easily accessible to the ocean. It is protected by the winding maze of waterways within the vast delta at the mouth of the Erinin known as the Fingers of the Dragon. These waterways are under complete control of the Tairens, who will not allow any ships to pass in or out through them without a Tairen pilot aboard. Perhaps unskilled sailors would be lost without a pilot, but for most voyagers, such as the Sea Folk, the precaution is laughable.

The expanse of land between the Sea and the city of Tear on the Erinin is large enough to support several towns, but the Tairen Lords will not allow even the smallest village to stand between the city of Tear and the sea lest that village become competition for the capital. All prime locations are secured for the Lords, and towns are taxed with increasing building taxes as they grow, preventing any town but Tear from growing large. The town of Godan was allowed to remain on the Bay of Remara only because of its strategic importance overlooking Mayene.

High Lords of Tear

Unlike most other nations, Tear has no one ruler, no king or queen. A council known as the High Lords of Tear rule together as a body. The members of this council must all be of a particular rank, but there is no fixed number of lords on the council; the membership has varied from as many as twenty to as few as six. All decisions are presented to the people as unanimous. The Lords of the Land – all the lesser Tairen Lords – then participate in carrying out the edicts of the High Lords.

In Tear only peasants toss dice. Lords who wish to gamble favor a card game called chop. Playing cards are hand-painted to depict various characters, with the rulers in the deck usually painted to resemble those actually ruling nations at the time the cards were made, with the nation's own ruler always leading the highest suit as the Ruler of Cups. In Tear, of course, this is a High Lord. Many idle nobles spend most of their waking hours playing chop, with only women or horses able to draw them away, and then only temporarily.

The Stone of Tear

The High Lords rule from the Stone of Tear, a massive fortress that dominates the city of Tear like a small mountain. The Stone is believed to be the oldest stronghold of mankind. It was built sometime during or shortly after the Breaking of the World, and was made using the One Power. Flows of Earth, Air and Fire were used to draw stone from every corner of the world and fuse it into a single massive structure without seam or joint or mortar. The Stone has been attacked and besieged over a hundred times, but had never fallen until the Dragon Reborn and a few hundred Aiel took it in a single night.

Deep within the center of the stronghold is the great vaulted chamber known as the Heart of the Stone. There, amid polished redstone columns and golden lamps, is the place where the great *sa'angreal* sword *Callandor* hung in its glittering crystal splendor until the Dragon Reborn claimed it. It is also there that the High Lords performed the Rite of Guarding four times a year, claiming that they were guarding the whole world against the Dragon Reborn by holding *Callandor*. Lords of the Land were raised to High Lords there. Before the Stone fell to Rand al'Thor, no one entered the fortress without the permission of the High Lords, and none but High Lords were allowed access to the Heart of the Stone. Even the High Lords only entered it as required for the Rite. For the most part Tairens did not like admitting that the Heart of the Stone, or *Callandor*, existed at all. Now that the Dragon Reborn has taken the Stone and opened the Heart, they can no longer deny either.

Treasures of the Stone

Callandor is not the only object of the One Power housed within the Stone. Deep in the bowels of the fortress, beneath the levels of the dungeons are a series of dusty storerooms filled with a cache of *angreal* and *ter'angreal* gathered from all over the world. The collection rivals that of the White Tower, though none are certain whether the Tairens collected the artifacts to preserve them, or to hide them. They ceased adding to the collection some three hundred years past, and never display their prizes. Some believe the collection only exists to lessen the stigma of holding the greatest of them, *Callandor*, for the Tairens hate and fear anything to do with the One Power or Aes Sedai.

The One Power and Tear

Before the Dragon Reborn came all channeling was outlawed in Tear, though, unlike in Amadicia, Aes Sedai were tolerated so long as they did not channel. Telling or possessing a copy of the Prophecies of the Dragon resulted in imprisonment. Whether this was because of the fact that Tear's fate was a part of the Prophecy, or simply a long-rooted distrust of all things connected to the Power, is unknown. Girls with the ability to channel are still sent off to Tar Valon the same day they are discovered, and are discouraged from returning.

The City of Tear

Outside of the Stone, the city of Tear is built on flat land. The inner city is protected by a high wall of gray stone.

The finer houses and square-domed palaces are all within this wall, set along streets paved with stone. Outside the wall the streets are unpaved, and always so deep with mud that sedan chairs and carriages do not venture beyond the inner city. Special elevated shoes must be worn by pedestrians who wish to avoid becoming hopelessly bogged in the mud. Only ox-carts and wagons travel through the unpaved districts.

The port district is called the Maule and is the rougher part of town. The district adjoining it, with its stone warehouses along the docks, is called the Chalm. Both contain inns, though they are cramped and often dirty, and the Maule also contains shops that cater to the sailors and working folk of the sea.

The city is protected by the Defenders of the Stone, an elite military unit that is housed in the Stone, but it is said by the poor of Tear that they are only there to protect the rich. There is no doubt that they operated with a double standard, for before the laws were changed, foreigners were allowed to carry their weapons, so long as their visit was only temporary, but locals other than lords who did so were subject to punishment under the law. Commoners were also prevented from obtaining any sort of justice in a grievance against a merchant or lord. Any commoner who pressed his or her case was subject to imprisonment or punishment. Any riots that resulted were simply put down forcibly by the Defenders. The arrival of the Dragon has begun to change things, and has made the formerly untouchable lords reassess their position, since commoners may now call lords before a magistrate without reprisal, but it will probably be some time before these changes affect the nation as a whole.

In most nations, the clothing of commoners is of similar design to that of nobles, but made of coarser and cheaper materials. In Tear, however, the dress of lords and ladies is quite different from that of commoners, no doubt in an attempt to further that uniquely Tairen belief that commoners are actually lesser beings.

Tairen lords wear colorful coats of padded silks and brocades with puffy sleeves, sometimes colored in stripes. Their breeches are tight to show a well-muscled leg to best advantage, and are often brightly colored.

Regular soldiers are uniformed with brilliant red coats with wide sleeves ending in narrow white cuffs. A gleaming breastplate is worn over the coat so as to let the sleeves show clearly. Their breeches are of the same tight cut as that of the lords, though not quite so brightly colored, and are worn tucked into knee-high boots. Defenders of the Stone wear black and gold coats with puffy sleeves as well as plumes of various colors on their rimmed round helmets to mark officers and under-officers. The soldiers of a particular lord wear that lord's colors on their puffy sleeves.

In contrast, common men wear baggy breeches, usually tied at the ankle and held up by a broad colored sash. Some few wear coats, but unlike the lord's, theirs are long and dark, fitting tightly to the wearer's arms and chest, then becoming wider below the waist. Sometimes low shoes or boots are worn, but more often bare feet or clogs are preferred for traversing the mud of the poorer quarters. Most common men wear cloth caps that hang to one side of their face, or wide conical straw hats to keep out the sun.

Dockmen and other laborers wear the same baggy breeches, but go bare-chested or with a long vest in place of a shirt.

The noble ladies of Tear wear long dresses with neck-lines cut to bare shoulders and even considerable bosom. Silk is the material of preference for most highborn ladies, and their dresses are often adorned with a lace ruff and a tiny matching cap. Tairen widows wear white, and have been known to don the color while their dying husband still lived. No self-respecting lady is ever without her tiny porcelain bottle of smelling salts.

Common women cannot afford the luxury of either silk, or long dresses that would be ruined in the ever-present mud. Their dresses have chin-high collars that reveal nothing, and ankle-high hems. The dresses are often adorned with pale-colored aprons, usually in a combination of two or three of progressively larger size, each smaller than the one beneath it. Hats, when worn, are wide-brimmed straw often dyed to match the aprons.

Anyone, regardless of class, who wishes to walk through the outer city must go barefoot or wear a special shoe called a 'clog,' which is actually a small wooden platform that fastens to the soles of the wearer's existing shoes to lift them clear of the mud. Bamboo staffs are also favored by many to help in the difficult process of traversing Tairen streets.

A Rich Nation

Aside from the Stone, Tear is best known for its oil and horses. The oil is produced from olive farms throughout the land, and is exported through the port. The olive farms are not owned by the peasants who work them, but by the lords who grow fat on the profits. Tear's chief rival in this industry is the tiny neighboring city-state of Mayene, and their oilfish. Because of the Tairen desire to

control everything, Tear has spent a great deal of its history trying to annex or control Mayene, but has never completely succeeded. The result of this failure has led to a national hatred of Mayene that is second only to the hatred of Illian.

Tear has no rivals, however, in the breeding of fine horses. The deep-chested Tairen steeds are undeniably the finest in the land, having superior speed, endurance, and beauty. Much of the forest land, including the great Ogier grove that stood just outside the city, has been turned into grassland to pasture the great herds of blood-stock.

The Fingers of the Dragon are home to many different large schools of fish. As a result Tear's fishing industry has flourished.

Tear also exports large quantities of grain. For the last twenty years most of their grain was sold to Cairhien to make up for their lost production. When the Cairhien royal house fell to riots, they could no longer buy the grain and Tear was left with growing stores and no market. The Dragon Reborn forced the High Lords to give grain as aid to Cairhien, so they might buy it again later, and to sell their surplus to their enemy, Illian. Only an outside force could make Tairens sell to Illian, for Tear has a long and bloody history of war with that neighbor. Tairens are always ready to go to war with Illian, despite the fact that there has never been a clear victor.

The wealth from all Tear's commerce is great, but only the lords have profited from it. In the city commoners live only in the outer city unless they are house servants. In the country they live in conditions that most other nations would consider unfit for livestock.

MAYENE

*'I will see Mayene and all its ships burn
before one Tairen lord sets foot in my city.'*
— BERELAIN SUR PAENDRAG,
FIRST OF MAYENE

Sigil   A golden hawk in flight; the Golden Hawk.

Banner   A Golden Hawk in flight on a field of blue.
Sometimes called Paendrag's Banner by Mayeners.
Fringed in gold if flown when the First is present.

Capital city   Mayene.

Mayene rests on the end of a peninsula in the Sea of
Storms, hemmed in by the looming bulk of Tear to the
west and the Drowned Lands to the north. It is actually an
independent city-state, rather than a nation, though Tear
claims it as a province despite Mayene's protests. What
fragile independence Mayeners have is maintained
through their one major asset, the secret oilfish shoals.
The lamp oil produced from the oilfish here rivals that
from the olive groves of Tear, Illian, and Tarabon. That oil
is the major source of Mayene's wealth and her fragile
independence. Despite Tear's provincial claim, no Tairen
knows where the oilfish shoals are located, and the
Mayeners are determined to keep it that way.

The ruling family of Mayene claims to be descended
from Artur Hawkwing, and uses the Paendrag name. The
man or woman who rules Mayene is styled 'the First,'
which once meant the first lord or lady. Currently the
First is Berelain sur Paendrag, a young ruler who also

acted as regent of Cairhien for a time. Originally there was also a single 'second' lord or lady, but over the last four hundred years the tradition changed so that several lords and ladies held the title at once. On some occasions there have been as many as nine second lords and ladies.

Because of the constant threat from Tairen assassins, all high lords and ladies are trained in basic self-defense, so that they need not rely solely on their personal guards for protection. The city-state itself is protected by the Mayener Winged Guards, the First's personal guard. Their gleaming red breastplates and red-streamered lances have been seen at the forefront of many conflicts throughout the history of Mayene.

Chapter 31

Holidays and the Calendar

 THE CURRENT CALENDAR is the Farede Calendar, created by Urin din Jubai Soaring Gull, a Sea Folk scholar, and promulgated by the Panarch Farede of Tarabon, who was the first Panarch and who tried to make Tanchico the intellectual center of the known world. Recording years of the New Era (NE), the Farede Calendar sets the first year after the War of the Hundred Years as 1 NE. By 50 NE the Farede Calendar was in general use.

The Farede Calendar sets 10 days to the week, 28 days to the month, and 13 months to the year. The months are: Taisham, Jumara, Saban, Aine, Adar, Saven, Amadaine, Tammaz, Maigdhal, Choren, Shaldine, Nesan, and Danu.

The calendar's named months are used almost exclusively in official documents. In everyday life, everyone from nobles to commoners reckons time by seasons, and

fixes dates by days or weeks from or to this or that feast-day, usually the major holidays.

Several major feastdays celebrated in every nation from the Aryth Ocean to the Spine of the World are not part of any month. Sunday, the longest day of the year, comes annually in Amadaine, but is not a day of that month. The Feast of Thanksgiving is celebrated only once every four years, at the spring equinox, and the Feast of All Souls' Salvation (also called All Souls' Day) is marked only once every ten years, at the autumn equinox.

There are far too many feasts and special days to be listed here, and of course they are all well known. As for those which are celebrated only in particular localities or regions, there are literally hundreds, perhaps thousands. They range from King's Days and Queen's Days (the Taraboner Calendar of Days, listing all feasts, festivals, and holidays, records both a King's Day and a Panarch's Day) to Harvest Week Festivals and Blessings of the Nets (in fishing communities), to festivals celebrating yearly increases in flocks or herds. Illian and the region of Altara around Ebou Dar in particular are known for their multi-plicity of celebrations, which often run one into another. All other days of the year are considered working days, for commoners at least, but during the course of a year, depending on exactly where they live, folk can count on at least 105 to 116 days when no work is expected (beyond that directly associated with the observances).

Given the way in which these days are set, one feastday or festival inevitably overlaps another from time to time. Both are then observed in an even larger celebration.

With the exceptions of the Feast of Lights, Sunday, the Feast of Thanksgiving, and the Feast of All Souls' Salvation, there is considerable variation in the way

common feastdays and holidays are observed and/or celebrated. Arad Doman and Illian are noted for the grandest celebrations, Illian and the region of Altara around Ebou Dar for the most libertine, and Cairhien (with the notorious exception of the Feast of Lights) for the most reserved.

The following is a brief list of holidays which are, if not all universal, widely observed.

The Feast of Lights

The last day of Danu (the shortest of the year) and the first day of Taisham. (Thus the last day of the old year and the first day of the new.) In many localities the second day of the Feast of Lights is called First Day or Firstday and is considered a particular time to give charitably.

High Chasaline

The twelfth day of Taisham. Also called 'the Day of Reflection.' A feastday, often with dancing that night (public in villages and smaller towns; usually at private gatherings in larger cities), on which you are supposed to reflect on your good fortune and the blessings of your life. It is considered bad form to complain about anything on High Chasaline, though that taboo is not always followed strictly.

Chansein

The third day of Jumara. A day of wild indulgence in food, where the object seems to be to get other people to eat as much as they can hold and more. People carry hot

pastries filled with meat or dried fruit, sometimes stuffing their pockets or actually carrying bagfuls, and hand them out to everyone they see. It is considered extremely ill-mannered to fail to eat every crumb. (The Borderlands; Arad Doman)

Feast of Abram

The ninth day of Jumara. (Tarabon, Amadicia, Ghealdan, Andor, Altara, Murandy, Illian, Tear, Cairhien)

Lamma Sor

Celebrated the day after the first quarter moon (called a 'knife moon') of Saban in the Borderlands. Nothing is eaten but bread and water, salt, and oil. Also called the Day of Remembrance. It is a day of prayers for those who have fallen defending against the Blight, and for those who will fall.

The Feast of Fools

Celebrated in Tammaz (in Arad Doman and the Borderlands) or Saven (everywhere else), the exact day varying according to locality. A day in which all order is deliberately inverted; the high perform lowly tasks (running errands, serving at table, etc.) while the low do no work and give orders to their usual superiors. In many villages and towns the most foolish person is given a title such as the Lord/Lady of Unreason/Misrule/Chaos or the King/Queen of Fools. Not an honor sought, but for that one day everyone has to obey whatever orders, however foolish, are given by the chosen one. (Called the Festival

of Unreason in Saldaea; the Festival of Fools in Kandor; Foolday in Baerlon and the Two Rivers.) Note: In Tear, Illian, and the southern half of Altara, the time between the Feast of Abram and the Feast of Fools is considered the most propitious for a wedding.

Winternight

The night before Bel Tine; spent visiting and exchanging gifts.

Bel Tine

Spring festival celebrating the end of winter, the first sprouting of crops, and the birth of the first lambs. Date determined locally.

Tirish Adar

From the rise of the first full moon in Adar to the rise of the next moon. In most northern countries, no one sleeps more than an hour or two a night during that period.

Feast of Neman

The ninth day of Adar. (Andor, Cairhien, Tear, the Borderlands)

The Feast of Freia

The twenty-first day of Adar. (Illian, Arad Doman, Ghealdan, Tarabon, parts of Altara and Murandy)

Dahan

The ninth day of Saven. Supposedly the anniversary of final victory in the Trolloc Wars and freedom from the Shadow. Most historians believe the date was arbitrarily chosen.

Asadine

Ten days before Sunday; a day of fasting, with no food taken between sunrise and sunset. (The Borderlands, Cairhien) In the Borderlands, the day after Asadine is considered an especially propitious time to wed.

The Feast of Maia

The sixth day of Amadaine. (Andor, Ghealdan, Altara, Murandy, Illian)

Bailene

Celebrated the ninth day of Amadaine. (Arad Doman, Tarabon, Amadicia, Tear)

Genshai

The third day of Tammaz. Brightly colored ribbons are worn by both men and women. (Tear, Illian, Amadicia, Tarabon, southern parts of Altara and Murandy)

Mabriam's Day

The eighteenth day of Tammaz. Any sort of labor is avoided, and some go to great lengths to do so. The food

is always cooked the day before, but some rise and dress in the dark on the theory that they have thus done that 'work' before the day began. One feature of Mabriam's Day is that young women traditionally play tricks on young men. These tricks are supposed to indicate the young woman's interest in the target man, but the young women work in groups and try to keep their actions as secret as possible. There are traditional forfeits if a young man guesses who is responsible, ranging from a kiss from the young woman who thought up the trick to a kiss from each in the group. Celebrated in villages and small towns in every nation.

Tandar

The ninth day of Maighdal. No one is supposed to let Tandar end still holding a grudge or having a disagreement with anyone. Although the intent is that the quarrelers should be reconciled, it is not unknown for festivities to be marred by attempts to meet the letter in quite another way.

Low Chasaline

The eighteenth day of Maighdal. In most places a day of fasting.

The Festival of Lanterns

The first day of Choren. Paper lanterns, often brightly colored, frequently fancifully shaped, are hung everywhere, in windows, in trees. (Arad Doman, Tarabon, Amadicia, Ghealdan, Altara, Murandy, Illian)

Bel Arvina

The first day of autumn; a floating feast, date determined locally.

Amaetheon

The sixth day of Shaldine. Everywhere except in the Borderlands this is a feast remembering the dead, not in a sad way, but joyously.

Shaoman

The twelfth day of Shaldine. Particularly oriented toward children, who are cosseted, praised, and given gifts. In many places groups of children go from house to house, where they sing songs before the door and are rewarded with small gifts or sweets.

Danshu

The last day of Nesan.

Sunday

A feastday and festival at midsummer, celebrated in many parts of the world.

Chapter 32

The Prophecies of
the Dragon

 SINCE THE TIME of the Breaking, and possibly before, though any such prophecies have been lost to myth, the Prophecies of the Dragon have grown, telling of a man who will be both destroyer and savior of the world. That man will be able to channel, and he will be the Dragon Reborn. He will be destined to fight the Tarmon Gai'don, the Last Battle against the Shadow. The Prophecies also state that he is the only hope of the world for salvation.

These prophecies are not fully understood, for nothing in a prophecy is ever exactly what it seems. For this reason, and for the fearsome nature of the return of one who once destroyed the world, most people either avoid or ignore the Prophecies. They are in fact outlawed in many nations. But they have led to doom for many male

channelers who believed that the Prophecies referred to them.

The first of these false Dragons, as they came to be called, to rise high enough for note was Raolin Darksbane in 335 AB; his followers went so far as to attack the White Tower (unsuccessfully) when he was finally taken. He was followed in 1300 AB by Yurian Stonebow, Davian in FY 351, Guaire Amalasan in FY 939, and then Logain in 997 NE and Mazrim Taim in 998 NE. Other men claimed the title without rising far, but until Logain, false Dragons were very rare, because very few men could channel strongly, and most were taken and gentled long before they were a real threat.

In the last few years more false Dragons have appeared than ever before, with the trend culminating in a young man named Rand al'Thor, who is believed to be the actual Dragon Reborn of prophecy. It is believed that at least one of the two surviving false Dragons has already proclaimed him the true Dragon Reborn. Such an occurrence has never happened in recorded history, and indeed many of the Prophecies appear to have been fulfilled, including the fall of the Stone of Tear and the claiming of *Callandor*.

Now Rand has created a Black Tower, in direct contrast to the White, and has begun to gather men who can channel to help him fight the Shadow. These men are being trained in a manner that somewhat resembles the training at the White Tower. They begin as 'soldiers' because each is there as a soldier to fight the Shadow, as well as any who oppose justice or oppress the weak. At a certain skill level they are raised to become 'Dedicated,' and are given a collar pin in the shape of a small silver sword. Those who progress far enough in their training will be raised to

be 'Asha'man.' The name originally meant one who defended truth and justice for everyone, a guardian who would not yield even when hope was gone. Each Asha'man is given a gold-and-red dragon to wear.

With such unusual events occurring there can be little doubt that the Wheel is turning toward the Last Battle. The White Tower has split and the Black has risen, and men with the ability are embracing the Source despite the certain doom promised by the taint on *saidin*, and joining this young Dragon in his fight against the Shadow. The Wheel has turned, but it has changed with the turning. The Prophecies tell all while revealing nothing. Only the Light may know whether this is the beginning of salvation, or the final destruction for us all.

Index

Italic page numbers refer to primary discussions and lists.

channelers); five threads of (Five Powers), 10, 16, 20, 50; healing by means of, 27, 38–39, 101, 215, 309; living constructs made with, 28, 266–67 (*see also* chora trees; Nym); nonliving constructs made with, 29, 53, 127, 213, 327, 399; Ogier *steddings* shielded from, 264, 267; persons strong in, 31, 62, 68, 80; and severence from True Source, 14–16, 107 (*see also* gentling; stilling); Talents linked to 122, 302; Talents unrelated to, 266, 278, 281; tools for working with (see *angreal; sa'angreal' ter'angreal*) as a weapon of war, 49, 147, 163, 223, 304

osan'gar, 48
Osan'gar *90*
Osendrelle Erinin, 148
ounce, 190

Paaran Disen, 25, 29, 31, 33, 52
paces, 190
Paendrag line. *See* Artur Hawkwing; Berelain sur Paendrag; Luther Paendrag Mondwin
Paendrag's Banner, 405
Paitar Nachiman, King of Arafel, 355
Panarch of Tarabon, 386–87. *See also* Farede
Panarch's Circle, Tanchico, 389
Panarch's Day, 408
Panarch's Legion, 325, 386
Panarch's Palace, Tanchico, 387, 389

Paral, 33
Parenia Demalle, 307
Pattern, of the Age, 3–8; boring into, 36, 45, 59 (*see also* Bore); effect of balefire on, 50; thinness in, 45, 53; Traveling and Skimming, 36, 37; and Ways, 273; 'Will of,' 205; and World of Dreams, 277, 299
Peace of Rhuidean, 252
Pedron Niall, Lord Captain Commander of the Children of Light, 175, 177
People of the Dragon. *See* Da'shain Aiel
People of the Sea. *See* Sea Folk
Perfumed Quarter, Illian, 395. *See* Sea Folk
Perrin Aybara ('Goldeneyes'), Lord, 281, 347
philosophy, 6
pikemen, 327, 330
Pit of Doom, 57, 61, 101, 148
Place Where Shadow Waits. *See* Shadar Logoth
population decline, 288
Portal Stones, 37, 224
pound, 190
Power. *See* One Power
present Age, 9, 10, 91, 99
prophecies, 6, 415; about Aiel, 246, 251, 252; about the Horn of Valere, 396. *See also* Foretelling Prophecies of the Dragon, 144, 400, *415–17*
Prophet of the Dragon Reborn, 390, 391

Qichen, 265
Qirat, Seanchan, 210
Qual, 48

WINTER'S HEART

Book Nine of THE WHEEL OF TIME

Robert Jordan

Rand al'Thor, the Dragon Reborn, is slowly succumbing to the taint that the Dark One has placed upon saidin – the male half of the True Source. His Asha'man followers are also showing the signs of the insanity that once devastated the world and brought the Age of Legends to an end.

And as Rand falters, the Shadow falls across a stricken land. In the city of Ebou Dar the Seanchan, blind to the folly of their cause, martial their forces and continue their relentless assault. In Shayol Ghul the Forsaken, ancient servants of the Dark One, join together to destroy the Dragon.

Rand's only chance is to hazard the impossible and remove the taint from saidin. But to do so he must master a power from the Age of Legends that none have ever dared to risk – a power that can annihilate Creation and bring an end to Time itself.

Winter's Heart is a triumph of epic storytelling, and a magnificent addition to a landmark series in the fantasy genre.

THE ONE KINGDOM

The Swans' War Book One

Sean Russell

From their home in the Vale of Lakes, a group of young traders embark on a quest to make their fortune. Carrying a cargo of ancient artefacts, their journey along the River Wynnd will take them into a world both strange and terrifying.

For the One Kingdom is a far more complex and dangerous place than the adventurers could have imagined. In the aftermath of a terrible war, political upheaval and family rivalries threaten to plunge the land into a new dark age. The past, it seems, is far from forgotten.

'A master of intelligent fantasy – subtle, well-crafted and gripping'
Stephen Donaldson

'Magic and mystery blend in abundance with an intricate cast of characters . . . An engrossing read'
Robin Hobb

'A perfectly plotted, beautifully written fantasy'
Publishers Weekly